# Push My Life into a Duffle Bag

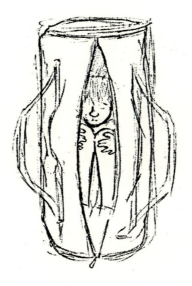

## John Roger Schofield

PublishAmerica
Baltimore

© 2008 by John Roger Schofield.
All rights reserved. No part of this book may be reproduced, stored in a retrieval system or transmitted in any form or by any means without the prior written permission of the publishers, except by a reviewer who may quote brief passages in a review to be printed in a newspaper, magazine or journal.

First printing

All characters in this book are fictitious, and any resemblance to real persons, living or dead, is coincidental.

ISBN: 1-60474-603-3
PUBLISHED BY PUBLISHAMERICA, LLLP
www.publishamerica.com
Baltimore

Printed in the United States of America

To Joani Lee

I hereby wish to dedicate this book to one Jason Johnson…whose patronage greatly encouraged me to continue my writing endeavors!

# Chapter 1
# April Is the Cruelest Month

This is how it was on that day. This is what it felt like. This is something that sticks with you, even though you want desperately to forget it. Sorry: there is no forgetting this.

For one thing, bathtubs: the way they look, the way they feel, the slick slide of their whiteness and all that they hold, will always summon vulnerability and feelings of powerlessness in me. On that day there was a bathtub.

For another thing, numbers: the way they need incessant calculation so that we can figure things out correctly and not lose any precious time. Numbers vex me. I fear the final sums when I crunch them; I fear the incorrect whether it is money, miles, or love. Numbers. This equals that, and here's your future. On that day I wasn't good enough at the numbers. Now I'm obsessed with being right. I am right.

One more thing: trust issues.

I don't remember what day of the week it was. I don't remember how old I was, perhaps five or six. I was young and tiny, that's for sure…barely old enough to accomplish chores and figure out people problems. I remember that it was April. I don't know why I so clearly remember this; perhaps we were learning calendar basics in school…a picture of a cartoon bear in a yellow raincoat with a humorous umbrella: floppy, broken, everything soaked.

The street we lived on was a little breezy. The trees were shivering in the wan sunlight. I think they were eucalyptus, maybe an old birch in a front yard or two. California suburbia. Cracked gray concrete sidewalks. Random children filling in the grassy spaces.

On this day my stepdad had an errand for me. It was simple. I'd done it before. He liked me doing big-boy things, and I liked to see him be proud of me, proud like a shadowy boxer is of his weaker left hook.

My errand was to help our poverty, our minimum-wage lifestyle, by pinching pennies—by trading in glass Coke bottles for small change. The small change would then be diligently saved for critical surgeries, college education, or a new two-story house overlooking the lights of our pinnacle city: Stockton, California. Small nickel change. Recycling. An honest errand.

I was handed a crusty, cardboard box with twenty-four empty bottles in it. My stepdad hadn't bothered to rinse them out, and I could see smear-dried brown cola along the inner walls of glass. If he'd cared about recycling, he'd have rinsed them. He only wanted quick coin.

Twenty-four bottles. A dime apiece when traded in at the local, what was it? A gas station? A corner grocer? I can't remember. However, what I do remember is that it was only three blocks north of our house, up on California St. a mere mile away from Saint Joseph's Hospital: the extravagant white building not at all dissimilar to another one (ten miles north) where I entered the air of this world in 1975. Ah! And that little city map just jolted my cobweb memory: it was a *liquor store* that gave dimes for bottles…a liquor store indeed. Childhood memories are foggy things.

This liquor store was quite prolific, replete with windows covered in gaudy ads for cigarettes, vodka, and Jack Daniel's signature road sign to hellish oblivion.

A perfect Stockton street. City of progress. Recycling. My errand.

Caleb glared down at me from the paternal heights of the ceiling. He spoke, "Now, when you git there you'll see Jack behind the counter; tell him you got some recycling and hand him the box; he'll count the bottles and give you the cash. Hold it in your right hand, nice and *tight*, and *don't* let go 'til you give it to me when you git back. Thank the man so he doesn't think you're an SOB," he mumbled, turning away. He then chuckled and sat down at the yellow kitchen table to do his daily ritual of poring over the used car/junk ads busy, buzzing, bitching, and pleading to indigent buyers all over the valley. Cheap ink. The paper crackled in his hands.

There was faint sunlight coming through the kitchen window; it put a golden sheen on his russet-colored hair and made his white-shirt shoulders glow like distant thunderheads.

"Okay," I squeaked and leaned back to support the unwieldy box that was glass-heavy to a small boy. And out the door I went. Into the April breeze.

I don't remember the walk to liquor store, but I do remember my stepdad yelling to me through the loud artillery of a Harley wailing by, "DON'T LOSE THE MONEY!" He didn't tell me to be careful or look out for hell's angels. Don't lose the money. $$$.

PUSH MY LIFE INTO A DUFFLE BAG

I did indeed make it to the liquor store, and distinctly I remember pushing the heavy box up onto the counter and being very nervous as Jack put down his magazine and peered down at me.

"Hey—what's this you got here?"

I could smell a musky moustachey odor diffusing from his breath. He looked into the box, mumbled, "Oh...uh humm," and began painfully counting with his gnarled fingertip, slowly touching each bottle with each number spoken.

*I looked to my left and felt childish avarice creep into my thoughts as I scanned all three flavors of Big League Chew in the Big League foil bags that looked like they contained adult tobacco. Hunks of shredded grape, watermelon, and bubble gum-flavored deliciousness danced like mute perfection only two feet away from my sweaty little eyes.* Big League Chew. It's quiet presence calmed me. I mused over baseball and gum. I felt a shred better.

"Well, you got twenty-four bottles in here, son," said Jack, interrupting my furtive gum love affair.

"Yah, there are twenty-four bottles in the box," I stated.

Jack slowly scratched his Wrangler ass and opened the cash register with a greasy clink sound. Over in the back corner of the store another dirty, trucker-looking fellow was leaning into the glass door and staring at the varieties of domestic piss beer, apparently indecisive over which to gulp down that evening over T.V. and T.V. dinner.

I shot a glance over to the magazine rack and saw two big high school boys trying to stealthily snag a magazine or two that were wrapped in plastic at the back of the rack. You know the kind. Mom told me that they were really bad and would rot my brain. Anyway, the boys didn't seem to care. They were pimply and really cool because they were in high school and all grown up. I remember them standing there as if it were yesterday.

"Don't fuck around, boys. If you want a *Hustler* you gotta buy it! I don't give a damn about your age!" hollered Jack over my head.

It startled me like a gunshot. He said the "F" word. He openly addressed the big high school boys.

They looked at each other, giggled like shiny cockroaches, and grabbed three magazines. Then I realized, to my acute horror, that they were coming to stand *right behind me*—to *wait*—to *buy* said magazines. I wanted out of their way, out of their sardonic gazes. I tried to let them go ahead of me to the register first, but Jack belched.

"NO! They can wait their turn. Now, you've got twenty four bottles at a dime apiece, so…I…owe you…two dollars and forty cents for recycling."

He started fingering coins in his greasy hand, unwilling to give me a paper dollar. Time started creeping…l i k e a g l a c i e r o v e r f l y p a p e r. The trucker guy was now standing in line behind the high schoolers with his case of aluminum beer: cheap, American, and guaranteed to help you forget your Stockton life.

Jack kept counting, using pennies only it seemed.… Time began perspiring.

I grew painfully nervous and felt like bolting for the door. I couldn't handle being surrounded by big scary strangers with monsters in their hearts and bad booby magazines in their hands. One of the boys was peering at the cover of his magazine, eyes pubescent and palpitating. The other huffed and tapped his sneaker on the floor. I risked a glance at his magazine and saw blonde bangs, lip gloss, skin, poisonous eyes, and felt my little heart put its bloody finger on the little trigger of my lungs and pull back slowly: CLICK!

Jack had finished counting out the coins. Finally! Thank goodness! But no…something was wrong. He'd messed up!

"*Two dollars, forty cents*, son. Here you go," he muttered, his hoary hand held high over my dewy forehead as if he were going to shower me with grimy pennies.

I put up my tremulous hand. White baby fingers. He filled it up. I looked over the change as fast as I could, not really knowing what I was looking for, but feeling in my heart that Jack had got it wrong. Something was off. He took the crusty box off the counter. The Big League Chew began to melt.

A fly landed on my forehead. I brushed it away and blurted out, "This is too much! You owe me only *two dollars* for the recycling!" I looked him right straight in his furrowed Busch-Light eyes. "This is too many coins."

I was right. He had counted wrong. I hoped he would nod his head, take away the extra coins, and smile broadly at me. Then of course I would get the hell out of there. But that is not how it all went down.

"*No*. They're a dime a piece, and you had *twenty-four*. Have you got to the part 'bout multiplation in your schoolin' yet, son?"

I started putting copper pennies quickly up on the counter in collocation one by one to hopefully prove my point and also avoid his intimidation.

"No. No. No. I got it right. Trust me, son, and take your money." He chuckled in annoyance.

## PUSH MY LIFE INTO A DUFFLE BAG

The trucker in line behind me bellowed, "Oohh! Ha! This munchkin's got attitude."

Jack grabbed my hand turned it over harshly into a cup shape. Then he shoveled all the pennies I had started counting on the scuffed counter back into my hand in one harsh motion. Apparently Jack was not going to let himself be intimidated by a little boy. He was going to show me just exactly *who* the good multiplier was.

One high schooler coughed; the other huffed (again) and barked, "Come on, kid!" Braces filled the air.

The stress was palpable, but I wasn't gonna let it mess up the final money numbers. "No! I think it's only two dollars—two hundred cents for recycling." I implored him with my upturned brows to rethink his rules, his math.

He frowned at me angrily. He'd had enough. "Just you wait one minute now! Dammit! You're makin' me do this, you know. And do you see the line you're holding up? You need to show some respect to your soooperiors, son!" He walked over to the phone.

Time fell over and corpsed. Then it began to stink. The coins in my hand began sticking together and emitting a pungent odor of irony copper and salt-germs from a billion liquor store-sinner hands.

I thought about wheeling around to see the line behind me, but stopped myself at the last millisecond. I did NOT want to see the big people! Drowning swimmers do *not* want to see the black-eyed, great whites below them!

Jack pointed at me and picked up the phone. "Just one second everyone, *dammit all."* he declared. He dialed quickly. "Yeah, helllllloh Caleb, it's Jack; yep…say, I'm gonna tell you right now somethin' that needs fixin'. Your little boy here seems to think I'm givin' him the wrong change for the recycling.… Yep, yah.… I know: $2.40; yep…dammit."

"I'll fer shure tell him; yah, okay…*see yah real soon."* He slammed the '70s phone down on its clear plastic horns.

During this dreadful conversation all I could do was stare-focus on the face of the black haired slugger on the grape package of Big League Chew. It was a way to try to be somewhere else, perhaps on a quiet, green ball field. I could feel frustrated heat from the high schoolers on my moist neck. It was like an old yellow light bulb was being held an inch from the skin. It was horrible. And so I decided then and there that I would take whatever amount of money Jack wanted and jog (not run/but no way in hell walk) out of there.

More and more people were now in line: I could hear a belligerent woman's voice chatting with a laconic man about having to stay overtime at work when she should have been off at eight a.m.; all he kept replying was, "Shit, ah shiiiiet."

Jack then pig goaded me with a poke to my ribs. "Two dollars, forty fuckin' cents. Now git home! Caleb's waitin' fer yer ass, and times a-tickin'!"

I balled my fist around the coins. I wasn't sure if I was at this point angry enough to throw down the change and push over the cigarette lighter display (if I could even reach it—a mere gosling among smoky foxes), or, scared enough to start crying and run full speed for the door.

I did neither. Instead, I did what I've done ever since. I nodded and walked out. I faked robotic tranquility and indifference.

The trucker laughed at me. "STUPID FUCKER," muttered one of the boys—the worst words ever. They hit me like a frozen snowball in the back of the head. The eloquent couple toward the back continued bitching about work and the spike in cigarette prices. They were oblivious to my tragedy. They didn't care about me.

I made my exit. A cool breeze hit my forehead as I pushed open the glass doors, seeing a sticker on the outside glass that read, "This establishment is alarmed by Viper Industries 24 hours a day." There was a picture of a viper face with its jaws open, tongue out, fangs apparent. I let the door swing back sort of hard after I pushed through. My mighty revenge.

My stomach felt like swampy slime soup as I walked past the dusty, white ice machine and onto the sidewalk. I immediately began avoiding cracks and large ants on the concrete walk. This game regained my sense of order and peace after all of the liquor store stickiness—the immense and sudden vanishing of kindness.

The breeze was still blowing; it felt assuaging, it felt light blue against my moist skin. Luckily, there were tons of ants on the sidewalk that day, so I had lots of careful stepping to do and plenty of little faces to pull as I avoided minuscule landmine exoskeletons.

Caleb had told me to hurry home, but I took my time in order to quell my nerves and also delay the thunderstorm waiting at home. I believe I was too young at this time to form any strategy for dealing with his anger. Later on in my youth I would become smart at befuddling both his and my mother's anger. Wit was key.

## PUSH MY LIFE INTO A DUFFLE BAG

The cold sun moved a touch overhead and brought me inexorably into the grass of our front yard. I put my hands in my pockets. The house loomed large. *It looked like an ominous old man crouching over me as I moved slowly toward its front and center. Wrinkles. Mothballs. A livid old skeleton man, like a time bomb ready to push my limbs right off my body with his explosive indictments, "YOU'RE LATE! YOU'RE RUDE! YOU CAN'T MULTIPLY! YOU DO NOT RESPECT ADULTS! YOU ARE A WORTHLESS STEPSON! JUST A STUPID KID!" Its old fashioned timbers creaked in the pollen breeze.*

I felt so guilty I could puke. But what had I done? Why was I about to receive punishment? Why was I swimming in sticky concrete filled with writhing, crunchy insects of all sorts; especially black widows and pincher bugs (the brown kind that are under every brick in a nice garden)? There were no answers.

Regardless, I was in deep trouble. It was only a matter of stepping through the door to receive that trouble. I suddenly stopped. I walked off the concrete walkway, stalling. I paced over to the juniper bushes on the right side of the lawn and started squishing the little white-blue berries betwixt my pink forefinger and thumb.

Any moment there was sure to be a scream from inside the suburban dungeon as soon as the step dragon noticed my presence within his fiery lair vicinity. Any moment now…I was sure of it. But no noise. Nothing.

I looked again at the house. The old home appeared to be sleeping on his early fifties foundation.

The pollen continued to blow around. *I squished more and more berries.* Then I heard the strident pinch of the phone ringing inside. It stopped ringing—grasped by a dragon's claw. Now was my chance. The phone might just throw off the pulse of the anger flow from Caleb, saving me from his yellow teeth.

I walked up the three porch steps—one—two—three—passed the cheesy earth-tone foldable lawn chairs, and pulled back the aluminum screen door, holding it back with my left hand whilst pushing open the real door with my right hand. (The door could be pushed open easily without turning the knob—which was broken and scheduled to be fixed by Caleb and his rusty tools sometime before the U.S. collapsed in the same decadent manner of its Roman grandfather). I then entered the musty living room and took three paces in, then stopped.

I could hear Caleb on the phone, murmuring in baritone spurts, barely masking his fire-nostril temper. I don't know who called to this day. It doesn't matter. From where Caleb was standing, in the phone/desk/junk room off to the left of the living room, he could not see the front door. So I was quite invisible for the moment.

I walked to the *more invisible* right side of the living room and put my hand on the corner of the harvest-gold velour couch. It was soft and '70s to the touch. It matched the drapes. It matched only one of the lamps.

Dust. Gloom. I moved quietly into the kitchen (only a wall separating Caleb and I) and immediately opened the fridge, determined (I think) to create everything fine and dandy. I got out some orange juice. I got out my favorite Snoopy glass from McDonalds. I poured cloppy juice that was sour and needed a desperate stir. I didn't stop to stir. I just drank it down with a tremor in my esophagus. I did all this with my free left hand, not daring to let go of the $2.40 in coins that my right hand held hot and smelly.

The phone conversation on the other side of the wall continued, "No...no, no, no...well...I told her *that* already, now, didn' I?...I know, but she shoulda known that...mmh.... But *she shoulda still known that* 'bout them.... They always fuckin' do this—it's what they do; you know that as well as me.... She's bein' stupid is what...uh huh...well, just tell her that...that'll shut her up; *damn* broad...uh huh...uh...yeah, yeah, okay, fine.... I don't care what you say, just *deal with it!*... Anyway, listen, I gotta go. The kid's home."

I wasn't invisible.

"Yeah...oh yeah...*e x a c t l y*...you guessed it.... Listen...I *mean* it.... Deal with her...'k? She's just a stupid, stubborn bitch."

Eight second pause.

"I know; I'm just tired...gotta shitstorm of a headache.... I won't.... Listen.... I won't; don't worry; I'll learn him good.... Okay, see yuh." The phone clicked into the receiver like a cold colt revolver being cocked.

My breathing freneticized; all four feet of me remained motionless. I looked down at Snoopy. He was sweating too, but only because of cold orange juice, not because of being a bad dog today. I put my glass up on the gold-flecked counter top so I wouldn't drop it and turned toward the fridge like I was going to make another happy selection (perhaps a blueberry yogurt with fruit on the bottom?) and create everything okay.

Then I heard footsteps on phone-room linoleum. Then I heard them on shag carpeting. Then on kitchen linoleum. My ears flooded bright red. My palms flooded salt. He was standing behind me. I could hear his breathing.

He leaned against the wall lazily with one shoulder, his head cocked sideways in a manner that displayed mockery. He peeled his eyes, staring hard at the back of my duck-fluff head, and took a deep breath, huffing it out like a proper fairy-tale devourer. He spoke, "Hungry? Well, you ain't gettin' shit. Not 'til tomorrow; if I had my way not for a fuckin' week. You'd starve."

I still had my back to him; one foot turned inward, my hands were together in front of me, soothing each other as best they could.

"You'd better turn 'round, boy."

I couldn't. I was all sloppy orange slushy.

He bore down on me like a lion—so fast that I had no time to flinch. He clutched me by the shoulders and spun me around and then grabbed the sides of my head, squishing my ears painfully—his face two inches from mine. His eyes—steel gray and veiny—shot nail knives of hick wrath through my milky vision and into my soft, vulnerable brain. "DO YOU LIKE BEING A SON OF A BITCH? DO YOU THINK YER A SMART LITTLE SHIT?"

Little boys seldom have answers to questions like these. I didn't. I couldn't answer. Pure fright.

He was cussing tremendously. He shook me. "YOU LISTEN, AND YOU LISTEN GOOD! YOU NEED TO LEARN SOME RESPECT AND STOP GIVIN' US SO MUCH TROUBLE! YOU NEED TO QUIT BEING SUCH A LITTLE PRICK AND START PULLING YOUR OWN WEIGHT 'ROUND HERE!"

I was five or six. These words confused me.

He paused. Violent thoughts flashed across his pupils. "WHERE'S THAT DAMN MONEY?"

I held up my right hand and opened it quickly. He let go of my head and snatched up the coins, then stood up straight, looking them over (counting, I'm sure) and finally wiped his forehead with the back of his hand.

What a stressful day for Caleb. He was sweating, his eyes pulsating, and his bony, sunken hick face seemingly even more stained with tobacco and ignorance than ever. He looked like the kind of mad woodsy man that you'd read about in a newspaper: His family strewn about the red house, slain by a sappy axe or a kitchen knife, rusty-dull. Lots of work. Dismemberment. Elbow grease.

He counted the change again. "TWO DOLLARS AND FORTY CENTS! WHAT THE HELL ELSE?"

I gambled and shrugged my shoulders. I mustering a sincere I'm-sorry face. It pissed him off—he threw the handful of hot coins directly at my chest as hard as he could. I backed up and squinted as they hit me, but I didn't turn from them. They felt like fifty billion rocks from the sharpest of backwoods gravel driveways, rocks that had baked all day in 100 degree July sun. It hurt.

"SEE? THAT'S WHAT HAPPENS WHEN YER A BRAT! WHEN YER A SELFISH LITTLE PRICK!"

My heart got hot and began to hurt.

Caleb grabbed my hand; we walked quickly/awkwardly to the bathroom. He yelled, "ARMS UP!" My arms shot up. My lips quivered, but I didn't cry. I couldn't. He pulled my shirt off and threw it to the side of the toilet, then stopped. "You take your shoes and pants and socks and underwear off right now, and stay *right* here." He pointed to the very spot I was standing.

He left the room, his head shaking back and forth with frustration. I could hear his dragon footfalls all the way to Mom's room and then the faint sound of the sliding closet door moving along its aluminum track.

I jerked spasmodically, realizing I had *not* started undressing. I plopped down on the chilly floor. I tore off my right sneaker, which was already loose since I wasn't very good at tying laces yet. Then I went for the left, but it was tighter. Mom had tied this one that morning to help me out, and she'd done a grown-up job of it—tight and confusing. I couldn't get it off.

The laces were webbed in a thousand patterns of knots and loops. Spiders would hail it as the best ever. I couldn't get it off.

The cold sweat started exuding, my heart raced, I pulled and pulled and forced my face red, my little vessels standing out on my forehead and neck, my teeth crushed together, panicked, etc. Then I heard dragon's feet pushing the floorboards again, fast and loud, so I abandoned the shoe, stood up and tried to pull off my tan cords over my shoe.

I didn't work. I hopped around for a half second and then fell into the wall, accidentally knocking over the tiny mauve trash can with the bumble bee cartoon on it (little smiley face, little stinger shaped like an arrow coming off its butt, little dashed line curving behind it to show where it had been buzzing).

Somehow I didn't fall over. I caught myself by grabbing the towels hanging above me. What a mess. I was panic-panicked and starting to breathe in frenzy. But I was too late.

"What the hell are...I TOLD YOU TO!"

He pushed me over hard and held me down: crushing my tiny naked torso into the linoleum with his left hand while his right ripped off my shoe (I remember my Achilles tendon hurting for weeks afterward), then my pants, then my sweaty Scooby Doo underoos, throwing them all in a hurry to the same place he threw my shirt: beside/behind the grimy toilet.

While being held down I noticed a leather belt balled up in his fist against my chest—its buckle colder than the floor against my skin.

"GIT UP!"

I scrambled. I got up.

"Now you're gonna learn how sick yer mom and me are of you...the way you been acting," he tersely declared, turning away from me and wrenching open the bathtub curtain. He looked over the white tub from right to left as he closed his other hand tightly over my soft upper arm.

Bruise and blood pressure. *I was completely naked. From this point on my memory fills with white ceramic sorrow. It's almost like I was not the small child in the tub; I was not the boy being whipped by leather and iron. No. It was some other kid. It was some brilliant six-year-old actor in a powerful, academy-award winning movie about the ravages of child abuse—filmed in black and white—silent, almost, so that you can focus, you can feel, in all horrible vicarious monstrosity, the force of brute adults upon the bright light of children.*

*We watch as innocence flows unwillingly down the grimy drain along with the mucus blood. We watch, in slow motion, the angry face of the stepfather exacting all of his hatred, all of his misfortunate life upon the skin of his young dependent. We watch the screaming. We watch the breaking of hope, the fluid birthing of fear, and we wish we could pay good money (that instant) to somehow magically ascend out of our theater seats and enter the black-and-white movie with nothing but our bare fists, our clawed fingers, and our rage—to rip the fucking head off that heartless monster!*

*Lots of hot air in the lungs. Lots and lots of it. The ripping off of heads is the extent of my hatred for Caleb during this time. It is something I am willing to release, but can't find a real way to release it. Every time I think the hatred is gone, I find it waking from some red canvas cot in some small, dark attic space within my spirit/mind/being.*

*It's hard. It's hard to live with something awfully bloody that you can't forget even though you try and try and try again.*

I was naked and scared to death. And I knew right there and then that I was going to be spanked, and that the leather belt was going to be used. This made me feel squeamish and pitch-black guilty because the belt was reserved only for times when I was really disobedient or for when my stepdad seemed to want to make it known to me that my punishments were far *worse* than the ones he lightly exacted upon my younger brother Sam.

Caleb liked Sam. Sam came from the blood of both Caleb and my mom. I did not. I came from Mom's blood and some other person's blood: a virile shadow's blood.

We both looked into the tub for about two seconds—he preparing, and me noting the pallid appearance of the gallows pole.

I lifted my right leg to get into the bathtub but didn't do it fast enough, apparently, because Caleb pushed me against the tile wall so that my other leg flopped in. It was at this moment that I smelled the fermented, hop smell on his breath. He had been drinking while I was at the liquor store. Nothing new. Every hoarse breath he sucked in and pushed out stank of yellow beer—perhaps an entire six pack (and why not? It was his day off, after all), as he huffed and struggled to hurt me good. There wasn't even a wisp of a cloudlet of fresh air in the small bathroom, no real oxygen anywhere. Caleb's pores exuded alcoholic foam. He stank.

What was odd to my young, terrified mind was that Caleb had not turned on the water once I was in the tub; for some reason I thought he would perhaps swat me a couple times and make me bathe right there and then—thus making me go to bed super early as punishment, isolating me from my mom whenever she was to come home. This punishment would be a bad enough one, a lonely one. But Caleb had something else brewing.

He shook out his belt; it came lolling out floppy straight, like a dead water moccasin that still had some wet poison drying along its teeth. He looked me straight in the eye. "Time to be a man—you *know* you deserve this," he preached.

My lip began quivering uncontrollably. I stood with my naked body vulnerable to his scrutiny. My hands where shaking, half covering my tiny genitals because I didn't want Caleb to see my private parts. I felt so bare and wretched.

"You turn around and bend over. I've had it with you!" he growled, then belched, filling the tub airspace with a tepid Budweiser cloud that coated my mouth and nostrils.

Unfortunately, I did not bend over. Instead I started kind of hopping, my face contorted, pleading for reprieve, pleading for only a bath and straight to bed.

I couldn't look into his face, so I stared at his white tee-shirt. It was old and had small holes here and there (a couple under the armpit, a bigger one right against the ring by the neck, and a couple by the missing pocket) and had pen marks along the bottom. Some pen he'd tried to use wouldn't give forth its ink, so he scribble-forced it to flow on the rough cotton.

I noticed his jeans, too: scruffy and blue-brown with the obligatory Stockton working-man oil stains down by the calf and halfway up the thigh. Checkin' oil and fixin' trucks, motorbikes, and whatever else had an engine was a favorite pastime of Caleb's breed.

But back to my beating. My pleading submission was no use. My hopping only exacerbated the situation. The dragon became livid, frothy fomentation. His hoary eyebrows shot up, his eyes yellow white, pulsed with freshly stirred venom. "YOU BEND OVER *NOW!*" He forced my head down.

My eyes focused on my feet. My toes gripped the tub frantically. I did not want to bend or be hit too far over and fall foreword. That would be catastrophic to my pain mitigation plight. If I were a shattered deer under a salivating grizzly I would play deader than venison in a jerky jar. With my right hand I braced myself against the mildewed tiles of the cold, gritty wall.

The first lash fell, and it hurt worse than any sting from any wasp, any bite from any dog, or any spanking I had yet received in my five/six years of scurrilously surreptitious Caleb punishments. It hurt so bad that I forgot where I was for a moment. My face eased away from its painful grimace into a bewildered stillness. I looked almost placid, as if I were at the zoo seeing a big, warm lion for the first time. My hand eased its grip on the tile, my toes unclenched the tub, I let myself go with every blow of the belt—swaying in delicate motion as they fell into my lower back, my butt, my upper thighs.

The pain was too intense to be felt. This was a distinct "nothing" sensation, because all of my other spankings had hurt with every single hit; this one, however, hurt too bad to be understood. Each lash blended into its predecessor, and I couldn't feel when exactly a new lash struck, but I could hear each and every strike. And they sounded bad. They sounded worse than they felt. The lashes felt like a raw steak being pushed into by a harsh wooden spoon again and again. Numb and pressure. The sound, though, was wicked evil; it went deeper than the skin, puncturing the muscles and cracking against bone, making all things brittle and ground beef.

My mind raced with severe concern over what my backside was beginning to look like as Caleb remodeled it with his hellish meat-sculpting tool. I imagined redness and pus and wrinkles and other weird things like hairy spiders falling out of the cracks in the skin.

*An image of a large factory just East of Stockton that I had seen on the way out to my Grandma's house began to cloud my thoughts. It had large columns of smoke billowing out of pulsing chimneys, as metallic sounds clang-echoed and hammered.* It was a real-life monster factory, I was sure. And I began thinking that my back was going to soon look like I had monster surgery there. My behind would forever be bumpy and irrevocably shredded for life. These hallucinations were probably a gift from God. I firmly believe this. To this very minute I firmly believe this.

Perhaps His immense love for children made him touch my brain with a sort of Holy Spirit morphine. Madhouse endorphins danced like sugar plum fairies before my serene amazement.

The big warm lion at the zoo stood up on its hind legs and waved a fluffy paw at me. The sun made him glow like beautiful fur touched with solar fire. I quickly handed my blueberry cotton candy (a new flavor!) to my mom and waved back. The lion then nodded in reply, got back down on all natural fours and began grinning. His teeth looked pallid and prickly, menacing; they started growing bigger and bigger and sharper and sharper. Then I finally felt the true, excruciatingly full pain of the giant tenth lash. The buckle and its protruding hole-spike pierced into the topmost part of my sacrum, awakening me from the colorful zoo.

Now there was no mistaking where I really was. Now there was immediate and inexorable pain; a pain that I can remember to this day if I close my eyes at night before I fall asleep and focus all of my sad memory wells. I gasped, my eyes full of hot saline. My toes gripped the tub. My hands gripped the yellow tile. My heart took a needleful of 100-proof adrenaline. I was sure that my bones were now showing through my skin. This was punishment horror that I was having a hard time computing; by far it was the worst whipping I ever received under Caleb.

After this tenth lash, Caleb paused—and it was very quiet for a few seconds, just the sound of his cathartic breathing. I definitely wasn't going to make a sound. He scratched the back of his upper thigh, the nails making noise on the rough jean cotton. I started straightening up my back.

"OH, NO YOU DON'T!" he screamed, like a dog trainer, breaking a frightened pup of its remaining will. "WE'RE NOT DONE YET, BOY, NOT BY A LONG SHOT!" I heard the buckle make a chingle noise against the bath tub, and right there and then realized the reason for the immense pain of this spanking: He was using the buckle side of the belt.

I wanted to die. Caleb began the next procession of lashes. I don't remember how many more there were. When he finished huffing and puffing and whipping and exacting and hating, he stepped back from the bathtub. I glanced at him as he slowly examined his belt.

*"Shit,"* he mumbled, deep under his moustache. Then he wiped his belt on his jeans, examined it again, looked angrily sideways at me, held it under the running water of the sink, wiped it off on his jeans again, and looked at it once more.

"Good thing I didn't use my new one," he nervously chuckled. I just stood there, shaking and waiting, my body all aquiver. I wiped my bedewed eyelashes and snotty nose. The mucus was clear like hot glue. "'Cus if I had, you woulda stained it all up like the messy kid you are," he said, his words getting faster toward the end of the sentence. I didn't understand his exact meaning. I thought he was talking about my sweat or snot. But how could snot get on the belt? Maybe snot could come from my bottom if it was hit hard enough. I didn't know. Maybe. Gross stuff was part of being a human body, Mom had told me. I shouldn't be ashamed of that, but I really was, especially as I watched Caleb cleaning his belt, carefully wiping off the brass buckle with crumpled toilet paper.

I hung my head downward; I couldn't look at him anymore. Then I noticed a slender ruddy-pink line that ran down between my peach feet all the way to the drain. Caleb quickly reached over me and turned on the bath water, nice and warm. I watched the pink line get cloudier and pinker as the warmth engulfed it. I stood up straight, my backside stung with raw pain, the type of pain that doesn't want you to move a muscle. I grimaced and looked at Caleb beseechingly. He looked away and further adjusted the water until the temperature was perfectly comforting. A warm bath for a boy who had taken his punishment well.

I then began touch-exploring my back slowly with my right hand. I did this furtively, watching Caleb as he looked at himself in the mirror, straightening his moustache and fixing his dirty flaxen hair, an absent-minded ritual of his. I could feel redness and seeming divots in my skin. I imagined them as gaping apertures that revealed my skeleton and blood.

What was palpably apparent to me at that precise moment was this: the buckle spike had punctured a few times. Cat o' nine tails. Small rippings of flesh. My very own flesh. Bathtub horror.

I intently felt a super painful hole on my upper left thigh and noticed immediate pinkish fluid running down the backside of my knee, then my calf, then my heel, and ultimately into the warm water, swirling and clouding and disappearing. I looked at my finger. The pink was red on it.

The entire bath was now filling up. But the water wasn't a nice silver. It was a strange silver-brown-pink that made it look warmer and made it smell sort of metallic like the sweaty coins I had held for so long earlier on that spring day. I swished the water with my tremor hands. It felt good. The punishment was over. I never wanted to take the recycling to the liquor store ever again.

"Well, git in," said Caleb, looking away from the mirror just long enough to get annoyed with the sight of my stupid, nude little body, hovering over the water like a quaking dog who is unjustifiably nervous to bathe.

I eased into the water. With every inch the warmth filled the scrapes and holes of my posterior. I distinctly remember a tingling sensation that seemed to warn me that it was dangerous, even poisonous to mix one's blood and skeleton with water; especially bath water—with all its mildew, soap scum, and spider parts left over down in the dank drain hole. I worried.

I swished the water around more and more, slowly, nicely, so that Caleb would see that I was being cool—that I was not sad and not worried. If he even saw a hint of a crybaby in me he'd be quick to flog me again; if not with the belt then with a chain—or at least vitriolic grown-up words that would lodge in my head forever. I swished the water. I was fine.

"Now you take yer bath, and *I don't want to hear any fuss*; here's yer towel—I don't want to see any yucky kid stains, so wash up good," he ordered, taking two steps backwards out the door. Then he stopped and gave the final blow. "You've got five minutes; yer mom will be home really late tonight, so there's no point to you staying up to meet her."

My illusion of post-punishment equanimity vanished. I wasn't going to get to see Mommy today. This hurt, especially because her touch would have been the spiritual/corporeal healing salve for my surreal wounds on this day. Deprived of her, I would now have to face the nightmares of a night where my bed would be "stained" with yucky kid pinkness or glue mucus. It was going to be gross, and it was going to hurt no matter how much I scrubbed.

"So...when yer finished up put your pjs on and hit the sack, *you hear?*" he ordered. I think his six pack/wrath high was coming down now, and he was beginning to get one of his dehydration headaches. He never drank any water.

I nodded, accepting without hesitation my final sentence: sleepless loneliness.

The dragon walked out. Seconds later I heard the T.V. fire up, some car chase and gunshots.

My bath was miserable. The water lukewarmed and got even pinker. My sores tingled. I peed. I'm sure that wasn't good for my holes and insides, but I couldn't help it. My muscle control was all mixed up. I vaguely remember forgoing any soap use. I was sure it would sting like wasp stingers and deep cat claws. I did rub the wet soap bar against the yellow tile, though, so Caleb would smell soapy smell and believe I had washed thoroughly.

I couldn't sit down at all, which made my tiny thighs ache as I squatted in the pink pee water. If anything were to push against my raw backside I was sure I'd squeal. So, I squatted pitifully and swished the water for five minutes. I hated these minutes. I hated the tingling.

The last thing I did was pour a capful of VO5 golden shampoo into the water, down by the drain and fluff it around—not enough to make bubble foam, but just enough to take away the faint urine smell. Then I got out and dried off, patting my bottom gently and being extremely thankful that the towel was a pale pink. The drying sores stung and made me hate the bathroom.

Caleb then arrived and yelled suddenly, "Pick up yer *damn* clothes and git to yer room!" Headache for sure.

I did as he ordered with awkward celerity, moving by him in a flinchy, performance-art way. He must have noticed this because his hand went up like he was going to swat me as I walked away. Thank God he didn't.

I was still sweaty, still dirty, still shaking. I looked out my bedroom window: the windy breeze was still doing its spring work: scattering juniper berries into the street. The sun was not down yet. I looked at my Mickey Mouse clock on the wall and worked hard to read his black hands: five o'clock: a ludicrous hour for a five/six year old to go to bed. Luckily, my body was exhausted.

I pulled on my fuzzy, baby-blue pjs and stood in the middle of the room for quite some time, listening for Mom's '73 Nova to come rumbling up the driveway. I never heard it. I only heard T.V. crashings and the popping open of aluminum cans. A sated dragon in the living room.

My thoughts must have been muddled. I don't know. What do little children think about after abuse? When they're alone, when they're sure that nobody will ever want to look at their backsides unless to laugh, point, and explode with awe? I don't know what I was thinking, what I was doing.

My room was light blue, a boy's color. The Mickey Mouse clock was red and black, of course. My bed was probably dark brown. The carpet was shag, earth-toned, and held a musty smell that evoked images of suffocating people and breathing bugs. These were the colors in my room, a room that was eerily darkening with the onset of early spring dusk.

The small figure standing still in the middle of the room was white and pink. He was pink and red. There were small holes in his back, poked there by a belt buckle. There were deep scrapes in his back, scraped there by a leather belt. There were red bruises, too.

Caleb had set me straight. I had been being a little brat, and I would be careful never to be again.

# Chapter 2
# Caleb in His Entirety

Caleb: the dragon. No, the great white shark—sharks are scarier and more real. Caleb was my stepdad. In a lot of ways, that sentence sums it up. There was a lack of connection; we were faulty wires. There was no love between the two of us. I can't remember anything lovely or genuine; if there was it would have definitely been *only* from my little heart toward his.

I remember wanting desperately to be his number-one buddy, wanting to let him know that his jokes were funny and that he was cool in my personal board book. I often laughed extra hard for him whenever he was being witty in his own hick way. I probably looked ridiculous, and it must have been very apparent that I was trying too hard. After all, I was an apple-juicy child; I read like an open book filled with giant, colorful illustrations that helped Caleb's obtuse mind follow along and find out what I was up to.

On most days he didn't care to read me, though, but I can't blame him. He was a redneck whose mind was feeble and whose appetencies were far from noble: trucks, cars, models of trucks, models on trucks, cars, ladies who weren't models but were nonetheless sexy and skinny, being tough, playin' baseball then softball, and mind-numbing piss beer. Life for Caleb was simply workin' for the weekend.

He liked the word, "shit." He liked dirty jokes. He liked being against everybody.

Like all good mental midgets he'd had his glory days in his youth and perpetually lived in his memories of them. He was a great baseball player whilst in high school (in Linden—not too far from Stockton—and every bit as stinky) and maintained the school records clear up into the early '80s for, I don't know, RBIs (?), homeruns (?), lowest ERA (?)…something like that. This was back in, like '66 or '67; lots of sporty, grassy baseball. I wonder if he ever listened to *Revolver* or *Sgt. Pepper's Lonely Hearts Club Band,* etc. Probably not.

Caleb reminded us daily that he would have been in the majors for sure-fire lucrative decades, and consequently, we would have had a big, fat house on Lake Comanche with a sparkly gold (Caleb's favorite color), Ranger bass boat. Life, it seemed to him, would have been "nice and easy" if old Vietnam hadn't robbed him of his adolescent life dreams. Adolescent skill. Athletic glory. Money in the bank. Mind the main chance. If only.

I fully believed him every time he brought this up. I'd hang my head, shake it, and then look solemnly into his sandpaper eyes. *You're right, Dad; that war was bad—so much SHIT has happened to you. It's no fair; it's no fair at all,* I would think to myself and say with my disciple puppy eyes.

(Whenever I wanted to be in line with Caleb's life and being, I would cuss inside my thoughts. This gave me instantaneous big-boy pleasure. After all, when I grew up, I was going to follow in his and all men's footsteps: I would cuss and be tough and work for the weekend. I would have a moustache too, and unkempt facial hair that would show how hard I worked, from sun up 'til sun down, and how shitty life and Vietnam had been to me. I couldn't wait to have my first ice-cold Coors Light, which was Silver Bullet new at the time).

Speaking of Vietnam, Caleb never talked about it. Now, don't get ahead of me and start thinking that, like all good vets, he saw all kinds of death, misery, and bloody-faced friends over there, their red guts exposed in the humidity, and therefore never could quite talk about "Nam" with his prosthetic family, never could quite walk down the grocery store aisle and pick out some bananas without a stinging sense that napalm was about to obliterate the entire fruit section.

No. Let's not jump to that bittersweet Nam conclusion, that glorious Tim O'Brien thesis concerning the human spirit vs. total horror, total loss. A war story is really a love story. A gunship in the river. Rice paddies. Junglefied green berets. Nothing like that.

I have a sneaking suspicion that Caleb never saw any combat. He wasn't in the army. He wasn't deep in country, surrounded by VC. He wasn't rushing legless heroes to the choppers landing helter-skelter on a hot LZ. No. Save your breath, Mr. Johnny Cash.

Caleb was in the Navy. He was out at sea using a greasy skillet in the ship's bowels: the mess hall. I know for a fact that he was a cook. This is barely noble, if you consider nourishment noble.

From '67-'70, Caleb most likely *never* fired an M16, but he may have fired a dishwasher or two. I am picturing hash browns and eggs now, peppered with tiny peppercorn shrapnel. Ketchup for blood.

Weird: Caleb in a war. He most likely had nothing better to do in life than join up or get drafted or whatever. I'll assume here that he was a lucky (no combat) loser from the very beginning. He had lost the preseason game of life before the first grassy pitch. There would be no major leagues for strapping young farm-team Caleb, just an extra innings game of puttin' food on the table for his sexy, red-haired "broad" (my sweet mother), his son, and his brat stepchild.

Caleb speaks forth from the past. "Didja know that *I* was chosen—I was *still* in high school, mind you—to play ball at the *Orioles* farm team camp over in Maryland? *Didja know that?* Didja know that, um…what's his name…hall of famer…pitched to me—fast balls, mind you…and he pitched over a 'hunnurd in those days, and I hit ev'ry damn one right straight down between the shortstop's legs—*doubles.* I tell you what! *Every hit a double! One a triple!"*

Caleb would confabulate like a bard of old, weaving his glory story, his love of baseball and triples. I would smile broadly, fully stretching the muscles of my face, and nod again and again, and again, and again, and again, and again, and again, and look at Mommy and smile, she would smile, and then I'd carefully look back at Caleb, encouraging him with my smile to be my number-one buddy and tell me more of our vaporous home on Lake Comanche. I still imagine, to this day, that its well-dusted shelves are full of glittery golden trophies and World Series Oscars for best baseball man of the seventies.

"Can *you* believe that about old Caleb?" he asked, with a pointed finger to his sternum again and again.

*HELL, YES, I CAN!* my mind would sing and shout as I really declared, "Oh, yeah," glistening with filial pride, picking at my mashed potatoes, rolling buttery green beans into them and making them disappear in shallow Idaho graves.

Ah, a typical yet delicious childhood dinner memory: Caleb all aglow. It's Friday night circa 1981. Mom is relaxed. Sam is in his brown plastic highchair, his face covered with an instant-potato-mash beard, unkempt; I'm being the best number-one buddy I can be, laughing extra hard, wishing I was wearing a white tee-shirt that proclaimed in black fuzzy letters, "NUMBER-ONE

BUDDY." There is a breezy semblance of a real family, of the genuine love bonds that, in fact, did not exist in our house.

No. No genuine love betwixt those walls. It was rather a weird half-love, a house of constant love-trying, love issuing out like warm, rosy spider webs, but never sticking. Our lives were guilty lives. Our lives were lazy lives. There were annoying ghost whispers of selfishness and loathing floating around the insulation behind the old sheet rock. You could almost smell it; especially on hot days.

Our family followed Caleb's lead, and Caleb was not a good leader. He was what lots of men were, are, and will be: scared. And if one is scared, one becomes mean. So he beat me, physically and vocally. Looking back, I think he hated me and was too dumb to know it.

On the other hand, he was quite clever in hiding my bruises from my mom, or maybe he had intelligent ways of keeping me from bruising. Maybe he had a profound, hidden knowledge of the body and could exact punishment on it without manifesting the physical signs of that punishment.

Perhaps his one mess up was the time with me in the bathtub, but he covered his ass there by telling my mom this weaselly gem of a tale. "He's *always* messing with the steel rake in the backyard, trying to be good and do chores, but then I see him bein' stoopid out there, tryin' to twirl it like a ninja weapon or somethin' and fallin' over on it and stuff; dumb kid; *I keep tellin' him those rake spikes'll get him.*" And he glares at me good. And my mom believes him. And my mom looks my backside over and slowly shakes her head, her dumb finger up to her dumb mouth. Dumb concern. And I die a thousand deaths right there in my own room.

Despite this and other such personal hells, I still adored my stepdad, and I mean, adored. Caleb was my best buddy, cooler than sliced bread, cooler than Chewbacca.

I remember standing in our quiet kitchen one morning before school and telling him that I wanted a tattoo just like his. It read, "Born to raise HELL!" I would definitely get one as soon as I was an adult and big enough to play real varsity hardball. I thought this would shine forth as ultimate devotion and Daddy adoration. I had even mentioned almighty baseball. I wanted to follow in his cleat-steps!

But, smoldering Caleb saw it as me being haughty and wanting to use *profanity*. He was holier than that. It pissed him off. I could feel him beginning to hate me. He stared hard at me, lowering the gray, crumply classifieds. "If you do, I'll whip you one good," he mumbled.

This confused me. There was no further explanation. I glanced at my mother. She was slicing tomatoes on a dark-orange cutting board. She raised her eyebrows at me like, "You should know better; I agree with your stepdad; profanity is a sin for kids."

But I wasn't being sinful! His tattoo was cool, a family point of pride; we all agreed. He would show it off at picnics, and everyone would smile and then take merry swigs from their silver cans. It was fun. Good fun. It was a cartoon: tough and honest; so why the whipping of one *good?*

"Tattoos aren't for you. And if I catch you cussin'..." he stopped, flexed his paper and then whistled low, a whistle that translated to, "Oh, shit, will you ever get it?"

I could tell that his russet head was nodding in time with the warning whistle. My lip trembled as tornados spun inside my ribcage. I turned and left the kitchen, retreating to my quiet bedroom. I organized my stuffed animals. Why did he always bite my head off?

Caleb's tattoo read, "Born to raise hell!" in red on his upper right shoulder. It had a picture of a cartoon devil, scurrilous and raisin' hell with his pitchfork/trident-looking thing. This tattoo was a man's way of playin' ball with the world, a fact that justified the profanity. So I thought I was justified in wanting one just like it. I was wrong, of course.

It was extremely apparent to even people over in China that he did NOT want me for a buddy, but I refused to believe it; I would win him over. Cute kids in the movies did it all the time. Try, try again.

But then one day, I stopped trying. Instead of loving him, I opted to fear him. This was only a natural decision for a soft six-year-old boy, after replacing his head a thousand times a day. I then became an easily frightened child. What made the frightening worse was that my imagination was indeed huge and beautiful, able to spin a million scintillating tales, a God-ray gift from above. *Thus, the monsters got bigger and hairier. The walls got more and more jagged and more and more covered in spiked, aphid-covered vines. The aphids' mouths and legs were shiny and crackly. I cringed at the sight and sound of them...so much munching and bending.*

The house got creepier daily; Caleb got creepier hourly. I could see it with my own two eyes. He was slowly, subtly transforming into a great white shark, and nobody else seemed to notice! He was turning into Jaws, the biggest shark in the world! One night I stayed up way past bedtime and watched *Jaws* on TV with Caleb; it was the Sunday Night NBC movie special; it scared the shit out of me, and I remember not sleeping well for at least a week.

*And so Caleb grew darker and colder toward me with every passing season, pulling more and more giant yellow barrels down deep under the black water, showing his evil strength and destructive power. I shot the harpoon that attached these barrels to his back. It was a feeble attempt to keep him at the surface, by my boat, so I could tell him how tough he looked and how fast he swam and how much I wanted to be a slippery shark, too—great and white. But he couldn't hear me; he was too busy water-logging barrels and destroying my cute little tug. I was either going to drown or be eaten by him. Wooden boards were snapping in two, rivets were coming loose; the metal hull was scraping apart upon endless rows of bony teeth and razorblade fins. The end was nigh!*

There was no joining his team. He was a shark. I was a boy. And it was going to be cold in the ocean.

I made up my mind to swim fast toward shore, toward Mom. I was not one for drowning. I was smarter than that. I gathered my imaginative weapons and waited. I watched. I schemed. I feared. I lived not the typical life of a five-to-ten-year-old boy. No baseball for me, only shark swimming. Only water-logged blood in the home waters.

## Chapter 3
## Beasts in the Dark Water

I woke up. Fast. There were noises inside the house. There were scuffled footsteps in the hallway, some creaks in the old walls. My little body began to pulse quickly.

Quiet. For almost like a minute. No more footsteps. Was I imagining footsteps? Was I dreaming them? I listened. Quiet. Still. I pulled the covers up close to my chin and tried to make my breathing nonexistent. My toes clenched. Ten little clenches. Quiet like crazy.

I looked directly at the shadows in my room...from the orange street lamps through the hoary tree arms through the cold glass windows to my walls. Shadows. Weird shapes. Monstrous. Imagine.

*There it is again: scuffled footsteps! I DO hear them!* They were moving again. The noises were moving for sure. But they seemed to be moving toward the kitchen, not my doorway. Good. Thank God.

I listened hard, as hard as a child can. They faded from noise to nil. I wished to Almighty God that Luke Skywalker was standing in front of me: his confident face and light saber aimed at the black square of the doorway, ready to Jedi the hell out of Caleb if he dared enter my room, his light saber light blue and buzzing with hero fireworks!

I also wished to God that Indiana Jones was standing next to Luke, his brown leather bull whip pulled back, his Colt revolver aimed at the black square of that hellish doorway, ready to punch the hell out of Caleb with leather, bullets and fists.

I wished some more heroes into the air. And I listened.

Sweat ran down through Indiana's stubble. He looked at me with Harrison Ford's classic stress/anxiety/confusion face. Worried, but ready for hell. They would protect me. My heroes.

But they wouldn't. My heroes weren't between the door and me. They weren't there. I was alone with only my blanket for a weapon, and it could only soft somebody to death through paroxysmal giggles.

*And there are the scuffled footsteps again!* They're moving about like a bloody wolf in a dark forest of furniture trees and hollow-wall earth-works trenches. Was he hungry, this wolf? Was I like a hot little steak? If this wolf was really a great white shark, Caleb, he wouldn't try to eat me, but he might come in and hurt me.

No. That's too easy.

He might come in and murder me. With an axe. He would finally be through with me, rid of me. Then he could enjoy my mommy's thighs without any bratty interruption from an acquired child. Although I was very young, I knew some things. I knew they did sexy adult things at night, like kissing and rubbing, and I also knew that Caleb wanted to do sexy things during the day too, but I was always in the way, taking away some of my mom's precious attention and time. There would be more black lacy underwear, boobies, and Chapstick if I were out of the picture.

So he would murder me, if not tonight, then soon, and at midnight, when the world was ice quiet. He would be like a smoky phantom with a purple cape. He would get away with it by telling my mom that I had run away, like all spoiled brats do. She would believe him, and they would kiss for a long time, strands of sticky shark saliva falling on her milky boobies.

Midnight. I listened harder. These mute foot sounds were life and death. Then no sound. No creaks. No scuffles. I had to do something, to *move*—requiring noise—but…but if he heard me…he might rush in and kill me.

I weighed the possible consequences of making noise. *Okay, so if he hears me he might kill me—to keep me quiet or something; or, on the other hand, he might be waiting for me to fall asleep so that he can murder me without a sweaty wrestling match. Hmmm. So if I stay quiet, he will come in and murder…maybe.*

Both options sucked. I was going to die either way. I didn't know what the hell to do now. I was a weird Hamlet in a weird confessional. I vacillated over my upcoming action. Anxiety.

I listened hard…nothing! Not a sound! No sounds for a couple minutes now. They'd be back for sure, any second now. I knew in my heart they'd be back, a black fog in the hallway with a purple cape!

I really didn't want to get murdered. I had to see Mommy for breakfast in the morning. There was a new box of Golden Sugar Crisp in the cabinet; I had seen it earlier that day when Caleb had grabbed some tortilla chips. There were also cartoons on tomorrow, too: it would be Saturday. Yes, tomorrow would be good. I did not want him to kill me quite yet, but I hadn't a doubt that he would—at midnight—the most *perfectest* time. And after the killing, he'd hide my limp body under the bed, behind my Tonka tractor play sets and my stuffed Paddington Bear. (I never played with him.) He'd use the pink bathroom towels to mop up the blood and mucus on the bed.

I looked up at my Mickey Mouse clock; it read… *"Shoot! 11:05 p.m.!"* I knew that both of Mickey's hands would converge on the twelve in a matter of minutes, and that that meant midnight. (We were learning time telling in school, and I was good at it; my teacher had given me a red star on three of my clock chart papers) The middle of the night. It would be darker and quieter than ever, ice-ocean quiet, and shark Caleb was gonna swim out of the kitchen to come chomp me to shreds! Rows of white-triangle razor teeth sinking and sinking and ripping and bruising!

*Now or never! I have to do something now or never!* Good thing I had come up with a plan over the last couple days. I vividly remember planning this plan on art paper with a red crayon. Manifest—plan = I shot out right out of bed. Noises be damned!

Over on my heavy blue dresser was a thing of Scotch tape, and in the bottom drawer were empty Coke bottles, hidden under my corduroys: five bottles that I had one by one stolen from the recycling, careful to not let Jaws find out. The bottles were a glassy rattle alarm to wake me up on stuffy murder nights. The tape was to lock my bedroom window.

Sometimes Caleb would go out on the wilting lawn to check the sprinklers and have a smoke late at night. I knew he *was not* doing anything productive out there. He was simply planning another way, a secret way into my room in order to kill me without Mom knowing. His purple cape was hidden under the big rock by the coiled hose.

The coiled hose image got me thinking…maybe he wouldn't hide my body under the bed. A girl at school had told me that dead bodies started stinking like cheese after an hour and a half. Maybe he'd take my dead body out the window and hide it behind the drive-through bushes at the McDonald's we frequented. A shark could swim there as fast as the wind on the sea. And this shark knew a shortcut through suburban coral roads into the kelpy back entrance of our favorite oil-slick restaurant. He could hide my body there really fast, at like, one a.m., when it was super black and everyone in the ocean was snoring bubbles.

Nobody would ever find me in those bushes; they were huge, dusty, and dark green. Plus they were full of spider webs and moths: nobody would go crawling through them to smell my cheesy body. One time I saw a dead crow way back under those bushes. It was on its back with its mouth open. There was dried blood on its beak. There was a definite cheese smell. A feet cheese smell. The girl was right.

I shuddered at the thought of moths and spiders eating me, my mouth agape—with blood coming out of it—whilst people drove on through for their happy meals and orange drinks. Yuck. I didn't want to be scary cheese. Hence, the tape and bottles. He would not catch me asleep! I was already out of bed and one step ahead!

This was my plan: if he came in I would scream bloody murder for my mommy and wake up the whole neighborhood without caring if it was bad-boy behavior. Even baby Sam would wake up screaming bloody murder. I would scream that loud—loud enough to make Caleb's hairy ears bleed the same way he made my nose bleed again and again.

I stopped quickly half way over to my dresser. The scuffled footprints started up again! He'd heard me! This was it! They were swimming out of the kitchen and down the hall toward my bedroom door!

I trembled; I had to hold my pee back with all the bowel muscle strength I could muster. Now was the time, and I wasn't prepared! I hadn't the sand for the scream I needed, and now Jaws himself was going to eat me! I braced my hot little lungs and filled them with stagnant air. I was *so* ready to try my voice at audible salvation.

But then the footsteps stopped again, and it was instantly quiet. But then again, right then, the floor creaked just once about ten feet down the hallway. I exhaled silently and quickly inhaled again—more oxygen ammo. I was all electric.

Suddenly, the footsteps resumed—fast—but back toward the kitchen! Now was my chance to set up the bottles that would throw Caleb's attention off me and give me enough time to scream the scream heard round the world. I ripped the bottom drawer open and pulled out two bottles (my hands were too small to hold three). I accidentally clanked them together, making a glassy noise that sent sound waves through the water—out my door and down the hall!

I stopped. My mouth agape. A big, huge, fat mistake! But there weren't any noises coming from the kitchen in reply. I stood up and bravely paced over to the bedroom door that was open about a foot to let hallway cottage-cheese ceiling air in. I strained and listened, one of my ears seeming to turn sideways like an alert fawn in a field of mountain lions.

No noise. My forehead was damp with salt water. I glanced to my left: there was the little blue chair that I used in the mornings to sit on whilst I tied my shoes. It was part of the plan. I put the bottles down by the door and moved toward the chair. I got behind it and picked it up. It was heavy. I had to be very careful not to make huffing noises. I put it behind the door (4/5ths closed) and stood up on its shiny wooden seat. It creaked loudly! *Another mistake!*

But still nary a cricket of a sound from the kitchen. Tick. Tock. Tick. And then I finally heard them: footsteps ringing out on the linoleum like a freight train! All too quickly they were on the hallway carpet and picking up speed!

I held tight to the back of the chair with one chubby hand and with the other I stretched as far as I could toward the bottles on the floor—mere inches away! Thoughts of Luke Skywalker stretching his hand toward his light saber in the Hoth snow cave and having it zoom into his Jedi fingers *just in the nick of time* flashed before my blizzard-blitz imagination.

I wished I were a Jedi! I needed those bottles! If anything I could use them as brown-shiny dual light sabers and cut up Caleb's face. Then I could tell R2 to start up the X-Wing, and we'd get the hell off that frozen planet! I would be free up in outer space!

I stretched and stretched—the bottles sat motionless. The dark side clouded my thoughts.

The finsteps arrived on the other side of the door! I shot up straight. My eyes exploded with wetness. My courage dissolved. *This was it:* I was to be murdered by chomping or broken bones, or Caleb was just going to punch my lights out and put me under those bushes where see-through, white spiders would gorge their bellies on my soft, wet intestines and liver.

The door slowly slid a few inches across the carpet. Its hinges creaked like a wicked banshee with a blood clot throat. I froze. I leaned back to avoid the encroaching door. It hit the bottles. Clank. It pushed them slowly forward. Then it bumped into my chair and stopped.

Mickey froze. His black hands stopped. The door moved back five inches, confused, and then slid adamantly forward 'til it hit the chair leg again. *The door was a blind, giant squid slathering its tentacles this way and that on the deck of a creaky boat lost at sea. Soon one of the suction tentacles would find exhausted sailor, me, grab hold, and rip me down into the cold sea, straight into the beaky mouth, where my skull would be crunched into bits whilst my muffled water screams turned to blood and boney bits of brain. Then jaws would come quickly and tear my legs off before the squid beak could swallow them, a black sea feast of flesh and bone! This was my fate!*

The door hit the chair leg again: this time with a slight bang. I freaked out and lost my Spartan will, backing up too far on the chair and losing my precious balance. I remember this fall with absolute clarity. It was a foggy sensation of losing control of my will and my body, something I hate, in the form of falling.

Gravity pulled me seemingly up then down—through the vaporous curtains of dark night air. I fell over the back of the chair—somehow, like a successful pole-vaulter, and landed in a moist pajama pile on the shag floor with a dull thud sound. Unfortunately, my foot caught the top of the chair (perhaps only a bronze medal?) as I descended and rocked it enough to send it careening silently down upon me. It hit me and trapped me under its woody ribcage—a frenzied sailor in a cage for dinner.

Now the door was free to swing open and the tentacle free to suction-clutch me!

The gaping black space behind the door widened, and I could see a gray silhouette staring down on me as the bottles were rolled aside.

I struggled under the chair to get a large chunk of air so that I might scream bloody murder, but I couldn't get enough due to the fact that I had started crying in hot convulsions. No more courage. McDonald's bushes and spiders were all I could think about.

The dark figure glided into the room like a phantom. The dark figure hovered before me. The dark figure reached over to turn on the light. Click. Light painted everything with a crystal coat of yellow safety.

My mom's face beamed with concern, confusion, and love as she looked down on her little son, writhing in agony under a chair. "Son, what *on earth* are you doing?" she said, gliding quickly forward and lifting the chair off me.

She didn't yell. She didn't exclamation point. She was robed in compassion and decency. She picked me up in her strong arms and wiped my nose and eyes. "Why are you up so late....what is all this mess?"

I sniffled and turned back into a small-year-old boy—innocent and free to cry about not knowing why anything in this crazy world happens. Moments before I had been in the military and seemingly twenty-five, planning, evading, and being a stealthy Jedi. Now I was back to being Tallene's little boy. I let my head rest on her lower neck; it was warm and soft. Then she sat me down on my bed and crouched down in front of me. She glanced at the bottles, the chair, the Mickey clock, and then looked me straight in the eye with love that only a mother can exude.

"What is all of this, son? What are you doing? Why aren't you in bed?" she questioned, smoothing down my sweaty hair and pushing it back off of my forehead.

What could I say to her? How did I answer? To be honest, I don't remember. Of course, I didn't say that I had been enacting a strategy to keep her husband from killing me. Rather, I'm sure it went something like this: "I had a bad dream, Mommie, about a big squid with a mouth, and I was trying to keep his mouth from coming in the door!" I stated.

Her eyebrows furrowed. She hugged me tight and said, "No, no, no, sshh. There are no squids in this house, son, just you and me and Sam and Caleb. Don't you worry. It's just your bedroom in the dark. But you know what?" She pulled back from me and looked me in the eyes with a big radiant smile. "Your bedroom never changes; it's the same in the dark as in the light and looks the same when you're awake as when you're asleep, so you're always safe. No squids, no monsters, only your Star Wars action figures and your stuffed animals and other toys. See?" She pointed at them, and then we both looked around the room quietly (me still holding tight to her, the sweat drying into my fuzzy pjs) and I nodded, playing my part. She tucked me in and kissed my cheek. "If you need me I'm right down the hall, baby, okay?"

I nodded again. I believed in goodness again.

"No more giant squids, huh?" she asked.

I smiled and wiped my eyes, nodding my head a million times as if to say, "Of course not, never again will I fear squids. They are *not* real." Unfortunately, Jaws was real, and he was snoring in my mother's bedroom.

"Okay, I love you, hon..." she soothed, and turned to glide like a regal ghost out of my room, but then stopped to take note of the two Coke bottles on the floor by the open door.

"Where did you get these?" she questioned.

"I saved them from the recycling. I like to drum on them with pencils and practice music lessons, but only when you guys aren't home so that it's not loud." I started to panic, thinking of Caleb, the coins for used bottles, the neon liquor store, and the whole poopy mess that was "recycling." Please don't tell Caleb. You can take twenty cents out of my piggy bank, but *please don't tell Caleb.* I like the bottles, and I am quiet with them so that they don't break. I like them; *please, Mommie!*" I declared, trying to make a sound case so that I wouldn't be eaten in the morning.

She paused and looked at me with a strange, cute expression. "Okay, Lovey, we'll keep it secret so that you can drum like 'Animal' on the Muppets and rock and roll all you want. Sound good?"

I loved Animal. He was my favorite Muppet. His psychedelic colors and hair were so cool. I smiled as my eyes brightened. I nodded like a trillion-chillion lightning strikes.

"Where should I put them?" She picked them up and held them before me.

She was being extra awesome! "In the bottom chester-dror," I said, pointing with vigor.

She opened it and chuckled, seeing that there were others bunched in around my winter sweaters, nicely so that they wouldn't make a sound when the "dror" was opened.

"You are very clever, son." She chuckled again and shook her head as if to say, "My crazy little guy!"

I giggled. All was Christmas and candy cane joy at this moment. My mom was the coolest and I was her son. We were both cool, and really funny when we worked together.

She placed both bottles in amongst the sweaters and wrapped them up nicely. "Oh, and this will help," she muttered, opening the drawer above it and pulling out a pink tee-shirt that I didn't like wearing because Caleb said it was a girl's tee-shirt.

"I know you don't like this one," she muttered, unfolding it. She shut the shirt drawer and stretched it out over the bottles in the sweaters, completely covering any sign of brown glass in the cotton folds. "That'll do," she said, almost as if she were as mythically cheery as Snow White; then she shut the drawer quickly in order to show me just how quiet she had made the Coke contraband.

I giggled some more. "Yeah," I said.

Then Snow White stood up and clicked off the lights. "No more squids or monsters, Lovey, only sweet dreams, okay?" she asked.

"Yep, and light savers [sabers—I pronounced it wrong 'til I was eight], too, Mom," I declared, proud of myself for being so tough.

"Remember to only drum when the babysitter is here; if you do when Caleb is home he'll want those bottles for recycling. He'll take them away from you, so be careful with them and have fun…but *don't* let him see them," she whispered, then smiled at how oddly peachy-sleepy her firstborn was.

I gave her a thumb's up in the mild darkness of my bedroom. This made her chuckle like a raccoon with a nighttime secret all the way down the hallway. My heart was glad to hear this. Indeed, to this day I fully and colorfully remember my mother's sweet feminine laugh. It was like radiant cherry blossoms in springtime. I miss it so.

The gentle night then ushered me into slumber land. The thought of being murdered melted away, and for a good eight hours I was just a silly boy asleep in a room filled with action figures and armistice. My mother's lighthouse was keeping night watch on my tugboat, and Jaws was in some distant sea, snoring bubbles deep down in the salty blackness.

# Chapter 4
# Conception History
# (A) Lodi and the Kids

Before me there was my mother. And she had been a child once, somewhere in California, and for some time. Her parents weren't the best, but then again, how many of us actually have parents who are the best?

After childhood, she became a high-school kid in Lodi, at Tokay High, just a little north of Stockton. Lodi was a nicer, more peaceful place, but still a bit farmy like Stockton, and very, very hickish, especially back in the early seventies.

Bio data: Her full name was Luella Tallene Jones. To this day I keep her last name as my own: Jones, a good name, a true name, the only last name in my past worth keeping because it reminds me of her. I will always love her.

My mother was a typical high-school kid looking for flirty fun around every corner in the breeze way or cafeteria, but also trying to magically get good grades without a lot of effort. She was a young woman in her adolescent years, slightly rebellious, staying out late, striving for worthless style points in the sardonic eyes of the "in" crowd, and maybe, just maybe, kissing a cute boy now and then for kicks in chrome-bumpered automobiles. Vinyl seats. Lip gloss.

I wish I could go back in time and be invisible so that I could watch my mom raise her hand in American History class, watch her drink a Coca-cola on a crisp fall night at a football game, watch her pick out the perfect mauve bell-bottom outfit for the first day of school sophomore year, etc. I wish to observe her young and fully alive (within a tiny glass capsule), before debts, affairs, and all the other life demons became her style, her wont. Before Stockton. Before me.

Her youth years interest me greatly. They're like May sunshine on an echoing green, fragrant and rolling on forever. I wonder what little Tallene was like. Was she a giggly girl? Was she vapid? Was she unpopular? Was she shy, a loser, or was she *"in"*? And that begs the question: what did it mean to be "in" from 1971-1974? Did it have to do with marijuana? I hope she was just *barely* "in," but not enough to sell her soul.

More questions: what did she look like aside from all the foggy photographs of her in high school? Was she a late hippie? A free spirit? Did she listen to Led Zeppelin and Black Sabbath, or, at the far other end of the sonorous spectrum: the burgeoning Carpenters? Wait...did she listen to Yes, and thereby become cognizant of myriad possibilities? Did the sky open for her, or rather, did the ground?

Maybe she listened to all of the above, and maybe it all happened forever. Maybe not. Maybe none of the above: option E on the S.A.T. Maybe music wasn't as important to her as it was to me when I was in high school in the earliest nineties, an orange-and-black butterfly wing popping out of a silent chrysalis.

I wish I could walk by her in the breeze way. I wish I could stop her and look her in the eyes, two hands on her shoulders, and say, "You're doin' great! You're a beautiful girl!" but then I'd start crying, and that would probably freak her out. So maybe I don't wish anymore.

I remember my high school years. They were a roaring grizzly bear juxtaposed to a sunlit sterling rose, death and dawn all at the same time, teeth and morning dew. High school is such a brutal time. It seems frozen to me, almost, spinning off in the black galaxy reaches of old memory, like a golden friend who still owes you a good amount of money and pretends it's forgotten.

I think I hate high school. I know I hate Tokay High, and yet I never attended there. But I was conceived there. I was conceived on the coldest concrete floor of the breeze way, with silent metal lockers looming overhead, with black, ancient specks of smashed-solid gum here and there, with the night and the trees and the football field aglow with high school sports. Everybody focused on the boys in uniform, tackling and chugging through the yards on the grassy field of play.

Frost. Red noses. Everybody there together, cheering, booing and being. Everybody, that is, except for two members of the student body, young and randy. One of them, my mother: Tallene. One of them, a boy named Stewart Vega. They were losing their virginity as teenagers, a road that many choose: to get it over with: the mystery of sex: the pain of sex: the ephemeral pull of sexual coupling, intercourse, screwing, fucking, doing it, getting it on, etc. My poor stupid mother and that ghost of an asshole, my father.

Apparently, Mom was fond of darker boys, because Stewart was Italian. He had dark hair and dark eyes. He was a Vega, Catholic and Californian to the core. He was fond of lighter girls. She was very white with fiery red hair and blue eyes, a color palette altogether foreign to him, intriguing to him. She was a Jones, busty and awkward. Unlike Stewart, her family was not a part of her, in that she didn't really know or care for her heritage. She really wanted only to escape it. His family was too much a part of him. He had no real self-identity autonomous from the honorable family name.

Tallene and Stewart were opposites, but high school always seems to blur the culture lines when it comes to kids, because kids don't really know who they are yet or what they believe in. They're just trying to survive their time in its clawed hallway clutches.

The Vegas had inveterate roots that clung down deep into the Lodi soil and ramified outward into all directions of California's central valley. The Vegas were prominent. They were bankers, librarians, contractors, realtors, and later would become newspaper writers and editors. Vega was a name somewhat well known and repeated at dinner parties, company meetings, and little league games. Sometimes their money was the topic of conversation, for they had a good amount of it. In short: they could afford things, therefore: Stewart could afford popularity. And his parents liked him being popular in the American business microcosm of high school. After all, young Stewart was carrying on their tradition.

On the steaming Tokay lawns, he was the big man on campus—smiling, joking, involved, flirting, but never raucous or ribald like other popular boys. He was more reserved, thanks to his Italian-Catholic upbringing.

Stewart was a third-generation American. His great grandparents were Italians who had made the move from the vine-ripe fields of rocky Italy to the fertile business soils of America way back in the day, and from them the torch of the family name was passed on over to California where it began to truly bloom in the fifties and sixties.

It reminds me of the intriguing fictional story of the great Corleones. Ellis Island. Big dreams. Tommy guns. But the Vegas ran legitimate businesses, of course. And they didn't whack people.

However, they were every bit as tenacious as the Don in climbing society's golden ladder. And Lodi was their ladder: a good place to be if you were concerned with climbing, because the lines of social hierarchy become quite visible during the sixties and seventies. There was the lower class: mostly farm workers or factory laborers, immigrants, vagrants stuck in middle California with no way out and not enough guts to head for the big cities. Then there was the massive, burgeoning middle class (even *before* minivans): mostly white and involved in profitable Lodi businesses. After all, "The business of America is business," as Calvin Coolidge would say.

There were obvious growing pains: stormy and distinct racial differences in Lodi at this time: thousands of poor, farming Mexicans, busy, busy, busy Italians, picnicking whites, nonexistent blacks, and one or fifty-three Asians. There were buildings slammed right up against farmed fields, which were skirted on the other end by mini malls and last-minute baby-boomer housing developments going up at the speed of a rotating Creedence Clearwater Revival record. (They wrote a song entitled, "Lodi," which contained these telling lyrics, "Oh, Lord, I'm stuck in Lodi again.")

Central Californian progress. Not exactly San Francisco, but not exactly Timbuktu either. Happy Purgatory.

Lodi was incontrovertibly not part of the urban "in" crowd. Sacramento, an old friend, was now in the "in" crowd, which made matters worse. Ever since becoming cronies with Oakland and (gasp!) San Francisco, Sacramento was always making fun of Lodi for its dowdy old clothes. And Stockton always threatened to beat Lodi up. So here we have a rock and a hard place and a "city" trying to be a "city," a place for kids to grow up feeling insecure about their home community. Oakie kids. And I don't mean dustbowl, Oklahoma migrants, I mean oakies spelled like a dusty, young oak. Yes, oakies with miserable attitudes, with fragrant manure stuck between the cracks in their shoe treads.

Even though Stewart was popular, he still had the stink of immigrant posterity about him. And he had the enormous pressure of a family name/pride to uphold. Golden sons have burdens of heavy gold. He had a terrible balancing act to maintain: being a kid, yet also being living gold bullion.

Practical examples: should he smoke this joint during lunch out behind the gym? Should he hang with rebellious partiers—just because they would advance him in social status as the big man on campus? Should he, too, be rebellious? Should he sleep with Veronica or Susie—or nobody? Should he be a good Catholic and a total square? How does one be Catholic and cool if he's not the pope? Should he stop answering so many Algebra questions correctly? Should his big Chevy truck be bigger? Greener? Sparklier? Was he tough enough? Should he focus his outfits more? Did this teacher really dislike the stench of family pride about him? Are those guys racist over there?

A million questions. Kiddy problems to solve. And then even more problems: Stewart Vega was born with a stern, laconic face, replete with deep set, dark eyes. He looked internally thoughtful and slightly angry, even when his face was entirely relaxed. Now, on the other hand, if he *was* smiling, he was smiling all the way—happy-happy—and his big face radiated. This was a very inviting expression, but seldom occurred, due to the fact that Stewart was oft quiet unless he was engrossed in convivial conversation.

Another strike against him: he had a bad temper (which could ignite almost anywhere) passed down by his late father, who had died when Stewart was a little kid. The only memories of his dad were mostly bad ones: the temper, the bad beatings in the stairwell, the angry words toward his mother, tempests of fire hidden from society quite well as the Vegas progressed. I don't remember exactly how his dad died, but I think it was a car accident, a liberating, yet sad event involving crunched steel and pulpy blood.

Stewart's widowed mother, Margaret, became obsessively protective of her only son after that. She was obsessed with his comings and goings, successes and failures. His close friends often called her "Mother Hen" for her incessant pecking and meddling. He found a little release in their jovial mockery. He secretly hated her for pushing away cool kids who were just becoming new friends. Sometimes it seemed as if she in fact *didn't* want him to be popular. The great parental paradox. A mother's righteous, all-knowing, all-seeing love.

Her beautiful son would have only the best friends: those who passed her crazy qualification standards. Her beautiful son, who wasn't really all that beautiful. He was *not* an attractive lad. The pretty girls would *not* date him, much to his frustration: woody kindling on the smoldering temper.

He was a large guy, not all that fat, but like an NFL lineman: big and meaty. The sight of him would make you want to put down a hearty meal of potatoes and beef and sauce, perhaps a giant mug of lager, then nap in a giant recliner with a fuzzy blanket over your soporific bulk, inhaling and exhaling steadily, peacefully, indeed automatically like a hibernating grizzly.

Stewart's large body rendered him largely insecure. (Side note: his small penis rendered him even more insecure. If he ever in fact did land a pretty girl he was sure that at the moment of manly-triumphant unveiling his penis would incite laughter in the lucky lady and terminally turn her off. Big body, small pecker; it wasn't fair. High school boys have the dumbest obsessions.)

The one big thing in Stewart's favor was his charismatic personality. He was quite funny and very sensitive toward others. Usually. He was also witty. Such charisma propelled him actual concrete popularity by the time he was a senior, earning him lots of free beer at numerous parties…good times minus the golden hotties. And thus Stewart advanced despite the odds against him. No Ellis Island would hold him back. He would dominate the school in the end, and he would definitely, finally, at some point score with a pretty girl: her clothes in a pile on the floor, her armpits all sweaty.

In the autumn of his senior year Stewart found said pretty girl: she was a fifteen-year-old white lass with freckles, no real popularity, and a family with a conspicuous dearth of power and money. In fact, her family was dirt poor. Her dad, Ray, was in prison. Had been for a couple years due to drug charges. Apparently he was a truck driver who took "uppers" to stay awake on long stretches of I-5. Truckers have to deliver their freight on time if they want to make any money, so one could surmise that he was just trying to do his job completely and efficiently. Well, the money he was *trying* to earn stopped flowing after he was arrested for whatever those "uppers" were. They must have been stronger than No-Doz. Knowing a bit about his greasy nature makes me think he was just your average junkie, always looking for a fix because he could never find satisfaction with his life. Unlike most truckers, he loved flashy things: flashy clothes and flashy Cadillacs. My mother told me that he continually lived beyond his means. Through such irresponsible spending their already-indigent situation was driven into the very bowels of the great black beast: debt. Ray couldn't give a shit that his little family hadn't much food in the old cupboards; as long as he and they lived an illusory life of luxury, then everything was fine, flashy-dandy fine.

His wife, my grandmother Lulu, lived the same way. She was obsessed with every frivolous gadget toy that hit the market. Like an insipid child, whatever the T.V. told her to buy she bought in order to fill the void of being grossly ignorant, perhaps to fulfill the prophecy of being ignorant.

Bliss. Blindspot Cadillacs. American waste. Land. Slender little filtered cigarettes.

With Tallene's dad locked up in prison, Lulu began working various odd jobs to keep the bills from crushing her. She made one smart move in divorcing junkie Ray in 1972. Then she fortuitously met and married another flannel-wearing truck driver (a real tough guy, a man's man) in 1974 named J.R. Barjager. Surprise, surprise: he was an actual good man among creepy creeps.

He was honest. Hardworking. Rare. Elbow grease. His buddies addressed him by his truck-driver-radio call name, "Bear Hunter," for he was wont to hunt actual bears up in the deep northern woods during beef jerky-n-beer-hunting season. J.R. owned many big guns.

Ray would never have hunted bears. Too yellow. Caleb lacked the balls, too.

Believe it or not, J.R. had been Ray's good buddy for years. I don't know if Ray knew that he was quietly sweet on Lulu all that time. I do know that old Bear Hunter moved in for the kill slowly and methodically after Ray was put in the pokey. I like J.R. more than Ray. I'm glad he married Lulu. He straightened her up a bit and turned the T.V. down and eventually off.

There wasn't anything flashy on him save his dirty-bronzed belt buckle with a grizzly standing upright on it ready to lunge and his big-rig keys constantly jingling. Even the shirts he wore were tough: red, black, and flannel. He was quite the foil for old Cadillac Ray. I now recall J.R.'s stone face. He was my true grandpa.

With this brief family history it is easy to see that teen Tallene (her name was cleverly derived from an old Angela Lansbury movie) had it pretty rough. What made it rougher is that she was stuck in the mud of oakie land. Tragically, she hadn't the critical thinking power at her age to logically break down her position and choose the correct roads out. Who really does at fifteen? I sure as hell didn't.

My mom simply ignored her lame situation, sweeping it under the rug, and focusing sharply on all the current, scintillating teenage issues: magazines, the opposite sex, fashion, and dancing…things that reek of triviality to seasoned adults. Kind of. And her fucked-up family obliged. They couldn't care less if she was out late every night and her grades were dropping like the flies on their windowsills. A murky fog crept into Lodi. Mom couldn't see. She stumbled down the wrong roads.

Enter stage left: all obligatory highway robbers hiding amongst the roadside thicket. Tallene's innumerable teenage male peers were of no help. Sadly, they wanted her only for her immense, brand-new breasts: personal points of *immense* insecurity and distress for her. They were already D cups by the time she was a freshman, and she wasn't at all chubby—maybe just ten pounds overweight—pleasantly plump and juicy to the hungry eyes of your average horny high-school boy. Her long, flowing red hair only invited more and more prying eyes to examine her young body…eventually ending up on the voluptuous breasts, almost popping off the buttons of her little '70s shirts.

Adolescent boys in Lodi definitely knew who Tallene Jones was, and oh did they ever talk about her, not because she was a slut—no, no, she was far from it—but because of her natural motherly endowment. And they had many derogatory names for her that thrilled their little masculine senses and aroused their little Ur father forelimbs. High school boys can be such pricks.

# Chapter 4
# Conception History
# (B) White Roses

They met in the breeze way on a chilly October day in 1974. It sounds so romantic and fated, but it wasn't. It was just a couple of awkward kids connecting in an awkward way. It was chance. It was me.

It was half way through a Wednesday lunch period. Stewart was walking through the breeze way in order to reach the bathroom at the far corner of the school, over by the ceramics classroom. Nobody used this bathroom; therefore, it was a quiet and peaceful place where Stewart could be alone when need be.

Today was a bad day, his temper was bubbling orange lava deep down within his guts, and he was trying to defuse it. He'd gotten an F on a geometry quiz; it was his third F on one of those damn quizzes. He studied hard for the tests and got Bs, but kept absent-mindedly forgetting about the quizzes and then just plain gave up trying halfway through them when none of his answers came out right. His fat, balding teacher informed him after class that the quizzes in the long run equaled more total class points than the exams, since they were so numerous. "Why even have shitty exams?" he sarcastically muttered under his breath as he left the dusty classroom. Momma Mia was gonna love seeing all these little Fs dancing around like little demon imps on his report card. He was sure she'd have some choice words for him; Stewart hated her choice words.

Right after that, in P.E., he had been shown up in basketball by a kid half his size and three years younger than him…only to be taunted and laughed at by his own teammates every time the kid blew by him for a graceful lay up. He was a senior—he should have crushed that kid, but the kid was playing fair, and Stewart wasn't honorless. Maybe he should have crushed Chris and Carlos—starting with their testicles!

*PUSH MY LIFE INTO A DUFFLE BAG*

The final blow: Fred Hall in 4th period slighted him in front of everyone by making a loud comment about the party last Friday night at Sheila's house. Fred had caught Stewart fooling around with tipsy Rhonda in the parent's bedroom's bathroom upstairs. Rhonda wasn't the prettiest thing, and Stewart sequestered her up there so that nobody would find out. He thought he had been successful. Nobody noticed them leave. The alcohol was too busy flowing, and Zeppelin was too busy booming.

He was wrong. Just when he got her shirt off and began to explore her giant milky breasts (he'd been secretly wanting to see them even if it meant kissing Rhonda) Fred pushed the door open with an intoxicated girl of his own.

Stewart was mortified. He was caught. He felt dirty all over, and worse, he felt his hands and feet slipping on the glimmering social ladder. He had slipped down a few rungs, and the last one undercut him in the chin. Rhonda was ugly. The door had not been locked. Regret.

Fred alerted the entire school through his laughter. Then he began a publicity campaign to alert all of northern California, complete with pamphlets, buses, loudspeakers, and volunteers. Fred was a real prick.

He hadn't said a word to Steve that night, only nodded, like, "Yeeeeaaaahhh…. Allriighhht, mannn…. It's coooooool…. Reeeeeel cooooohll." He was pissed drunk, of course. Stewart thought he might not remember, but come to find out he sure as hell did remember, and he sure as hell did blab the whole mess to everybody, beginning by spilling the story open in 4th period Biology like a beaker full of poison vomit.

Dammit. Big man on campus fondles big Rhonda. Shit. What chick would date him now? Stewart's eyes sank back in his head as the hot blood surged through his quiet face. He was smart enough to get away from people and punch the wall when things got bad; he hated people seeing his father's temper in him. So he decided to get away to collect his frustrated thoughts before he blew up and tarnished the Vega name, a name he sometimes wanted to rip.

Thus: bathroom #7. There would be nobody in there; no stage fright, no clouds of pot, no animalistic jock fights ending in red-faced freshman stuck in the vomity trashcans—no pee puddles under the urinals, no flies, no noise…nothing but solitude and the faint smell of crusty bleach cleaner on old tiles mingled with the fainter smell of ceramics projects being burned alive in a kiln on the other side of the wall. Crackly-hot glaze.

Big Stewart hurried quietly past chatty girls, nerdish underclassman, and them and those and they: the young, soft coteries of baby adults. His expensive dress shoes clapped on the shaded concrete hallway and frustrated him with their noisy clatter. He wanted total silence from at least himself, if not everybody else.

But everybody else was clamoring and yammering away: there were myriad sudden noises (very annoying). A hairy guy over in a dark corner of the locker breeze way to Stewart's left exclaimed, "Hell, yeah, I know her!" to his mop-top, acne-scarred little rat friend. They were having an exciting conversation, apparently. The hairy guy glanced quickly at Stewart as he shuffled past at a clappy-dress-shoe distance. He slowly pointed, grinning to his little pet rat. Stewart breathed deeply in order to calm the black thunderheads and kept up a steady pace.

His serene bathroom was waiting just about three hundred feet away, past the two swaying eucalyptus trees that guarded it on the lawn between the breeze way and the mauve ceramics building. His bladder was empty. But a full bladder was never prerequisite to entering the sweet pungent silence that was Men's Restroom #7.

He had his Opeechee notebook to journal in if the onus of his various shames overtook him. He could draw people being cut to pulpy steak pieces, their faces wide-eyed, wide-mouthed, by massive swords swung by robots or, or…yes, elaborate scenes of rusty, smoking tanks rolling over the sharding skulls of literally brainless idiots who were too dense to get the hell out of the way. Bloody drawings oft soothed him.

Sometimes he drew his mother being drawn and quartered by Clydesdales, but these were always destroyed quickly. If his mother ever found them he would be drowned in a pool of bubbling Alfredo sauce; but she would never find them, especially not the ones where she was topless—stars on her nipples.

On this perhaps fated chilly day there was a gaggle of nubile Lodi girlies blocking the breeze way exit betwixt Stewart and #7. They were standing in an oddly shaped oval of oddly spoken youth colloquialisms in the form of cheese-sandwich lunch gossip. They were standing right smack in the middle of the double door exit. "Stupid girls." Each displayed the trendy clothing of post-hippie/pre-disco flair. "Stupid girls."

They were all juniors: important girls, penultimate girls with important issues to discuss: tampons, shoes, conditioner, Nixon's innovative foreign policy with the Soviet Union.

*But why oh why are they blocking the damn doorway!* thought Stewart. Maybe they couldn't decide which way to go…the grassy quad, the cafeteria, or the oak-speckled lawn in front of the Drama building. Maybe there was more than one gaggle leader among them and an epic, implicit struggle of who would win the lunch location today was furtively being fought whilst they bantered over who got really shit-faced on tequila at who's house and who was surreptitiously making out with whom everyday in the lower dug out of the ball field after school. Perhaps they didn't use the word "surreptitiously."

Regardless of Stewart's scrutiny, the point of the matter was that this group (possibly eight—some pretty, some not so much) of girls was blocking his lissome exit from Tokay central to his precious quiet time. And by the time he saw them it was almost too late to apply the foot brakes and move toward a pretext locker off to the side in order to figure out how to smoothly pass them.

He couldn't just walk up and say, "Excuse me," and squeeze past. That would only be possible on a cool guy day; he was too shy, too angry, and too damn bad at strategy. They looked to be whispering about him now; three of them turned their frenetic mascara eyes toward his big direction.

*They know.... Shit,* thought Stewart.

And there was Rhonda on the left side in the back. She looked to be giggling. Was she a part of this torture? Had she been paid to wag her behemoth breasts in his tipsy face at Shiela's dumb party? It was probable.

Everybody was always out to shoot down the popular big Italian, especially if they were white and didn't drive sparkly green trucks.

Perhaps he would roll over Rhonda's cheap-shit pinto with his big V-8 Chevy pick up. *Then everybody would know I hate her and her fuckin' fat body.* His words were black smoke. He was cussing a lot now in his head. He then determined to blow right through them like a big sweaty comet. They were *not* an impenetrable impasse. They were stupid girls, stupid bitches, even. He was not stupid. They would not waste the last (he glanced at his gold Rolex) 17 minutes of precious lunch left! But then he noticed Rhonda coming around the gaggle to the front *to greet him* personally with romantic retardedness!

Yikes!

His heart picked up and his neck and forehead moistened. He stopped. He quickly looked away. Could he pretend to check a locker? Did she know where his true locker was? If she or they did he would look like the biggest, spineless coward ever.

*Screw it,* he thought. He turned to the right and walked over to a locker. He fumbled slowly with the lock. Rhonda stopped her fat advance. She was still a good ten yards away.

Maybe he could turn around and go out the breeze way the way he had come *and then* go around the red tile building the long way to get to his lucky #7. It would work…not efficiently, but it would work.

He turned back and surveyed the path. Stewart was a methodical young man, brightly scheming like a mafia spy in the alleyway shadows, his Opeechee loaded with thought drawings like a tommy gun loaded with lead. *Dammit!*

It was much worse behind him—a large group of loud and bawdy stoners (two of them appearing to wear Black Sabbath tee-shirts and oily hair down to their asses) were advancing on him at a distance of twenty yards and closing: they had that swagger in their marijuana stride that told Stewart they were looking for a weakling to smoke. He wasn't a weakling—they usually ignored him, and he them (two different worlds plus Stewart was big and could handle himself in a fight)—but today was different; Rhonda's older brother, Mike, (an ashen senior with a moustache and supposed knife scars on his upper arms) appeared to be leading the pack of stoned wolves.

Did he know about the bathroom fondling of his ugly little sister? Did he care? Was he murderous when it came to his poor family? These and several thousand other questions raced through Stewart's sweaty head. Well, if they spotted him and then rushed him he would unleash volcanic amounts of frustration and big man fury upon them!

"I'll beat them to hell!"

He wasn't afraid of fighting them, he was a cornered animal, but he just might lose if he fought all *eight* of them—hell, even if it was just four of them, and he won the stupid fight (with his stabbing granite fists all blindly plunged) then for sure the other four would get him in queue the following days-weeks-year. They would get him with collective choke holds. They would get him with finger-pointing, racial taunts leading to parking lot baseball battings and jagged key scratches on the beautiful, finish of his beloved Chevy.

These guys were fucked-up. They played dirty. They didn't care about anything, not even their futures. And they would never leave him alone. (No more separate worlds.) A big "wop," blacklisted.

*How did his sister not become a stoner?* Stewart thought. At this point, Mike swept back his auto-shop oiled hair and spotted Stewart over by his own locker.

"What the fuck, dude?" Mike hollered.

The smoky wolves awoke from their hypnotic strides and stared at Stewart.

*PUSH MY LIFE INTO A DUFFLE BAG*

"What are you doin' by my locker?" Mike hollered again, this time a bit quieter, recognizing the bigness, the likeableness of Stewart Vega and his golden watch.

Stewart didn't want to deal with this crap right now. The gaggle of girls quit honking and intently watched the showdown between Stoner and Italian. Things got quiet. A tumble weed bounced in the wind across the floor, and a lone coyote howled somewhere off in the distance.

Stewart used theatrical diplomacy. He shook his head violently like he was lividly pissed off that he'd thought this was his locker only to find out it wasn't, and that there was the reason that his combo wasn't working. (He was a grizzly, they were wolves, they would not jump him once they beheld his huge wrath!)

He took a big breath, big enough for everybody to notice his rising temper and rib cage. Then he put his hand up toward the stoners in order to say, Not now! I'm *seriously* confused and angry *for no good reason*, but I'm a high school boy so it's acceptable behavior!"

Then he really said this: "Sorry, Mike, dude; I'm fuckin' out of it." He was glad he remembered Mike's name. Stewart glared at them all right in their beady little eyes: they were insignificant dogs.

Stewart used a sonorous stoner register of voice so that the smelly Sabbaths would not interrogate him any further. They loved it when you used the word "dude" and "fuck" in the same line. They loved brazen idiocy.

Stewart was also sure the use of the expletive and the display of wrath would move the stupid girls out of his way. He turned toward them and walked right at the girly gaggle. The honking geese seemed to be finally silenced, their yellow beaks shut tight by the sight and fear of a real, live grizzly bear.

He was finally respected: half of the oval moved aside to let the great grizzly through, careful not to be brushed by any part of him, fearing he would turn and chomp them all in two…blood besoaked feathers floating in the breeze way breeze. Rhonda was nowhere to be seen. He hoped he'd made her cry and run away like a little crybaby. She could dry her tears on her sweater pillow breasts. He stomped right through them and left the stoners standing by Mike's locker in a purple haze of vexation.

*Now, onward to #7 before I destroy something,* thought Stewart.

It was right here at this very moment in time that Stewart Vega caught a whiff of delicious rose perfume that had arisen off of the moist neck area of one of those numerous girls. Roses diffused like lucid fireworks into the delicious autumnal air just outside the breeze way, fanned by the boughs of the eucalyptus trees. The fireworks sparkle-burned his nose and mouth.

His mood snapped into absolute change: instead of red, he saw light pink, pastel and pretty. He saw soft, bouncing skin and glossy, licked lips in his mind's eye as he moved away from the girls without a sound save his clapping shoes.

One of the girls smelled like roses. He loved roses. His Italian mother had them eternally planted, white ones, wherever they housed for whichever season. He could almost eat the white petals, he loved them so much. All demons of shitty angst fled his mind in absolute fright at the immense sight and smell of holy white roses and their sweet perfume. Stewart was spun about.

Before he reached the corner of the ceramics building, he glanced back at the girls. All of their backs were turned. They were honking again, two playing tug of war with an unfortunately large worm, save one: a cute little red head. She had watched Stewart walk over the grass and under the trees. He felt uncomfortable because their eye contact remained locked for an unreal amount of time. Then she smiled and lightly bit her bottom lip with her front teeth. A flirt. A nice flirt. A beeeeautiful flirt.

Stewart's big heart got all mushy. He smiled back and nodded his dark head, relaxing the stern in his face. She exhaled cutely and then turned back to the goose-down jamboree. It was very summer-lightning strike, even in the fall. White rose lightning.

Stewart walked over to the bathroom door and entered his sanctum. He had escaped the sticky trappings of Tokay gossip gunfire for the time under a rose-blossom canopy. And best of all—he had earlier stolen a ceramics-class metal folding chair and installed it in a hidden corner of bathroom #7. And since nobody frequented #7 (maybe not even the janitor) the orange chair had remained. It was his thinking throne—a philosopher's throne, unadulterated by the dirty haunches of his peers. He was glad to see it was still there.

Later that same newborn day, Stewart fortuitously bumped into rosy redhead Tallene whilst rounding a corner on his way to 7th period. Just like in a Hugh Grant movie (forgive the anachronism), they literally bumped into each other, and she dropped one of her books, which he, of course, with gentlemanly grace, picked up for her. Here she was again in all of her quiet, cute little alba rose glory!

He would not be nervous. He would not say something inane. He would turn up the charm and glow like a new world for her, full of adventure and fecund love. He would win her. She was very pretty. So he simply *had* to win her.

As it turned out, they both bucked up the courage to talk a bit right then and there. Lucky for me they found a way to communicate. Remember: this is high school, so most kids would have merely spit out a few words of greeting, nodded their heads, and giggled like chickens about it later).

"Sorry about that!" bellowed Stewart, his furrowed brows and stern face relaxing into a big sonsy smile.

"Oh, no, it's cool; you couldn't see me coming around the corner," she chirped, her eyes quite flirty, which is surprising because she hadn't yet mastered the art of flirt.

Then there was a peaceful pause, a palpable gap in the air. Stewart scratched his head. Tallene tapped the spine of her book slowly and looked out over the lawn to the left: it was a blustery day: orange leaves, chilled grass, crystal clear sky…explicitly romantic. Cold, wan sunlight imbued the entire valley with a dusting of lambent magic. The kids were enchanted. Neither of them wanted to leave the other's company.

"You're name is Tallene, right?" Stewart took a shot. (A socialite friend in U.S. History class had told him thus.)

"Yes!" She beamed with youthful delight, leaning against the red tile wall. She looked like a little harvest bunny, rows of wholesome corn and hay bales.

"How'd you know?" she asked.

Stewart didn't permit himself to get uneasy; he spoke boldly. "Oh, well, I asked Jamie what your name was after I saw you at lunch; I've never heard of that name before."

"It's from a movie, probably my mom's favorite: um…*A Lawless Street*," she said, feeling dumb that she'd mentioned her mom—how uncool. She then let her book arm fall to her right side comfortably and looked out once more over the lawn in order to regain some confidence—she couldn't continue looking up into his face—it was too commanding, too senior in all of its maleness. She could smell a faint musky pomade smell exuding from him. She liked it. A lot.

Stewart unconsciously glanced at her buxom bosom whilst she looked away. The breeze was blowing cold. She turned her head back at him. He looked up. And then they talked awhile longer about nothing and everything in order to seal a date in the near future. And thus, she would be taken after school to one of Stewart's favorite Italian restaurants in downtown Lodi, Vito's Vino, in his big Chevy pickup and then onward to a trite movie containing a plot visually grainy and early '70s;...a plot in no way as brilliant as *One Flew Over the Cuckoos Nest* or *The Deer Hunter*.

Tallene, like most young women, noticed the fleeting glance that Stewart gave her breasts, but instead of making her feel insecure and judged it actually made her feel like an attractive woman. Validation.

Somehow Stewart was okay to look at her sexually. She even wanted him too. She was tired of always being a friend to the popular guys and never a date. She was tired of being the *only* junior who'd only *kissed* boys, but never gone any further, and therefore had no dirty stories to tell her girl friends when they chewed the fat, honking like lovely geese. She was ready to go further; so was he.

Stewart was delighted to date a knockout redhead who was known around school to be a groovy, but quiet girl. She was acceptable and would both bolster his social climbing and perhaps satisfy his seventeen-year-old lust, a lust that was like a mute forest fire, consumed the entire Sierra Nevada mountain range daily.

(I remember being seventeen and hornier than a triceratops. I remember wanting to have adventures in girls' chest regions. I can relate to my vaporous father, even though I do not care for him in the least. I wish I could say that I relate to my teenage mother, but I'm not a woman, and I won't be pretentious over the powers of my imagination. Teen girls are infinitely different from their male peers. For one thing, they don't have as strong a desire to explore our chest regions or our tent pole nether regions, no matter how many shallow-brained teenage boys fantasize that they really, secretly do.)

So my parents had their first "dinner and a movie" together. Then they went out again...to another movie. Stewart was patiently planning to fool around, but this time Tallene insisted that they take her *new* '71 Ford Mustang (a car payment beyond her means). He obliged, thinking quickly to himself, *smaller space = closer bodies.*

At the time, my mom had a job at the local K-mart (Yes! Can you believe K-Mart is that old?). She'd saved and saved and saved her minimum-wage dollars to make a down payment on the scintillating little sports car. It was creamy white. J.R. was very proud of her. He was hard-working and loved that his cutesy stepdaughter had worked hard toward a goal and hunted that bear all the way down. He helped her pay for it, of course.

When she drove up, Stewart thought the car looked pretty damn bitchin'. It's growling engine excited him. America. On this, the second date, the fooling around officially began. Swirls of tongues and awkward saliva complemented groping hands and the tiniest of grunts. They acted like experienced, worldly movie lovers though neither of them knew what they were doing. At one point they conked heads together quite painfully; she laughed and rubbed her head; he feigned a laugh, but became frustrated that the conking had cooled down the hot love for a moment. Boys will be boys.

Stewart was a restless lover. He had something to prove. And Tallene let him. She gave up her soft white body so that she could feel love as it existed in *Cosmopolitan* magazine. "I'm in love," she mused. Grunts in a Mustang. True love grunts. She was a lucky young American girl. Her beautiful red hair draped over her naked shoulders as the big Italian man explored away upon her glorious twin mountains. He might as well have had a backpack and climbing gear.

School pushed forward a good three weeks or so. Stewart's lasagna Momma became inquisitive over this white girl he was seeing. "What's her family like? Is she beautiful? Why don't you bring her over for dinner? She better be good enough for my baby boy!" she bellowed over and over again to the great annoyance of secret-seduction Stewart. In his mother's Italian Catholic eyes, *nobody* was good enough for her only son. He was gold bullion legacy. Vineyards. Vintage heritage. Stewart stayed out of the house as much as he could whilst dating his ephemeral alba rose. It was like he had swum to Sicily from the rocky boot to escape his powerful momma.

Lulu and J.R. Barjager didn't really look into the matter too much. Their girl was free to do whatever she wanted as long as she didn't run away. J.R. was too busy truckin'. Lulu was too busy gossiping. Their daughter was, in their eyes, the luckiest high school girl in the valley—*free* to make her own decisions, "and her own money," sayeth Lulu, flicking a slender lady's cigarette into a bright pink ash tray shaped like a '58 Cadillac. "Enjoy your high school years, babe. They're the best years of your life, trust me," she inculcated.

"I will, I will, *I will*," my mom bantered back, smiling, and heading out the aluminum screen door to her exorbitant Mustang.

# Chapter 4
# Conception History
# (C) The Deed

Night.

Football game.

"I'm on the drill team," she said.

"Oh! Okay, I wasn't sure if you were a cheerleader or what; I'd heard different things from different people," he said.

"Nope, not a cheerleader; maybe next year." She smiled and made a nervous look toward him with her eyebrows raised as if to say, "Wouldn't it be exciting if *I did* make it as a varsity cheerleader?"

He looked out at the football players: they were running around and hitting each other in the cold air. Then one of them caught the ball and looked cool doing it so the crowd exploded with sports orgasms. Stewart asked Tallene, "Did you see that one?"

"Nooooo," she whined, scanning the field with concern.

They were at the last game of the season. They'd seen all of the movies playing in town, so there was nothing else to do but come to the ultimate high school social event. (There was no way in hell they would even set foot within 100 yards of each other's houses/parents). Stewart regretted it. He wasn't too into sports even though he feigned interest in order to please his jerseyed friends and maintain big-man bullshit.

He wished tonight that he and his buxom bunny were out at Lake Hogan, in a tent, clothes off, nobody around for miles. He'd been secretly contemplating losing his secret secret virginity with Tallene. He really needed to get it over with. Everybody around school assumed that he'd slept with numerous chicks, but he hadn't. Big Stewart had never steered little Stewart into any port whatsoever—partially because Big Stewart was overly obsessed with thinking little Stewart too little. His porn magazines gave evidence that all other males in the *entire* universe had genitals like that of horses and emissions like that of donkeys, so he concluded that he was irregular and tinier than Tim.

His insecurity over his big body and the fact that he was not really a "looker" had kept him from the sexual act. Certainly the first female he got naked with would giggle and run when they beheld the splendor of his man boobs jiggling upon his hulking frame.

Certainly.

But then again, maybe not! Because Tallene was different; she was not so quick to judge people. She seemed to like him just fine: all of him (although she hadn't seen or felt his penis yet). He felt confident to move forward to the fleshy sweat level of sexual intercourse with her as soon as possible. He was highly horny and he couldn't wait to have her bare body pressed against his shirtless chest. Electric.

His mind drifted from the game as the crowd erupted yet again: another football guy leaped like a jaguar upon the fumbled pigskin. Unbeknownst to Stewart, Tallene was feeling almost the exact same way. She was sick of being a virgin. She was in love with him according to *Cosmo* and other such tomes of serial verisimilitude. Something in the fall air was churning her blood into a magical romance stew. She felt like kissing him a whole lot. She felt like licking his face and neck, like getting a little crazy. And why not? She was young and sizzling, now was the time of her life…a time to grab hold and electrify!

The night got sweetly thick around them. The game got quieter, more distant to the couple sitting in the lower left bleachers, sort of apart from everyone else, and *right by the exit,* thought Stewart.

Stewart was at full speed now. His heart picked up and sent blood to the baby places as his mind experienced image after image of her naked, her arms and legs wrapped around him, the sweat, the deep breathing; this hypnotism hypnotized him. He stared off into space, unaware of the game or even his actual, physical, pseudo-girlfriend who sat right next to him. His magazines were the research supporting this vaporous lecture of earthly delights.

Tallene studied his face and divined that he was being a tired, quiet boy. Sometimes boys acted solitarily strange, but *not* tonight! Tonight was the night; her mind was made up: he would listen for once; she would wake him up. She'd learned earlier about the power of phallic symbols in one of her magazines. She was eating a hotdog slathered in mustard. She put her hand softly on his thigh.

He looked down at it like a stupid, tranquilized bear. She squeezed her hand. He electrified awake and looked up into her face.

She then took a big bite of her hotdog: slow and sexy like they do in the movies: women who know what they want, when they want it, and have meaningless martini men wrapped around their manicured fingers; women who wear hats in any season and actually pull it off.

Stewart's heart pumped pink lava within him. She was horny, he could tell; he was smart. This was it: *the time was now* as it had never been before. He must right *now* get her away from the myriad sports morons and...and...well, *I know damn well what!* he thought to himself.

It explosively dawned upon his erect brain that tonight would be the night! He had *never* seen her behave this way before! I mean, sure—at the movies she'd made out and licked his ears and let him feel her chest, *but never anything below the waist!*

Never!

And now she was applying pressure by his polyester thigh and eating a hotdog with mustard dripping off of it!

*#%@@^!^**$/#!

He could think *only* in crazy exclamation points and BIG, ERECT WORDS just like all boys all over the world all over the galaxy all over the universe do whenever the sexy ghost of sex comes rapping at *their very own* window in reds and purples, *with thousands of breasts swirling and glistening!*

Stewart was turning into pure 100% testicles. It was already ten p.m. The game was in its 4$^{th}$ quarter. Panic set in. Time was almost up. Time was about to loose all 1,000 people out of the sports area and end the night. Decisions needed to be made. Stewart quickly/firmly adjusted himself and stood up, bringing Tallene up with him by taking hold of her hand.

She dropped her hotdog and, as they scurried away—out the exit and toward the dark school grounds, reached into her bell-bottom pocket, pulling out a stick of Juicy Fruit and plunging it into her moist mouth. Her body was flesh lightening and ignited rose fireworks. She could feel the blood coursing through her. Rhythms of lovely.

Stewart was randy, yet frustrated: he didn't know where to take her. It had to be somewhere isolated: a prime location for clandestine copulation, one where they would be unobserved, entirely alone. He did not want another Rhonda experience. It had to be dark, too. He was fat, and his penis was mighty small. It would also have to be indoors, somehow, or else they'd freeze their butts off, and she'd get turned off, and his penis would *shrink!* (It got horrifically *smaller* when cold, incontrovertibly re*cock*ulous to behold!)

Where to go? They walk-jogged away from the field and toward the orange-lit school buildings and lawns. They rounded a corner by the A building and proceeded onward past the sleeping giant gym. Stewart would hold back his volcano lust in order to earn a great location, but would she wait? Yes. She was giggling. *We're still on!* he thought, sweating in the chilly moonlit air.

Tallene had never been so excited in all her life. It was so romantic: rushing away from the football game, the crowd, all of the stupid girls and cheerleaders who were not about to have *sex* like she was! *Fools!* She was so emotionally into it that she wasn't even afraid that it might hurt or that she might become very, very uncomfortable.

There was a reason for her ease besides the "romantic" nature of the ensuing encounter. Reason: She and Stewart had been secretly sipping Rum through his silver flask during the game. Nobody saw them do it, but they did it. And alcohol wasn't allowed on school grounds.

Stewart loved rum, and she thought he was very manly and groovy—in his big green, huge-tired truck—a flask of pricey Caribbean rum in the glove box. She had developed quite the taste for the liquor over the past two weeks.

But this was the first time she'd drunk with abandon, feeling like a "bad girl" amidst her good football peers. Rum had supplied the warm rush of sexuality that she was caressing in her evening soul. Stewart had had only a couple swigs and wasn't aware that she was tipsy and hiding it quite well.

"Here we are!" he declared, his jaw trembling with cold sex. They were in front of the breeze way entrance, and to their utter joy and surprise the chain and lock that were usually hanging tight around the handles were nowhere to be seen! Had the janitor had rum that night too? What luck!

"Should we?" he motioned to the door…then thought how much cooler it would've sounded to say, "Shall we," like James Bond.

Tallene's eyes widened; she nodded, licking her lips like a little vampire.

From the point of entrance into the dark breeze way until the next morning, Stewart did not ask any more questions. He was in charge. His powerful hormones and driven wiring took over and exacted their lust upon my young mother. It was like a pervert switch went off in him and set the whole world ablaze. He pulled her into the darkness of the breeze way and shut the door, wishing desperately that he could jam a crowbar between the pole handles and lock them in forever. He hoped the door at the other end of the hall was locked, but didn't have time to check; his pants were already over 200 degrees Fahrenheit.

"Over here," he gasped, pulling her over to the right, into a locker alcove of utter darkness—where the orange light coming through the windows from outside didn't reach. He then turned on her and grabbed her head, frenching her as fast as he could. It was hasty and jerky: tongue in and out, heads wobbling, hands sliding around on polyester with love sibilance resonance. (If it had been Thanksgiving, he would have shoved the whole juicy turkey into his piggy face.)

Tallene didn't think it all too absurd; she drunkenly loved it and frenched him right back, hard (for the first twenty seconds, that is; then she got a little hesitant because he'd had never acted this way before). The rum in her took over and made time slow down and speed up and slow down and speed up. She careened in Stewart's big Italian arms.

It was right there and then that Stewart became the definition of impatience: he stopped kissing her and forced her arms up, pulling off her brown shirt with force. Before she knew it, her bra was ripped off, the old plastic parts of it scraping her painfully. And now he was in her chest, going crazy with what she was terming in her rummy head *passion!*

Then he grew even more impatient: he forced her down on the ground, convinced that she wanted love as wild as it could be—and oh, he would give her what she wanted! (Stewart, the five-minute stallion.)

The concrete was cold as her bare back hit the pavement, her breasts jiggling with the fall in the darkness. She sighed, laughing like a romance novel of ravished maidens and husky knights with bulging armor that was reading hotly before her. "Heeere," she moaned like a drugged arena rocker, helping him unbutton her bell-bottoms.

Stewart abruptly pulled off her pants and then wasted no time pulling off her panties. He moved in with his head and hands: doing some awkward pressure stuff down there, then becoming more restless than a child: standing up quickly, kicking off his shoes, sliding off his pants, his sweaty underwear, and descending his full body weight on top of my little mother.

He was still wearing his shirt and socks—not fair: she HAD to be totally, completely, and irrevocably naked, hiding not one inch of her young naked body from him, but he could keep his shirt on and hide some big insecurities from her. It really wasn't fair, but he was making the dominant rules. Piggy rules.

She squirmed under his bulk, rubbing his back with her cute Elvin hands, white as snow. He huffed and puffed like a wolf, panting on top of her, feeling the dirtiness of the grind. Her back was getting sore against the freezing concrete; her butt was numb; her panties lay crumpled ten yards away.

And then it was finally time. Stewart forced his way in, pushing apart her thighs with frustrated glee. She became instantly frightened, but bit her lip and kept quiet. It did not feel good. It just hurt. Like hell was inside her. She was certain she was bleeding and felt what can only be described as tearing, although the pain was more complex than that. Stewart drove on and on like a Chevy piston. This is how they did it in the blue films; this is how it felt. He loved it!

He kissed her for approximately five seconds then quit in order to focus fully on the fucking, which lasted about thirty seconds because he couldn't physically take the immense female softness for very long. And so he withdrew; from darkness into darkness.

The deed was done. They felt sticky. The rum was wearing thin. The night was over. Neither of them had even thought to use a condom. Neither of them had any: they were ignorant virgins.

On that October night, I was conceived. Good old 1974. I'm actually glad they didn't have a condom; wouldn't you be?

Immediately after the school's squawking gossipers announced that teen Tallene Jones was preggers, Stewart ran like hell, hiding behind his strong and arrogant Italian Momma Mia Margaret who declared lividly to the Jones' in no uncertain terms that her family, the great and powerful Vegas were "a [rich] Catholic family, very religious, very pious." They could never have any dealings with a [poor] trashy, nonreligious family whose father was in prison for drugs!" She also sang the malicious song of, "And you cannot prove that my good son Stewart is the father. Besides, he's a virgin! And I can prove it!" and the argument ended there.

Lulu and J.R. weren't smart enough to refute Margaret's Corleone thunder and seek legal action. DNA was inutile in the '70s. My mother was too destroyed by it all and began silently closing off to the world like a white rose closing up in the first frost of the life season. She quickly dropped out of high school (junior year) and took on full-time, minimum wage hours at the local K-Mart.

# Chapter 5
# Father Figure Fishing

Believe it or not, there were actual times where Caleb and I got along, where we somehow enjoyed each other's company as if we were of the same blood. These occurrences were boldest and brightest in 1981-1983. They were times of real peace, real childhood. The Californian delta was the stage for these special one-act plays, right around where it winds by Stockton and perfumes the air with moisture and the beneficial echo of nature: its peace, its wholesome joy, quiet animals, and muddy reeds.

I love the outdoors. So did Caleb. At the time, I was six-eight years old; this is a magical time in a boy's life, filled with frogs, old barn adventures, dusty-gravel bikes, and stained-red Popsicle mouths. Good times. I thank God that I was able to have a few good times myself amidst all the chaos and fear.

The good times happened on certain Friday nights: random bright lighthouse lights on a calendar of Jaws blackness. Caleb would finish up his man-work at The Midvalley Truss Company in town and then book it home so we could get an early start. I remember my mom telling me numerous times that Caleb had called from work and was thinking of "heading out to the delta tonight" and that he was "feeling fishy" (one of his witty phrases). As soon as I heard these somewhat familiar words my little heart would mutely race in my little frame. My face would flush, and I'd try my best to subdue infinite joy so as not to get too excited; it seems to me that every time I got too overtly excited the fishing grandeur ended up not happening. Caleb's last hour at work would turn sour and he'd get home pissed off and looking to get piss-beer pissed before unwinding in front of the tube.

When he came home like that, I knew that I'd better not even remind him of catfish lest he swat me for taking him at his afternoon word. Caleb was tricky; you had to play your kiddy cards just right if you wanted to secure the good times.

On the nights where he came home ready to rock and roll with the sturgeon and cats, he'd be jolly as a hick in a gold mine with hot apple dumplings in his tummy. He'd get off at five. and roll up the driveway in his dusty truck, ready to turn into nature man: supreme ruler of fish. I'd get the peremptory order to "make sandwiches 'cuz we'll be starvin'," and rush off to the quiet kitchen with glee.

It seems that every time we went fishing we ate the same thing: bologna sandwiches. I'd construct them with care, spreading on Best Foods smoothly as if I were Klimt painting perfect kisses. Wonder Bread was always the canvas, and American cheese was always the second coat, protecting the painting from the sunlight fading effects of moist bologna...always stacked by the threes so that Caleb and his awkward stepson could have copious amounts of protein: important when wrestling mammoth cats at midnight.

Yes. Tasty times.

When sandwich construction was over I would proceed to the next step (all steps memorized with a sacred duty sense), which was to wrap them all (always six) in cheap tin foil, folding them in as carefully as the ancient Egyptians folded in Ramses. They continually became silvery crumpled by the time they were unveiled for eating, much to my anality disdain. I wanted Caleb to see how much I cared about our protein rations.

I did my fishing packing quickly: food, nature gear, like backpacks filled with old, faded beach towels for God knows what (wipe the dirt off the fish?) and a kiddy blanket. Oh, yeah: plus my red Mickey Mouse flashlight too, with fresh double A's [child-sized], never forgetting anything lest Caleb's mood be soured like tired milk.

Then I'd be right by his side, ready to grab anything he wanted: nets, poles, three in total; he was usually the one to get these from the garage because I was wont to bang them together, rendering them hopelessly entangled, the great and mighty delta lantern, jackets, Mom (if she wasn't cleaning at the hospital), so that she could kiss us goodbye and wish us fish.

I was the supreme fishing squire to my knight, Caleb, in shining weekend armor: fishing pole glinting in the setting Stockton sun like a broad sword ready to strike at the heart of Saracen fishdom. Indeed. We would battle the mighty fish together, nicely; like Templar gents.

I was very glad that my brother Sam was too young to fish. Let him stay at home in his pee, slobber, and poo. He was just a dumb baby baby.

I gleamed like a supernatural boy-comet as we bumped along in the big truck, Caleb's work stuff all over the floorboard under my dangling sneakers. We headed out to north Stockton all the way toward Eight Mile Road without saying much, sometimes listening to not-quite-yet classic rock, rock playing on some inane valley radio station at a volume of 2 out of 10 so as not to disturb the chance occurrence that Caleb might wish to dispense Delta wisdom to his worshipping squire.

Sometimes he'd tell me of his delta heritage, how he'd ride his bike all the way from Linden without getting tired (the prime of youth) so that he could visit his Aunt out on the island she then owned. Ah, and the name of it was weird and holy: Ringetrack island. "Those were the good old days; she owned the whole island, and I would hang out there and fish and look for treasures and stuff. Did you know that *Cool Hand Luke* was filmed there? Yep, Paul Newman himself ran through my Aunt Eleanor's chicken coop!" he would serenely bellow, the evening trees rushing past the truck windows with graying foliage.

He absolutely cherished the Paul Newman stories. He told me that old Aunt Eleanor even watched some of the filming. It was a closed set, but she declared herself worthy due to the shotgun fact that she "owned" the island or whatever. She didn't see what all the fuss was over the Hollywood-glorious, Roman demi-god Paul. "He ain't *that* good lookin'. He looks pretty normal to me; I've seen better lookin' men on the ferry boats—and those men ain't pampered!" I don't think she ever said this, but I really would like to believe she had.

I want old Aunt Eleanor's image to be missing three teeth and boxing Caleb behind the ears every day just for being "an ornery, property-line wanderin', no good, whipper-snapping little runt of a dirty, chicken-stealing varmint!"

Yes. I love it all: the muddy delta complete with its benighted denizens and all of that Mississippi analogousness. It deserves such embellishment. After all, "Paul Newman ran through Aunt Eleanor's chicken coop!" Caleb watched Hollywood "in action" as a hillbilly towhead on a bicycle with clumps of dirtwax behind his ears.

There was an important stop along Thornton Road right before Eight Mile that was ritual for us: The Bass Hole liquor store. After all, Caleb needed beer like bears need honey, especially after a long day of stalking white-tail deer at the Midvalley Truss Company.

Ah, let us now look at the menu of sumptuous Bass Hole delights: Coors, Michelob, Budweiser (the king of beers), Pabst, Miller (High Life—if you're feeling culturally saucy). Um…there were various others of which a light-yellow color ensured tasty perfection of product—without upping the price! Caleb wins—beer for mere change, it seems.

Later in life I discovered that there were *better* beers available in the world; you only have to pay a little more for the intelligence and culture that goes into them. I am more than willing to pay this price after living under Caleb's cloud of redneck frugality. "They won't trick old Caleb with their fancy labels—I can see the damn price plain as day!"

He liked getting more bang for his early eighties buck, and I took this mode of living as incontrovertible gospel. Caleb was my god, but more like an emotional, conditional Greek god with vehement glints of mortality than the God of the Gideon's Bible: available to my hot little hands every time I opened a dingy motel night stand drawer—which was seldom.

Little child me adored The Bass Hole. Being in that dusty liquor store meant we were fishing—*fishing! Fishing, I say!* We were indeed on an adventure as if we were pirates on a palm-tree and turquoise-translucent sea looting adventure in the spicy Caribbean.

I loved watching Caleb pick out his twelve pack of whatever was on sale and then, later, picking out for myself one of two holy items: either a yellow Hostess cupcake (with the white frosting swirls on top!) or a home-run yellow lemon pie. *Oh! What sweet felicity!*

I'd also get to purchase three Hawaiian punches that would last me the night. Delish. Acute memory tastes on the tongue. Preservatives.

The man who was behind the register at the Bass Hole was a black man, and he knew everything about fishing the delta. *It seemed to me at the time that he was perhaps born under the muddy waters of the delta so that he'd be eternally knowledgeable. His mother must have worn a maternity snorkel, and the doctor must have been a wise and ancient, barbel-bearded catfish who studied medicine at the Aquatic School of Ichthyology.* I watched carefully as he bantered with Caleb, trading fish stories and beeping the beer through. He wore a white V-neck tee shirt and had a gold watch with a golden catfish that swivelled around counting the seconds. It was a cool watch, and Caleb made a point to have him show it to me every time we were there. It was so cool. I would make a point to get one as soon as I was grown up in high school.

The Bass Hole was also where we secured ammunition for the upcoming battle at sea: chicken liver, stinky clammy goop, and salty-brown crawdads (dead) were common ammo fare. Caleb selected chicken liver almost every time, believing it to be the rocket launcher amongst various machine guns. I was oft glad he eschewed the scary looking crawdads. I never wanted to get near them, much less touch them. Yuck. I tried my best to hide my squeamish girliness over the slime nature of catfish bait. Caleb wasn't scared—so I would be less scared than I really was, but scared none the less, actually. I didn't want him to call me a "pussy." Whatever the word meant, I didn't like the sound of it.

We bid the black man good bye and hopped back in the big truck. Caleb fired up the engine and we rolled onward toward Eight Mile Road. We had work to do: happy work. Happy work that required beer, which in turn made it happier work. Fishing nights were the only times where I actually *wanted* Caleb to drink his beers down. Somehow he never got angry drunk when we were out on the delta. Believe you me, he drank his fill of beer, but never got belligerent—only misty eyed over, I don't know…nature, or the delta, or childhood recollections. His father probably beat him up a lot. His father probably took him fishing a lot. Memory. Redolent, earthy water smells. Cat tails. Millions of cigarettes.

When we finally arrived near the molasses waters of the delta, Caleb turned off the main road and onto a dirt road that ran parallel to it. It was a secret road that only he knew. I hunkered down a little in my seat and put my finger to my lips. "Ssshhhhh." Eventually we ended up by a metal gate that read: NO TRESPASSING. Caleb launched out of his seat, and jimmy rigged the lock, opened the gate, and hopped back in the truck: the engine humming low as if the truck itself was being stealthy, knowing that monster catfish were at stake.

"This used to be old Eleanor's land, *dammit*, and I'll be damned if we can't fish here," he mumbled, lighting the first Camel Light of the night to improve his fish-assassin instincts. I nodded and was careful not to crinkle the clear Hostess packaging in my moist hands. This enchanted road wound on down to the levee and then kept going until Ringetrack Island was in sight. Good old Paul Newman and chicken coops.

Onward we crept until we came to the perfect place that suited Caleb's innate senses for the evening hunt. Caleb pulled the rig into a secret, bushy hiding spot (perfect camouflage against Luftwaffe aerial reconnaissance) and then we jumped out, closing the doors softly like phantom soldiers. We grabbed our M16s and mortars out of the back without even opening the tail gate. We

*PUSH MY LIFE INTO A DUFFLE BAG*

slinked like silent human cougars down the rocky (low-water level) shore to the water. Caleb scoped out the spot, decided it was good and we began setting up bivouac. The tiny white flies could be seen bouncing on the quiet, swirling waters; it was so peaceful that even a child could perceive the importance of the natural world and why we had to fight for it.

I loved it out there. It almost felt like Caleb was my real dad, like he truly loved me. Consanguineous. One salient fact of fishing that made it super army to both of us is the fact that we would fish until the sun came up…*all night*! To a young boy, staying up all night is tantamount in awesomeness to a bungee jumping adventure for an old boy with muddy dreadlocks.

All night. Awesome. Perfect conditions for me to be Caleb's buddy because I was ready to stand catfish sentry through even the darkest hours of the night. I would impress him, that is until about eleven or midnight, when I'd get cold, cranky, and super-duper tired. (Hardly any little boys can stay up all night, not even if there are horror movies to watch. No, the wee hours always conquer them in the end. Only at, say, age twelve do they begin to successfully deprive themselves of crucial growth sleep.)

Whenever I began feeling whiny and tired, the novelty of fishing seemed to vanish, along with my fear of Caleb. Sleepiness made me selfish and courageous. I could care less if I upset Caleb. Luckily, this didn't matter much because by eleven p.m. he was feeling pretty good in the slow steep of weekend beer and fish.

He'd merely say, "Tuckered?" and then take me up to the truck (all the while glancing over his shoulder to see if the three poles were wiggling with the electricity of hungry depth beasts. He was probably glad by this point to have me put safely away for the night. No longer would I be throwing rocks in the water and scaring the fish. No longer would I be complaining about hunger, mosquitoes, or being cold. No longer would I be depriving him of his precious night silence…man vs. nature and all that.

Yes. With me asleep in the vinyl hedges of the truck, he was free to be a lone man with no real worries, only fish to think about—and loads of delicious, orange-fire-tipped cigarettes to enjoy. The Marlboro man—who smoked Camel Lights.

At the moment of the very first cast of the night, I never ever had the forethought that I would get tired in less than five hours and give up the dad bonding for sleep. No, I always set out to stay up all night, with words like, "I'm not even gonna sleep a wink. I'm gonna fish and fish and fish and fish until the ranger comes to replace the fish cuz there'll be none left!" I'd boast in a jocular tone.

Sometimes I'd even make Caleb giggle with my wit and goofy sentences. I think the sugar from the Hawaiian Punches and Hostess cupcakes sharpened my wits the same way two cups of coffee sharpen the wits of an ad executive.

On this particular fishing adventure, the night was still younger than a tadpole. Caleb examined our bivouac and uttered a "Dammit" under his moustache. "You forgot the igloo," he muttered, nicely, so that the night wouldn't be spoiled. He wanted us to be good buddies too, apparently. He trudged up the rocky bank toward the truck and was back quick as a wink.

The sun was setting in oranges and smoky pinks. The birds were making odd, eventide delta noises. The crickets were tuning their violin legs. Caleb set about finalizing the campsite. He set up the two beige folding chairs—they promised leisure and comfort. He grabbed some extra matches, smokes, and two flannel blankets from the duffle bag. I was proud that mine was big and green like his.

Since the stars were popping out one by one overhead, Caleb began to find a prime spot for the big lantern, positioning it on a pair of rocks that he'd constructed into a stalwart table shape to support the lamp weight all night long (*important* because if the lamp fell over, we'd be up a dark creek without a paddle). Ah, yes, the dark green lantern. It was the holy symbol of outdoor adventures. It was freedom.

Oddly enough, I don't remember ever seeing Caleb with a flashlight, and I don't remember ever using my Mickey Mouse flashlight on fishing trips. I believe I packed it only to feel like a responsible green beret or because I liked Mickey Mouse, etc.

Anyway, when the lamp was in place, the night began: Caleb leaned over it carefully as if it were a holy relic, lighting it slowly and letting it hiss and burn with a sweet sibilance that charmed me right down to my little soul socks. To this day whenever I hear a camping lantern hiss I am flooded with ineffable rapture. The lamp gave a dull glow at first, but soon was beaming brightly as if Tinker Bell herself were trapped behind the glass! The rocks glistened like dragon's jewels. Caleb's moustache turned golden before my eyes, his eyes sparkly and noble: the greatest fisherman of all the ages.

"Okay, now we're ready. Grab the tackle box and the igloo and put 'em down by the poles," mumbled Caleb, making consummate adjustments to the holy light. I stumbled quickly over the rocks and did my task with summer lightning coursing through my veins. Caleb joined me by the poles and began connecting the two parts that completed the their respective lengths, then unwound the line from the reels, threaded the line up through the pole holes and let out enough of it to apply a hook, sinkers, and perhaps a bobber if he didn't want to run too deep. He knew that cats weren't always on the very bottom of the delta and often experimented with different depths: building a fishing empiricism tantamount to a general who'd written the book on war strategy based on smoky battle experience.

I picked up a rock and dusted it off, turning it over and contemplating it.

"You're not gonna throw that in the water are you? 'Cuz if you are we might as well go home right now," Caleb declared, looking sideways at me as he bent over a pole.

"No way, man," I replied. After all, I was *too cool* for that kind of crap (I mean: that kind of *shit)*; I dropped the rock and stood closely by Caleb, ready to help.

"Good, 'cuz I got a good feelin' about the cats tonight. I think we'll catch us a big one; go get me a Coors," requested the fish master. I hopped over to the igloo and procured a yellow wet can and then delivered it post haste, therefore beginning the refreshment exuberance of my stepdad. It's funny, he never called beer "beer." He always called it by whatever brand he was drinking at the moment (whatever was on sale), like he was some kind of great American piss beer sampler, acknowledging the name and distinction of beers that didn't deserve distinct acknowledgment because they really didn't inherently have any distinction; they were all the same: swill.

(Luckily, I didn't have these odd critical thinking skills when I was approximately eight. I thought Coors was awesome, and I wished I could drink it by the truckload. I also thought Stockton was Disneyland. Children are so full of hope it's ridiculously awesome.)

After a few cool, crisp, refreshing swigs, Caleb began the ritual of finding three perfect places to mount the poles in the rocks—not too far from the water, but not too close, just close enough to get the chicken liver out there a good ways and down down down down (keep going) down down down deep in the murk where the lunker monsters sexily glided.

I remember how scary catfish looked when I was a boy. They were indeed monstrous, scaleless, gray-fleshy garbage disposals with molester moustaches. The pukey gurgling sound they made when you held them up didn't help. They are still the juiciest, slimiest of $H_2O$ creatures.

"Hey, why don't *you* try a cast, boy!" Caleb hollered from the furthest pole, a good ten yards away. My courage blossomed. I had been waiting for this moment since the last time we went fishing—when I unfortunately cast *horribly*: screwing up the line big time and making Caleb frustrated to the point of his famous fiery frumpled eyebrows.

This time, however, I would redeem myself. I would show him that I was a man's man! "Okay," I twittered, not wanting to give away my intense swell if inner bottle rocket butterfly emotions. I hopped over to the pole to my right that was all ready to go—already mounted in its little castle of rocks—fully loaded with chicken liver dangling in the eventide air about a foot from the dirt—ready—waiting; this is what a polished rifle must have looked like to an infantryman at the outset of Gettysburg! I would cast like a motherfucker! It didn't matter that I didn't understand the implications of that word.

Caleb cast the furthest pole out out out into the delta; it hit the water with a kerplunk in a perfect onomatopoeia type of way. He let the sinker sink the goods, and then reeled the line in about five feet in order to set the distance just about right. He waited. He saw that it was good. He set the pole in its respective stone castle and angled it beautifully, like the leaning tower of delta, toward the cool, muddy waters.

I watched him with passion in my heart: I was seeing Zeus himself performing some epic feat of Athenian strategy (or Jove performing some epic feat of Roman strategy, or maybe Dagon performing…etc.). Then Caleb lit a fresh cigarette and *finally* came up to where I was about to burst with anticipation over my forthcoming Olympic cast of wire and hookery. Caleb gave me a slow example of how to cast, which I had seen before, but I watched and nodded like a good pupil.

THEN HE HANDED ME THE POLE! (Yes, it was this exciting.) And told me not to "worry about the distance to the water's edge. The sinkers will do the work for you; remember—it's all in the wrist—just like throwin' a baseball—and don't think too much about it—just feel it through." He was full of these types of workin'-man sayings, whether it pertained to driving a truck, painting a wall, or toasting toast, it was always about "feel" and "going with the flow" and "not thinking too much," manly wisdom of the ages, seasoned with briny mud from the California delta. Good honest stuff that a man could build a life upon.

Despite such solid instruction I was nervous; I wanted so desperately to cast well that I began worrying that I wouldn't. And then, of course, I self-fulfilled that stupid prophesy and cast horribly, almost hooking Caleb's ear with the be-livered treble-hook! I most certainly did not use my wrist. I *flung* my whole entire body forward with all my kiddy might, and my right foot slid on some muddy rocks. *Scrape! Scrabble-Scramble! Sclump!*

This sent me into a magical dance that wobbled the pole as my thumb came off the line release button, curtailing the flow of line and snapping the hook and sinkers into a whirling pattern that brought them back toward us instead of the water.

They whizzed overhead at the first pass, but on the second they smacked Caleb in the side of the head—leaving bloody, black liver smears in his dowdy hair and barely missing a nice, flesh hook lodging in his prominent red ears.

*Shit. Shit. Shit.* If I had no fear of being smacked, I would have said "Shit" right then and there to put a good, heavy tombstone on the grave of my failure. But I didn't cuss. I merely screwed up my face in an, "Oh, *poop*...I'm *sooo* sorry," manner—eyebrows raised and lips parted, pulled back.

Caleb stood still for a moment and then felt his liver hair, glaring at me. "You weren't listnin', were ya?" he accused.

I protested, "NO! I was listening...I just got stuck in the rocks!" I squealed, looking down at the evil rocks around my sneakers. Curse them. *A pox on them.*

"Nah, you didn't listin'; you never listin', so you'll never learn to cast, and that's *your* problem!" he bellowed, putting me in my place and fraying some of the edges of the great flag of fishing. He took a long, Vietnam pull from his cigarette and quit looking at me, opting, rather, to look out over the graying waters and thus refilling his sense of riverly peace. After a couple delicious moments, he returned his gaze upon me, exhaling an old faithful amount of smoky steam and said, "All right, no problems while fishin', right? Right. Gimme that pole."

I relinquished the sinful pole with reverence to the reverend and watched as he made it all better, casting so damn far out that I was awestruck. *WWHHHHIIIIZZZZZZZ* went the line, and way out in the wet distance I could barely hear the sinker slap the water. It was a cast full of muscles. I loved watching him cast. It was encouraging and it was one of the rare times that I felt safe and proud with him. He was my dad. And he was a peaceful dad…that is, unless he started blabbering about almighty baseball once all of the baited lines were "swimmin' pretty" out in the "stew."

Caleb loved baseball over everything. He seemed to live life through the lens of the game, always using baseball aphorisms like, "Keep your eye on the ball," and "It's time to bring in the designated hitter." I hate to say it, but I think a lot of my life love for baseball comes from Caleb's inexorable inculcation of the game into my malleable brain as a youngster.

Caleb and I were quite comfortable with each other whenever baseball was on the conversational menu. We could honestly relate, even though I didn't have much life experience with the game. On this night, Caleb threw the opening audible pitch as soon as the sun dropped behind the valley bleachers and the scoreboard lit up with moon advertisements and star stats. We sat back in our slowly warming aluminum and beige nylon (was it nylon?) folding chairs and settled in within our snug dugout. "It's pretty out here," I said, feeling important.

"Yup," he replied. "It smells like that good grassy smell, like out on a cold mornin' ball field," he artfully expounded. I looked over at him, loving him, loving baseball and fishing, hearing only the wondrous song of the lantern—hissing and beaming like heaven itself.

"If anything is as good as fishing it's baseball, right?" he questioned rhetorically.

"Yeah," I replied, getting up and walking over to the cooler, procuring for myself a delicious Hawaiian Punch; it dripped with ice-cold ice bits. Caleb had to open it for me; it was too cold, and my fingers weren't strong enough to snap the top.

"Can you grab me another Coors?" Suddenly Caleb was becoming super happy, as if God, Jesus, and the Holy Ghost were all working on him because he was in close proximity to the hypnotic Jordan Delta. "Have you heard of Fernando Valenzuela?" he asked, cracking open his beer.

"No," I answered, taking a crisp swig of delicious red kiddy wine (I actually had heard of him before, from Caleb, of course, but I wanted to hear of him again).

"Well, yuh know, he's a new rookie pitcher for the Dodgers, and he, oh boy, he's gonna be a Hall ah Famer. I tell yuh what, boy, he's damn good. Damn good, and he works hard…reeal hard; he's been clocked at over a hunnerd!" hollered Caleb, getting excited and leaning forward in the creaky chair.

I smiled, nodding intelligently as if I were the Oakland A's sportscaster guy during the pre-game show. "Yeeauh, he's good. He 'minds me of Nolan Ryan when he was jest startin' out for the Mets back in '68; did yuh know that if Vietnam hadn't fuc-...messt up my baseball plans I would-a been a rookie *the same year as Nolan?*" (He didn't give me time to nod—he was already winding up—the good times were already happening.) "Yep, I woulda been. That was back 'round the time I got to practice out in Baltimore with the Orioles. I hit the ball *hard* and *fast* that day, man. I tell you, I bet they were thinkin' of signin' me on if old Uncle Sam hadn't stept in and *robbed me*. Nolan Ryan...how'd he get outta Nam?" Caleb thoughtfully mused (that is, if he was capable of musing). He became cigarette quiet for a minute.

I was well studied in Calebry by this time and knew that now was not the time to say anything, but to let him play out his little witty drama: the lead character in his vaporous workingman soliloquies: silently working out the workings of time and mankind through alcoholic, philosophical midwifery. He took another pull from the shrinking Camel. The crickets put up a beautiful night serenade behind the lamenting, Shakespearean Caleb. Then he just started gabbing again (all the while keeping an acute eye on the silent poles lest a fish try to trick him like Nam did).

"Nolan Ryan is one of the best, man. So is Jim Palmer. He could pull any team outta the crappiest innings just by takin' the mound and teachin' any batter a lesson or two on strikin' out. I tell yuh what; I seen him do it again and again. Yeah, he don't walk no one; he's from the old school of talkin' the talk— and he's not out there just tryin' to break records like some of these young punks is. Hell, no—he's jest tryin' to win the games, and that should be the only concern of every major league ballplayer. Right there, win games and quit whining about who broke what record and who did this and this and such. HELL...yuh know?"

Oh, boy was he preaching now!

I nodded and banged my make-believe baseball mitt Bible against my knees. He was righteously right; who did these young punks think they were anyways? I took a giant swig of my Hawaiian Punch and wiped my red sticky lips with my hairy forearm. Caleb continued his litany, "I tell you, the *day* Rickey Henderson is outta baseball is the day it'll be 'bout the game again and not 'bout money and records; he oughta be a basketball player he's so flashy and ornery. What a baby! And he's only been in the majors fer like a yeeer!

Some second baseman oughta *accidentally* clean his clock the next time he tries to steal! Shit! Breakin' records! Joe Morgan and Willie Mays didn't steal bases to break fuckin' records. *THEY STOLE 'UM 'CUZ THEY HAD TO!"*

He was on fire.

The unbridled cussing was a sure fire sign that Caleb was in his campfire lantern element: weaving and confabulating stories with alcoholic joy the same way the old thanes in the mead hall did. Being out in the fragrant outdoors only intoxicated him more. This was the romantic man: ranting and raving and happy and bitchin' and fishin' and hairy and flannelly. The Marlboro Camel man was enjoying himself too much to even consider beating me for existing.

I'm sure that many other men have great memories of fishing with their fathers or stepfathers or grandfathers or even their mothers. There is a definite something about it that cheers the heart, young or old.

If Caleb was talkin' baseball, then the time would most certainly be between nine and eleven. Usually by this time, the fishing was golden. When I say "golden," I don't mean we were catching anything yet (usually the catfish started biting around midnight), what I do mean is this: I was having the time of my life.

I remember specifically the physical motions of Caleb, whether storytelling, reeling in a monster, or just kicking around the night rocks. I would study him intently, without the knowledge that I was "studying" anything. He was important to me because I remember him, all of him: the good cowboy and the sick fuck.

A few times when fishing, a cat would bite early, before I got all testy and went to sleep up in the truck. When this biting occurred, Caleb would quit the oral tradition, the whistling, or the envisioning of Paul Newman covered in chicken feathers. He would *and did* shut up instantly—with one open hand extended toward me in a vertical "Ssshhhh!"

One of the poles was jerking slightly on its end; then it stopped jerking; cats were tricky and usually waited for Caleb to be at the height of his buzzed confabulations before delicately trying to remove tasty morsels of chicken liver surreptitiously from the landmine treble hooks. But Caleb was too smart for them.

The end of the pole jerked once more—immediately causing an electric-air-chain-reaction that made our man blood course faster and hotter. The hunt had begun. Caleb glanced over at the furthest pole and then at the other closer one: neither was being touched; only the one in the middle was catching any action.

It jerked again! And…then, three seconds later…the biggest jerk of all—making the very tip end of the pole curve like a night moon scimitar for a good two seconds!

Caleb waited. He never moved in for the kill too soon. He wasn't to be tricked by catfish coquettish teasing. He was superbly skilled at the delta dance.

I put down my lukewarm Hawaiian Punch—slowly, turning it slightly in the dirt so it wouldn't spill—and looked to Caleb for coaching. He threw a quick man-glance at me that read, "Don't move a muscle—I got it."

Thus began the epic bodily fishing movement of Caleb that I'll always remember, a veritable ballet. He stood up and took three or four paces toward the jerking pole, ignoring everything else in the night, eyes fixated on its every move. His legs somehow ended up in a bow-legged stance, as he got closer to the pole. Then, he leaned low and put his left hand on his left knee, eyes never leaving the goal. They darted back and forth from the pole's end to the dark water. In this final position, Caleb's right hand moved up to his mouth and placed the half-smoked cigarette firmly in his leather lips for a long enough time to take a hurricane pull, sucking the very life from its bright orange tobacco entrails.

(I can hear it echo in my night thoughts even today: that sonorous drag: the crackle-ember-fire-vapor.)

After exhausting the cigarette's soul, Caleb moved in for the kill, throwing the cigarette to the ground as if it had burned his fingers—then he leapt upon the pole and took it from its rock castle as if he were a starving man and it were a free pot roast. He heaved the pole back toward his right shoulder, pointing the top of it straight up and back over him, looking like a mighty warrior hero, defying the gods, striking them with a fishing pole broadsword born of holy water.

Ah, the hook was set! The fish didn't have a chance now, no matter how strong or slimy it was; it was no match for the sinewy, workingman arms of the Marlboro Camel man. As he reeled the hidden beast in we hoped (to the same river gods we'd just defied) that it was a catfish and *not* some stupid striper. Those worthless fish really pissed Caleb off; they continually stole the bait we worked so diligently to apply and caused nothing but wasted time and trouble. Caleb wished they could all be eaten somehow by some specially planted carnivorous fish with an exclusive taste for only delta striper. I don't think there is such a fish in existence, but it was a cool scientific idea.

He also hated perch because they were "bony and fought like pussies. Nobody can eat 'em—no meat on 'em!" he'd holler. "Damn stripers and perch. Somebody should've given Luke Skywalker scuba gear and a waterproof light saber; he'd have taken care of them all!"

Luckily, most times a fish was securely caught on our brown treble hooks it *was* a catfish. Perch never stayed on for some reason, and stripers only took the bait and left the hook to dangle uselessly in the muddy-murder coldness. So this time, like many, we were happy when the beast was finally exhumed from the dirty depths. It was indeed a juice-filled, biggy, fatty catfish—with sharp barbells and black eyes and a gaping mouth that reminded me of numerous scurrilous creatures in that Tatooine Cantina in *Star Wars*. It was gross. It was harrowing to me just looking at it from a safe eight foot distance as Caleb cautiously moved toward it in the dark shallow waters; it might be hiding a dagger, after all…for one last strike before the death croak.

He yelled nicely at me, "Bring the lantern down here!"

I grabbed the lantern and scurried quickly back down to the shoreline like a thirsty muskrat. I was just in time to see Caleb grab him up out of the water with his bare hands and hold him high. "GOTCHA!" he yelled with glee, for he held in his hands at least one minute of victory over his shitty life. This seven-pound cat magically became the major leagues or a well-paying job or a private house on Lake Comanche complete with silvery Ranger fishing boat immortality.

Yes! A plump catfish.

"Here—hold him fer me," he moved the fish toward my downward arms—a test of manhood, which I always failed.

"I CAN'T; I DON'T WANT TO; it's ugly!" I whined, moving backwards out and away from the lantern's yellow light.

"C'mon, you'll have ta do it sometime. How can we call you a fisherman if yur sceered of the fish?" he huffed.

I shrugged my shoulders and begin to panic over my validity. I don't remember Caleb ever getting angry with me over this, though.

"Okay, whatever. Yuh know yer gonna help me clean this sucker, though, when we get back home. It's a right of passage into manhood, boy." He chortled, putting the squirming cat into our special green cooler thingy that was full of death ice for the freezing fish. He closed the lid without ceremony.

No time to waste; onward to the next greedy cat. The delta was full of gilled avarice.

After a few battle recovery minutes of silence, we resumed chat. Every time a boat went by in the black distance (green lights blinking), Caleb would comment disdainfully, "What are they doin' out this time of night? A boat that big shouldn't be out on the delta, sceerin' the fish and oilin' up the water." He hated big boats, but I think he secretly wanted to own one, especially since they had big engines in them that he could tinker with.

When the night was finally concluded, we bumbled and bumped our way back home. Eight Mile Road looked resplendent in the newborn sun. I felt like a soldier. The views from our halftrack truck were grand: fresh yellow fields painted with fresh orange sunlight. Black birds with red dots on their wings darting this way and that. We had fought all night and now were bringing home the spoils to our great She-Emperor.

(Iced catfish equaled gold, jewels, spices and virgins...oh what sweet conquest! We'd been methodical in our hunt. First we caught all the fish in the entire delta. Second we dried it all up. Third we burned it. Fourth we sowed its muddy soil with loads of salt. One, two, three, four; never again would the Barbarian Catfish Ostrogoths attack the decency of our hoplite-laden truck!)

Mom, the aforementioned She-Emperor, had a staunch rule that pertained to fishing days: no fish (prisoner), dead or alive, was allowed in the house (Rome) unless it was cleaned and ready for freezing or feasting. So, as soon as we got home we took our armor and hung it up in the armory storage shed and then took our monstrous booty out to the backyard for a thorough cleaning. We cleaned them on newspaper, always.

I remember the smell of the carcasses, the way they were slowly drying, the way they stuck to the newspaper if you left them in one position for too long. The headlines and advertisements would darken and get all sticky.

Caleb used his good-old-boy-from-Linden Buck knife. It was bigger than your average buck knife and had gold tips at the ends of the ivory-looking body, chasse, fuselage, holder thing.

Like most boys I was fascinated by the cutting and guts and blood, but unlike your average American boy who revels in such gore (later to go on and play varsity sports without fear, without blinking a trophy eye), I was hesitant. I liked seeing all the goo, but didn't want to get too close lest I become gooey or the dead fish rise again in my nightmares to "gut" me, vengeance treble hooks dangling from my bloody mouth.

I watched Caleb clean, vitiating the fish (guts pulled out in one long sweeping motion, then the heart and lungs and other lifeless crap) with consummate skill; he was so damn tough.

I held the hose and extra newspaper if we needed it. I enjoyed holding these squire objects because they kept my hands full and safe from the ghoulish work before me. If for some reason I didn't have newspaper, I'd bring along my Mickey flashlight with the pretext of, "I have this in case you [Caleb] need to see the guts better...or if you need to see in the catfishes' mouths." To me, these responses seemed valid, but to Caleb, they must have sounded retarded. He knew I was afraid and for some reason let me be (thank God). Maybe it was because I was being a good and patient helper. Maybe he loved cleaning the fish and didn't want to be bothered by a stepchild who would clean them wrong. I don't know. But he never made me touch the guts.

However, I did have one proud responsibility. I *alone* carried the freshly cleaned fish into the house from the backyard autopsy table. Caleb wrapped them in fresh newspaper and handed them to me. This never really scared me; their yucky guts were gone, and they were hosed off so they were "clean," plus they were rolled in thick newspaper. On the other hand I remember feeling the slimy weight through the paper and worrying that at any second they would flop alive and clutch my little white wrist in their frigid sharp mouths! Yikes!

But they never did.

As soon as I made it into the Roman house, my mother beamed at me, wrapped in her greenish bathrobe, emitting a yawn every minute while the Yuban dripped and whistled with electric heat.

"Whatcha got there, son of mine?" she sang.

*"FISH!"* I bellowed, my chest full of organic fireworks.

She took them from me and told me to go get the rest. I hop-hop-hopped out to the back yard and was handed the last two fish (it seems like we usually caught approximately five—well, Caleb did—after I was nestled in the truck) with the words, "There you go, tasty ones!" bursting from Caleb's exhausted morning lips...tuckered out from twenty beers, thirty cigarettes, forty crazy stories, and 10,000 gusts of delta night wind.

I ran full speed into the house with both excitement and a morbid Murphy's law sense that if any of cats were to bite me it would be the last two. Mom turned when she heard me burst into the sleepy kitchen. She smiled. "And whatcha got this time, little fisherman?"

"MORE FFIIISSHH!" I exploded, mishandling them and dropping one that hit the linoleum floor with a frozen thud.

I jumped back—had it come back to life?

No.

Mom chuckled, picked up the fish and moved it toward me in a macabre dance of "I'm going to get you!" (Somewhere back in the 19th century Camille Saint-Saëns was penning a masterpiece entitled, "Danse Macabre.") Her eyes were radiant with consanguineous fun.

I stood my ground. "It's not alive!" I did a crazy, twirly dance move on the linoleum in order to augment my argument and show that I wasn't scared of stupid, dead catfish. She giggled and stuck the remaining two monsters in the freezer, tucking them in to sleep with the other fishes. Their newspaper blankets would keep them warm, I remember thinking.

We waited until dinner to cook them in tin foil coats and butter. The oven always turned them crispy and delicious. I think I was one of those rare children that actually liked the taste of cooked fish that had been caught by his own (step)dad. Most kids find fish repulsive, cooked or no. They opt, rather, for watermelon sugar candies. But not I; I was too proud—I picked out the bones without fear or frustration and smeared the butter round and round the white meaty chucks. Even the crisp black skin didn't bother me. I don't know, maybe I've got some sort of Nordic innate love of fish within me. Or maybe I just wanted Caleb to be proud: I was eating delicious fish, I was earning my keep, and I was *not* being a prima donna like Rickey Henderson. I was certain he didn't eat fish, 'cuz he was a pussy.

Caleb's hoary mustache filled with butter crust as he chewed and chewed, devouring the carcass before him. He worked quickly, knowing that the sooner the protein was consumed the sooner he could wash it down with a cold one. Eating fish that you yourself had caught was always high on the list of manly things to do. He reveled in such things. *I think he would have literally exploded with glee if he ever got the incredibly odd chance to eat the fish he himself had caught upon a table that was a clean-idling engine that he himself had fixed—all the while wearing the baseball uniform he himself had worn at the Orioles training camp back in the early seventies. Incontrovertible ecstasy... Later on, the police would find only a solitary moustache basted in salty butter. The whole thing would seem fishy to them.*

    The day after fishing was always a let down. Caleb would be grumpy and stubborn; he'd stay on the outside of the house "fixing" things and doing God knows what. This grumpy day was usually Sunday, a day that never meant church or Sabbath relaxation or even family-together time. It was a day like any other. You were either working or playing and not really putting a lot of effort into either. That was life for us in Stockton: lazy, with the smug guise of carpe diem.

    In reality, neither Tallene nor Caleb cared much for drinking deep from the cup of life. They'd both had shitty lives so far…so there wasn't a dream left in either of them. All they seemed to care about was "getting by" and going fishing or shopping now and then. It's hard to put into words, harder still because I'm seeing it darkly through the memory lens of child-me. And all I see is stupid oakies. And I love and hate them and love and hate them and desperately want to forever escape them. And I really do escape them one step at a time by striving like crazy to really live my own life: to see the world—to expand my knowledge—to imbue each day with culture, history, and truth—to love and genuinely connect with others. All that kind of stuff: the stuff that matters, the stuff that burns hotter than the sun within my breast.

    Those Stokes and Jones and especially that house depress me. And yet, though I hate to admit it, I love it…somewhat fiercely. Like most folks tethered to cloudy personal histories, I wish I could go back in time and be invisible there…be invisible in order to love. I wish I could glide unseen through the rooms of the house and witness the oakies in action. I'd love to see my mother alive and healthy again. I'd love to even go fishing with the great white shark again. I'd love to watch him cast. However, no matter how much I wish, my pennies sit motionless and corroded at the bottom of the well.

    I wonder, what am I really wishing for? Perhaps the peaceful Jordan delta.

# Chapter 6
# Blueberry Muffins

Our humble Stockton home on 542 East Wyndotte St. was never safe enough for me. The entire time I was there (roughly 1977 to 1981) I enjoyed the comforts of home, but never felt completely secure. Caleb was a big reason. He was a loose cannon.

My mom was another reason. Though I love her dearly and want to look back on her with only the serene thought that she was my courageous rock of stability, I cannot. She was very insecure and became codependent and soap-opera dramatic as the years wore on. I wonder now if she had some chemical problems going on within her perpetually unhealthy body.

She had an addiction to diet pills that poisoned her to the point of having a kidney transplant at the young age of 26. Actually, the pills weren't the only cause; genetics had something to do with it. Alcohol most certainly did not. My mom was nowhere near alcoholism. She drank less than your average American, so that makes me wonder what else came into play. She had weight issues for sure. And those most have been somewhat innate. She struggled and floundered daily in the area of weight management and also depression. I have a hard fight with my weight every day of my life, but I don't let it get to me the way she did. Then again, I don't have an alcoholic husband who berates me verbally, cheats on me, and is a son of a bitch. I'm also six feet four inches, not five feet two inches.

But back to the son of a bitch: Caleb was a problem in every area of our lives, but he put food on the table a little bit better than did my mom, so she stayed with him. Her various odd jobs couldn't keep the checks from bouncing up and down in our paltry bank account. I remember her working, doing something. I don't know what she was skilled at besides cleaning up patient puke and perhaps answering phones at a family hospital, as a house cleaner, and as some sort of small-time tax accountant. I hope she crunched numbers well. She did indeed take care of paying the bills at home so maybe math was a forte of hers.

Managing money certainly wasn't, nor managing her eating habits. I often wonder about her and Caleb managing their relationship. I also often wonder about the state of their sexual relationship all of those years. Was there good, healthy sex: that practical peanut butter in the relationship of marriage that holds the two pieces of cheap white bread together? I'll never know. They're both dead now. I'm certain her weight issues affected their sex life. I'm also quite certain that Caleb mocked her efforts.

Sam, my little brother, Caleb's son from my mother, was born in 1980. I never felt close to him because he was more special in Caleb's eyes than I. Therefore all types of subliminal sibling rivalries ensued throughout the eighties.

All this stuff is quite foggy to me, and dense, dank, like a field all soggy and unable to be heated up with purifying sunshine. Permanent fog and twilight. The flickering light from my red Mickey Mouse flashlight didn't amount to a hill of beans back in the eighties; the dark murk of Stockton was too thick and unwilling to change. It was similar, paradoxically, to the waters of my beloved delta in its inexorable nature. And we were all treading it.

*Caleb was the biggest, ugliest shark-catfish hybrid in those waters. He was a blind, ignorant bottom-feeder. One could easily see him in Plato's cave allegory: He would be sitting Indian-style on the cold stony floor way back deep in the furthest reaches of the cave, only nefarious bats for friends, loving the play of the shadows on the wall in front of him, the campfire ablaze behind him, and considering those very shadows the only display of life. The shadows would look a lot like trusses and titties.*

Odd, yet salient fact: Caleb lived in a seedy hotel when my mother first met him. I consider this symbolic of his transient, unobserved, and unrecorded life. On and off blinks the neon VACANCY sign in the dark night. He is forever shirtless. He is forever pissing in the wind. He is forever knocking me around the house.

I was perpetually in the path of his toothy jaws. Even when I got a little older he continued slapping me around with words and dry hands. I'll remember one such incident quite vividly until the day I die. Sam, Caleb and I were all in the car, and it was sometime in the evening, possibly seven p.m. on a weekday. Mom was at home having an Avon meeting in the living room with a group of other subsocialites—discussing make-up and women's early '80s shenanigans. This was one of her various odd jobs.

I know for a fact that I was eight years old, so the year was 1983, which makes Sam a mere three years old, but I don't remember him being in a high chair. In fact, he was in the front seat with Caleb, hopefully wearing a seat belt. I was seated in the middle of the back seat, looking out between the two of them at the massive golden arches approaching in the distance. Yes, Mom was too busy to cook tonight so we boys were grabbing a healthy and cost-effective dinner at McDonald's.

My hot little mouth salivated with anticipation for smooshed cheeseburgers with two pickles and little bits of onion.... or, no... chicken mcnuggets (no I will *not* capitalize this word) with sweet and sour sauce and french fries...; such luscious lumps of grease waited in their heated bins for me that very second!

Caleb was laconic and moody. Sam was quiet too. The radio was playing that same just-barely-classic rock at a conversation killing volume of three out of ten. I was restless. It was dark already, and rain was drenching the windshield, making the golden arches melt and seem to jiggle in a dazzling fashion, as if they were doing a seductive dance in order to lure us into obesity and Americanism. I longed for the pungent smell of fast food.

Ah, and there it finally was—that ubiquitous McDonald's smell that emanates from every single one of their greasy stores no matter where you are on this greasy globe.

I salivated and was, to be frank: turned on. I began tapping the back of the front seat. The vinyl thumped. "Knock it off, boy, dammit," spurted Caleb. He was in a funk. Apparently the delicious smell wasn't vivifying his spirits.

Sam was still quiet; he seemed almost thoughtful, looking out the rain-streaked window to his right into total darkness. Maybe he had the supernaturally quiet child gift of seeing ghosts. I don't know; he sure as hell stared off into space all of the time. Perhaps he was just dense or not as frenetically sensitive and alert as I. His hair had an Alfalfa cowlick bloobie sticking up in the back. That's what we called sleep hair that stood up, "bloobies." It was funny and very cute of us to coin such a word. (Although we were a half-assed family we still had our fun). I think my mom made it up.

Earlier that day at school I had heard an older kid tell a funny joke at recess. It was definitely a grown-up joke. I had laughed pretty loud so that I would seem cool, but it had taken me all day to entirely figure out the joke. At least,

I thought I had it figured out. I had also debated all day whether or not I should tell it to my stepdad. It was right up his workin' man mirth alley.

Somehow whilst figuring it out I had memorized it and now had a humor bullet in my cerebral gun, ready to fire. I had an itchy trigger finger. If it hit Caleb just right, I would be his burger buddy and a real sarcastic gunslinger. Both of these things I desperately wanted to be. So, now I waited for the eight-year-old sand to actually sling the gun.

We pulled up to the drive-through, a modern convenience, and Caleb began ordering for us all. I let him do it because my radar said he was not to be messed with, and besides, he usually knew what I wanted. I listened closely. "Yeah…uhm…two Big Macs, a large coke, six-piece chicken nugget with barbeque sauce (the only thing at McDonald's that Sam would put in his tender baby mouth), two small orange drinks…and…ah…[I crossed my fingers and toes] yeah…how 'bout a Happy Meal…with a cheeseburger in it…. Right? Yup…goood…heah…hey, scratch one ah them orange drinks and make it ah small strawberry shake, okay?"

*What? Strawberry shake? Was today frickin' Christmas?*

We never got a shake because Caleb always called them "a damn rip off." He looked at both Sam and me with a 2-by-4 smile on his moustache. "A treat for two quiet boys," then pulled forward to secure our golden edible treasure.

I immediately intuited that we would all share the shake; Caleb was far too cheap to get us each one, and I knew that Strawberry was his favorite flavor no matter what the confection or drink. Regardless, I was just excited that I would get one big slurp of delicious strawberry sugar ice, plus a Happy Meal! And, do you know what comes in a luscious happy meal? *A luscious toy!*

Caleb's funk must have changed; behold the vast wonders of fast food! I would wait until we were parked (to give Mom and the gals the house for a while) and eating like juicy hogs to unleash my radical joke. Sam wouldn't get it, but he was just a dumb baby.

Caleb put the car in park and let it idle to keep the heater churning. I heard the crackling of greasy papers in the front seat and then saw Caleb's head lunge forward into his dripping double decker big mac burger. He mumbled an "mmm" through his chews and onion-flecked moustache. Sam was quietly sucking on a chicken nugget, Caleb was too busy to open Sam's barbecue thingy and hold it out for Sam's dippy messiness. I looked down at my happy meal. It was still locked up in its colorful cardboard box. I decided to tell the joke before opening it; I couldn't wait! Then the food would be that more satisfying, and we could all giggle between gulps: a perfect guys' night out!

"I've got a funny joke!" I blurted out, making Caleb's head jerk with surprise.

He turned around and took a slurp on the pink shake. "Okay, out with it—and it better be damn funny," he happily declared, pointing a secret sauce finger back at me. He was in the mood for fun. I could tell because he was smiling and still eating his burger like a contented hog whilst listening.

I took a swallow of courageous, stuffy, rain-car air and began my grown-up joke with pride. "It goes like this: I don't drink, I don't smoke, and I don't cuss!"

Caleb smiled, his jaw muscles working away on the beef.

Then I delivered the glorious punch line, "Damn! I left my cigarettes at the bar!" I exploded with laughter to show everyone just how funny it was, knowing that Caleb was a dirty blonde hair away from exploding into a genuine paroxysm of ultimate hilarity. But He didn't. Instead he exploded with rage. He smacked me hard across the face with the back of his hand. I was electrified with painful surprise. My brain jumped in my skull as the little candle of good times had a bucket of Caleb's caustic acid dumped directly upon it.

He was *pissed* at me, at my stupid joke. "What did you say?" he hollered. "WHAT DID YOU SAY?" he *screamed*.

I shrugged my shoulders and pushed my body back into the vinyl as far as my legs would permit.

"Repeat the joke!" he ordered.

I did, awkwardly, between sobs of hot tears. I was terrified. Before I could finish the punch line he smacked me again—harder than ever. I squealed quietly.

"Repeat what you jest said, the end of the joke," he ordered.

I didn't want to. I would rather lower my foot into the salty mouth of a bloody great white shark. I would rather hold a live, slime-squirming catfish in my ungloved hands. I would rather pull weeds in the muggy sun all afternoon at J.R. and grandma's. I would rather…I would rather…I would rath…so of course I repeated the joke for the last time and received a harsh man-punch to the right shoulder. I don't know why the shoulder; he might as well of just punched me full on in my eight-year-old face; I know he was just itching to.

I broke down crying.

"Don't be a pussy!" he yelled. "It don't go with yer tough-guy joke! Do you like cussin'? Is that what you want to teech yer little brother? There's no way in *hell* he's gonna cuss and be a smart-ass brat like you! You wanna suck a bar of soap when we get home?" he blasted and blasted and blasted me away. My head was bit clean off. The joke had failed.

Before we left he grabbed my unopened happy meal out of my trembling hands and threw it out the window. "You get nothin'!" he declared, pointing at me once more with his withered finger.

We pulled out of the black, wet parking lot, past the dark murder bushes, and onward through Caleb's back road suburbia short cut all the way home. The lights in the house were glowing orange through the living room windows. Cars I had never seen before were parked along the street in front of our house. Nobody had dared to take Caleb's parking spot due to Tallene's severe warning.

I wanted desperately to see my mommy, but like on all beating days, I was cut off from her by Caleb's ingenious methods for keeping my tears and bruises hidden from her. I would not be consoled and loved that night. I was sent straight to bed, with the final judgment of, "No seein' yer mother 'til tomorrow. We'll go in through the back door. (Huff) I'll fill her in on how BAD you been today."

What an asshole. What a monstrous pile of shark shit. My glorious happy meal lay uneaten and cold on the wet asphalt; it was all I could think about as I tried to sleep. Shiny black ants were probably formicating over the soggy and vulnerable burger.

Three glass coke bottles were standing up directly against the bottom of the door. The window had ten separate rectangles of scotch tape sealing it shut to the frame. I had been doing this on and off now for almost two years. It's easy to see that I had it hard, but not as hard as *some* kids. I just had to be careful.

Yes. Careful and cautious.

Everywhere.

Except one place, a place where I was completely safe from Caleb and completely allowed to just be a kid. You'd probably think it was at my grandma and grandpa's house (J.R. and Lulu) in Lodi, but it wasn't. Their house was fine, but not immune to visitation by the great white shark. In fact, Caleb kind of liked hanging out with J.R., the "bear hunter," because he was a tough working man who made a good deal of money annually at "the yard." Caleb would get funny around J.R., like he was hoping for a "fatherly" hand out or free beer. I think my mom noticed this and quietly enjoyed it. He looked a tad bit ridiculous and ineffective next to big old J.R., who was an honest man: his yes was yes and his no was no. Proverbial.

When I look back at J.R. I sure do like him. He was the only stable male "patriarch" figure in my young life. I respected him because he was strict but fair with me, and he let me be a child. I feared him healthily, and I admired him a great deal, the way a child would admire and lionize a real live G.I. Joe.

When I got out of line he would spank me, but spank me fairly and somewhat painlessly compared to the bursting black hell Caleb would unleash upon me. Most times, no—most likely all of the times I truly deserved J.R.'s spankings, and each of them were endorsed by grandma Lulu. Yes, discipline was a good thing with them. There were no scary tricks at their house. And there was definitely a good amount of fun at their house.

There were a lot of days where Lulu would sneak me off to the village toy store when J.R. was at "the yard." Once there she'd let me roam the aisles at my leisure and ceremoniously pick out one special toy at a reasonable price. (I remember that toy store with ancient glee that stirs my heart with joy even today. It had a Tudor-style thatched roof, and course white stucco.)

Would I pick a Star Wars action figure? A Tonka truck? A Tonka tractor? A squishy plastic Tyrannosaurus Rex in red and yellow? Hmmm...I would patiently wait with a fastidious air until I actually got inside the toy store in order to see everything they had and then make my selection logically and with distinction. Such an important, shrewd, and businessesque child was I. Toys were important things, not to be messed with. They deserved respect.

When the bear hunter got home from work (if I was spending an entire day at their home) he would (of course) see my new toy and a playful smirk would appear on his wrinkled face. "Good grief! Whatcha got there, boy?" he'd sing, happy that his solid money had allowed me to be a child and play heartily with my toy in the same way he played heartily at the yard. Americans should always play after they've worked. It's funny, most of my relatives used the word, "boy," when addressing me. Use of this word is pungently indicative of gentle hickdom.

I loved the way J.R. took interest in the toys I'd continually receive. I had no fear he'd be upset over the money that was spent. He even sat down many times to have a good look at them. Then he'd tell me ways I could maximize my fun, especially if they were manly toys with weapons or engines.

One time he set up a ramp composed of two trucker magazines leaning against a propped up book. He showed me how I could jump the toy dirt bike (my selection that day) off the magazines and make it do a three-sixty in the air before it landed on the carpet. I must have done that for hours. J.R. was sweet and awesome, a good combo, indeed, a good grandpa figure in my life. He smelled like pipe tobacco and old, hairy forearms with brass watches. Straight 30 weight oil in his blood.

Lulu was also very kind. She had no qualms about spending money on me. After the toy store she'd walk me over to the village confectionary and purchase one big, blue raspberry popcorn ball. I loved those messy popcorn balls; they turned my tongue, teeth, and lips blue. Then we'd perhaps run a few errands. Lulu was always on the go.

It was fun getting toys and popcorn balls. Nobody spent money on me at home, yet; Caleb made sure of that. I sometimes imagine Lulu's license plate frame thingy reading, "Born to spoil my grandkids!" But I don't think anybody manufactured vanity license-plate-frame-holder thingies back in the earliest '80s. In all actuality her license plate frame holder thingy probably just read, "Dick Smith's Valley Value Ford," or something similar. Business and boredom.

Considering all of the above, Grandma and J.R.'s house was both fun and pretty darn safe, but there was one place that was even *safer* then their house, indeed super safe because now I refer to it in my memory as the safe house.

I had a great grandmother back then, the mother of Lulu, named Mildred Foster. She was still young in the early eighties due to the fact that she was born in 1917. Like most oakies, the Joneses married and had offspring young, which in this case worked out because Mildred was still young and active: able to be my favorite person in the world next to my beautiful mother. To be entirely honest, Mildred was my savior.

She filled me up with sunlight and toasty grandma love when I was running on nothing but fright and the gallows. She was compassionate toward me and loved me in a way that was entirely genuine and more real than the navy blue Velcro sneakers on my feet. She thought I was interesting. I thought she was hope.

I called her Granny, and I spent more time with her than anyone else save my mother. By virtue of this I was at her one-bedroom apartment quite a bit.

It had a quiet, open air carport that became my movie play area: I could set up entire battle field scenes for my Star Wars guys and take my delicious time enacting gorgeous war stories complete with symphonic background and complex plots that would make George Lucas himself jealous.

Granny didn't have a car, so the carport was always spacious, save a few sundry gardening supplies that lined the walls...gardening supplies that made perfect earthworks and fortified bastions for battle. The rake made a perfect trap for my jeep/tank thing, popping its tires and ripping at its treads as the guys (veritable fish in a barrel) abandoned its burning hulk (there were mines) and ran for cover behind the immense bag of potting soil under a hail of withering fire: lasers, bullets, rockets, plus thrown swords and light sabers. I really should have had a little kitchen sink weapon to throw; it was indeed warranted.

Granny let me play by myself as long as I wished. Sometimes that meant hours. The sun's rays would shadow the carport in five different ways; when it got to the fifth stage (finally hitting the kitchen door) I knew the battle was over and that I should get up and see what Granny was up to. Most likely she was reading *Reader's Digest* or baking something delicious. Her apartment was quiet and as comforting as a down comforter in winter; it contained a methodically-ticking wall clock made of pine and iron, sea shells and glass animals (ensconced in a light dust) which lined the display shelves in the living room, and a comfy, pumpkin orange couch with a fully automated kick out leg rest. I loved kicking out that leg rest, picking up a *Reader's Digest,* and pretending to read just like Granny. There weren't a lot of pictures so it took some real effort.

*We existed like eternal, lambent angels in a golden realm of sweet isolation, Granny and I, she too old to care for the world and I too young to care or know anything of the world. We were miles away from my home, miles away from the thunderstorms. Many, many miles away.*

My mom told me later in life that Caleb never even knew where Granny lived. He couldn't care less about her or me, so when I was out there he most likely loved it, thinking that in a way we cancelled each other out. Granny lived far out in East Lodi, apparently a bad part of town at the time, yet paradoxically safer than safe itself. I never felt fear whilst there. The only gunshots I ever heard were backfiring jalopies.

I stayed with Granny thousands of times between the ages of three to ten. What made these times even better was the fact that my little half-brother never came with me. Not once. He wasn't of blood relation, so Caleb didn't think it good for him to get involved with "too many confusing relations. He needs to know *only* his *real family relations*," he'd preach.

Whenever I was at Granny's, Sam was at grandma Flora's, Caleb's miraculously normal mother out east in milk-weedy Linden. She was really humble. She was a good woman, the type who'd feed you hot split pea soup and glazed ham in an instant if you even seemed to look hungry. I know not how Caleb turned out to be such a patent moron; maybe he was secretly adopted from secret, bigger morons up in the Sierra Nevadas.

But back to Granny: being in her early seventies, Mildred was naturally set in her ways. However, she was always perfectly kind, and to be entirely honest, "her ways" were actually quite cute, even to me as a child. I think I was more perceptive of human behavior than most kids, probably because there were so many hyperbolic, Dickensian characters in my life.

One of Granny's pet peeves was as follows: I could never, under *no* circumstances bring over the Atari video game system that Mom got me for Christmas in 1984 (an exorbitant gift and my favorite toy). Granny was convinced that it would permanently mess up her TV, somehow distorting the frequencies and garbling the electrics with futuristic problems. Her rabbit ears and tin foil would not be able to handle the powerful effects of the modern Atari…or something like that. Helmeted robots with bright red eyes would crunch microchips with their silver claws whilst chanting "deviation!" and we'd all be lost. This was a ludicrous fear. It was unfounded and a perfect example of blue-hair fretting. But I didn't care. I actually believed her, I think. So her TV remained undefiled by Atari. Fine and dandy. I had myriad other, more 1920s-ish baubles to fiddle with. I always followed Granny's rules.

One early eighties toy that Mildred dug (evidenced by her constant purchasing of them for me) was the imaginative display toy that went by the marketing name of Colorforms. If you grew up at this time you probably had one or two of these glossy cardboard things. Colorforms came in a box that contained a display board that a child could lay flat upon the carpet or hang on the wall. On the board was a depicted scene of fancy: usually a general motif for whatever marketed toy or movie theme the board was displaying. Then (and now for the fun part!), there were about fifteen little squishy, flat plasticky things that stuck to the board; each of these was an object or a character that you could move around on the scene to create displayed fun tantamount to jumping into the netted pool of multicolored balls at Fun land.

There were many Colorforms: Marvel Superheroes, Smurfs, Star Wars, Cowboys and Indians (you might think this theme had died out in the '50s, but no), My Little Pony, Mork and Mindy (a lame dress-up set), Sesame Street, Scooby Doo, Garfield, and a stupid little construction site one that looked like a Tonka dig scene, but was hopelessly generic—no kids wanted this one. Oh, and not one kid wanted the gross Human Body Colorform. Who wants to scientifically place organs on a flesh-colored human body board? Sick nerds, that's who.

I positively adored Colorforms because I could show Granny what I had created, and she would display it on her fridge and leave it untouched until I came to visit again. Yes, she was that cool.

I remember the Star Wars Colorforms mostly. I believe there were like five of them in full detail. This equaled rapture! They were my incontrovertible favorites.

The first one I owned was the scene with Luke Skywalker and Darth Vader at the end of Empire Strikes Back where they were dueling with light sabers, and Darth was using the force to chuck objects, like metal boxes and Sky-City hose things at Luke. They were standing, if *you* placed them there, on that skinny platform over the endless abyss, with yellow lights seeming to blink in the background. I'd sadistically make Luke fall again and again off of the platform—just like in the movie that I saw with my mom in the movie theater. We had delicious Tab soda pop and Junior Mints that day.

The next one I got was the Hoth battle scene at the rebel base. It was spectacular. There were AT-AT walkers and snow trooper storm troopers and laser cannons mounted on ice snow hillocks and A-Wings and rebel troops in dirty white wool suits (to keep warm) with goggles, and bellowing Tauntauns (those two-legged beast things with 70s horns) and run on and run on and improper sentence structure and I really don't care because this Colorform was so damn cool!

I think the other, later ones were Ewoks on Endor, Jabba's scary palace, Yoda's House in the swamp, and a most peculiar one that was only available for a limited time. It displayed a sumptuous bedroom all in purples and reds, with candles and incense and a giant bed with handcuffs on the headboard. I guess it was Han Solo's bedroom in the Millennium Falcon because it came with a Han figure and a Princess Leia figure that had transparent silk robes you could easily take off—then you could just as easily stick both Han and Leia to the bed and play "make little rebels." I think it was entitled: Galaxy Copulation, or something like that. Oh! And it came with a complimentary purple cassette tape of Isaac Hayes singing the sex in Wookie. Yes, I remember this Colorform clearly...and I think I made it up in my little nine year old head after seeing Princess Leia in that golden slave bikini for the first time: the first fleeting stir of sexual blood in my young frame brought about by visual movie stimulation. A George Lucas curve ball. I'm glad Granny never saw *Return of the Jedi*; she would've covered my eyes, and I would've been frustrated.

All imaginative dross such as this was easily conceived and mentally birthed due to the wonderful *chunks* of time available to me in the isolation of the east Lodi safe house. Oh, what adventures I had, like a pre-pubescent Luke Skywalker—winding and wending my way through Alderaanian air castles in the sky replete with action figures, Hot Wheels, and rubbery dinosaurs.

Granny encouraged me daily to rev my imaginative engine up to four-thousand rpms. She was entirely affirmative. And she continually had delicious "junk" cereals waiting quietly for me in her dark mahogany, faux-finish cupboards, cereals like Lucky Charms, Fruit Loops, Sugar Smacks, etc. My mom never let Sam and me eat these cereals; it was always generic raisin bran. But at Granny's I could count on brand name sugar in all of its saccharine glory. Let the milky goo run down my face! Let the Corn Pops pop in my sanguine cereal heart like little heaven grenades of flavor-flash! Granny knew how to please! She loved me with toys, cereal, and (best of all) conversation.

I remember one such conversation quite clearly. Let me preface it by telling you that Granny had a humble, peaceful way of talking to me as if I were as old as she, having precisely the same amount of life experience and empirical wisdom. She never doubted that she could learn something of significance from everyone around her, whether they were a lifetime friend or a seemingly insignificant child such as myself. She was such a role model...a being of light...a heroine.

I arrived early that Saturday morning, around six. The year was 1981. My mother and Caleb were going to spend the weekend up at Lake Tahoe—playing the nickel machines at Fredo's Hotel and Casino. Money would be wasted. I had no college savings fund, by the way.

Usually my mom went by herself to "get away and clear her head in the pines" as she called it. But this time Caleb went with her; perhaps they were getting along swimmingly and thought loud sex at Caesar's would be a nice change from seldom, mute sex at home in Stockton.

Whenever my mom went to Tahoe I went to Granny's, which was fine by me. "Have fun, Mom!" I squealed as I hugged her, sending her happily glissading up to the serene mountain lake.

"Now you be good, and follow all Granny's rules, and go to bed when you're told, okay?" she ordered, before shutting the heavy '70s car door.

I nodded, looking proud, so obedient—such a good boy.

"He's a gem, honey…don't you worry about us…and don't spend too much money up there. That's how they get you!" she jovially declared to my gambling mother. Granny despised gambling; she had a deep enmity for it due to her experiences with her daughter Louis's first husband Ray, the Cadillac fool, the waster of all good things.

Tallene smiled goofily and shut the door. Clank. The big-ass engine started up and idled as we all waved and waved and waved some more. I actually was glad to see Mom go, partly because Caleb was half asleep in the passenger side and partly because Tahoe made her happy. I don't think Caleb wanted to go, but my mom had insisted he go this time. She was feeling romantic and trying desperately to rekindle their suburban love back to hotel grandeur. Later in life she let go and quit trying.

I hope the pines were good for them. I hope he dropped his surly Do-we-have-to? attitude. He hated ever going anywhere. His paradise was in front of the TV, forever shirtless.

The car roared off into the hazy morning distance. I knew that if I were good all weekend my mom would give me a silver dollar from Fredo's. I already had seventeen of them. Eventually I would use them to buy my first car, a cherry-red Ford Mustang. This was my naïve plan, anyway.

When we got inside the sweet and cozy little east Lodi apartment (through my beloved carport, of course) my nostrils were met instantly with the smell of blueberry muffins!

Granny led me directly to the mauve oven and opened it quietly so I could see the incubating doughy glories. They were "almost, but not quite ready," she hummed. I drooled slightly and ran over to my red backpack. I had something to show her. At school the day before I had prepared for my visit to the safehouse by drawing a picture of Granny's apartment the way it looked in early spring: with pink and white cherry blossoms blossoming on the trees out front and the sunlight white bright with clarity on the glowing concrete walk. I thought myself very smart because the current season was fall and I was not very old, yet knew of the seasons in exquisite detail. I was proud of my sensitivity toward nature. So was Granny. She held it high and gasped, "Oh! Isn't this nice…you've done a very good job, young man. Is this springtime?"

I nodded, about to explode with blushing pride. My heart was racing; I lived to impress her.

"Oh, yes, the blossoms are the spittin' image; I am impressed that you've chosen a season different from the one we're in. You're very smart; usually boys don't notice how pretty and varied the different seasons are. Very clever and very good of you; you'll make a fine grown up someday!" she cooed, patting me on the head on her way to the British Museum display case: the Frigidaire and it's mounting magnets. I nearly sprouted wings. Her words and the morning and the hot blueberry smell were too much to handle. So I did a little turn around and swivel dance lightning quick whilst Granny's back was turned. It was necessary to manifest some of the joy I was feeling into furtive performance art. Kids do a lot of furtive performance art.

"You know, I think our muffins are ready now," Granny said, walking over to the oven and peeking in at them. The crack of the opened door let out a scintillating mirage of steamy dreamy. Once more my salivary glands punched in on the biological time clock.

She began singing a little 1930s tune about blueberries, falling stars, and skylarks on the boughs of a willow whilst taking out the hot tray of muffins and setting them carefully on the stove. Two pink plates were then placed beside them. The plates looked like flowers; the edges were petal shaped. I loved these plates and insisted we use them when I visited. Granny conceded, forever calling them, "the Great Grandson Plates."

"Are you hungry?" she asked.

*Hell yeah!* I thought, then answered, "Yes!" like a good boy.

"Good! Why don't we sit at the table; can you fill up my coffee mug and put it at the table? Oh, and there's some orange juice in the fridge for you," she said.

That was another great thing about Granny: she lived a kind of "serve yourself" life that was hearty and frontier; it helped me to be confident and take initiative.

I grabbed her mug, carefully filled it with black coffee, no cream, (*Hearty, I say!* like Aunt Eller in *Oklahoma!*) and whisked it over to the table, a trail of vapor followed the mug's movements like the spirit of all happy breakfasts ever. Then I procured some juice for myself and grabbed two flower pattern napkins, placing them with utmost care on the table. I think my salivary glands were working for overtime pay by now.

After gliding over to the table with the steaming muffins, Granny took her sweet time painting whipped butter on each one by turn. I worked hard at being a patient boy, but it didn't work. She intuited my actual impatience and merely chuckled at it, saying, "Patience is a virtue, darling."

I sat back in my chair, restless, but chirping morning glory in my juicy heart. I glanced downward. My sneakers could almost touch the linoleum. I was getting so big, almost seven. I wondered if I would/could drink coffee today. That would *irrefutably* impress Granny.

I cautiously reached across the duckling yellow tablecloth and coaxed Granny's coffee mug toward me. It, like everything else, was a famous relic: It was of usual shape, white, ceramic, but it had a picture of a Pomeranian dog on it: smiling and cute with its little pink tongue out. A "fuzz ball," Granny called it. Before I was born she had two Pomeranians: Adam and Eve. Apparently they were awesome and she missed them dearly. She would continually joke that when they were alive they were "out of the garden and naked, but still not ashamed," to which I laughed heartily, never understanding the Biblical allusion until the day she cracked open her ancient Black Bible and read me the fanciful story in Genesis about the very first man and woman. It was a good tale.

As I sat there at the table my mind followed a chain-link thought pattern from Pomeranian mug to Adam and Eve and ultimately to God in all of seven seconds. Then the image of a solid black Bible stuck in my head. So I glanced over at the coffee table in the adjoining living room: there was the Bible with early morning sun from the window making it glow like holy fire—like the Word Himself. The Logos.

There. Right (over) there. Now that I had spotted it for a good five seconds, it was cleverly cancelled. I'd quelled my obsessive impulse and it was erased from my edgy mind; now I was free to explore the silty depths of Granny's coffee.

I pulled the cup close. It was dark and smelled like forests somehow.

I looked up at Granny, *still* buttering, humming a post-ragtime ditty. "Granny, why do you drink coffee?" I asked.

She finished painting and looked up at me like Socrates. "Because it's delicious!" she asserted, as if quoting the illustrious Dr. Purdy (concerning potatoes) a confident spark in her ancient face. I grinned, satisfied with her philosophy, and looked back into the mysterious coffee crystal ball before me. It was enchanting, beseeching me with its warm vapor to *drink drink drink.* But I hesitated.

"Should...can I try some?" I asked politely, wanting to grow up, to impress.

"Sure, but just a little, because it's got some caffeine kick to it, and I don't want to mess up your young healthy rhythms," she said, walking over to the cupboard to get me my own mug. Here we have an example of her treating me like an equal: my *own* mug, not a sip from hers, but my *own* mug to explore the coffee palatabilities at my own leisure. She let me be *me*, not her or anyone else. She celebrated me for my me-ness. Another thing: she used the word, "rhythms" quite a lot. I think she felt earthy or spiritual or up to date with the '70s cultural jargon when she said it. It's funny, some parts of her were stuck inexorably back in 1938, and yet other parts were striving for 2000. Granny led a myriad-thoughted life indeed.

At that very moment in the history of time and space the almighty mug was placed before me. My first taste of coffee. The beginning of a beautiful relationship.

I looked up at her; she was smiling with her eyebrows raised, waiting for me. "Should I put milk in it to cool it down?" I asked.

"No, I put an ice cube in it, and it's gone, so it should be ready. Try it black first. That's how the cowboys drink it," she sang, patting the table with a confident smack to encourage me.

I wanted to be a cowboy. They shot pistols at tumbling tumbleweeds. I hovered over the surface of the dark waters. They swirled and gave up a pleasing aroma of forest earth. I looked up at Granny again, feeling scared that I would hate the taste. "Muffins are gettin' cold; dive in!" she exhorted.

Ah, and here we have my first taste ever: the coffee swirled over my tongue like a vigorous silken ghost of flavor and folly. And I hated it. I grimaced and was shocked that so many adults in the world were morning masochists.

Granny laughed out loud and got some brown sugar and cream from the kitchen. She poured out half the coffee and filled it back up with the copious cream, swirling it around in my mug—making a sweet dessert drink. Then she handed it back. "There, try that...I think you'll like it now," she said. I did indeed like it. I drank down the whole damn thing before even looking at a muffin. I think God created sugar and cream with children's tongues in mind. Forsooth.

After finishing my "coffee," I moved on to the blueberry muffins.

We took our time peeling off the paper pants of each muffin and let ourselves slowly delight in the texture and tastes of the whipped butter and berries of moist doughy blue.

We chatted at length concerning east Lodi and how it used to look back in the fifties; you know, how much better, cleaner, and safer it was back then…when things were simpler. Granny asked me if I missed the old Woolworth's Department Store down on 5th. I did, of course; I explained to her my reasons, "They always opened the door for you back in those days; they'd even direct you to the best brown leather penny loafers in the perfect size. Nowadays at stores they couldn't give a rip about *service*…you know?"

She nodded. We were both in our early seventies at Granny Mildred's breakfast table. We were old friends. Truest friends.

There are some other important things I remember about being at Granny's house. There was a little (even though it seemed big to me at the time) wooden music box that played a pleasant tune. (Is this a ubiquitous/obligatory item at all grandmother's houses?) The tune was "Raindrops Keep Fallin' on My Head" by B.J. Thomas, made popular in 1970 by the hit movie: *Butch Cassidy and the Sundance Kid,* starring Robert Redford and Paul Newman (*Again!*—this time he isn't running through a chicken coop on the delta; instead, he's humming a pleasant, swain tune through a music box). Like all good children, I liked to turn the crank on that music box for too long, eventually annoying Granny. All children at all places for all time have a strange compulsion to make the music slow down down down and then speed up to a ridiculous speed: Dum dum deee dum deee dum deee dum. *(Insert image of Newman being hilarious and Redford being quick on the draw.)*

If Granny wasn't making blueberry muffins, grilled cheese, or root beer floats, then she most likely was making the classic Mildred Foster cookie: cheesy, but delicious. These cookies started out as plain old chocolate chip cookies: dry, chunky, and banal…but then they magically morphed into veritable edible butterflies when she added the finishing touch: a crimson crown to each one: a cherry hard candy. Yes, chocolate chip cookies with bright red candies in their middles. Cheesy times ten.

As a child, the cherry candies radiated, of course, with the delicious promise of fruity sugar gliders in my moist mouth. I craved them and obsessively picked off each one, placing them aside as "dessert" for after the cookie meal. Funny.

Even as a youngster I was deliberate and meticulous in my eating tasks. Whenever I saw other kids wolfing down meals without paying close attention to the order in which things should be eaten, I would writhe with scorn. They were uncivilized brutes in my culinary book.

Couldn't they see the brilliant ceramic plate map before them, how it was a battlefield where mashed potatoes declared war on turkey and sent in the gravy cavalry—setting in motion the steamy hegemony of dinner domination? All the while, cranberry sauce declared ,"Switzerland!" and stayed put, frightened and jiggling with vacillation. Oh, and the stuffing heaped up its bready defenses in order to be ready to soak up the gravy blitzkrieg…and on and on and on. Did *not* the other children see all of this?

Potatoes must be eaten first to give the others some breathing space. Then the stuffing must be eaten, because its bulwark defenses are making it boastful. Nothing could defend itself against my little mashers! The turkey must go next—for mid-battle protein—and lastly, that dammed cranberry sauce! "Neutral, eh? *Taste my masher daggers!*"

Eating a meal was a holy time of microcosmic dramatics. The napkin to the lips = the curtain closing on the dark stage. Fin. Burp. Satisfaction.

Caleb never implicitly played with his food. I figure he hadn't the brains for it, so he never understood. But Granny sure did. She must have had a few billion Shakespearian dinners during her life. And that makes me smile.

I remember watching the Muppets at the safe house. It was by far my favorite show for a couple years. Granny thought the Muppets were "colorful and silly." I thought they were awesome. The only bummer was that I had to abide by Granny's rules, and that meant that I had to watch some TV that she liked in order to watch what I liked.

She claimed it was good for me to "understand the shows that other generations have enjoyed," so that I could grasp "universal comedy" or something. She was right. I want my kids to watch *Seinfeld* someday.

The shows I had to watch with her were *The Odd Couple* and various Bob Hope specials. They are classics, I suppose. The former was and is funny to this day, but grainy in film and plot. The latter…well, I don't remember anything but polyester suits in light blue, and Bob Hope's sweaty bald head and face cracking jokes with charm and old wartime debonair flair. Granny didn't really *make me* watch these shows. She just liked me in the room with her. What's truly humorous and weird is that our two generational favorites *epically* merged in one movie when Bob Hope made a celebrity cameo on *The Muppet Movie* in 1979. What's weirder is that there's now a movie house in Stockton named the Bob Hope Theater.

Granny had this stash of old comic books she'd bring out so that I could studiously ignore Felix, Oscar, and Bob. I remember once, well... hearing this one woman in an illustrated scene *breathing!* I don't remember who the heroes or villains were, incidentally, but I *do* however, and this is gravely important, acutely remember thinking, feeling, and indeed, hearing this. I swear she breathed *out loud!*

Needless to say it freaked me the hell out. I threw the comic book at the nearest wall hoping the impact would kill the breathing woman. I was severely frightened and reluctant to look at the old, possessed comic books ever again. I suppose now that I was probably hearing my own strange comic book breath bouncing off the graying pages before me. I don't know. Regardless, I never told Granny of this spirited fiasco. I didn't want to offend her by telling her that her old comic books were breathing and scary.

I don't know what else to say about Granny Mildred. She was a sweetheart. She was a glowing light of hope to a bruised little kid. I can still see her warm angular face. She must have been beautiful in youth because she was beautiful in old age. Gwyneth Paltrow in her earliest twenties in the late 30s, if you will. I wish I could talk to Mildred today, just for five minutes, over coffee and cherry candy cookies.

Now her body lies in the cold ground. Dust to dust. But her radiant soul...now that's another story. She died of colon cancer in 1986. I'm glad I got to have breakfast with her many, many times. I'm glad I got to watch Bob Hope with her. I'm glad I got to hear her laugh. She was my granny. The best Granny in the world. No, the universe. Thank you, God, for her. Take good care of her.

# Chapter 7
# Middle: The Little Pawns Move Around
# (A) The Oxford Circle Gets a Droid

Middle childhood. Is it like middle age? Is it a strange, uncertain time where a person looks at him/herself in the mirror and thinks, Who am I today? Am I who I want to be? Am I being true to myself? What the hell does "being *true* to yourself" mean? It sounds like a pile of crap. Just like being stuck smack dab in the middle of certain *things* in life is crappy. *Things* meaning the bad things.

Do you remember the stupid ages of, say, ten to fourteen? The word "puberty" ring any old bells? Insecurities that secretly last a lifetime? Any thought of puberty repulses most people in an instant: visions of trite drama and symbolic, hackneyed acne. Insignificance. Emotionalism. Foggy kids jogging in stupid P.E. circles for no reason whatsoever. To be honest, people should be repulsed by puberty. It's a natural reaction to something awkward and sour, like rotten sour cream.

I hate puberty. Such a pockmarked design. It happens way too fast, or too slow, for that matter; and kids are cruel, so very cruel, like dictators with loud voices and beards. Nebulous, bitter and dreamlike: this middle childhood.

I don't care if some happy hippies with myriad degrees believe this time is golden, in that it's a poignant storm of memory for people, a blossoming time of natural personhood, beautiful and chunky like real life. Bah! For me, and I know this is merely subjective, the bulk of this age was stomach acid, fear, cold oatmeal, and complete vexation.

By my troth, my kids (someday out there in the blue) will be compassionately helped along by a cognizant father who remembers the shittiness of those years. They won't be left alone to their silent dog paddling in the bilge of "Who am I?" I will throw the wet tennis ball of adult understanding within reach. They will paddle slowly, but effectively. All will be okay. A mere game of fetch. Answers whenever they need them. I suppose this might be naiveté on my part, and I just might fail in helping them through middle childhood. But there will certainly be hours of earnest prayer. The darker Psalms kind. I will have faith, I hope.

Around 1986 I began the first green tendrils of puberty. I suppose I was an early bloomer. In fifth grade my body started growing hair in places I didn't expect. Some guys were jealous of me, but I would have rather been a late bloomer and had more time to figure out my body before it blew up around me: all hair and craziness. Because I truly and really didn't have a dad at this time (Caleb and Mom's relationship was disintegrating) nobody told me what was going on or what would happen next.

My mom must have been too embarrassed to sit me down and save my social life by showing me important things like *deodorant* and *showers*, etc. From about '86-'88 I stunk to high heaven of dried sweat and B.O. I *wasn't* at all aware of this. I thought I was okay and simply smelling like a man should. After all, Caleb stunk sometimes…when he was around.

So these were the stinky junior high years. I never ever wore deodorant. And on most days I could definitely smell myself. It was somewhat obvious to me that I stunk, but I didn't know if I should ask my mom about it. So I didn't. I distinctly remember playing vigorous sports like basketball and baseball and getting drenched in boy-man sweat, and then just going on from there for days without showers or any kind of grooming. I must have had a solid inch of dried sweat salt crystals covering my shiny skin.

Glorious. Beautiful, athletic, golden youth…like the Greeks of old! It's all pretty gross. I was hopelessly stinky, like a orange newt slathered in pond poop.

I remember wearing my radical black Reebok sneakers every day for *two* years—and *never* wearing socks. My feet reeked of athletic fungality: rotten potatoes of sweaty skin behind the cool guise of pop cultural b-ball shoes all black and half-laced! Real hot.

My friends would sometimes mention my B.O., but we'd just laugh it off and continue to stink together. (I was the stinkiest by far). I think now that they were putting me down and trying to candidly and mockingly tell me that my body sucked and was bothering their olfactory lives. What a horrible situation stuck back in a ruthless time. Not even Tears for Fears on the radio could make it any better.

(Nobody bothered with the simple altruistic task of handing me a spray can of Aarid; I thought that only moustached, Magnum P.I. adults used such spray cans. And yet, I had a minuscule cheesy moustache myself: therefore I qualified. Alas.)

I finally clued in to the fact that it was within my power to NOT STINK by the time I was a freshman in high school. One of my shaggy friends posed a question to a bunch of us mulleted manboys. "If you could take one thing along with you to a desert island, what would it be?" [Later in life (college) the question would sound like this: "If you could take one *record* with you to a desert island, what would it be?"] We quietly stood there for a moment by our lockers, lookin' rad in our Reeboks and cheap jean jackets; then I blurted out, "MY PILLOW! Definitely my pillow, man."

They all laughed at me, and I was like, "What?"

The shaggy questioner answered his own question the correct way. "No, man, no, not me. I would take m*y deodorant*! Everyone's heads nodded in time, except mine. My eyebrows crumpled in confusion, then I nodded. Conventional wisdom.

When I think really hard about the junior high years I can remember lots of jokes hurled at me concerning my odoriferousness. From the ages of nine to about fourteen I was the butt of all odoriferous jokes. I think I secretly liked them, though, for, though they stung, they kept me in the middle of popular conversation. My peers couldn't forget me; I was always as near as their nose. Therefore I was perpetually *in*. I think now that a few hundred showers would have been more pleasant to me (and my skin) than being the odor ghost of the junior-high campus hallways. Indeed.

Once that desert island joke answer, "deodorant!" hit the audible air I was afire with the dawning realization that I could actually fix my conundrum by means of a common adult product. So, I began intermittently filching my mother's Aarid spray can during mornings when she was busy toasting toast or stirring bitter orange juice concentrate. I only used it once every three days at first, but then I fortuitously saw a Mitchum add on the television that told me this important info. "Use of Mitchum *every day* can drastically wipe out body odor with its powerful...blah blah blah."

That commercial saved me. I stole my mom's Aarid every day from that day on. Then I actually worked up the courage to ask her if I could purchase my own. Then I did indeed purchase my own. And then I felt really rad because I began buying sporty brands like Right Guard and began feeling like Darryl Strawberry getting ready for a big game. Pure power. Baseball in my armpits. Big League Chew forever.

Unfortunately, I still wasn't brushing my teeth nearly enough. Only twice a week would the fuzz in my mouth be removed. I was still odoriferous. Indolent, too.

To add to the middle-child drama of my life at home, I started noticing that Caleb and Tallene were not getting along too well. They were like two wolverines fighting over a rotten deer carcass: Their marriage.

I know now that Caleb cheated many times on Mom. I think that she grew tired of his cheating and eventually gave up. Stockton is the perfect place to cheat and give up: dusty, frustrating as hell. I think Caleb's cheating began getting worse right around the time Mom started dipping in and out of St. Joseph's hospital, beginning her new career of chronic illness in 1984.

Before I tell you about that I have to get you up to speed about where we lived at this point in our collective life. We abandoned the old house on Wyndotte Street in 1981. Now this sounds bad at first, but it really wasn't. St. Joseph's hospital (virtually our next door neighbor) needed to expand—desperately; apparently Stockton was only getting sicker. So it "purchased" our house directly from us so that it could raze it to the rocky soil and pave a freshly hot parking lot. The cemetery by our house, of course, stayed. The dead could continue sleeping. The worms could continue feasting. The living could start *moving*. And we did.

What was cool about the whole Jones/Stokes diaspora was the fact that St. Joseph's didn't exactly "purchase" our doomed old house in the cash sense of the word; rather, they purchased us a *new* house. And if I remember correctly, Mom got to *choose* where it would be. Very fun. The ultimate shopping adventure.

Anyway, we ended up in a way nicer part of town—indeed much nicer than we ourselves as oakies were. We moved to Regent Street—a street loaded with fine red brick homes and very close to the intelligent grandeur of the University of the Pacific. (Go Tigers.) And thus, we felt like a collective Dorothy in a richer Oz. It was nice and weird, especially for Caleb; he wasn't accustomed to California hospitals buying him houses.

(The exact street address of our new life was 611 S Regent St. How important a sound resounds when that name resonates in my sonorous memory. I remember us standing on fresh-cut green lawns: oakies in Oz.) Our old Wyndotte house couldn't compare and was soon forgotten. Its dead history is actually quite interesting, though, and worth a brief overview:

## JOHN ROGER SCHOFIELD

The Wyndotte house was built by the "bear hunter" himself: J.R. Barjager! Before or after he married Lulu, he built the house for his old and ailing mother (her dusty name escapes me). She lived there for a time, alone, unobserved; I remember my mother making token visits to her every once in a blue moon. She continually brought Earl Grey tea or cheap tea biscuit cookies from Gemco. Token visits; those two words sadden me.

In 1976 J.R.'s mom started going nuts with dementia and a '70s form of Alzheimer's. I'm surprised J.R. ever even found out that she was sliding off the lucid, living path; despite his kindness toward me, he hardly ever looked in on his ancient mother. He figured he'd built her a house to comfortably die in, and therefore considered his duty to her finished. I don't know. I'm sure he still loved her, just had no time, with "the yard" and all. The work world is unrelenting.

So finally, the old crazy lady went to a home somewhere in the setting sun hills of Stockton. And young Tallene, with a fresh peachy-chubby baby on her hip (me) wound up with a house and no mortgage payment. Somehow it was paid off at some point by J.R.'s work world. $$$. We were lucky youngsters all around.

Mom started working as soon as we settled, and I started growing and pooping my diapers both proficiently and prodigiously. Then Caleb hopped on board in 1979. Then Sam was born in 1980. Then St. Joseph's began its grand sterile hegemony: veritable Romans with golden latex gloves.

And thus, in 1981, the Wyndotte house was *demolished* and we descended out of the progress tornado in an Oz with a red brick house. How ironic would it have been if the bricks were yellow? Did I mention that the house was paid in full by St. Joseph's? Well, it was. And we were lucky once more: no mortgage...*again!* Our new house was, as the local muckymucks called it, "Off the Oxford Circle." Sweater vests and pipe smoke floating over impeccable green lawns. Who knew Stockton had such intelligent flair?

I remember seeing this one professor guy every day; he lived across the street and drove a nice new Volvo. It was dark beige and matched his corduroy sport coats. Erudition. Sagacity. Volvo.

What's rather funny about our move is that, after about a month of living off the Oxford Circle, Mom started dressing us boys a bit better. Everyday our clothes had to be straight, unfaded, newer than old, and in style. Sam and I both got new *Member's Only* jackets—well, knockoffs—from the local K-Mart.

Mine was mauve, his: navy blue. I can't believe they made those jackets in our tiny sizes! Sam was only about two years old! The jackets were shiny and made sibilant squibbly noises whenever I'd run my fingernails across them. I did this a lot to pass the time. *Squib, Squib.*

"Listen, Sam," I'd say. *Squib.* Then he'd turn his head away from me in order to look for more ghosts. He was always distracted and disinterested in my little histrionic shenanigans.

The bad news about having no mortgage payment is that it allowed my mother to put money in other ridiculous elsewheres. Money was not her forte (twice bankrupt). Our monthly—sometimes weekly—new clothes are a perfect example of this. Her various jobs didn't afford us much cash. ("Avon calling," hospital pseudo-janitorial work, dowdy retail.) Caleb's paycheck pretty much paid the bills. Her money just seemed to disappear on trifles that would sate her dramatic whims: food items, clothing items, candy, movies, trinkets, and God only knows what else. She loved to shop: whenever she was in a depressive state she'd head out to drug herself with new stuff from K-Mart, Price Club, or, her favorite: Gemco—the first Wal-Mart, if you will. Her pretext of shopping at *only* thrifty locations afforded her cover from Caleb's watchful billfold eye. But he was annoyed with her spending, nonetheless. It whittled his affection for her away like bark off a branch. I think they had separate bank accounts for this reason.

Ah. I am reminded now of the myriad times she headed up to Tahoe to assuage her lower-class demons by wasting crucial funds (no matter how small) on those damn nickel machines. I love my mom, but she did some dumb stuff. A character rife with correct responsibility traits seemed to forever elude her.

She was so scattered. Bits and bits on the world floor. Scattered especially when it came to relationships. She was eternally jealous of Caleb. Therefore, he began feeling trapped. Thus he cheated with younger, thinner girls, starting, I'll surmise, around 1984. As I said before, my mother's health began declining at about this time. Her kidneys began to slowly shut down due to a caustic mixture of bad Jones genes and those shitty diet pills (all six billion that she tried). I think she was obsessive/compulsive about those little colorful things. She became dependent on them, and her body chemistry never leveled out once the pills took over.

She began hooking up to a dialysis machine that year. She kept in close contact with it for two years. She started gaining more weight at about this time. Caleb frowned and scratched at his tawny thighs. I remember thinking the dialysis machine looked like R2D2 on steroids. It grossed me out to see her hooked up to that thing, though she said it wasn't so bad. In 1986 Mom finally had to have surgery on her kidneys. Both were shot. However, she was able to get only *one* transplant: a fresh new kidney from some dead high school kid who had one too many at some dead high school party, sad and forgotten. Twisted metal. Distant. A donor. *I'm sorry, kid.*

That kidney kept her alive. But still, her failing body continued its descent into Macbeth chemistry madness for a few more years. When she got home from the hospital she couldn't move much, so I attended to her as best I could with juice, toast, and blueberry yogurt with fruit on the bottom: her favorite. She was rather gracious and amiable for being in such bad shape. Her bed became her real home during this time. This is precisely when I perceived the black fog rolling in: obese, sick Mom, vanishing-magician Caleb.

Surprisingly, my mother didn't drink. I'm proud of her for this. Her kidneys probably wouldn't have had a fightin' chance if she were like most other hard-drinkin' rednecks. Good for her. And good for Caleb for never bringing home female-ish tasty alcohol, say, Bartels and James wine coolers, from that liquor store up the street.

Less surprisingly, Mom never touched drugs. She had bongloads of friends who touched them plenty, but she never partook. More points for Tallene. I don't know if Caleb partook. He most likely did: a wreath of victorious pot leaves 'round his sun burnt head.

Incidentally, here is a bit more on what my mother actually looked like. She had blue eyes, very distinct, bright-blue eyes. Her hair was red and frizzy, hard to maintain. It was often dyed to make it a more stylish red, colors like "Auburn" and "Rose" and "Russet."

I can smell that toxic hair dye goop right now—all clear plastic glovey and thick. It makes me sick. Towards the end she must have dyed her hair close to twenty times in order to hide the graying toxicity of oncoming death. Despite her frenetic efforts her life eventually bleached out in the same hospital room that she had cleaned numerous times for other hair dyers. I can hear the white machines humming; millions of droids on steroids.

And now we arrive at Ogressa, a barfly friend of my over-trusting mother with an old-world name. Oh, man, was she ever a classy lady! My mom put her in charge of the house while she was in the hospital getting her new, golden, teen kidney.

Caleb was already fulfilling his new vanishing-magician role by this time: a veritable caped ghost who would haunt us for only a half hour on Saturdays: he'd come in, grab some beer, scratch Sam's head, and then truck on out the door toward some unknown and nefarious adventure.

Ogressa hated Caleb, so the fortuitous circumstances worked out swimmingly. It was lucky for Ogressa that she was profoundly ugly, or else Caleb would have tried desperately, numerous times, to mount her in our own house, and Sam and I would've had to cover our ears with our striped pillows. That would have been bad, but regardless, her being profoundly ugly (hideous dark hair, unkempt, short and scraggly like a witch hag's; fat fish belly body; pock marked face! The horror! Jagged teeth, too!) made things pretty ugly anyway, due to the fact that she found solace in various drugs of an illegal nature (speed and pot, mostly), all of which were sold daily to shady, scurrilous, Stockton strangers in the middle of our very own living room.

I remember not quite understanding what was going on, but feeling unsafe whenever those shadow people came over. I hated life while Ogressa lived with us. She was in her late thirties, yet smelled like she was in her mid one thousands. She continually used the words "rowdy" and "cunty," applying them to everything in life or even in the kitchen cupboard. I didn't know what the latter meant back then. I thought it had something to do with being out in the country.

Lucky for poor little Sam and me Ogressa wasn't with us for too long; Mom returned from the hospital after about a month and took over the house: our very own maternal sloth, high in a tree of torpidity.

Despite the doctor's warnings, the pill jungle grew darker and deeper with every passing day. Poisonous plants vibrated here and there. We were lost in the undergrowth. My mom the human sloth. She quit dressing up. She only wore what was comfortable and stretchy. She quit "doing" her hair, but continued dying it, of course. She quit cleaning up around the rooms of our beautiful red brick house on Regent Street, just off the Oxford Circle. She quit energy. She quit aspiring. She just relaxed.

And I drastically came out of my childhood stupor and began being the man around the house. I woke up to our sad state of affairs. What a jolt! Me, the man of the house. Not Caleb. Weird. I was getting bigger now, and Caleb was losing any and all semblance of his former Great White status. He was now looking more like a barracuda—sharp teeth—but wiry, and getting smaller all of the time due to the pollution of the sea by beer, cigarettes, and no multivitamins or EPA. He was beginning to wash up on the shores of the mid-'80s…and only younger women could keep old Caleb alive. Or so he desperately thought.

Mom noticed that Sam and I began floundering like little starving flounders in the cold Atlantic once she began floundering, so she tried to help us out by buying us lots of things. If she loved new things, then she figured her sons and everybody else on the green planet did as well. She was at this time the quintessential American parent, buying our love and ostensible welfare: movies, comics, candy, McDonald's, plastic toy ephemera, tapes of vapid pop music, we seemed to have it all raining down on us like crunchy honey from heaven. She figured the red-brick neighbors would think all was okay if we had the semblance of new freshness about us. "Those Stokes boys sure are cute in their tiny jackets! Look at their fresh transformers. That jet-guy one is purple, baby blue, *and* navy blue. Oh, how classy, a veritable mélange of Stokes savoir-faire!" they'd say, puffing their pecuniary cigars with peculiarity.

Yet, despite our freshest Optimus Primes, my heart's feelings about our life on Regent Street continued to darken. I knew things were getting bad. I also knew they were getting quite shitty.

The one thing during this time that I'm forever glad happened to me personally is the fact that I indelibly changed. I got up off my comic-book keister and started cleaning the rooms in the house. I started looking after Sam a whole lot better. I had to change because my mother was high up in that mossy, metaphorical tree doing absolutely nothing. The more she was in bed the more I picked up shoes and placed them in the closets. The more she lazed around in her fuchsia robe the more I put dishes in the old dishwasher and got Sam endless bananas from the fruit basket in the kitchen. I started watching him like a hawk for any sign that he was hungry. If he was eating normally I knew that all the Joneses' ducks were in a row, and I could feel somewhat at peace. And this was a time where one had to grab any wisp of peace by its little wisps as fast as one could.

On another note, and to finally speak nicely of my mom, I will add here that she did, in fact, work a little during the sloth duration as an accountant for a fine upstanding Stockton Mormon man by the name of Brigham Smith. I remember having dinner at his house one Sunday evening and not being able to wrap my little American mind around the fact that his wife was blatantly Japanese. I thought white people were supposed to marry only white people by law. I was utterly confused, thinking that perhaps, since he was a Mormon it was okay or even something he had to do—as a missionary to foreign peoples. I mean: didn't they knock on doors and stuff? Maybe they had to marry the foreign people that joined their cult so that they would feel cool and even hip in the Mormon crowd.

Retarded thoughts such as these buzzed around like drunk flies in my head as I watched his Japanese wife scoop blackened soy sauce rice into her mouth and nod as her husband said something about the ever-productive Latter-day Saints and their righteous, busy-bee ten-speeds. Conversions by the bike-load, apparently. The beehive was simply buzzing at the moment.

Mom never entertained even the tiniest thought of joining their cult, even though old Salt Lake Brigham did his best to win her over with the good faux news and dreamy neo polygamy. Tallene's old Pentecostal roots wouldn't let her move even one religious inch. "Planets? Our own *planets* when we die? Don't you believe a crazy word he says, boys, even if he's a very nice man. Just be polite and don't ever discuss religion with him. He's super chatty about Mormonism; I know you both know that Jesus loves all of us, which is true, but he's not dying to give us planets," she'd say as she got up to help me remove a load of towels from the massively loud drier.

Then I'd follow with the logical question. "Wulll, then, what's he really dying for, Mom?"

And she'd look at me, hot towels plopping out of her arms onto the dusty floor, where they would inexorably soak up dirtiness and ruin all my efforts at Godliness, and reply, "I think he's dying to have us be good...so the good in the world can balance out the evil."

*This is how she eternally saw religion and Jesus: good vs. evil. Both were cosmically balanced. If you were good you were a Christian and would go to heaven, where there were puffy clouds and snowy white beards forever billowing in the apple blossom breezes. If you were bad you were evil and went to rock-and-roll hell where it was hot, and the chubby devil guards goaded you like a hot pig with hot trident stick things. Easy as that.*

*Not one ounce of scholarly philosophical or religious midwifery, erudition in exegesis, empirical sagacity, eschatological knowledge steeped in veritable years of diligent hermeneutical study and scriptural explication, or even the honest admission that one ultimately doesn't know a thing and therefore must seek for years and years to arrive at a statement of stalwart belief.*

Good vs. Evil. That's it. Entirely. And don't you ever confuse it with all that highfalutin mumbo jumbo! So we must be good. That was the key to heaven.

Thus, I guarded my little heart against Mr. Smith's smarmy grin from that day on. He wouldn't get me. Mom was right. He was innocuously crazy. The bike helmet probably had lead in it. Yes, he was crazy, and so was his Oriental wife. And their marriage was implicitly illegal and would result in children with messed up color skin and messed up eyes. I was sure of it.

# Chapter 7
# Middle: The Little Pawns Move Around (B) "[I] Shut the Fuckin' Door!"

 Caleb wasn't a good communicator. He communicated only with trusses and titties. Mom wasn't a good communicator either, though she thought she was. Her mind wasn't honed enough to ever rise above personal strife. Relationship demons hopped around mockingly on her bed at night and whispered crappiness 'til the early sun finally scared them away. They perpetually crept out of the shadows of daytime talk-shows, *Days of Our Lives,* and grocery-store romance novels complete with rippling pects, hidden daggers, animalistic sex, and myopia.
 I suppose Tallene and Caleb could have sought marriage counseling, but it wouldn't have helped. To think of them with a counselor is quite funny. Caleb would most definitely get hot under the collar, stand up in his dirty jeans, and proclaim something like, "Yer tellin' me yer gonna sit there and tell me that feelin's and talkin' on and on and on 'bout feelin's is more important than getting' down to bus'nis' with yer broad? And let's be clear an' honest, since we're s'pos'd to, Mr. Degrees on the Wall: I mean, bed love and doin' the nasty…you know givin' it to her!"
 Yikes.
 The sad thing is that Tallene would feign support in favor of the counselor's views on the marriage, but really, really, down deep she'd side with the scrawny litany sitting next to her. She'd be secretly, sexually turned on by his manly bombast, imagining his shirt magically unbuttoning right there in the counseling office, revealing them-thar (nonexistent) pects, salty and old with spice. Sex was one of her Achilles' heels.
 *Alas! Their marriage was nothing more than a ship doomed since the day it was christened with a 40-oz. bottle of beer, a ship complete with*

*rotten timbers and a hole in it the size of a sand shark. The hole was in the hull, you see, poison leaking deep into the wound under the brackish black water. Goodbye Love Boat. Did you really ever have a chance?*

I often wonder how they managed to stay together for even eight years. Lust was something they used to plug the leak. For sure. It would have been so good for all of us if my mother had dumped old Caleb way back in, say '82, just enough time for Sam to enter the world and have a home for a while, but not enough time for Caleb to whip his shark-skin belt.

Yes. I wish it happened that way. But it didn't. So no crying over spilled milk. The past is set in its ways like old concrete in a foundation. Period.

My childhood is what it is: formative. And I really like who I've become. I like myself today. I'm no longer in the middle. Far from it. Early grief in life begets…I don't know…something good, like a disciplined or careful or cognitive or responsible personality. I'm no longer in the middle. Dammit.

Caleb and Tallene were together for as long as they should have been and no longer. Mom *finally* made sure of that! The reason for her I'm-completely-done-with-him attitude was Caleb's furtively blatant screwing around. She got right-hand-raised reports of said screwing around from friends and relatives. Enter upstage left: Kris. My aunt. She was the one who first caught him in the act.

Kris was like an older sister to me, but technically she was my aunt. She was and is five and a half years older than I and is my mom's sister, a *later* sister, the final offspring of my mother's mom Lulu and swanky Ray.

J.R. Barjager naturally and chronologically became her stepdad once he married Lulu, and was very strict with Kris from day one; he was from the old school of child rearing and hardly *ever* let her simply be a kid. This is really weird, because he totally let me be a kid. Maybe he felt as if he had to get all the Ray-ness out of her with good old discipline. He had myriad chores for her, daily, and she did them with a keen smile. She had wits enough to realize that if she appeared to stay within J.R.'s set boundaries for her she could live a secret life of freedom. She was a quick one. And pretty to boot!

It bums me out that J.R. was such a drill sergeant with her. Seriously, because Kris was 100% awesome. And I mean it. If he would have been a touch easier on her, then later (in my rebellious high school years) I wouldn't have been so cold to him, so, "See ya hopefully *never again*, old fart," as I slammed the aluminum screen door again and again. I felt I owed him this blistering coldness because I was forever a symbolic protector of Kris, forever her ally, her golden nephew/brother. In all actuality, we protected each other from the evil hick forces of our famously fucked-up family. What made our relationship even stronger were the many halcyon days we spent hanging out at Granny Mildred's when we were younger. Kris enjoyed hot blueberry muffins with melted butter as much as I did.

Unfortunately, my little brother Sam didn't. He was never close to Kris; he was too off in his own world, hearing God whisper to him in his sleep as the ghosts sang him old songs. He was preoccupied, like the ocean at night. He was also preoccupied, when lucid, with big daddy Caleb, his vanishing buddy.

Sam's disinterest in Kris worked in my favor. Kris was all mine, somebody I could truly love. She helped me grow up. She showed me how the boyfriend/girlfriend world of adolescence worked: we'd go out on pretend dates for fun and see a somewhat horrific eighties flick or hit the mall together. I learned that it was okay and even awesome to hang out with girls (even at the mall, with tough guys in jean jackets all around us!) by physically walking around with Kris. Even when she actually had boyfriends, I would ofttimes still venture out on their actual *dates*. She was that cool, letting me come along, even talking me up to her various boyfriends using hip lingo like "rad" and "bad ass" and "bastard." Her rugged equanimity knew no bounds. She even helped me pick out my signature junior high, pro-baseball hat: navy blue, New York Yankees; I wore it for three whole years. She said I looked like Don Mattingly; I smiled and felt like high school.

Most times, we (me, Kris, and her killer boyfriend Richie) would surreptitiously head out to the delta islands, looking for adolescent adventure. We'd find dusty places to build illegal campfires so that we could sit back and throw sticks into the evening blaze. Comfort, real comfort.

Kris and Richie would awkwardly smoke Camels, offering me one again and again: box extended, one cigarette popping out above the rest. I'd decline, a slight tremor in my lungs, pretending I didn't like the Camel brand because it was too *burnt* tasting. Really I was afraid to smoke at the tender age of eleven-thirteen. Kris never told Richie that I was a cigarette wussy, she only aided my smoke screen pretext by adding that I smoked only Marlboro Lights, whatever those were. Then, as if on cue, I'd slowly run my fingers through my tiny mullet to make sure it was flowing in the delta breeze like Don Mattingly's incontrovertibly would. Good times with cigarettes. Good teamwork. Once I heard Richie mention clove cigarettes, and I was utterly nonplussed; I pictured a cigarette packed with green four leaf clovers, their greeniness popping out the ends; an Irish good-luck smoke that made one crave marshmallow cereal.

I don't know how Richie put up with me being at those delta campfires so many times. I was dorky and seriously must have annoyed him in that he couldn't french my hottie aunt Kris while a was farting around with them. Exacerbating his frustration was just how hot she was: hair like Elizabeth Shue in the *Karate Kid*: sandy colored and shoulder length, a cutesy face that looked very young yet somehow twenty-six at the same time, cuffed, acid-washed jeans that showed off her slender, long legs, *and* she wore lipstick, eyeliner and blush: a woman with real hips and attitude!

Despite his annoyance he was continually convivial to me. A nice guy. Well, that is, until he and Kris eventually married way way tooooo early in 1989. Within the first year he gave her a black eye and a fat lip. She didn't take shit like that. Good old smart Kris. Quick as a whip, she filed the papers the next day. Goodbye, Richie. You lost someone spectacular. Fool! Come to think of it, he looked an awful lot like the bad guy in *Karate Kid*: Johnny, all spikey hairspray hair and a surreal, made-for-TV clay face. He also looked a lot like a rebellious Ricky Schroeder.

Kris was the perfect person to concretely report that Caleb was screwing around. She had a lot of heart and really cared about her sister. She caught Caleb sex-handed on an early evening at a ball field in northern Stockton. The sky was orange and beautiful. If memory serves me correctly then the story goes that it was in the fall. Kris was out on one of her numerous dates and was driving around all lovey-dovey with some farm boy when they fortuitously pulled into the parking lot of the ball field in a very quiet part of town; lots of huge, old shade trees. They were going to park and fool around with collective glands and nerves. Youth: blunt and red-blooded. As they pulled into the parking lot she noticed a beat-up white Datsun pick up. The truck looked very familiar.

"What the shit? That's Caleb's truck."

"Who's Caleb?" asked Chad.

"Uh," face peering through the windshield, "he's my sister's husband; he's a punk. Wait; stop!" hands on dash, "STOP the car!"

"Okay."

The CRX slowly pulled to a stop about twenty yards away from the white Datsun. The sun was sinking in the distant hills, over yonder in the stew of the bay area. The air was still. Thick. Moist. Indian summer autumn warmth.

"Whaddooyou wanna do?" asked Chad, impatiently.

"I don't know. Look." She points. "The windows are all fogged up; is the truck moving?" asked Kris, eyes fixed on the small truck: her sister's life.

"No, it's not moving," said Chad, looking around nervously, frustrated that a damn truck was ruining his chance to score; all he wanted in the world was a safe place to explore the workings of a lacey bra.

"Okay, I have to see—to know for sure. Pull up to it slowly, as quiet as you can, and roll down my window, please," ordered Kris. (The windows were automatic and expensive).

The sporty red CRX crept closer. Still she could not yet make visual sense of what was going on. Closer still. Within ten yards now. Still couldn't tell. "Dammit, I don't know." Her eyebrows furrowed, her detective candor determined. "Pull up closer, but turn your wheels toward the driveway out so that I can see inside the truck, and then we can get the hell outta here if it is actually him," she ordered.

Chad nervously obliged. She was so cute that he'd do anything she'd say as long as it earned him make-out time. Boys will be boys. The CRX pulled closer still, and then its little muffler suddenly coughed on all the exhaustion of creeping around in a gravelly parking lot. It coughed loudly, right as the car turned, enabling Kris to see through the foggy windows: a mere eight feet away!

A hairy head popped up, shoulders straining as they supported the brawny-scrawny frame of an alerted male redneck. He quickly rolled the window down in order to fling some fuck words out the window at the pervert intruders. As he awkwardly rolled it down, Kris saw a slutty girl (who looked no older than eighteen) pop her head up from under him and look backwards over her naked shoulder, straining her peachy neck.

At that instant, Caleb's sweaty eyes met Kris' directly. Their instincts sharpened and their pulses quickened. Fear grappled nerve endings, and faces became odd for about three seconds.

Chad tried to look past Kris to see if the girl was topless, but kept his left foot on the brake pedal and his right on the gas: a quick release of the left and a push of the right, and they were the hell out of there before the pissed redneck could even get the key to the ignition. Chad couldn't see any breasts, only the girl's sweaty forehead and messy hair.

"DON'T YOU TELL THE OLD LADY OR I'LL FUCKIN' KILL YOU!" Caleb tremulously squealed, like an injured pig. He pushed the girl down under him and out of sexual sight.

Kris shook her head and glared at him with utter hatred. His threat didn't scare her; she knew he was a weak, burned-out shell of a man. A stupid wrestler of strumpet girls.

The CRX exploded out of the parking lot, rocks spraying up onto the back window of the little white truck, making a crack in the upper left corner. The crack looked like a star scar. Caleb yelled, "SSHIIIIIIIT!" and pushed Shelly out of the way, wiping away the back window steam to see the star. "DAMMNN LITTLE PRICK!"

He considered chasing after them, but knew his truck had no real power and that CRX looked new. The kid behind the wheel was definitely a lead foot. He squished his forehead and salty eyebrows with his vaginal fingers and slowly growled, "Shiiiit." Shelly rubbed his bare thigh and suddenly became quite embarrassed, looking down at herself and realizing that she was very, very naked.

Everybody in the family knew Caleb was sleeping around, but now somebody reliable had actually caught him in the act, somebody that Caleb already hated and considered "nosy and feminist!" It couldn't have been more perfect. This was the final nine-inch nail in the coffin. Finally.

Once it was all out in the open, Caleb put up a tough front, repeating to every hillbilly he knew his own personal take on the rocky relationship. It was the only time he ever used a somewhat working metaphor, which he filched from a TV talk show. "Well, it's better to take a big hammer and shatter the dam and let it drown the whole damn town than to let it trickle for years and years and have everyone dry up with thirst. I don't fuckin' care about her. Let her talk. Let that cow know the truth! She's a cold bitch, maybe even a fuckin' DYKE!"

F-word power.

When Kris told me about what she saw I considered it a big strike against Caleb, but he wasn't *quite* out of the game yet, my game, that is. I still wanted him in our family. But then it became awfully hard to keep him in the game because, out of nowhere, came a big, sizzling strike TWO right across home plate. Then strike THREE! And FOUR! And FIVE! Etc.

He was out. The big umpire stood erect and did his sovereign, sweeping movement to the right, "YEEERRRRRRR OUT!" And Caleb whirled his bat at the dugout like a big baby.

By November 1986 and on into '87, Caleb could care less who saw him doing what. He was gonna prove he could do whatever he wanted whenever he wanted. He was truly "born to raise hell!" He seemed to especially like having me "see" him cheating. He began blatantly caressing women's shoulders and touching their hair in front of me, at the liquor store, the Midvalley Truss Company, etc. These were women I didn't know, women whom he apparently *did* know. Quite well.

These same women had houses and lives all their own, but sometimes we'd visit (just the two of us—never Sam) for an afternoon or so for no apparent reason. Of course we were there so Caleb could quickly wet his Stockton whistle whilst I was sequestered away in the living room or Datsun. All the while my mother was stuck at home, a sloth, recovering. Caleb was finally free to chase the slutty sluts like a dog with a red rocket.

Strike TWO: one peculiar afternoon we were in western Stockton for a couple hours at this lady's house. She had red hair like my mom, but it looked dyed because her eyebrows were black; she also reeked of musk. It wasn't the first time we'd been there; it was about the fifth, but I didn't mind because the lady, Sheila, had a son a few years younger than I, and he had superb amounts of old Star Wars Action Figures. He even had the ATAT walker from Empire Strikes Back. It was huge, very expensive, and made real laser noises! So, this kid, Barry, and I got them all out on the carpet in the den and took turns choosing guys from the pile for our personal militia in the same way two team captains pick kids one by one for tetherball militias. I ended up getting the coolest guys because Barry was like seven and a dolt. I easily convinced him that he, in fact, didn't want Hammerhead or IG88 or Boba Fett; *no no…* he wanted only "cool" guys like ATAT driver guy, random doctor ewok, R5D5 droid, and headless Obi Wan Kenobi. Yes.

He fell for it. I was a persuasive little cheater. Barry even felt sorry his militia was so much more kick ass than mine and tried to give me jacket-less Yoda. I declined. My militia would win, of course. Annihilation of the retard guys.

Whilst Barry and I began The Battle of Den, Caleb and Sheila attended to matters in the bedroom. Privately. Exclusively. Under the pretext of, "Sheila's a client; we gotta finalize some truss transactions in the back. She's buyin' a lot a steel, so we'll need privacy; it's grown-up business. You guys stay out here."

He said it all so nicely I believed him even though I was eleven. I wanted to believe him. I focused on the battle and felt responsible for keeping little Barry entertained with his toys (which I secretly still enjoyed playing with).

Caleb was a liar. It wasn't a steel transaction. It was a bodily fluids transaction.

Soon enough, the battle waned, and headless Obi Wan was armless and legless. My militia beautifully steamrolled over Barry's, and he began wrapping all his dead guys in toilet paper…something he'd done the last time we came over.

I was tired, hungry, and dying to go home.

My agony and boredom made me brave, and I decided to tell Caleb it was time to go, so I marched straight back toward the bedroom, my sneakers scuffing on the three-tone brown, post-shag carpeting. I was a big guy now, in junior high. It was time to go home. Two hours was enough.

I put my clammy hand on the brass door handle and then suddenly stopped, hearing the obligatory bed springs bouncing in that sinfully silly way. I didn't know what that sound meant at that time, so I opened the door and pushed my body over the threshold, declaring, "I'm HUNGRY!" tilting my head to the left for effect.

Then, quite shockingly, I saw it all: a mountain of floral blankets on the bed, a mountain earth quaking up and down. Caleb's bare back was part of the mountain, like a dirty-white glacier. He whipped his head around and yelled, "SHUT THE FUCKIN' DOOR!"

I ran out. I was beyond scared. Things became quite clear to me. But I didn't tell Mom. Perhaps all the bathtubs kept me quiet.

Infidelity. It reeks to this very day like a corpse on fire. Selfish sin is powerful folly. Folly is the profound wasting of a good lifetime. Proverbial. I prefer the straight and narrow. Though it's never easy, it's the best, the absolute bestest best.

There's one other salient story from this time that I simply must tell. It's a prime example of Caleb's horndoggedness and penchant for idiocy. It involves me being stuck with Caleb at a ranch house out in the boonies for a solid six and a half hours, not to mention the many hours before that spent at a sunny softball game.

Caleb was first the baseman for a softball team (oh, the hick accolades): the hot Stockton outfit, "Lauderdale," which played games in some musky league. Weekend warfare, if you will. Again, it was a softball team. The ball was soft.

One hapless afternoon I got talked into going with him to a game in the solstice month of June. This was a few months after the whole Sheila thing. The game was a tight one; it ended up going into extra innings, but Lauderdale pulled out a victory, and then there was hoopla galore. A bunch of hicks hopping around: women and men: breasts and spandexed bulges bouncing up and down in the grassy sunset. It was pretty hot out, and everybody was sweating. There were a lot of moustaches crisping in the heat. I could hear them.

Then one of the leading hicks hollered, "Let's have a victory party out at Dick and Jezebel's!" So we all got in our respective pickups and 4-by'd out to the dead hills out past Linden.

The game ended at seven p.m. We got out to good old Dick and Jezebel's at approximately eight p.m. I was stuck there until 2:30 a.m.

Sam wasn't with us, of course. He was safe at home, protected from seeing his dad turn into a drunken sailor. I, however, was not, and was poised again and again to see him party animal it up: drinkin', humpin', cussin', and pissin' all over the shitty hinterlands.

It's a wonder I didn't start drinking earlier than I did; perhaps my conscience was still whispering to me of vital truths and the straight and narrow. Jesus was hovering over the party, and He was looking directly at me. He was very concerned.

Caleb's conscience, on the other hand, had apparently fallen overboard whilst intoxicated about three miles out from the balmy coast of Nam in the late '60s: "Me love you long time," and such.

I forgot to mention that the game was actually a tournament game on this day, so the partying was to be justifiably fierce. When we first got out to the ranch house (one floor, long, 1960s red with fake white/brown rocks on one third of the siding = classy) I noticed immediately that there was a trampoline out back.

Fun. No, really. I got excited. I would head for the trampoline. Solitary bliss awaited me. I proceeded to politely ask an already-buzzed Mrs. Jezebel if I could bounce, and she said, "Of course, darlin'." A long-nailed finger against my cheek. Hmmm.

So I bolted for the trampoline and bounced copiously, for about an hour, I bounced like a pubescent bunny, all by myself, with the aaa'dults livin' it up with zest about twenty yards away, paying no heed to my accomplishments.

I tried to work my courage up so I could do a radical flip. I practiced and practiced doing half flips and landing safely on my back, my tiny mullet flapping in the country eventide breeze. I was scared that I might break my neck if I landed wrong, so I was being extra careful. I was likewise scared of doing a painful back flop off a diving board when I was trying to do flips at my buddy Brett's tiny pool. I was continually and irrationally frightened of hurting my body...inflicting medical complications that would haunt me all of my paranoid days. So I took my time practicing on the trampoline. I had an innate and empirical sense that I was going to be at good-old beer-and-softball Dick and Jezebel's for a long time.

I took my time. Bounce. Bounce. Bounce. Sadly, I was never able to do a full flip. I was not radical enough. After an hour, I gave up and convinced myself that it was better not to break my neck than snap it like a calcium twig whilst flipping gloriously. (I never had the rock-star guts to do semi-stupid things; I'd rather watch stupid people do them and get really hurt. Then I could point my chubby finger and laugh just loud enough to be cool, but not loud enough for them to hear me lest they come over and beat me up; even with their bobbing broken-neck heads they were still tougher than I. I was privy to this knowledge and reminded of it every time I looked down at my fat, white, adolescent belly with its little hairs: scant and out of any sort of collocated order.)

The valley sun was gone by now—way below even San Francisco. The Rice-a-Roni street lamps were flickering on right about now, I thought to myself. Orange and yellow. I decided to look for Caleb. I found him drinkin' it up with several hick blokes (American/British oxymoron) over by the horseshoe game range thing, all sandy and usually neglected. Apparently Dick and Jezebel loved recreational materials.

"Can we go soon?" I painfully inquired.

He ignored me.

So I left him to his million lagers and wandered over and into the brightly lit house through the sliding glass door that had a stained-glass rainbow thing dangling from it by a gold string and a clear suction cup. It read, "Howdy, friend! Welcome to our spread!" Images of a black clad robber reading the rainbow sign and letting himself gently in, his gloved hands slowly pulling at the aluminum handle (like Darth Vader's hands pulling at Leia's throat) crossed my tired mind.

Didn't they know they were inviting rape and pillage with that stupid sign? "Stupid people," I muttered, entering the house. The ranch kitchen was to my left. It was honey toned, like everything in my life at that point.

I stopped and listened. Absolute quiet and clean stillness. Nobody was in the house. The air was cooler than outside; it felt nice on my summer skin, after my Olympic workout on the trampoline. The chicken clock atop the fridge read 9:33. It was later than I thought. All the piles of hicks outside suddenly let out a large whoop; it startled me good. Apparently some golden hick had wrung a perfect horseshoe or dropped his pants or farted into a beer bottle for kicks. Everyone whooped again. Now he was probably pissing into the fire. I peered out the kitchen window, but could see nothing but bumbling Sodom silhouettes in front of the massive bonfire ablaze with clambake saturnalia. They were moving around like revived rock 'n' roll revelers from the '70s.

I was very hungry and very thirsty. Not very rock 'n' roll. So I went over to the massive fridge: it was one of those new kinds with twin vertical doors and an ice dispenser. I had seen one like this on the Cosby show, but never in person yet. I pushed the ice dispenser with my dirty hand. Ice spat out and smarted my forefinger. Oops. I bent over and hurriedly picked up all the glass shards of inert water. If Caleb saw me do that he'd call me a stupid kid—especially if Mom were thirty miles away (which she was) and his buddies (especially hot broads) were around to jeer and tell him not to call me that, 'cuz then that gave him license to walk over and put me in a full Nelson saying, "Awww, but he likes it. He likes me when I call him that, right, buddy?"

Then I'd smile and feel like a stupid kid: trapped, sweaty, and fat in my XXL Oakland A's shirt, his friends smiling at me, their beers sweating, the big-breasted broads taking mental note of my burgeoning man boobs. Good times.

Once I'd scooped the ice and patted it into the large silver sink, I opened up the Cosby fridge. Theo wasn't in there, but Dr. Peppers were. So were Coors Light cans, a Herculean watermelon, bologna (the smell of the sweet delta and midnight wafted through my beleaguered brain), rotting green beans, and three French's mustards—all of them half full. I shook each one just to find out. Then I shrugged as if I were in an ABC sitcom about life, being tired, being "just a kid," having kooky parents, and ceremoniously grabbed a Dr. Pepper. I was definitely not going to be bothered with finding and asking the electrically inebriated Jezebel for one.

I never talked to Dick. He scared me. It would be like talking to a white Mr. T. He was bombastic as hell, but ironically got quiet whenever he was at bat—

striking out three quarters of the time. He was impotent too. Caleb told me once, driving home from practice. I still didn't know what it meant, but had images of Jezebel in red lingerie—sprawled across a satiny cream-colored bed, her eyes saying, "Come hither," every time I thought of the word.

My Dr. Pepper tasted sugary sweet to my cavity teeth as I thought of satiny-satany Jezebel. My loins felt the little jolts of tickle and tease lightning bugs. Caleb's horny friends often inspired my loins to their earliest life since his friends lived as if they were eternally eighteen.

I looked around the living room. Might as well kill some time. Pictures of vacations in Cabo and Hawaii and other hot '80s sun-and-sand destinations. *The Beach Boys somewhere were writing "Kokomo" for all the martini and hoola-girl baby boomers the world over, rich or poor—it didn't matter. They'd all purchase the white cassette single for their respective Dodge Caravans or Lamborghini Diablos.*

One picture had Jezebel standing next to a beefy hunk fishing-guide guy with a blonde mullet and a Quiet Riot tank top, who held out a big swordfish that he/she had just caught. Behind their dreamy Cabo smiles on the railing of the boat were several bottles of Corona and one bottle of pink sunscreen. ("Aruba…Jamaica…oooh, I wanna take ya…")

I clicked on the TV and watched it for about an hour. Hicks came in and out during this time (not Caleb—he being the premium jokester afire outside, drunk off his ass with numerous soft-ball sluts hanging on his tanned, tobacco'd, and tank-topped night arms). Everyone of them made some dumb comment to kiddy me as they came in, like, "Diiiid you have a beerr?" or "Waaatchin' some ttvee?" or "Havviin' funn, son?" They all tried to make me feel better, like I was part of the party and loving it all, and in no way should make their consciences feel guilty about such oceans of alcohol on a Saturday night in their thirties.

(Didn't they need to get some sleep for church tomorrow?)

One lady was actually *so* intoxicated that she blurted out this gem, "You get a littllle ollder and get a little spiiicier like your pop, then yoou just might geeet to seeee these here tiiiittties!" and she bent over (right before she bumped into the sliding glass door) and squished her lime green tank-topped, size D, redneck breasts together. I could see the cleavage plain as day; freckled and milky white; fireflies buzzed in my parachute pants. I grinned and pretended not to care, even though my heart was racing like and SR-71 Blackbird at full throttle.

She was gross, but she still had breasts. And they were big. Very Big. Big. Like Tom Hanks in the movie *Big,* but not really at all. To this day I still can't believe she said that to me.

At about ten 'til midnight I noticed two thirty-something chicks (and I remember using the word "chicks" in my head back then) and one almost-handsome Rickey Sharp (all-star pitcher—only twenty-five but treated as though he was part of the washed-up gang because he was showing early signs of choice-loser choiceness) come in through the glass doors behind me and move in a slow, drunken dance back toward the ranch recesses of the house.

They went right by me. I was infinitely interested. The red question of *SEX* was in the air. I turned toward them, swiveling the LaZboy and slowly waking up from a TV catnap stupor. The chicks were talking baby *sex talk* to him and walking backwards like kitties in heat; he was giggling and letting them pull him along to their orgasmic den of painted-lady herpes. I quick-like turned the TV volume up a hair, to remain a ghost in the house.

When they were out of view I jack rabbit jumped up and looked out the kitchen window: bonfire still ablaze, hicks still carousing with mighty gusto: Caleb the ringleader. They'd moved on to Tequila and Whiskey ("beer before liquor") and Dick and Jezebel's Run DMC-looking silver boom box (were these people rich?) was blasting out some choice, "More than a Feelin'" Boston. The party apparently was just beginning. And at that one special moment, I was actually glad, for I was about to be a spy ninja. I was about to see a few things I'd never seen before!

I tiptoed down the hall and felt my stomach swirl and my heart race once again with every footfall of sneaker to carpeting. Would this be it? The first time I was ever to see real boobies?

I listened: The two chicks were still "ooing" and "ahhing" and there was the soft sibilant sound of scuffled clothes. I heard some giggling. Quite suddenly, one of Rickey's white Nike cleats hit the opposite side of the wall right next to my face! *Yikes!* I backed up. They were one room closer to me than I thought they were! Stupidly I had almost walked right passed the open-door threshold of the red sex room! *Stupid. Stupid. Stupid.* I stopped and collected myself. I was mere inches away. Why hadn't they shut the door? All the lights were on in the room, too. It was brighter than the hallway in there. Weren't they ashamed of possibly being caught?

I still hadn't wrapped my mind around the fact that TWO girls and ONE guy were in the red sex room; wasn't that against California laws or something? My mind immediately thought of Granny Mildred's big black Bible glowing in the one p.m. skylight sunlight atop that desk at her mystical apartment. That Bible surely didn't like what was going on in this room. That Bible was surely, deeply saddened by it.

Then I heard a painted lady's voice, "How you feelin', Rickey?" and then some giggling and kind of stupid sounding moaning, like an animal slowly dying in a latex trap. Fireflies started biting me in the crotch.

I HAD TO LOOK! I had to. Yes. *Had to*. Now or never!

I wished at that rapid moment that I was superman and could look through the wall without being seen, but all I could really do was peer around the corner and risk being seen....and the hallway light, though dim, was for some stupid reason *on*, and I couldn't turn it off, or they would, for sure notice. "Damn it," I whispered, outstretching my chubby fingers at my sides.

I glanced behind me. If someone were to come in from outside...No. I didn't let myself think about that.

More and more words were coming from inside the room, like, "Waayyeeet...yeah...uh huuuuhhhh..." and a particularly lame sentence from Rickey's husky man voice, "Ohh yeah, this is...umm...better thaen baasebball...yeeeeeah...you gals are reel better than baseball combined," followed by more animal-trap noises.

It occurred to me (like a lightning strike!) at that very moment that I was amidst what I'd heard referred to as "porno." This intriguing word I'd recently learned the definition of at school thanks to my rat-faced peers. And, though I grasped what it meant, I hadn't yet ever seen any porno in my young innocent life.

There I was: at a live porno show, holding my tickets, all a-tremble, and not knowing what the hell to do. I was electric, the good boy in me hesitating. The bad man giving God the finger. Pandora's box lay before me. I just had to open it! But did I have the sand?

Suddenly, out of nowhere, like an M-80 *exploding*, about a billion merry drunks bumbled into the living room from outside. I froze, then acted, because it was *now* or *never*.

I peeked quickly around the corner into the red sex room.

[GASP!]

"HEY! SHUT THE FUCKIN' DOOOR!"

Ricky's other cleat hit me in the shoulder, and I bolted away toward the safety of the merry, redneck coterie outside. But

I
saw
boobies.
For the first time ever.
I
saw
boobies.
Four of them.
Really fast I saw them.

And they were big and sort of saggy and droopy. They didn't look anything like what I'd ever pictured: a sort of motherly beauty and fullness, a gracefulness. No, they were nothing of the sort. There were stretch marks on two of them, but I didn't know what stretch marks were, really, so I ignorantly surmised them to be scars from a knife fight at a local bar.

I also saw teal and pink women's underwear (being worn) and, unfortunately, Ricky fully naked. He was very big and hairy down there. Later on I would look down to my own self and wonder if I would ever grow into that kind of look. Later on I would also learn that what Ricky was, was referred to as "hung" by ignorant males.

(Rednecks put a lot of stock into the size of their male genitals: it's a mark of mental midgetry; if you take an intelligent/wise road in life away from the lazy, redneck stew you'll find that genitalia doesn't really matter in life; there are better things to think about: like old elm trees, classic novels, and endless essential human truths worth elucidation. Yes, genitals are good for posterity, but not much else, unless you're a hick. Then they're the singular pride of your benighted life!)

Obviously, I got a lot of "Shut the fuckin' door!" between the years of 1984-1987. Each one stung differently. Each one stung mightily. The aforementioned one I completely brought upon myself. Though I didn't place myself at that crappy party, I did choose to place myself at that crappy red doorway. Indeed. Life is full of choices.

The rest of that night was spent wandering around the dark fields surrounding the house and trying to remember and inculcate the boobies I saw to memory. (Young boys do ridiculous things like this. It makes me honestly wonder what God was thinking when He made the decision to put that many sexually fire-tipped hormone arrows in an adolescent boy's growing body.)

At around one-thirty in the morning, I became frustrated: I'd had enough. I located Jezebel—she was still in full-on party mode: her blouse thing was unbuttoned entirely—showing her red lace bra with massive '80s Cold War missiles contained within. More to inculcate.

Didn't her inept blouse make Dick angry? Nope. He was passed out in the Tequila bathroom. He didn't care about anything.

I envisioned knife fight wounds on her breasts as I asked her if I could use the phone.

"Yeaah…why yyeee-esz, of course…yessssssssssss…you can *sertanely* yoos phones!" she stumbled.

I nodded. Yes. I was capable of using phones.

She led me slowly to the pantry room, tiny and dark, where she sultrily handed me the big '70s phone and rubbed the top of my head with her long red nails. (Impotent. Dick was impotent.)

"How yuuo doin', son? Yah havinn fun foniiiite?" she bent on down to my level (she was rather tall) and looked me in the eyes, then winked.

"Yeah, but I'm tired and hungry and I want to go home." I desperately determinated to her, glancing quickly at her red lacy bra.

"Ahhhh…. I noe, hony…I no-oh." She then hugged me for a good ten seconds and rocked back and forth—my kiddy face in her motherly bosom.

Fireflies awoke *again* and buzzed electrically around my tender testicles.

She kissed me on the cheek and then bluntly said, "You stink, little man…do you shower yet?" then she giggled rummily and sauntered out.

If you were to look up the word "vexed" in the dictionary, at that precise moment in time you would've seen a picture of eleven-year-old me with my eyebrows frumpled. (Dick was still impotent. Red. Satin. "Come hither.")

I called Mom. She was irritated and worried. "Where the hell are you?" Not "you guys," but "you." By this time she only thought of and cared for me; Caleb was a dick, and she realized it.

She made me get Jezebel back on the phone. (She'd only gone as far as the Cosby fridge) so that she could give my sober and respectful mother a map to the house of sin. There wasn't a hint of sloth in Mom's voice.

When Tallene dusted up the moonlit gravel driveway, I knew I could finally get the hell out of there. I was so tired I wanted to die. Mom didn't look for Caleb.

I told her I'd be in the living room, so she came through the front door, swiftly grabbed me, and we took off. She wanted Caleb to be drunk and confused and pissed off over my disappearance, which he was for a good hour or two before he sobered up enough to guiltily contact Mom, who didn't answer the phone, which should have rung like crazy about 86 times, but didn't because we were sound asleep and it was off the hook.

My mother was cool again, like back in the days of the night bottles. Her anger made her beautiful to me again. It would all soon be over for Tallene and Caleb, but sadly, only after I'd been beat up a thousand times and seen a few stretched boobies.

There was one more odd item of happenstance that happened that night: on our way home my mother actually picked up a hitchhiker. She never, ever, ever did this; in fact, she thought it was an extremely stupid thing for people to do, so when she pulled over I got a little scared.

Fortunately, the hitchhiker was a kindly woman about thirty years old named Wendy. She was heading to San Francisco to put some flowers in her hair or something. Didn't she know she was seventeen years late? Mom thought she looked pathetic on the road in the moonlight, so she helped her; this was just a glimpse of all the helping of kids that would soon well up in my mother.

Caleb was finally given the muddy boot in 1987. Divorce. Courts. Lawyer's fees that magically turned into forever debt. I didn't go to even one the proceedings, being merely a child in my twelfth year and craving only guitar player posters of Zak Wylde and Kirk Hammet, not colorful posters of family court "shit."

And this is a whole new can of worms. At this time in my young life I began my descent into adolescent madness like everyone else in the world. I remember not being home the day that Caleb packed up his gross stuff and took off. I think it was a Saturday, so no school, but I was purposefully at—well, somewhere; I don't remember. I came home later than usual for a twelve-year-old, and the first thing I noticed was that Caleb's big yellow and red neon MILLER HIGH LIFE sign was missing from the living room corner area. Today I cannot believe that I ever lived in a house that had one of these insipid signs *on its living room wall! (an exclamation point for the sake of taste)*

I also noticed that there was no beer in the fridge, which instantly gave me a pleasant *new* feeling…like springtime, a profound peaceful feeling deep down inside. No beer. No drinking. Just health.

I was very afraid of alcohol all the way up to my sophomore year of high school, when this irrational fear was surmounted by pseudo-friend Roy, a vice boy who taught me to enjoy Mickey's wide-mouth malt liquor.

A few months later Mom and I went to secretly check up on what Caleb was doing, how he was living. He'd been gone since the day the High Life sign disappeared. He had successfully pulled off the ultimate magician vanishing act of all time. Houdini turned in his grave, very upset.

Tallene had heard that he was living out in Linden with his brother, but she wasn't precisely sure. She hated him, but wanted to see what he was up to in that meddling, grocery-store-novel way. I was brought along on this trip as a safety alibi just in case we were to run into the great white shark out in his scary home waters. I remember my mother getting lost out in the hillbilly fields of Linden and saying, quite loudly, "FUCK!" as we almost hit a chubby, dusty, black Labrador retriever that ran across the hot road, seemingly out of nowhere.

Then she looked at me, sweat beads on her forehead, and said, "Sorry, hon."

I played it cool. "I don't care," I muttered in a smarting way. I did not like being in Linden. I hated Caleb. I hated their marriage. Their stupid divorce. I didn't care about either of them. I was twelve and I was so tough—a rock, an island—feeling no pain—never crying, like Simon and Garfunkel. I was typical.

I scratched my head and huffed out disapproval of my mom's vapid driving. She kept driving and ignored me a little—too interested in sneaking around her ex-lover's affairs to even consider disciplining her mulleted preteen: the ass.

We eventually drove past Caleb's brother's house, spotted it, affirmed it, drove past it again, read the address slowly, circled it longways, then stopped by the side of the road, in the dirt, at a safe viewing distance: behind double-thick aquarium glass—safe from the jaws of Caleb the shark.

We got out. The sun was high overhead and hotter than Satan's breath. Tallene walked over to my side of the car, and we both peered over the scorched yellow grasshopper grass toward the shack. And when I say shack I mean shack. It was a shitty camper thing that was built into or alongside (connected to?) a house-looking rectangular thing, painted poop-brown several years earlier. There was the obligatory hick junk in the front yard (dirt and rocks littered with sparse dead grass), but no cliché items like mattresses, dead refrigerators, or a car with no engine or vice versa. There were no other houses for miles around. Nor people. Just the sun, the grass, the stench of shack and spiritual death.

It was the clearest day ever, but it felt like we were in the midst of the greatest fog ever recorded in the California valley. A lethargy fog—a body odor—of shacks and the souls they devour. I noticed a grasshopper on the hood of our old car. He looked intently at me and leaned toward me as if to say, "Get the hell outta here! There's still time to escape with your life and your youthful vitality!"

I was Dante, and Tallene was Virgil. But we weren't smart, and this wasn't the *Inferno*. Not quite. Caleb was definitely *NOT* Beatrice. He did not need rescuing. He needed dying. And from the looks of that place and his white Datsun pickup parked next to it in the blistering heat, he was dying just fine.

I was happy to confirm that he was living there. In hell. It was his rightful prison.

My mom was too, though she was nervous about being discovered by the shark on her dramatic recon; she looked extremely overjoyed at the sight of Caleb's banged-up truck next to that trailer/poop-brown rectangle shack.

She looked at me and smiled, raising her eyebrows. "Well, there he is," she declared.

"Yeah, *DICK*," I said.

She didn't berate me.

She chuckled, adding, "Dick in a hole."

It was perhaps the dirtiest, bawdiest, funniest thing my mother ever said to me. And I love it dearly, cherishing it forever.

She slung her arm around me and we moved slowly back toward the car. Grasshoppers popped and sizzled all around us on the hot side-road gravel. Their yellow juices exploded out of their dust exoskeletons. Hell was frying up a silent burn of summer and afternoon: slashed, severed, and slit in two. Good riddance.

Hell laughed at us and with us.

Caleb, I'm sure, was shirtless and drinking with the warm flies in that very shack...on a cum-stained mattress passed down to his brother from the whores of their Stokes ancestors.

We drove away. Our backs had white wings made of white feather freedom, fringed in silver. Mom's novel was thickening. Millions of other life readers would purchase a copy; Caleb's folly would be scrutinized and all the women of the world would rejoice at his monstrous errors and ultimate downfall: a dick in a hell hole.

Weird. Relationships are weird. Some people do 'em right, and others make the human race look like a bunch of deaf-and-dumb pervert clowns. I really dislike clowns. They're scary. The red and white paint makes me feel like I'm gonna get cut up by a knife. Clowns really suck. Unfortunately for me, Caleb and Tallene both owned pairs of big floppy shoes. I'd seen both pairs in the bedroom closet of our Stockton home years earlier.

# Chapter 8
# Girls and Guitars Like Daily Bread
# (A) Heavy Metal…or No Metal at All

After Caleb was gone Mom had to find a way to make more money. Her body was inefficient, running at about forty percent its normal workday energy; so, she needed desperately to find a way to make money without physical exertion. This seemed impossible to her at the time. It still seems impossible to me when I think back on it. However, we got lucky: Ogressa was still hanging around the valley and one day gave my mom a quick barfly-gal-pal call. She was in trouble. Apparently she was only a few strikes away from permanently wearing a bright orange jumpsuit. She'd been busted for narcotics and other nefarious dealings again and again in a mild way, not enough of a way to put her away, but these busts were adding up, and big brother had his all-seeing eye fixed on her. He told her in no uncertain terms that her kids (lawbreakers themselves) could no longer stay with her in her ogre cave. It was a court order.

Her offspring numbered two. They were every bit as lackluster as Ogressa, with burgeoning drug hobbies all their own. Cloke and Orchid. The progeny of genius. Veritable scamps.

Now, here's the *reason* Ogressa was calling my mother. The scamps had just recently been released from juvenile hall after a wonderful two month vacation there, complete with initialed bathrobes and full room service. Exquisite California Juvy. They'd been busted for greeny joints rolled into their stonewashed jeans and public fighting or something like that. Broken beer bottles to the skin.

"Can my babies stay with you for a while? Honey? I promise to God they won't get cunty on you…not ever, or I'll skin 'em; promise to God! But can they? Can they please, honey? Tallene? Are yah still there?" importuned Ogressa.

"Yes. Certainly. Don't you worry about a thing," replied mother Tallene.
"Ohhh, honey, you've seriously just saved my life, honey!"
"Well, you're welcome, just, *please* watch yourself; I can't house them forever...you know my situation right now."

And my mother broadly opened her big arms. I guess it was the noble thing to do, but I really wish she hadn't. I think that picking up that hitchhiker on the way back from boozy Linden that night had taken away any fear she'd previously had of foreign felons being let into our lives.

And there was another, more pragmatic reason she accepted Cloke and Orchid: to her pleasant surprise she found out that the organization that placed the delinquents into our humble homestead (Charles Dickens Hall) punctually paid $350 a month for each foster placed therein.

This really got Mom off her indolent rear end. Money is a powerful thing. She cleaned up the house. She started taking more interest in life. When the miscreants arrived, wrapped in denim, switchblades, and street attitude, she provided a resplendent home situation for them. She really did the best she could with what she had, despite her limited energy and resources.

Charles Dickens noticed.

Orchid and Cloke reported that they liked Tallene's Oklahoma cooking and Tallene's "discipline," and then, after about five short months ($1,750.00 earned!), Charles Dickens Hall asked my mother hen if she could take any more rapscallions. They had tons of reprobates to choose from.

This was bad. She listened, mused over doubling her money, and complied. All in the same phone call. And onward came the *four-year* march of approximately *twenty-five foster kids*, all with greeny shoots of pot and pandemonium in their stonewashed hearts. Bad times for Sam and me. At first I was scared of them, but I eventually got used to the numerous young knaves. Sam didn't seem too scared of them. At least he didn't pay the myriad young caitiffs any heed. They weren't as socially engrossing as ghosts. Nothing is.

Our house worked out well for any and all scallywags: they could eat well, have a place to bathe and sleep, *and* sneak around the drug world of "Appetite for Destruction" juvenilia. Not one complained of life just off the Oxford Circle.

For the real kids of the house, Sam and I, the foster presence was like a black fog of vice wrapped around the neighborhood. And it took away all of our mother's precious attention. We took far away back seats in the greyhound bus that was our home. We dwindled in the corners like frightened mice.

We also were exposed to the wonderful world of drugs, real cussing, and sex. Yes. Sex. If the fosters had never come I most likely would have been too scared to ever dabble in such nefarious dross. Then again, my taste for heavy-metal music during this period may have instructed me on such things nonetheless.

Mom really liked her new career of feeding 21 jumpstreeters for $350 per mouth. In 1989 we had, at one time, mind you, EIGHT separate and distinct rowdy rascals in our home at once! That's $2,800 dollars a month. That's $33,600 a year. Tallene had no job at this time, of course. "I don't even need one!" she'd laugh.

During these years, the late eighties, I descended into what I call "heavy metal madness," like most white American suburban kids.

Bear with me now. If you could go back in time and walk through my killer room, you might find yourself unsure of your personal safety. Well, not really. It was all show; I was still a chubby coward, *but a coward who owned door-length Iron Maiden posters!*

That's right, ya'll. Three of them. All different. With lots of black and splashes of neon green and purple. Heavy Metal. I was waaaaaaay into metal. It became my supreme mother and father: always with me, always helping me, showing me the ropes of life, handing me the electric-chair controls.

Iron Maiden was the real teacher amongst all the other bands: teaching me general historical facts, such as Churchill's exhortative speech to rally Britain vs. the Luftwaffe, Napoleon's conquests, etc., a veritable audio Socrates or Benjamin Franklin at my disposal in the tangible form of glistening cassette tapes.

It ruled. And it blasted like strawberry fire from my K-Mart boom box, whined and sputtered from my expensive Sony cassette Walkman, and was on permanent playback in my entire world. You name the heavy metal band: I most likely had a taped copy of their music, that is, if they were readily available to a teen lost in suburbia.

Many of the choicest foster kids (namely: Mike, Otis, and Steve-arreeno) exposed me to the choicest metal: i.e.: Metallica, Maiden, Def Leppard, Motley Crue, ACDC (which I truly thought stood for "anti-christ devil children." This kind of scared me, but I pretended that this name made me stronger somehow. Megadeath, Guns 'n' Roses, Dokken, Skid Row, Black Sabbath, and also Ozzzzzzzzzy, post Sabbaath. I had them all. A consummate mélange, if you will. Randy Rhodes and Zak Wylde played their hot lixxx for my own personal pleasure. My self esteem went crazy, like a bull in a china shop.

I was the shit. I was a heavy metal guy. I'd finally found my social group. Back then, "metal" really wasn't known as "metal." No, it was only known as "heavy metal," which perpetually jostled my young brain into thinking of overweight strippers all joobily-boobily, leaning over me and loving me because I loved heavy metal, their boobilies slapping me in the face in time to the guitar riffs. Wow. America. Cable TV.

I had a subscription to various guitar metal magazines that were half printed just in black and white and on newspaper paper. So completely ghetto. I loved them; my mullet bristled with glee every time I opened a fresh one from our (off the) Oxford Circle mailbox.

I eventually got a cheap Ibanez knock-off guitar called a "Kramer" in 1989. I practiced my cheesy chops and hammered away on all six thousand frets with my hotdog fingers for hours at a time.

Sam started paying attention to me around this time. The enchanting ghosts could not match my radicalness. Music is stronger than death.

I studied the heavy metal mag tablature pages diligently so that I could play the *exact* licks of Kirk Hammet.... "MASTER! MASTER! Master of puppets is pulling YOUR STRINGS!" My playing, however, sounded a universe apart from Hammet's. I was merely a neophyte. A tadpole wearing faded jeans.

By far, my favorite band was Metallica. I owned and adored all their records. And my favorite record of theirs was irrefutably *And Justice for All*. 1988.

James Hetfield. Lars Ulrich. Kirk Hammet. Jason Newstead. They were my fathers to the fourth power. And the crazy solo on Shortest Straw was my anthem. Savage chops, like a wolf's razor teeth against a caribou rib, Hammet's digits on a maple neck. (Reading back over the above lines makes it lucidly apparent to me that at this time I was a dork. I was the dorkiest heavy-metal teenage dork.)

I forgot all about KISS. Well, secretly I was into them, too, because I really did "want to rock and roll all night." And my white and black make-up did indeed run with hot tears every time "Beth, What Can I Do" played through my puffy earphones.

Here's an example of what would have been considered the paragon of pleasure to me back then: being at the Straw Hat Pizzeria at around 7 p.m. with my buddy Brett...pumping the jukebox full of clammy quarters while "Sweet Child of Mine" blasts out of it—and then perhaps "One" and then (if we were feeling especially romantic over chix) "Shot through the Heart," "Pour Some Sugar on Me," and "Lay Your Hands on Me" and also (forgive the run-on: metal glory warrants it) Brett and I are playing the "Altered Beast" arcade game. Then...then...I was in *heaven!* And "heaven wasn't too far away!"

Wow. Somebody shoot me in the face. Why couldn't I have been listening to R.E.M., Sonic Youth, or the Pixies at this juncture? That would have given me a cultural jump way ahead of my peers! Early indie garb. Not leather. So much metal produced a lot of bad effects on me as I grew, but there was one concrete good effect: my mother actually got worried about me. Hooray!

One time she came right out and asked me if I thought the Iron Maiden skeleton guy on my door-length posters was evil—because she most certainly did. I felt a hot rush around my ears and answered, "No, not at all. Maybe if you're a baby or something."

She huffed and replied, "Well, I guess that makes me a baby!" and stormed out of the kitchen, abruptly leaving the soapy pans she had been scrubbing. I didn't storm out; I was too busy getting some freakin' Teddy Grahams. Chocolate Teddy Grahams: I was so heavy metal eating handfuls of chocolate Teddy Grahams.

I didn't see her again that night. She left five minutes later to go to some FFA function that our hick foster kid Kelsey was supposedly starring in; obviously, a busy life in drug trafficking didn't stop Kelsey from taking important time to show off her big-star goat creature that lived out at her uncle's. He was the type of man that didn't have time for her young refugee life, but could easily look after her big-star goat creature.

A burning enmity for my mother and her stupid fosters grew in my heart. I recited a mantra again and again in the shower one day, "She's so damn busy with those fosters that she could care less if I slit my own wrists with Sam's buck knife! Maybe I will! Maybe! She'd know then how much I hate them." I talked real tough when I was by myself.

But when she actually started to care, it only annoyed me. By this time I was into a threefold meal of evil: heavy metal, horror movies, and lip-gloss pornography—another benevolent cultural gift bestowed upon me by the ever-nasty foster punks (namely Otis).

One day I actually had the balls to hang up three pin-up centerfolds from Playboy magazine on the wall amongst my Metallica motif. This retarded display of, "I don't effin care about anything or anyone but myself," lasted all of two hours. That is, exactly two hours after these sexy images were pinned up, my mother came home from, ironically enough, Otis' mandatory juvy meeting, and bounded into my room to ask where Sam had gotten off to. As soon as I saw her sovereign visage in a room amongst the slutty images of Hefner, I felt my ribcage shake slightly with an angry beehive of nerves.

"WHAT THE HELL IS THIS CRAP?"

She suddenly, really *did* care. She walked right over to all three of my beautiful baby fantasies and ripped them all down; trying violently to swipe them all off in one fell swoop pattern for potent parent dramatics, but missed half of the middle one and most of the left one (I had pinned them up quite well). So it actually took her a second to get every last crumb of peachy paper off of the wall.

She looked funny doing this: fumbling violently, but I was too embarrassed and too incensed to fully grasp the physical humor at the moment. I charged directly forward to save my girls, my teen pride…my human right to playboy and sex. We abruptly collided, it was very awkward.

I said, "NO! Mom! THEY'RE MINE; I PAID FOR THEM, AND YOU OWE ME FOR RIPPING THEM!"

My junior high logic was inane and invalid. I paid for them? Like that even gave me the right to have them? In truth, I didn't pay for them: Otis ripped them out for me from his fecund intercourse catalogues and said, "These first hotties are free, but next time you gotta pay, see?" Did he think himself a Chicago gangster during Prohibition using words like, "see," at the end of sentences? Otis was stupid.

Mom and I met hands in the air: hers full of crumpled porn, mine full of empty fury. I clasped hers in mid air and didn't let go, so we ended up doing a magically slow dance with our hands raised together in the air like romantic orangutans. It was hilarious—sweaty—and there would be no compromises from either of us. We wrestled and wrestled away, but then she got downright feminist on my sorry little ass. "SON, NO! These pictures are sick and dirty, and what's worse than that is that they're degrading to women! THESE WOMEN ARE PROBABLY HOMELESS, AND PLAYBOY TOOK ADVANTAGE OF THEM!"

I'll always remember that quote. It's a magical tale of Little Red Riding Hoods gone wrong in a world of dark, woolen skies and evil wolfish playboys; perhaps it truly does contain a semblance of truth.

"No, they DON'T! They make MILLIONS of dollars!" I retorted.

Then she dropped a big grenade. "They are *NAKED!* COMPLETELY *NAKED!* AND YOU'RE OGGLING AT THEIR SHAME!" We wrestled and wrestled. Paper was flying everywhere like a peach madness hurricane.

"NO THEY'RE NOT!" I retorted again, "They've got different color lingerie on." (I could see Ginger's crumpled face in Mom's left hand; I motioned my head quickly toward her) "Look! Ginger's got *purple bras* on!"

What was I thinking? Purple bras? First of all, Ginger only had ONE bra on; secondly, it was completely off and hanging onto her elbow for dear life. The worst part about the above sentence was that I said Ginger's lovely name out loud, which meant I did, in fact, know her name and did, in fact, dream of her and love her and know that she enjoyed long walks on the beach and well hung men like Rickey Sharp.

We stopped wrestling. "GINGER?" My mother threw our hands down; crumpled porn flew all over the world, the universe. "GINGER?"

I nodded like, "Um YE-AH—duh—Ginger," like all men and women and babies everywhere in every climate throughout the world knew of the sweet and decorous Ginger and her maternal, breastly gift of sanguine love to all peoples everywhere.

"You know her *NAME*, son?" She breathed heavy and put her hands to her sheriff hips.

"Of course. Why not?"

I looked down at the ruined porn—such a shame: good porn—wasted. I would have to purchase more now from the old Chicago gangster.

"YOU know HER name, son?" Her voice trembled slightly as it grew into righteous anger, the anger of a lion.

"GINGER, *Mom*, that's her name. Big freakin' deal."

The phrase, "That's her name; don't wear it out," flashed across my mind; man, I'm glad I didn't utter it; my life would have been silenced forever; she would have whipped out a AK-47 and peppered me in the face!

She looked at me blankly. Then she dropped the Hiroshima bomb. "Do you MASTURBATE when you look at Ginger's naked body?"

I turned away and looked in desperation at my Dokken poster; it didn't help me find an answer. I turned back quickly and shook my cocked head in defiance. "I don't do that—*but Sam does!*" I yelled, full-on lying. Sam was only nine. If he was indeed masturbating, then the Guinness World Record people would be knocking down our door any minute now.

"*NO,* HE MOST CERTAINLY DOES *NOT!*" she yelled back; she was now winning the argument due to her atomic bomb use of the word, "masturbate." Even the sound of it made me cringe and lose all sense of sex sophistry. "But *you* do; *I KNOW* YOOU DOO!" she yelled and pointed at me.

"Whatever," I murmured, trembling, turning away from her Sauron's stare. I moved toward the door in an effort to escape, because tears were starting to run a marathon down my chubby, hairless cheek. I hadn't the stomach for the word "masturbate." I was still a softy, I guess. I was stepping through the bedroom doorway when my mother hollered, "I hear you in those long shower-baths that you take!—you're in there for *SO LONG* that the water runs *COLD!*"

My heart stopped. She knew I did that? SHIT! I was done for! I was a pervert and the whole world knew it!

"BETCHA DIDN'T KNOW I KNEW THAT!" she hollered as I raced down the hallway and onward out the door. I saw Otis on the couch staring at the TV right before I hopped outside. He'd heard the whole thing. I was mortified. I avoided eye contact with him.

*Somewhere, probably down in seedy-swank L.A., Ginger, Jasmine, and Simone were all sobbing and throwing expensive glass objects at expensive mirrored walls in an effort to burn out the pain of the fall of the House of Mullet.*

I walked for miles and miles of stinkweed pavement. I passed a liquor store, thought about stopping inside to try my hand at stealing a Hustler (Why not? The day was already extreme), but my conscience told me I'd wind up in jail. So instead I just walked on and on, kicking a billion rocks into the street. There were lots of big black ants racing across the sidewalk, so I took some mental refuge in avoiding them. Instead of going to jail I wound up sneaking into my broken aluminum-screened window at around nine p.m. I didn't see my mom again for like, two days. She was out doing Charles Dickens Hall stuff. But on my particleboard desk there was a note. It read: "Pornography is a disease. I love you." Succinct. Concise. Simple. Golden.

I ripped it to shreds and offered it to the Black Sabbath demons. The next day I dug out a few grubby bills from my secret, minuscule, Swiss-bank Reeboks box and handed them to Otis; he handed me the Playmate-of-the-Year Issue. She had blonde hair and reeked of rose-petal sin. I spiraled downward into sexual hypnosterbation.

I wish I could go back in time and punch myself across my room. I would punch hard enough to remember. Bloody lip or black eye.

During the foster years, Caleb came back into our lives as a sex phantom: mysteriously dropping in now and then, usually about six times a year. I say "sex phantom" because he came only for sex. Now that they were no longer together at all Mom and Caleb could couple at their leisure. They turned each other on again. It was racy and forbidden. Neither of them was particularly attractive by that point in the game, indeed far from it, so it's a bit peculiar to me now.

I hated seeing him. Oft times I'd quickly leave the house when he was there with excuses like, "Brett's got a new Nintendo game." (No, he didn't—he was poor too.) "I'm gonna check it out. I'll be back later." And nobody listened, and nobody cared. Good.

My mother gave me a lot of freedom as a youth; I could go and do pretty much anything I wanted; which wasn't much, since I was both a responsible teen and a coward.

Caleb didn't have an ounce of authority over me. He hardly said one word to me during the foster years. If ever he would have tried to enforce authority over me by telling me to, say, stack some wood, then I would have ignored him. I was physically bigger than he was. Taller than he was. Weighed more than he did. And I hated him. I really hated the old belt buckle scars in my back.

And now for a bit about the third sovereign triumvirate in my life: horror films. Horror films made me feel tough. *Friday the 13th, Nightmare on Elm Street,* and *Creepshow* were my favorites. Unfortunately, I could quote from them. Another horrible horror show that the generous fosters showed me was *Faces of Death.* Nobody should ever watch this filth. It sticks in your head like road tar and seemingly never comes out. Even to this day I recall the bear ripping off that guy's face and that drowned drunkard washing up on the beach. The airline crash, too. I don't know how much of what they filmed was real, but it sure looked real. The '70s and '80s had an indelible grisly note contained within the currents of their pop-cultural fancies.

I've had a dark fascination with the macabre for as long as I can remember, and I don't know why; some of it is natural curiosity and detective in nature, but some of it I believe to be simply and frankly depraved, an appetency for somewhat metaphorical human mud.

Those fosters, I tell you what; they were indeed a lot like the powerful/influential emperor in *Return of the Jedi:* enticing me daily to "Strike myself down with all my hatred and anger so that my journey toward the dark side would be complete!"

However, let us not go into the dark too far, for we must now, in all haste, turn our attention to the resplendent prince that turned out to be my conspicuous saving grace at this juncture: his name was Baseball.

Now, Almighty baseball (a healthy occupation for a youngster) was a sport I adored when I was an innocent child, before the totalitarian triumvirate took over during my adolescence. Not to worry; baseball would soon be back in my life, with force.

After four years of darkness (reaching its crescendo with an avid interest in serial killer psychology) I began feeling that I was turning into some kind of monster. Looking back, and to be entirely honest with you, I believe that the Holy Ghost was beginning to call me back from the edge of a very real, enchanting abyss of personal misery.

Josiah, my brand-new best friend from school, went to a mild Pentecostal church in north Stockton, so I began to attend said church with him at this time; just being there felt like cleansing fire to my entire person. Daylight to my darkness. Oxygen to my carbon dioxide.

Pentecostals, as the stereotype goes, are known for their shaking and lurching all over the church floor. But this church didn't do that kind of stuff. I wouldn't have gone if they had. I was much keener on attending a delicious Pentecostal church potluck held in the gymnasium than a spiritual vomiting session outlined in the bulletin. I really liked going to Josiah's church. It felt responsible. It felt clean like fresh snowfall on an alpine meadow.

Surprisingly enough, the renaissance of baseball in my life felt responsible and clean also. Around the age of 15 I began getting back into baseball full throttle, and adamantly forsaking and disowning the two darkest of the three evil triumvirates: the chix and flix. I threw out all of my magazines and movies, to the great joy of my mother. I remember ceremoniously walking them out to the Dumpster on trash day whilst she watched through the kitchen window, her hands on her hips, nodding her head with quiet joy in her heart. The victory was won, for now. Baseball and Jesus had swept the series.

Tallene loved baseball. It was totally healthy. She loved "healthy" things concerning her two sons. Therefore, she urged me to purchase more and more baseball stuff: big glossy posters, sharp cleats, cool white leather and Velcro batting gloves, and an expensive wool Oakland A's hat, my favorite team. The bash brothers: McGuire and Canseco. I loved the paternal attention. I was starving for it. And I sported myself out responsibly.

However, I held on to the third triumvirate of evil, heavy metal, because it increased my strength for pitching and swinging the bat. It's a fact, Jack: certain choice heavy-metal records actually help a person hit the ball harder! Thus, the fence got closer and closer each time I stepped to the plate, due *solely* to James Hetfield chugging on a monster riff through my portable boom box! It's a known fact that metal and baseball go hand in hand. Said boom box (loaded with huge Energizers; all six hundred of them) was as much of a necessity on the ball field as gloves, bats, or balls. Josiah and I positioned it perfectly every time, putting an extra, crappy blue baseball mitt under it so that it would be propped up to give us perfectly aimed and sonorously righteous metal. We'd usually listen to one of my "Best of Metal" Memorex recorded tapes: chrome bias, professional tone, because I was *in the know* about recording.

(I'd squeeze the ball hard and dig my nails into the white leather as Kirk Hammet dug his foot into the whah petal. Bad-ass felicity.)

It was perpetually sunny out on that public Stockton ball field; the grass was green, trim, and fragrant. The air was bright and delicious, but all the happy ball fields in the world couldn't prepare me for what happened next Mom started having an affair with Josiah's super Pentecostal dad.

Amon was his name. Josiah was a nicer-than-nice kid, really. The kid in a movie that everybody loves and pulls for, a golden heart with a big smile and beautiful Reebok Air Pumps: a hot new item back then, which made him extremely cool. This salient combination of niceness and coolness was quite rare in the early teen years. You were either a nice nerd or a cool asshole, depending upon many sociological factors.

Josiah and I instantly hit it off, due to the fact that we had the exact same purple Ferrari Testarossa Trapper Keeper. Plus: he loved Iron Maiden and the Oakland A's. We'd spend hours at his house (no fosters) leafing through our baseball cards and looking up Beckett prices whilst Maiden wailed out of his brand-new Sony boom box that was flaming red and looked like a cube.

His parents had money. Hence the Pumps and the big Sony boom box. Josiah also had a Nintendo.

We played Double Dragon like there was no tomorrow, especially if I spent the night. We'd punch and kick 8-bit bad guys in cut off jean vests until the sun came up. Then we'd wolf down an entire box of Lucky Charms, supreme bad-ass felicity.

Josiah was a great friend, even though I was entirely suspicious of his dad's intent concerning my mother. I had very real images of them in my head: rolling around in the sack, giggling and shushing one another. Yes, the years had not been all that good to me, but they had taught me to be alert and suspicious of adults. And I was. And I was correct in my suspicions: they were rolling around in the sheets like sexy steamrollers. This illicitly illustrious affair lasted from 1989-91—a nice workout plan for both Tallene and Amon amidst the end of the get-fit eighties! Leg warmers, head bands, and hand cuffs.

It went down like this: My mom's bank account was in a state of perpetual wobble, but Charles Dickens Hall was sending enough $$$ to keep us fed and warm. However, we had absolutely no extra money to fix the car or the plumbing or, in this here exact case: repaint the house. And it needed repainting. The 1960s paint over the slats had begun chipping and peeling off. Flecks of it, yellow-white and moldy, could be seen peppered across the front and back yard. Quite embarrassing.

This simply wouldn't do because Tallene needed to keep us up with the (other) Joneses on either side of our house and across the street—especially that professor guy with his sumptuous Volvo. The Oxford circle was no laughing matter. They already knew we housed foster kids, but Tallene wanted the neighbors to know that it was only because we were three little Mother Theresas—not because we were poor folk who scored a lucky house where they didn't belong.

"M u s t p a I n t h o u s e…and *fast*," hummed Tallene's cerebral social text.

Because my mom was my mom, and Josiah was my new friend she eventually met him and got to know him. And then she met his dad, Amon, due to their coterminous lives as parents of a pair of good friends. Amon dropped me off at home on weekend afternoons after Double Dragon or church. He was a good guy that way. He was handsome, a former police officer, and a good Christian. She concluded that such a stand-up guy had irrefutable experience wielding a paintbrush. He was also handsome. He probably wouldn't mind coming over for a weekend and painting up the old house for a few extra bucks as the boys leafed through Josiah's new Upper Deck set: the first one: 1989: Ken Griffey Rookie card in a plastic sheath. He was also quite handsome. It wouldn't take him any time at all to paint the place white, get a good workout in the hot sun, and water the seed of good friend relations. Sexual coupling is also a great relationship builder.

He sure was handsome. I don't know what Mom saw in Amon. He looked like Abe Lincoln in the 1850s, before the beard, before the stovepipe hat, before the Emancipation Proclamation. Abe Lincoln was not a hottie, that is, unless honesty turns you on. Actually, perhaps that *is* what turned her on: Amon's honest look and upright stature—being an absolute opposite foil of the great white shenanigan Caleb. Her old Oklahoma, Pentecostal family roots crept up and grabbed her! They whispered to her, "Go on and get him, honey!" And that's exactly what she did. Like a sooner racing after land: wheels of the bumpy schooner almost coming right off as the prairie dog holes pop at the under carriage! Honest Abe didn't stand a chance. Though ailing, Tallene was still very hot-blooded and slightly gap-toothed at the time—like the old Wife of Bath.

Amon came over and painted our house for an honest fee. And painting made him thirsty. Tallene brought him a simple glass of lemonade. The catalyst for all clandestine activity. It was a hot July afternoon. Stockton sizzlin', white paint dryin' all too fast. Honest Amon's brow all sweaty. He was hot. He needed refreshment.

He was workin' hard paintin' the old Oxford Circle house for Ms. Jones, "That benevolent, compassionate lady who takes in orphans and gives them a second chance at life. Heck, maybe I'll invite Ms. Jones to my church down on Ponderosa way. Yeah. That'd be nice. Christians cominglin' with Christians. Fellowship." Intercourse. "Yes. That'd be very nice." And—she was a redhead. He loved redheads. His wife was a blonde; he was tired of blonde. He was ready for something different, something dirty.

Okay, stop! Honest Amon most likely did not have these exact thoughts, these salacious plans. He probably only wanted to make a bit of cash doing some honest work (even though he really didn't need it) and help out his son's friend's mom. After that, he was only looking to retire to his peaceful home after gulping down some deliciously cool, crisp Country Time Lemonade…with ice cubes all jingly-happy.

He was a good charismatic Christian. He couldn't have had premeditated infidelity thoughts. But: I will never know if he really did or didn't. That's locked in the past forever. And it's so damn frustrating. The only thing I can be sure of is that my mother went after him like he was pure Illinois custard pie. She told me so later in life. "I trapped that man; he didn't have a chance," she'd regretfully lament.

What I want to know is why he didn't run like Joseph from Potiphar's wife. Were his legs damaged in some way?

After a few weeks of them completely knowing each other I became suspicious. I recognized certain voice inflections and nervous behaviors in both of them at key moments. I had recognized stuff like this before with Caleb. It was well learned and easily distinguishable to my trained senses. Mom had a blush that would pop up on her face unannounced whenever Amon was even spoken of. She also had a new, saucy minx-ish skip in her step. Steamrollers.

One day I couldn't bottle it up any longer: I flat out told Josiah what they were doing; he didn't believe me at all, though I presented my case, I thought, rather soundly. He said I was a bastard and that I just wanted his family to be shattered and poor like mine. His dad once taught him the quaint aphorism, "Misery loves company." He told me that this was the truth of the matter.

(Whatever, dude.)

It was obvious to me, wise sage that I was at fourteen, that Josiah was still just a kid, and I was a copious adult. Plainly he was not yet in tune with the dark side of life. No empirical rain cloud data in his pure, puppy dog brain. Still, he didn't have to be such a dick about it.

His mom and dad were "both to blame for his total *ignorance*," (a new word I'd learned in my first-period English class) I thought to myself as we sat there in his quiet room, once again leafing through baseball cards and being quite annoyed with one another's presence.

His mom didn't seem to know about the affair. She was very blonde (big hair; big bangs; loads of hair-net hairspray; loads of gold jewelry; loads of makeup; loads of female ostentation) and wore copious amounts of cheap, drug store perfume (Navy/Vanilla Fields). She really bought into and personally symbolized the whole Trinity Network: big money, big church, big bullshit prosperity preaching bullshit. She was a real "Christian" show off, reeking of mendacity and pious selfishness. She really made Christianity look stupid, the same way beer sloshing frat parties make brilliantly beautiful universities stupid. Poor God. Poor Professors.

Amon wasn't quite as show pony as she. He was less Tammy Faye, more—um, well, I'll come back again to Abe Lincoln: laconic, taciturn, noble? No, not really—he was doing my mother, after all.

I'll never understand how he and that bombastic, perfumed poodle ever got married. They seemed to agitate each other with subtle, pointed words (without fail) every time I was over. They weren't happily married. Poor Josiah was left to his expensive baseball cards, top-of-the-line Huffy mountain bike, rat-tail, and gold chain crucifix.

After the affair fizzled out in 1991 Abe and blondie remained married, as if nothing had ever happened. They never split up; the couple that prays together stays together.... *(Though I strongly doubt they ever truly prayed together a day in their life.)* I don't know if she ever found out, Abe was so darn quiet. Like a church ninja.

One very peculiar night Josiah told me something about his dad that I've never forgotten. We were at their house, completely alone, enjoying delicious banana splits, and thoroughly watching game six of the Battle of the Bay World Series in '89. "Why's your dad so quiet all the time?" asked I.

"Mm-im-mmm, I don't know," mumbled Josiah, a mouthful of chocolate-bleeding vanilla ice cream (Breyer's).

"Hmmm," said I.

Then there was a contented silence as we watched Mark McGuire stretch and scratch his cupped nuts before stepping up to the plate. I suddenly got the feeling that Josiah was going to tell me something juicy about his pop. His spoon had stopped in his bowl. He was staring at the carpet in front of him, not the TV.

The affair was in full swing: Tallene and Amon were hitting grand slams approximately thrice a week between the sheets. One horrible time I actually heard my mother scream out in thunderous pleasure. (She didn't know I'd run home to make a cassette copy of Metallica's "Ride the Lightning" for Brett). I instantly grimaced my face into a shocked frown, listened for a second through the wall, heard heavy breathing and the word, "Uh huh," and then felt rather sick to my stomach because my mom was getting nailed by a dead president. I quickly eschewed any recording ideas and silently made my exit. I still don't know where all the fosters were to this day; my mother was very good at planning genital trysts at perfectly secret times.

"My dad used to be a cop," he blurted out.

"NO WAY!" I exclaimed, dropping my spoon into the gushy Breyer's.

"Yeah, he was with the Lodi Police force five years ago," he muttered, squishing the strawberry ice cream area into the vanilla ice cream area, which bugged me.

Mark McGuire hit a double, then scratched his prodigious nuts on second base in front of ten million viewers. To relieve stress, the pitcher scratched his nervous nuts, then the camera panned over to a shirtless, obese male super fan with a giant orange "SF" painted on his breasts; he was eating salty hot nuts in a white and red striped bag. The whole world was nuts at this moment in time. (Somewhere, far away, a brindle-colored great dane's nuts were subtly gargantuan at that very moment in time.)

I glanced again at Josiah's ice cream—he was eating it sloppily—chocolate sauce and caramel swirled around all crazy, and the vanilla was losing its creamy-white pallor—and wouldn't you know it: there were nuts all over his ice cream. Big nuts, like McGuire's.

"How come he isn't a cop anymore?" I questioned, feeling hip because I used the word cop instead of policeman.

"I'm not supposed to never tell anybody else this, 'cuz my mom is serious about it. My dad doesn't ever talk about it these days, but I'll tell you, 'cuz you're my best friend, and you've earned it. *But:* you can't tell a soul! 'Kay?" declared/asked/whispered Josiah, retiring his well worked spoon into the drizzle of motley cream left in his bowl. (*He didn't even finish it all!* How disconcerting. I almost pointed to his bowl and said, "Aren't you gonna finish that? My family's poor; we always finish what we eat and are very thankful for it. You should finish it…all of it," but I didn't. I tried really hard to ignore his damn ice cream bowl and listen to his story—A.D.D. lights were flashing red in my head.)

"He stole evidence," whispered Josiah, looking me straight in the eye as if he had just said, "He murdered a baby girl in her cradle with a Rambo knife." I didn't really know what stealing evidence meant, so I just went ahead and asked him. He was my best friend; he'd never mock me for ignorance.

"He stole drugs that they got off some greasy spic in Manteca. They were holding it as evidence—drug evidence, and my dad stole it 'cuz he wanted to try it out," confessed Josiah, now looking down at his grubby-cold ice-cream hands. (He'd been the one that dished out the ice cream, therefore his hands were still grubby and gross—I didn't want him to touch me and had stayed at a nice three-foot distance from his sticky mitts.)

"He wanted to try it out? Was it marijuana or cocaine?" I asked, using the only drug words I knew at the time.

"It was pot," he said.

"Oh," I said. I didn't know that pot was the same thing as marijuana; I don't think he did either. When I heard the word I visualized purple crystals glowing like sin in a ceramic bowl, emitting a ripe smoke and foul smell that could turn you instantaneously into Charles Manson. Helter Skelter.

"Why'd he want to try it?" I asked.

Then Josiah used one of his sententious dad aphorisms again. "Curiosity killed the cat."

"Yeah, I guess so. So he got busted then?" I asked more and more.

"Yeah, he was fired from the Lodi police force and was dishonored or something; he'd never even tried drugs before, and he told me he didn't even try the pot, either—just kept it in his closet and began to feel bad about it." He began defending honest Abe. "He told me God convicted him to change his ways and confess, so he did, and my mom stuck by him and helped him."

"Wow," I murmured.

McGuire rounded third and scored on a hard hit line drive from Terry Steinbach. We both said, "YES!" and raised our hands. Then I became immediately fraught with worry that he'd want to high-five me with his grubby, ice-cream hand, but he didn't. Bullet dodged.

And that's all that was said about Honest Amon.

Josiah and I watched the rest of the game and my mother arrived to pick me up halfway through the ninth inning. She wasn't the only one who arrived. She arrived with a new foster named Dolores. Dolores made me nervous. Dolores was incredibly cute. I blushed and tried not to gape at her with my awkward baseball eyes.

Mom introduced us to Dolores, telling us that she was only a year older than we were, and beseeching me to hurry up so we could leave. She slurred a couple words. I think she was afraid Blondie might be home.

Awkward moment in time indeed: Infidelity—World Series—Dolores. 1989 was quickly becoming 1990. I was to be of driving age soon. I had shaved designs in my hair. I could read my mom like an open book. I loved loud music. I had seen lots of naked women and knew how their privates looked naked. I was in high school now.

I looked with quick disdain at Josiah's sticky, ice-cream hands and suddenly didn't give a damn about anything. I especially didn't give a damn that mom was cheating on Sam and me. She could do whatever the hell, no, "whatever the fuck she wants." I enjoyed utilizing the F word in my private thoughts.

Canseco stepped up to the plate.

# Chapter 8
# Girls and Guitars Like Daily Bread
# (B) Dolores: Trick and Trash

Now we've arrived at another problem: namely Dolores. More than any other foster, she was a very bad influence on me. Very Bad, with capital letters. Otis and Stevo and the nameless other vagrant ephemera that moved through our house like smelly ghosts each affected me in tints of gray and black, but Ms. Dolores affected me in tints of *red*.

She taught me all about sex. She taught me all about what she believed were the ins and outs of sexy sex, but really she didn't know much. Who does at the Trojan-engrossed age of sixteen? Not a one, but I didn't know she didn't know. I thought she was omniscient.

She was deadly, immediate, powerful. Carnal. She was Lolita. (I suppose that makes me a very young Humbert Humbert, for I was the enchanted hunter, forsooth.) Dolores was sixteen years old, had short blonde hair, cut in a sort of bob-looking shape, but grown out of its original proportions into an odd looking helmet; it resembled a sloppy version of Mary Lou Retton's hairdo in the '84 Olympics. So hot.

She stood entirely luscious at five foot five and was eternally ensconced in her beloved baby-blue denim: acid-washed and knock off in nature. She also loved Hypercolor tee shirts. (If you were young in the late '80s, then you will distinctly remember these bright tie-dye shirts that changed colors awkwardly when your body temperature rose—so that the armpits were always a different, lighter color than the rest of the shirt.)

Dolores was your stereotypical teen girl: giddy, vapid, and concerned more with her face and hair than starving children in Africa. Unfortunately she was also oversexed. Yes, even at sixteen—Dolores was oversexed; her boyfriend and she were virile bunnies, rife with both irresponsibility and a genitallyobsessive compulsion. Pop culture, of course, didn't help: sexy sex *all over* the tube, pop music hits (Bobby Brown rubbing warm lotion all over his bootyliscious, dancin' hoes—his jolly prerogative).

I don't think Dolores was quite right in the head. I think her father sexually abused her before Charles Dickens scooped her up into his white-feathered arms. Of course, she never mentioned being abused to Sam or me, so I have no proof. I don't think she ever told Mom anything of the sort, but I'll bet a thousand hard earned dollars that she was abused. Thus the very real and very scary problems. Indelible scarlet implications. She was confused. She was chatty. She was daring.

I, on the other hand, was not daring, so she shook me up good. The first thing that set my mind upon her like a crow upon a shiny object was the fact that she was very cute. (It's strange to me now that teens used the word "cute" back then to describe somebody's attractive qualities.) Even her bob haircut was cute. Not to mention her playful, precocious smile: all those little white teeth in a straight row.

*It's a good thing Caleb never actually met Dolores. (He totally disappeared during this time; probably runnin' from the law because he swiped a quart of straight thirty-weight oil from the local auto shop, and old Jethro behind the counter saw him do it: Run, Caleb! Run into the arms of some poor, blind woman.) Yes, it's a good thing indeed, because if he ever actually did meet her—methinks he would've tried to seduce her; Dolores for sure would've snuck out with him: fishing, perhaps, and giggled 'til dawn like all good neophytical, nympho-maniacal girls do; Caleb would've ended up in prison [Finally—he'd be the one with black eyes], and Dolores would've ended up heavy with Delta child. Textbook depravity rife with 1,000,000-ton sorrow.)*

I was supremely attracted to her. I could *not* get her out of my mind during those first few weeks and would often track her movements throughout the house, trying as best as possible to naturally end up in the same room as her. The television set became my best friend and ally at this time. Dolores loved TV.

I remember the first week she lived with us I couldn't picture her face properly in my head when I was alone so I began the mental exercise of naturally blending it with Kathy Ireland's face. Kathy Ireland was big at this time. Her swimsuit photos for *Sports Illustrated* ruled the visual male world.

This "epic" visualizing of Dolores' visage was quite silly of me. She didn't look like Kathy Ireland. Not in the least. Her face wasn't as round, her curves weren't so mature and womanly, and she was rather run-of-the-mill looking: like me and everybody else in Stockton.

Despite this, and although she wasn't a *Sports Illustrated* swimsuit model, I took my visual lionizing of her a step further: imagining her sexily supine on some white sandy beach with radiant turquoise waters lapping at the shore, the sun tickling her body with a heat salacious shine, the intoxicating smell of Hawaiian Tropics lotion wafting off of her golden skin—baking and sexing the air with possibilities. Her bikini was always red, and Metallica was always on a nearby jet-engined house boat (live!) playing their hit single, "One," through massive, water-proof, hot pink Peavey mains, mounted atop the houseboat roof. Ah, what a sweet dream—and I was the official spray-her-down-and-get-her-a-Corona guy—paid to please her and her alone.

Later on, in the moonlit jungle, she would thank me kindly for my unflagging devotion with ivy kisses and gracefully remove her red bikini slowly like it was made of rose glass. Then we'd—well, you know—ending with cigarettes and cold Vodka, her softly salty fingers stroking the duck wisps of my mullet as the sun painted the bedewed foliage with warm sexuality once more. (Oh, how nerdy school boys are. Men are nerdy too. Our minds continue to intermittently spin out such inane fantasies 'til the day we die; we just quit telling anybody about such things—around the sensible age of twenty-four. [Unless you're Caleb. Then you stop talking at age eighty 'cuz you're "hella honest," and "a straight, no bullshit" shooter]).

So, Dolores. Yes. She was my real life fantasy—before me everyday in the flesh. Nubile, rose-scented flesh. I was in trouble.

Nabokov tried to warn me about both her and my own self, but I wasn't reading quintessential 20th century novels at this time.

I was extremely happy that Dolores didn't attend a real high school (like mine). I didn't have to undergo the immense pain and pressure of seeing guys who were *more* heavy metal than I hitting on her or perhaps French kissing her in the cafeteria right in front of me. No. Her life was all under control. She went to some independent school where the boys were kept secretly/separately contained from the girls because all of the rebel kids there were wont to perform sex at the drop of a hat—or pants—or even if a pencil happened to slide off a desk during Algebra class. The teachers had grown tired of pulling

## PUSH MY LIFE INTO A DUFFLE BAG

the in-perpetual-heat teenagers off and out from one another. So, they were strictly separated: all the time.

But to my disconsolate chagrin, this did not keep the nymphet Dolores from arriving at our foster home without a previously installed boyfriend. Dammit. I hated him. I hated him a lot. A whole lot. He was eighteen and scary. He was six foot four and had a scraggly beard that looked like pubic hair on his greasy face. His name was Razor, believe it or not.

I never found out his real name. He had artfully fooled everyone into thinking it was his birth-certificate name—and so everyone I knew called him Razor without batting an eye. Dumb. So dumb they all were. Where did he get off thinking he could name himself something like "Razor"? His ego must have certainly been razor sharp; I think Razor was a name that gave him special powers and made him capable of stealing Twinkies and Swisher Sweets from every 7-Eleven in the valley. But I thought it just made him a jerk. Should I start telling everybody to call me Cougar Magnum or SR-71 or MC Porsche?

I thought not. I was *not that* pretentious. I was just who I was—take it or leave it. No bullshit.

Despite my mature logic, Dolores loved his name. She should've gone ahead and named herself Blade; then they could've robbed the Bank of Stockton with only switchblades in their hands and audacity in their blood.

She really thought he was the shit. And he really liked to have sex with her, so they remained coupled for almost the entire duration that she stayed with us at Regent Street, about one year: '89-'90. Mom was too busy with Abe Lincoln to notice all of the sex Dolores was having—even when it was performed in our own Christian home at 4 p.m.! I wish she would have woken up to the matter and really threatened Dolores with, "You'll be outta here, missy, if you don't knock off the knockin' boots with that pseudonym pig ne'r-do-well!" She could've at least given her a box of condoms. But she didn't. She just turned a blind eye and went shopping at K-Mart whenever Razor was over.

All the while, Sam and I were becoming anthropomorphic, inquisitive puppies, boarded at some breeding kennel: we salivated, sniffed, and wondered at all the pheromones in the air, vexed like the innocents we were.

Sam wasn't turned on by Dolores. He was ten. So really in all honesty I was the only inquisitive puppy sniffing the air. He was too busy sniffing the air for a Frisbee or a Nerf football—one of those killer black and hot pink ones with

153

finger grooves and turbo action; I was way too old for them, but still thought they were hot. I even tossed one back and forth with him a few times in the front yard like a good older brother—mostly at dusk so I could just maybe be outside at the perfect time to swiftly and surreptitiously see Dolores disrobing through her bedroom window that faced the yard, me, and all kingdom come, much to her amusement: she was a spicy little exhibitionist.

Many times Sam would think I was grinning because he was throwing such good Joe Montana spirals, but no, it was because Dolores was partially displaying herself in a red bra behind a very thin, single-pane window. And although there was a good amount of curtain in that window, and although she feigned to see me not, she knew, oh goodness did she know, that I was watching.

She loved to tease me. She'd show a little skin here and there, but never anything particularly and distinctly pertaining only to the female sex. The football would continue its rhythmic flight back and forth between us in the dusk light. Ofttimes I'd miss Sam by a good eight feet, and he'd have to sprint like a jackrabbit to catch it just in the nick time. I'd get pretty befuddled out on the spacious front lawn, feeling a nervous rush of blood coursing through my body.

And then, every damned time, Dolorous would walk over to the window and abruptly pull down the faded window shade thingy with a flash of tummy and a final (quick as a wink) red-panty display. Painful though it was, it still qualified in my book as bad-ass felicity. Dolores in her undergarments was pretty heavy metal.

I'd continue playing catch with dorky kiddy Sam for only twenty seconds more after the window shade went down. The show was over; therefore, my brotherly playtime was over. This was my recurrent pretext. "Okay. Sam, I'm pooped. I'm getting a Pepsi; I think *MacGyver* is about on, so, we're done," I'd mutter, staunchly holding on to the Nerf football so that he got the point. "Awww, c'mon—just five more minutes. You promised yesterday that we'd play longer today. It's not even dark yet!" he'd whine and whine and whine, like a smelly suckling shoat.

How annoying. Why couldn't he just throw the damn football with his ghost buddies? They could indeed come out to play now that it was dark out.

I wonder what Sam would have replied if I'd just been honest with him and said, "Look, no more tits, no more toss!" His golden, Caleb-posterity cowlick would've stood straight up like static, I'm sure. Then again, I don't think he knew what "tit" meant. He was quite the innocent ten-year-old despite my pin-up proclivities. Maybe those ghosts kept him pure by taking away his attention with shimmering, silvery ghost stories about willow trees and dead horses, spectral sonnets and the like. I wish they'd have thrown the football with him a few times instead.

Thinking back, Sam might have been a ghost himself. He definitely was vaporous enough. No more than a child breeze. Casper. The friendly shoat.

As the months wore on with Dolores living in our house the red just got redder: apples, tomatoes, and fire trucks. And crappy Razor began showing off, especially at night when we were all watching the tube because we were lazy American teens with no extra X-quotient to do anything productive.

One particular night he (quickly) licked the side of Dolores' apricot face whilst she was preoccupied with MacGyver leaping from an exploding pick up truck. She chortled like a parakeet and wiped her face, never removing her eyes from the screen. I pretended I hadn't noticed.

Five minutes later he did the same thing, achieving much the same results. I pretended again not to notice—I was too busy staring at Angela as she dropped a paperweight on Tony's Italian foot on *Who's the Boss?* But *dammit* I *had* seen him *licking* and *sullying* her Noxzema-clean cheeks!

Then he did it again. And again. Slower this time. He looked over at me, picked up the couch pillow nearest him and threw it at me, saying, "Hey, metal-head," his apt name for me. "LOOK!"

I looked.

Dammit: he licked her face once more (a big lick, like a Saint Bernard) and she giggled away, scrunching her angel eyes closed. He winked at me, immediately grabbing one of her boobs, which, thank God, she didn't permit in front of me, Sam, Otis, or the public at large. She pushed his paw away, declaring, "NOT NOW, Raze!" Not now. That meant that later he could.

I bubbled with hot lava jealousy and turned my attention toward Alyssa Milano, who had a black eye in this episode, but was still hotter than lasagna, a juicy school-victim vixen.

This repeated action (fooling around/grabbing of each other to show off) was a common thing in our foster home with little Bonny and Clyde. Even Sam was used to it by now; first he was frightened by it and would look down at his sneakers followed regularly by a question to me about what my favorite Bon Jovi song was or how many bases Rickey Henderson had stolen this year...*again*. He already knew these answers. He was just ten years old and extremely uncomfortable. Who could blame him? Even the ghosts hid betwixt the sheet rock in the walls whenever Dolores and Razor decided to be sexy.

After a few months of said crap, I became a lot less interested in Dolores. I was sick of her teasing. I, of all people, was jaded and bored with my real-life Kathy Ireland. I retreated to the safe controllability of my *Sports Illustrated* girls, with whom I got more action; especially with Rachel Hunter, who was currently way out on Mexico's Pacific coast getting her pictures taken by lucky sporty people who would *never* fully appreciate her as much as I, in fact, did.

Dolores. What a gal. She came to our house and teased me from October to May. She teased like the truest teaser defined and then hyperbolized with sugar on top. She once put her hand over my crotch in the kitchen and asked, "Nervous?"

My voice cracked as I looked down and answered, "I don't care...doesn't bother me." My voice cracked on the word "me," and she started to chuckle. I was trying so hard to be cool, thought the line was pretty suave, but when my voice cracked it all went to hell. My face began sweating profusely, especially up around my hairline, and I couldn't get enough little amounts of close kitchen air to stabilize my man courage.

She then proceeded to look me hard right in the eye and, while pushing her body against mine, snapped at the air right in front of my face with an animalistic jaw movement. It was the hottest thing that had ever happened to me. My heart broke the sound barrier. I still remember it to this very day, at my computer, with vivid clarity. Right after snapping at me and pushing at my body, she smirked and unceremoniously left the kitchen, leaving me in a dreamy stupor. I watched her walk out, staring at her twain-golden-biscuits butt as it slinked out of the kitchen. I imagined her gently smacking it a few times. Juicy.

By the time it was May, the crappiest guy in our galaxy, Razor, confessed to Dolores that he hated Stockton and would be moving to his dad's home in Yuba City. She was crushed, as crushed as a crawdad in heat under the tire of a young boy's chrome bike on a hot asphalt walkway by the dried up creek bed at mid-day in mid-July. Crushed!

(Crushed, but free, and not at all pregnant. I can't to this day believe that she somehow did not become "with child" during the time Razor was frequenting her establishment. They rarely used protection, only a condom now and again. [I know this because I saw used ones lying around the house in awkward locations: in the big jungle plant by the TV and behind the toilet paper stack in the bathroom cabinet.] Seeing these irrefutable articles of venery convinced me that they were doing it at an absurd frequency: rabbits being electrocuted.)

With Razor gone Dolores realized she desperately needed to get over his absence and assert herself elsewhere and with good speed lest she become bored. So she did. And not with Stevo and Otis. They were gross to her, common fare. She preferred more unique targets.

One fine early June afternoon, Dolores trapped me in the kitchen and told me a bunch of stuff (in blatant detail) that she and Razor were fond of doing. Just out of nowhere! She just sauntered in, stared deep into my eyes, and began chatting away about things she knew would alert me. She knew I would give her my complete attention for as long as she wanted.

Nobody else was home. Mom was at the Gettysburg address. Sam was at little league. The other fosters were making Molotov cocktails downtown. All I could hear was the buzzing of the air conditioning unit out my window and the red words tumbling off Dolores little lithe tongue. Words about stuff. Stuff she and Razor did all the time for both exercise and leisure. Dirty stuff. Stuff that I could barely believe because I was still ignorant and gun shy, though I pretended not to be. She saw right through me. She knew I'd done nothing sexual in my life save masturbation and was a virgin. (For some reason in the eighties and early nineties this word was used pejoratively in many pop culture teen movies) I instantaneously blushed at the very utterance of the word, indicating that I was, in fact, a real live virgin: chaste like a dewy daffodil on a fresh June morn.

So she kept talking. And I leaned gingerly against the counter, listening as if my life depended on it. She told me of their favorite positions. She was very descriptive, gesticulating smoothly, her eyes afire like she was speaking of the methods she took to murder somebody. I couldn't take it. Really. I was about to have a heart attack. I had to interrupt her, just to slow the planet down a bit.

So I blurted out an important question concerning her current topic entitled, Why I like whipping cream. "Do you RREEAALLYY do that?" my face quivering with shock and awe.

She turned away foxily and got herself an ice cold Pepsi from the ice cold fridge. "Yep," she uttered. The word floated out of her mouth and hit the floor slowly, sexily, like a dewy daffodil falling into a quiet fire.

"Wow," I said, furtively glancing at her jean pocket buttocks whilst she poured the Pepsi into a glass with ice—a thing that she regularly did; she always-always-always had to waste a good clean glass just so her soda could be, like three degrees cooler. That was sooo like her: cool and not caring what anybody else thought. Her way or the highway.

I could smell her Debbie Gibson Electric Youth perfume. It filled the air with swimsuit possibilities. I was certain I wanted her. I was a shaking, vibrating dachshund, a veritable horndog, a healthy American boy, more turned on than all the TVs in the land. But there was a problem: I was actually, physically shaking, vibrating, and trembling like a boy scout who has turned a corner on a trail and happened upon a grizzly bear, munching berries profusely. My right hip began trembling with nervous energy. Then my left. Then my entire body. Embarrassment flooded my heart and my chubby face blushed like a rose.

Dolores turned and looked at me. She could tell she'd bewitched me good. And she proceeded to push it a little further.

She laughed at me and said, "Are you okay?" as some Pepsi spilled down her chin and dribbled upon her light pink top (Jimmie Z surf shirt) leaving a sugary wet spot on her chest.

"Totally," I declared, steadying my voice. I tossed her a dishtowel. It hit her in the forehead.

We both chuckled.

(I was trying very hard to secretly gain control over my quivering muscles. I hoped to high heaven that my sports deodorant was working…or else I was for sure a smelly hog by now.)

Dolores looked down at the sugary spot and wiped at it slowly, but couldn't quite sponge all the brown cola color out. I considered going over and dampening the towel so I could apply my hands to her chest under the guise of helping her, but wussed out. She probably would have liked the ballsy attention.

The moment passed. I stayed by in my corner, stuck to the counter. I scratched at my shoulder. Time began creeping hot and glorious.

"I have *videos*, you know," she stated. (She appeared to be suddenly drunk, like a salty wench sailor under a lunacy moon of enchanting light. Her body swayed a little like a big ship on the sea.)

"Like…mmovies—of…TVVee?" I mumbled dumbly.

"No, not TV…better. Home movies of *me* in my bra and panties, and then the bra and panties go away, and it's just me: Dolores the movie star." She swayed. She was shooting for my full and complete attention. Her aim was dead center. Her eyes fixed on mine and smoldered with hell flame.

My heart squeezed through my throat, up through my sinuses, and finally squished into my skull with my brain—where they jostled for position to stare out my eyeballs at the female fire that was unfolding before us. We were missing only popcorn.)

"You're *naked* in it…in the home movies?" I croaked.

She nodded, scratching her warm thighs.

I looked down at her thighs and then quickly back up to her eyes. Her short blonde hair was beginning to smoke.

"Really? NAKED?" I was hopelessly lost and stalling for time. I didn't know how to progress the conversation into something tangibly steamy.

"Yeah, really. What? You don't believe me?"

When she said this I knew I had achieved a foothold. I wasn't so hopeless after all. I grabbed at the logically perfect answer to this. "No, no…you're probably not *fully* naked; you're lying. There probably isn't any home movie, either."

I put my hands on my quaking hips, defiant, and then the practically vexing thought occurred to me that Dolores didn't own a video camera—did Razor have one at his, um, where did he live, anyway? On the other side of the tracks, for sure. Then it hit me like a ton of hot bricks: MY CAMERA. I had received it as an exorbitant gift from my MasterCard mother on my 15th birthday. It was a gray Sony camcorder: the old type where you put an actual VHS tape directly into the side of the camera and shoot away: squealing kids in the pool, a wild moose at Yellowstone, your sister's wedding vows, Razor and Dolores Greek wrestling, burning calories.

My camera, of course. She must have been good about sneaking it because I hadn't noticed, and I usually noticed any and all small, subtle changes if said changes pertained to the usage of my personal stuff. I was a jealous owner of things—especially my expensive Sony camcorder.

"I'm not lying!" She was becoming feisty like an over-stimulated cat. "We used *your* camera, so there! And you never even knew it, cuz Razor is a ninja at swiping stuff!" she declared, grinning victoriously, glistening, and shaking the air with her sassy voice.

Right then it occurred to me that Razor would be in the videos too. *Damn. Yuck. Of course. That sucks,* said my thoughts to me, continuing with, *He touched my camera! He owes me money. But it's cool. I'll let it slide since Dolores is in the footage.*

"I knew you were using my camera for something; I could tell; it was greasy sometimes and the padding on the microphone was moved around. I could tell. I totally could tell," I lied and lied.

She put her forefinger to her mouth, contemplating me. Neither of us said anything for fifteen seconds, during which time my right hip began trembling again. I tried settling my nerves by looking at her as an equal (sex being) and not as a home video (hot) girl, reminiscent of the chick in all those Aerosmith videos I adored at Josiah's cable house.

It worked. Mildly. My hip simmered down. The kitchen remained warm and quiet for a few more delicious seconds whilst Dolores gulped down the last of her ice-cold Pepsi. It was a sexy Pepsi: all bubble slicks and sugar. The gotta-have-it slogan hadn't been born yet, but it already applied. She set the wet glass down on the counter with a clink.

I ventured to speak in order to keep the movie rolling, "I bet you didn't do it right. The camera's complicated, and you probably filmed the lens cap," I taunted, hoping she would hasten to prove to me that she had indeed done it right.

"We did too do it right. Come look. I'll prove it to you!" she ordered, racing out of the kitchen toward my room, which had a small TV and the only hook up for the camera. Did that mean they'd done it in my room—for convenience—in my bed? If so, I was pretty lucky.

I raced after her into my room. She grabbed the camera and worked it professionally—plugging in all the right things in the right places—a consummate Spielberg of human anatomy!

I was excited. I was absurdly excited. Christmas had never felt this good. Santa was wasting his time with toys and children.

Dolores' hands were moving rapidly, that is, until they suddenly just stopped. The camera was all ready to go. All she had to do was press play and turn on the TV, but instead, she set it down on the carpet, giggled, and ran out of the room. Right out. Just like that.

I watched her disappear through the doorway without any explanation and felt my entire young world instantaneously drop into the flaming tar pits of hellish despair. It was all a big sex joke. I was the butt. A trembling virgin butt. If I would have had a blowtorch right then and there I might have torched my imported door-length Iron Maiden posters. That's how crappy I felt. I gasped for air.

(No sex for me.)

Then, quite suddenly, she was back, quick as a turtle drinking espresso, with a black, heavy VHS tape in her hand. "I forgot the actual tape!" She giggled. (All trees everywhere bloomed as a billion bluebirds sang exuberant songs and flowers and rainbows and comets all exploded into sheer golden rapture!)

I would not have to torch my expensive posters. The world was good again. The open mouth of hell caved in on itself and pink flowers grew overtop it. Dolores popped the video in and took a deep breath—then pushed play. I suddenly realized what I was about to see. (A rocket took off.)

She pushed pause and looked me in the eye with a curvy grin on her Lolita lips. She asked, "You ready to *eat* your words?"

"I still don't believe you. This is going to be *Full House* or something stupid like that, Dolores," I declared, loving the sound of her name, loving the whole damn world of foster kids and all their inherent problems.

She pushed the red play button. We watched. I shook like a wet newborn puppy. She kept commenting on how fat her butt looked. I kept commenting on how it looked "fine," my voice cracking all the while. She stayed a good three feet away from me. I stayed a good three feet away from her. Then I noticed we both were trembling. Both of us together.

Sex was everywhere: flashing on the screen, dripping from the ceiling, burning in our mouths, swirling in our shoes between our socks and toes, slathered on my posters, tangled in our hair, glowing along our ribcages, and splashing around inside our eyeballs. It was beyond surreal and very poisonous to both our hearts and minds.

We kept watching. Five minutes passed. The video was blurry. Then she turned it off and took it out.

"See? I do *do it*, and I do video it!" she asserted. She sounded agitated.

"Fine, you win," I croaked.

We didn't do anything physical that night. We actually avoided each other like the plague. I left the house and walked to the ball field. I sat in the bleachers and watched the sun go down. The sky was orange. The air was warm. All was quiet. I tried to turn off my brain, but it kept flashing images of Dolores' naked body over and over again. I cradled my head in my hands.

In later weeks Dolores teased me again and again about the prospect of watching the tapes again (which we actually did a couple of times—once with

Sam, which I hated, but Dolores insisted that he see her privates too). Sam frowned and kept throwing his dirty baseball into his mitt while he stood there trying his best to contemplate what he was in fact seeing. Then he blurted out, *"This is gross!"* and ran out to the front lawn in order to forget it all by throwing the baseball repeatedly up into the air—really high—and catching it, all slick, like Will Clark. Baseball was his favorite thing in the world at that age. And he focused hard on it in order to shut out Dolores and the other fosters. Thus, he remained an innocent child.

To this day I'm very, very thankful that my little brother Sam wasn't a couple of years older—or he might have forever lost that precious innocence. He might have been videotaped like me.

# Chapter 9
# The Irish Invade
# (A) A Real Swimming Pool!

And now the wicked lasso of time will wrap around us and fling us back into the summer of 1985. No longer are we on the cusp of the '90s, ready for a glorious future, an escape from childhood.

No, no, the lasso has wrapped us up good. The lasso has flung us back. We need to learn a few more things. We need to see more things illuminated. Puzzle pieces if you will. And so the story goes: wicked and honest like a trotting horse. Worry not, there will be familiarity.

In 1985, Sam, Caleb, Mom, and I were all living deep in debt on Regent St. Situation normal: A.F.U. But then, out of nowhere, serendipity smiled upon us: this peculiar family moved in across the street…a fatherless family. I thank the Holy Spirit to this day for this wonderful event. It would drastically change the course of my life in later years. This family was made up of a smart mother and three boys around my age. They were the Finnegans.

At first, the Finnegans lived together as one big happy family in Chico, California, about 200 miles north of Stockton, approximately. I don't remember how long they lived in Chico, but they left there in June of '85. Reason: a month earlier their husband and father, Connor, was killed by a drunk driver along a late sleepy road east of Chico in the piney foothills up near Paradise.

Tragedy. But the Finnegans weren't quitters. They up and moved like lightning. They were determined to survive and later thrive. *Connor would have wanted it this way.* Sinead understood this.

Sinead was now the leader of the clan. She had to be brave. No problem. She was always brave, always hardworking, and always resplendent.

As I got to really know her, I began loving her for this, in a Platonic, respectful way. Deep down inside I began to wish she were *my* mom. I wanted in with the Finnegan clan. Desperately.

Sinead was a real go-getter for her boys. And this helped their post-father bank account considerably. Most families struggle when the "breadwinner" dies, but not the Finnegans. They did okay for themselves.

The Finnegans moved in across the street from us, but actually could have chosen a much bigger house on Regent St. (or any other posh area of Stockton) due to Sinead's gumption and Connor's financial planning. He'd been a prolific accountant and made a good salary—all the kids had Nikes.

I never met Connor. I'm sure I would have liked the man. After all, he had sense enough to marry the Irish Lioness, and oh how I lionized her.

As the story goes, the Finnegans *ended up* on Regent because Sinead was exhausted and just couldn't see any more houses around Stockton, too many realtors hounding her with smiles, shiny business cards, and butter-up cups of coffee. So she chose a quaint bungalow house just off the Oxford Circle, next to me and billions of crazy fosters. It was a fine enough house, red brick and very close to the University of the Pacific, Home of the Fightin' Tigers.

Sinead needed to finish up her degree in the field of pharmaceuticals, so having the U.P. at arms' length was wonderfully perfect. She was in graduate school. I was only ten, but knew that graduate school was something golden, something foreign to all Joneses and Stokeses that ever were, something smart and key to making real money and having leather-bound books—items that I had seen at one of my teacher's houses during a PTA meeting—coveted items that one must earn through diligence and maturity, through proven awesomeness. I was sure that the professor across the street with the tweed jacket and Volvo had leather-bound books; I'll bet he even had Moby Dick! (The smartest book ever, I'd heard.)

Sindead's boys, on the other hand, weren't so foreign to my world; they were neat and normal friends to meet and just plain grow up with: lots of baseball, swimming. They had a freaking *pool* in the backyard. My childish heart swooned with chlorine and barbequed hotdog delight—not to mention billions of bags of Doritos nacho cheese tortilla chips you could eat *while you were IN the pool.* We'd just set the bag on a floating hot pink raft device and eat until our lips were orange with deliciousness! and myriad suburbia Goonies adventures. They were my best friends!

Roll call: Brendan, Carrigan, and Seamus. Brendan was born in 1976, Carrigan in 1978, and Seamus in 1981. When reading those birth dates go ahead and contract them to read like this: '76, '78, and '81; it's way faster.

The coolest thing about the Finnegans' moving in was the practical fact that Brendan and I were the same age. When our moms met each other (paper plate of peanut butter cookies complete with Saran Wrap colliding with ceramic plate of Irish lace cookies) they joyfully clapped metaphorical hands whilst putting us together and acknowledging our common age of ten.

Brendan and I eyed each other suspiciously. He was wearing bright red floral jams like he thought he was in Hawaii or something. But then again, I thought, *He's probably cool 'cuz he's ten, and Mom said he has the big jet transformer guy: the purple and blue one, very expensive.*

I smiled at him. The sun looked down at all of us. A robin began singing in the distance. Then both moms gushed with more and more happiness: our common age meant more leisure time for them. We could entertain each other and hopefully keep each other away from the bad-boy Stockton crowds that were into making out and ruining driveways with their loud, hot-pink-wheeled T & C skateboards. More time for Tallene to worry about her kidney. More time for Sinead to worry about the memory of Connor.

We shook hands at high noon over a well-watered Finnegan lawn. Little Carrigan then approached me silently from the left, wanting to shake my hand, but I declined hastily, changing the subject to the military jet that was crunching the air over our summer pates. (I saw Carrigan earlier intently scratching his bottom. (Poopy, I was sure; he was only seven) as he eyed a fat bumblebee on a dandelion). I didn't want to shake his hand. He was a little dork. He would annoy Brendan and me in later days.

After the jet noise dissipated, I began noticing another boy—behind the screen door. The moms were busy chatting away like pigeons proud of their broods. This other boy was a mere ten feet away from us, pushing his little peach nose into the screen and making gross gurgly noises. He was four. He was Seamus. He was like half retarded/half autistic or something. He was irrefutably weird and in future days would frequently frighten me, because I was perpetually afraid I'd step on him and inadvertently make him wail bloody murder or something. I was nonstop uncomfortable concerning his presence.

He had repetitive, gurgly catch phrases such as, "Bbbooooyyyyssss," that were a studied, retarded mimicry of his mother's raised voice. "BBBOOOOYYYYSSSSS!" he'd holler, his beloved saliva song.

What made matters worse was that Carrigan was incredibly mean to him, continually pushing him over in the grass or in the kitchen, or into (gasp!) the pool, and hollering out a hyperbolized retarded voice when his mom wasn't around, "SSSEEAAAMMUS LLLIIIKKESS BBOOOYYYYSSS and is a FFFAAAAGGGOOOTTT!" Carrigan always had a bit of a potty mouth—even as a youngster towhead. Seamus would inevitably hit the floor again and again and again with a plump thud and, of course, *not* show any sign of pain or anger: rather, he'd gurgle with a mute expression indicative of the private nothing's-working in his power-outage head.

Although kind of retarded, Seamus was a somewhat okay-looking, acceptable four year old, wearing light-brown duck-fluff hair and the tiniest sun-kissed freckles. His eyes were a bit small, though, like little almonds of vacancy.

Unlike Carrigan, Brendan, the eldest brother, was kind and caring to little Forest Gump Seamus, defending him day after day and showing me how to correctly behave around him. Hmmm. Seamus. I haven't thought of him in years. I can see his gurgles. S E A M U S. I can see his gurgles in 3D all around me, juicy and genuine. It's seriously the tenderest name for a little boy with problems. He was lucky to have Brendan as an older brother—Carrigan received many a bruised shoulder for picking on poor oblivious Seamus.

I remember one time we were all changing into our bathing suits in the Finnegans' giant main bathroom (outfitted with black marble sinks) in the summer of '87—getting our fins, fluorescent snorkels, and clear-orange water pistols ready for a good four-hour, raisiny romp in the pool.

Brendan and I at that time were both caught in the eye of a storm named puberty, my body way ahead of his in hair and hormone, but we averted glances and treated each other with gentlemanly dignity whilst changing for the pool.

Carrigan was never allowed to change with us big boys; we'd push his gangly Gollum boy body out the door with threats like, "Perverts can't change in here!" Such threats bounced off him like water. He was way too uppity to feel pain when we ostracized him, the little rock of pride. I don't remember Sam being with us on this particular pool day; he was most likely out with Caleb, cruisin' for chicks at the bars.

Regardless, on this fated day there was a secret third boy in the Finnegan bathroom that we were unaware of: namely: Seamus, who was six now and oft times quiet as the surface of an alpine lake. (Maybe he could see ghosts like Sam.)

Brendan and I stripped down whilst confabulating over just how good Mountain Dew actually was and how it was way better than Coke or Coke

Classic. (It was neon yellow—we were sold) when I suddenly felt a wet hand on my lower thigh—the back side of it—right below my *complete nakedness!*

I jumped up as if an electric eel had licked me and there, to my great surprise and insecure horror was Seamus Gump—*under* the faucet, the wooden cabinet door half swung open—his face protruding out and staring blankly in the direction of my shame—sizing me up it seemed.

Before Brendan or I could berate Seamus and throw him out of the big-boy bathroom he gently reached his soft saliva hand out and closed the cabinet door with all the equanimity of a sleeping kitten in a shaft of sunlight. I was incredibly stressed out at that very moment in time: he'd seen too much of me: entirely *all* of my naked, small nudity. (Really, how much more ridiculous and insecure could I be? I was embarrassed and indeed mad at this little retarded child for "deliberately" seeing me naked when really he was off in his own world, just kind of hanging out under the sink; after all, he had nowhere else to be at that hour. Cartoons were concluded, mid-day grilled cheese and milk consumed, green beans and sloppy joes and bed time story about *Where the Wild Things Are* were hours away from now. Why not be under the black marble sink?)

He wasn't culpable of any crime, and yet I looked at him with lava accusations in my racing heart. *YOU HATE MY BODY, Seamus—JUST SAY SO—YOU THINK MY PENIS IS SMALL AND HAIRLESS!* Utter nonsense: Seamus was only thinking of how he'd just completed a small part of his ultimate childhood goal: which was to slobber on the entire world…one person, toy, puppy, or chair at a time.

Brendan then hurried to my rescue, rushing to the sink and pulling out the enchanted Seamus from his quiet plumbing den. He gurgled and pointed sternly at my chubby hands hiding my penis and testicles. I think I remember Brendan laughing out loud at the oddity of the fiasco. He was pretty mature in mind at this age and could logically find the quaint and subtle humor in simple things. I hastily pulled on my Oakland A's bathing trunks, yellow and green. The whole thing is pretty hilarious in retrospect.

Why was he under there in the first place? Why was his mother in the kitchen mixing up potato salad in a big wooden bowl and not being vigilantly cognizant of his Gumpish whereabouts? Why was I so ashamed of myself, cowering like a nude elephant atop a tiny footstool whilst an oblivious furry mouse scuttles slowly by—running its own important errands?

Maybe Seamus was organizing the Ivory bars under there, stacking them into a clean pyramid: an altar to pure cleanliness; who knows? After all the histrionics, we went on out to the pool. I tried to forget my shame by diving to the bottom and holding my breath.

There were many days spent swimming in that pool, healthy days away from the fosters. (Sinead made no bones about *not* wanting them around her sons. Tallene politely conceded due to the fact that I was getting fed and being a normal American boy), away from the '80s craziness across the street.

Brendan and I helped each other in school—especially math—which he was keenly adroit in, unlike dolt me. I helped him learn all about heavy metal and chix as the years slowly rolled over. It was a good trade off. Pop culture for scholarship. In the end we would all equal the perfect blend of personality adjustment: a beautiful American picnic bowl of chilled potato salad, if you will. Brendan continually adding his brilliantly pointed wit to all things, which seasoned this potato salad with a nice amount of cayenne pepper so that our tastes were toughened, and our tongues matured; Carrigan continually adding…um, I don't know…loud, shiny black olives? Yes, because I could wear him on my fingertips whenever I felt like it or throw him off accordingly. He was unneeded in the salad, in my less than humble opinion; Seamus would be the gurgly mayonnaise, the heart and soul of our picnic lunch. Without his objectively innocent candor, the rest of us (me the potatoes—it's my salad after all, Sinead the sweetest pickles) would be nothing! A potato salad. A live potato salad:

"Hand me a Mountain Dew. I didn't say *throw it*, Carrigan!" I yelled.

"Don't be a baby!" he yelled back.

"Gurgle." Fart. Seamus spilled apple juice.

(Laughter. All of us, including Sinead.)

Seamus loved apple juice over anything else in the world. His hands were eternally sticky because of this. It drove me bonkers.

But of course, it never ever drove Sinead bonkers. Nothing ever did. Her name should have been Patience or Constance. Even her hair was patient and constantly soft in the trendy form of a perm. She was also wise. The glasses she sometimes wore were indicative of this: see-through pastel pink frames with UV protection lenses (she told me thus) that were better for the eyes but very expensive. An ocular investment. Modern and savvy.

That same year, 1987, Sinead concluded her studies at UOP and graduated a fully capable pharmacist: a $$$ ninja, a super healer. She also married that year. The lucky dog was a man by the name of Luke Cromwell. Sinead made the decision that she would keep the Finnegan name for her and the boys. Respect for the dead. Very noble. Besides, Cromwell sounds just plain Leviathanical.

I was so jealous of Luke. He got to be Sinead's soul mate: a special, coveted name I'd heard on talk shows. I would observe them flirting in the kitchen as they popped popcorn in their new electric microwave for us boys on movie night. She'd spill melted butter on his hand, and he'd be like "HEY!—Whad are ya doin?" And then she'd giggle and apologize and then they'd go ahead and make out, sweeping dishes off the counter so they could begin making love in the "heat of the passion" (more talk show fodder). No, not really, but they might as well have done that. Soul mate's eventually mate; I was sure of it.

All I actually ever saw them do was politely, decorously kiss one another on the lips like two speckled fawns at dawn showing appreciation of another's forest company. Respectable. It made me sick with black opera jealousy. I hated it, but couldn't keep up the hatred for long being that I was genuinely glad in my heart for Sinead. (Women with kids needed to keep having "love relations" or "encounters," so that they could feel good about themselves and have exercise. It was scientifically true. I'd seen something about it on late-night PBS: the paragon of glistening truth. There is a great oxymoron hidden in there, "late-night PBS.")

I often wondered if Brendan ever heard them at night having "love relations" the same way I thought I heard a few of our fosters messing around. I never asked him, thinking he'd be like, "Dude, that's gross; that's *my mom!*" (like Bill said to Ted).

This bummed me out about Brendan. I didn't care if anyone asked *me* sexy questions about my Tallene. She had a body like everyone else, and I was sure she liked doing sex; Caleb incontrovertibly liked "doing it" (he always bragged about his giant hog and how it was fully automatic, words that vexed me and rendered Sam timorous).

At this time in my life, I believed myself to be pretty keen on how good sex was for humans, objectively speaking. I didn't, however, really understand the mechanics of it. Otis and Dolores hadn't yet graced our home with their carnal wisdom.

Even after Sinead married Luke (Skywalker, his name might as well have been, the x-wing stud), she continued to spend *unreal* amounts of healthily invested time with her boys. I don't know how, to this day, she did it: A's baseball games, bike rides, swimming pool again and again and again, new husband/kids movie nights, and other such flights of brilliant time management. She also finished school, did some medical job/internships, and properly mourned Connor. Was she supernatural? I wondered if Sam could tell just by focusing his special metaphysical eyes on her. Maybe he could see her hidden, diaphanous wings.

My poor mother hadn't any wings, just big floppy clown shoes.

Fast forward to the very sad year: 1989.

The Finnegans and Luke Cromwell moved away. Sinead made the protracted decision to get the hell out of Stockton. Even the brick façade off the Oxford Circle couldn't hide the stench of such a dying town, overrun with exasperated rap "gangstas," replete with mac10s and stolen sneakers. It was no place for her sons to be during their precious, formative teens. She looked into jobs elsewhere with her powerful resume and landed a delicious one up in the beautiful foothills of the Sierra Nevada: namely: Pine Grove—around 2,500 feet up in the mountainy, oakie, piney peacefulness—far from the Minas Morgul valley. The gold country. The heartland of California. A place even better than Chico and ten times closer to actual heaven than the town of Paradise.

I was once again quietly jealous. I wanted out of Stockton. Although only fourteen, I was keen to its dour stupidity. Plus, I was up to my ears in fosters by 1989, and old Abe Lincoln was just beginning to sniff the freshly painted bricks of our Regent St. house. Something was rotten in the state of Stockton.

I felt deeply that I was missing out on something in life. Something that naturally belongs to a growing boy. A sense of security, perhaps. A trust fund. Probably not.

I lived on the West Coast. For sure I would miss the Finnegan's warm gravity gravely. I would miss Brendan, Seamus, even Carrigan, who was still a little punk with a woolen, blue L.A. Dodgers hat that was way too big for his head. But most secretly of all: I would miss Sinead: my archetypal woman, the woman who landed a career job at Amador Sutter Hospital in Jackson, about six miles away from the Finnegans' new two-story country house. Brendan told me all the details over the phone. Long distance. When they left, Sinead took me aside and told me I could call whenever I wanted. She would accept all the charges. Her wings rustled quietly in the warm breeze. So I called them. A lot.

I decided to keep in contact forever; I had to. They were the only real people on earth. And I had a promised long-distance golden ticket.

In my tactile world, there was Mom, Sam, Abe, and the damn fosters, who actually, on a good note, seemed to be dissipating as 1990 rolled around. Otis left, with his half-ass evil packed in his SF Giants team bag in the summer of that year: his walkman on, volume at 11, "Take Me Down to the Paradise City" churnin' away. Axl Rose was his demigod. I remember he kissed my mom on the cheek by the front door when he left. She giggled and tore up; weird. Despite his nefarious nature I suppose he was happy that someone actually took him in and looked after him. I winked as he waved to me, stepping into that all-too-familiar, dark-blue Charles Dickens Hall bus. I don't know where he was going.

(He exposed me to so much porn whilst with us that I could have challenged Hugh Hefner to a grand, mansion pool side Porn Off!, a salacious quiz show where the questions and answers are as dirty as a fly's green abdomen. I would wear an XL red robe to conceal my girth—thus looking really hot and hip amongst the peachy centerfold bunnies, and I'd have my very first martini complete with a horny green olive.)

Once Otis left, there was only Dolores (video camera in hand), Rob (a bore, I don't need tell of him and his crappy leather bomber jacket), Tiffany (ugly and angry, forgive my candor), and like, one or two others that I'll probably place correctly in my head by the time I go to bed tonight. I don't recall them now. As I said earlier: there were like 30-40 different fosters within a five-year period: too many to mention. I've highlighted the top three: Otis, Dolores, and Stevo.

Ah, but I haven't said much concerning him: Stevo. I was told secretly by my gossipy mother (hand to mouth, eyes darting left and right even though we were the only two home at that moment) that Steve's mom burn-killed his dad by gently spraying an old mattress (while he slept on it) with copious amounts of kerosene and then throwin' in a diamond match to light up her bitchy-tattoo night. The police report later reported that he screamed, scorched, and rolled over into hell. There were some extra bottles of Jack Daniel's whiskey that fell off the window sill and broke forth into the flames, exacerbating the whole fiasco. Then it was further reported that said murderess dropped off her three-year-old son, Steve's nameless bro, at some Greyhound station in Tracy (where he sat picking his chilly nose and wishing his mom was a human being rather than a poison-fanged rattlesnake) and then took the hell off for British Columbia via I5; that was in 1986. Steve was 15 then and left home to consider eternity, God, the star courses in the fiery empyrean, and whether or not to put butter on the memory of his poor dead father. Human toast. Gruesome.

I don't think it really happened that way. My mom, however, did, and took special, special care of Steve, her "most fragile orphan," as she so eloquently called him.

Steve's Manson family mother was caught by Johnny Law and his moustache in Oregon and sent to orange-jumpsuit land, where she became a prison lesbian of the highest order: Butch. Nobody would ever mess with her again. She was a veritable Molotov cocktail in the flesh.

Though I was way interested in the murder story, I never broached the toasty father subject with Steve. I was afraid he'd karate chop me—karate was his chief hobby, like so many other uppity '80s Doo teens. (Very odd how popular that karate stuff was back then. "HIIIII YAAAH!" sixty billion rat-tailed male teens screamed as they chopped a balsa wood board in two. Adolescent catharsis times ten.)

I waited daily, with cautious, baited breath, for Steve to mention his mom, but he never did—opting, rather, to ignore me and pop giant red zits for seemingly ever. He had bad acne, poor fellow. Saucefleem, as Chaucer called it.

Steve left around 1989. Dolores alighted off to other faux-wood paneled sex dens in late 1990, surfing on a stream of silver astro-glide.

What seriously sucks is that *I* actually left very close to when all of them were clearing out one by one. So I never got to spend any real healing time with my mother; not until later—right before she died.

Before I truly left Stockton, I escaped a few times up to the Finnegan ranch up in the mountains. Their invites to come and visit did not fall upon deaf ears. In the summer of 1990 I actually got to stay at their house for two whole beautiful months…ah…my soupy Oakland A's heart swooned with delight. This was the fortunate and wonderfully-taken-care-of (by God Himself) time where I abandoned all the pop-cultural darkness in my life. This was the time where I once again started loving *baseball* in all its crisp grassy nature. My posters of Maiden, Zak Wylde, and various other "sex, drugs, and rock 'n' roll" prophets came down and were replaced with posters of Jose Canseco and Rickey Henderson. (Steroids rather than cocaine!)

*PUSH MY LIFE INTO A DUFFLE BAG*

Mom loved, adored, and cherished this change in my young life; it was evident by her brand-new house allowances for me, such as, "Whenever you decide to move out you can still keep your room, honey. I don't need it, and it'll be nice for you to have some space when you come to visit; I like all the baseball stuff, too! It's just so fun!" and she was being honest!

She thought Jose Canseco was "sexy, a tall drink of water," and would often, whilst in my room talking to me, look dazedly at his bash-brothers poster and act like she wasn't paying attention to what I was saying because she was so intoxicated by his black-shades visage and rippling-pastime biceps. It was always funny. "I'm sorry, what did you say, hon?" In a lot of quaint ways like this, my mom was very funny, very human, a consummate dearling of fun. I know I bash her a lot, but she was a good person—warm and cheerfully generous with all people.

She was golden. A true heart. My one and only mother. She raised me. She loved me. She loved me like Chopin loved the gleam of the faint eventide sunlight upon the sable lid of his beloved grand. That felt nice to say; that one was for you, Mom. May it cheer and warm your heart beneath the cold sod.

Under the grass… "The beautiful uncut hair of graves," as Whitman once sang it. I still love you and always will love you, Mom.

Okay. I'm getting a bit misty eyed at the thought of her sweet soul, floating off in the Christ ether with the fragrance of apricots and apple blossoms drifting silently in the solar breeze. Her ghost. Her spirit. Her light. Her misfortunes. Her folly. Her giant dust body not mattering anymore.

…

Now I'm not sure what to type. Right here. On this page. I am still in my body, stuck in the realm of hostile time, not free from it, like her. I wonder what she is thinking at this moment. I can't even imagine the "thoughts" of souls all brightly brilliant like quick lightning in a thousand shimmering forests of snowlight. I am only a blind owl within the numb night of a treeless forest seven billion miles south of that eternal, invisible, perfect and ineffable realm.

"Hoot hoot!" I say, the ground below splattered with corporeal droppings. "Hoot hoot!"

And time exhales and inhales, lit dimly by the far away glow of God.

…

Mom, I would like to tell you something right now. On this page. Forever. I am sorry you died. I'm sorry and I miss you, like God misses us. I miss you, Mom.

There is one picture of my mother that I treasure. It is a silly picture. It makes me giggle like a child when I see it. Then I grow quiet and my soul turns to cold water. In it, Tallene, the happy redhead, is seated in the foreground…a seventies foreground of graininess and Farah Faucet feathers. She is smiling like crazy. I don't know who took the picture. It was probably one of her barfly friends: Dot or Jane, et al. My mother seems posed. Poised. Ready to be in a great picture. She's sitting at a table about three feet away from the camera lens. She smiles like crazy, her hand just under her chin in a somewhat musing pose. She smiles like she's really happy. Her hair looks good. Her tan blouse, cotton-top thing looks good. It fits her well. Maybe she just bought it that day, and that there's the reason for her pose, her happiness, her unflagging youthful ebullience. I don't know. She smiles nicely. Like crazy. Like madness. Like divinest sense.

Now, here's something humorous for you. Here's the funny part. Here's the shaft of sunlight which pierces through the white morning mist that blankets the mossy grave yard in gold. Picture this: me as a child. I'm in the picture too: behind her at a distance of about, say, ten feet. I don't think I was supposed to be in the picture. If I was, Dot or Jane probably flippantly told me to say cheese for a split second, but never trusted me to actually be good and hold still for the picture. This is because I was only five: a funny, distracted child—there is a chocolate fudge smudge on the upper right side of my open mouth.

*Now*, this is important. *My mouth is open.* Why? Because I am about to fall off a chair that I'm precariously standing upon. I'm being a bad boy. I was up on a kitchen chair, probably wasn't supposed to be, but maybe was allowed to due to the picture taking. Maybe Dot or Jane took my disciplinary mom's attention away with the promise of an impromptu, three-second photo op—thus I quickly ascended (or was already on?) the chair and felt like a big boy. But not big for long. You see, I'm falling off the chair.

I don't remember this instance, this day, but it's verified by the picture; the most awkward picture ever recorded in the paternal world of the seventies!

I fell. Right off the chair.

And my oblivious mother is there too: posed, smiling like the July sun, about four feet from the camera. And her fledgling son is a few feet behind my her, falling off a chair, falling to the left, facing the camera, my mouth open and chocolaty, my face scared and irrational, my curly, seventies baby wisps frozen flying, my hands are over my head and curved toward my fall like I'm doing some hot *Saturday Night Fever* choreography. My belly's protruding like soft white dough, my underoos underwear is clinging to my poopee-contingent loins, my tiny tank top is striped blue on white like the cheesy sailors of old. And Mom smiles radiantly, clueless concerning my descent.

I wish I could go back in time and personally study the aftermath of this fiasco. I surely cried. Mom surely comforted. Dot surely lit a fresh Camel cigarette and complained about the smallish nature of her barfly breasts.

And Tallene surely chuckled and said, "All you need's a handful!"

To which Dot surely replied, "Easy for you to say, boobie queen of California!"

All the while I mournfully wiped my salty-red eyes and wondered what the crap they were speaking of.

Maybe. Maybe it happened this way. Perhaps. I'll never know. All I know is that my beautiful mother smiled and I fell. Hilarious and sad. She posed and I fell. Human and yet wanting to rise above human. She posed and I fell. And here we have a germane thesis statement for our mother/son relationship during the olden family years.

Hmmm. I don't know how to think sometimes when I remember my one and only mother. I miss her, I'm tired of her, I forgive her, I feel sorry for her, I want to talk to her, *I want to yell at her and shake her!* Is this how you feel sometimes, late at night when you're alone and more honest? A total, brutal wash?

# Chapter 9
# The Irish Invade
# (B) *"Up, Up, Up into the Foothills!"*

By 1991 I began seeing more and more of the Finnegans and less and less of my mom. This was fine and dandy to me by this point, since she was completely enthralled with the historical thrustings of the American presidency by this time. I'll boldly put forth here that she was a bit of a sex addict.

As the summer of '91 rolled around I made my silent exit from Stockton. Praise the Lord on high. And two months of pine tree bliss awaited me: trails to hike, bikes to ride, mullets to crisp in the sun! It would be halcyon forsooth!

Sinead came up with a brilliantly practical reason for my being there as a young man for such an extended stay: I was officially an official "babysitter" for Seamus. Brendan and I would be his guardians. We would make sure Seamus didn't stick scissors in his eyes, light the cat on fire, and/or show his genitalia to the neighbors. Brendan and I were real manly men by this time: both fifteen years of age…a valid babysitter age, trustworthy as hell. Come to think of it I was sixteen that summer. Our birthdays were coterminous, so half the year we'd be the same age, and the other half I'd be dominant and supreme.

If Sinead had faith that we could keep the country house from burning down and Seamus' eyes from exploding in bloody, minuscule, twain ocular tidal waves, then I believe we were, in fact, totally capable. Her female intuition was as solid as adamantium.

I remember that first, sweet catalytic phone call that changed my life and got me moving: a phone call from my good old buddy Brendan asking me if I'd like to "Come hang out in the country for the summer."

"YES! YES! Just lemme ask my mom! Hold on a sec." (Yes, I would like to move.)

"Mom?"

"Yes?"
"Can I move away for a little while?"
"Why not?"
"Exactly."
"Go ahead, honey."
"Totally."
"Will you write?"
"Of course."
"I love you; I'll miss your face."
"Ditto; bye bye."
"Bren? Are you still there?"
"Yeah."
"It's cool. She said yes; prepare for glorious, exalted grandeur."
"Totally; bring your mitt and your foundering heart."
"I will."

And I packed up and headed northeast. I was so excited I could've done a huge, heavy flip, if only that trampoline from the hick party were there I would have finally conquered it.

Tallene was excited, too. She knew I would have a blast and that I'd be well taken care of. She could smell the pines of Amador County, far off in the distance. They smelled healthy. Canseco pines.

This summer was the summer between my freshman and sophomore year as a Stockton Stag high schooler. I almost had my driver's license. I was becoming an independent adult. Or so I thought.

I forgot to mention that I visited the Finnegan country estate in the summer of '89 as well. It was only for a week, but man, was it ever fun! Because of that sunshiny trip I knew empirically that I wanted to visit again when Brendan called with his Godly offer. No doubt in my mind. To say "no" would have been like Santa coming down the chimney on a snowy Christmas Eve with a huge bag of gifts for me, and me standing there in my pajamas, waiting for him, arms crossed, and telling him to get the fuck out of my house.

And there is one story from that little visit that I must tell. Seriously now. There was a certain day during that time that was not as fun as all the others, and it just so happened to happen on July 4th, believe you me. (Plenty of imminent fireworks!)

So here's the tale: There was a group of roads, endless driveways and other such dusty car trails that led mostly to secluded retired folk hamlets called

"Surrey Junction," that was about a mile away from the Finnegan spread. The boys were fond of using these roads, endless driveways, and other such dusty car trails as an inexhaustible source of bike riding fun. Of course, this was '89, so there were no more actual horse-drawn surreys physically strolling down Surrey Junction (with pretty little fringes on their tops), but it was still pretty countrified. It was sleepy and hot, rural and thickly quiet, like napping coon hounds.

So, Brendan, me, Carrigan, and Sam (he was invited and had come along for the week, much to my implicit displeasure, but no Seamus this time: Gump worked alone—he was under the vast country sink back at the house; it had a soap dispenser in the shape of a cow with black-and-white spots glistening under a copious ceramic glaze) had made the decision one delicious morning to head out to Surrey Junction in search of biking adventure. It would be radical; we were all sure of this, as we filled our specialized water bottles and threw them in our backpacks alongside the half-full tubes of Ranch Pringles, licorice whips, and other assorted protein rations. We then exited the air-conditioned house and entered the blazing sunlight. We mounted our faithful steeds (assorted bicycles in assorted colors), who shook like thunder and whinnied like crazy for summer battle. Then we set out for the Junction, with Brendan in the lead. All the bikes were radical bikes, well...all of them but mine: a borrowed '70s Schwinn racing bike with tires that were about a millimeter thick—*not great on gravel*). We sped quickly through the first mile, which cut directly across Ridge Road, a busy highway, filling my bones with responsibility trepidation. (I imagined Sam hit head on by a logging truck, his ketchup corpse flinging into the blazing summer distance...the length of an airy football field, his flight finally broken by a resting, 2,000-pound mountain lion, who then in turn begins to feast upon his young corpse, as I am sent to jail for not being my brother's keeper.).

When we reached the glorious Surrey Junction (which Brendan had promised me would kick serious ass) we simply rode around, exploring various clandestine driveways for about an hour in the 90-degree pine-tree sun. Sap, rocks, and needles. I was afraid some bearded, sweaty hick would discover us on his NO TRESPASSING property and fill our buttocks with buck shot. No such thing happened, thank God.

(I think I saw Tom Sawyer race by on a vaporous parallel road—he had a new Mongoose mountain bike in fluorescent yellow. Huck too—he had a bike built by BMX that somehow looked like a big raft. Jim had made sure his tire pressure was correct for safety.)

The day got indeed more ballsy when Brendan and Carrigan decided to show us what they called the "G.I. Joe Hill." The name sounded cheesy enough, so I thought it would be nothing especially scary and agreed to visit said hill and conquer it. My Schwinn steed was just itching for such a conquest, her spokes puffing loudly in the heat.

So onward we went. It took about a half hour to get there.

"How far is this stupid hill?" I exhaled, supremely annoyed at how much I was sweating.

"We're almost there; take a chill pill, dude," said Brendan.

I wasn't offended. Brendan could say to me what he wanted whenever he pleased, and it wouldn't offend my sensitivity because we were on a level. I respected him and he me, deeply. If Carrigan had said the above I would have told him to fuck off and then felt a little guilty, since he was Brendan's little brother, and it would have been very awkward 'til I hopefully perceived a furtive smile on Brendan's face.

He hated Carrigan too. Carrigan was such a little rock of petulant arrogance, and he didn't even have any pubic hair yet! Ah! Such unwarranted audacity!

When we finally reached G.I. Joe hill we approached it naturally from the south, which put us in the perfect, top-of-the-hill spot to race down its steep, seemingly vertical length. Just my luck: G.I. Joe hill was set up to deliver the goods right off the bat. Awesome. Begin "Ride of the Valkyries" now!)

Of course, there was a good-sized incline to surpass from the south to get to the pinnacle goods, but it was in no way tantamount to the sheer, grave gravity gravel drop off that was hidden from my view as I chugged up and up and still further upward, gushing sweat and watching Sam to make sure he could make it. In fact, he couldn't make it, but then again, neither could I. We both walked our bikes up like big pussies. I blamed it on the hot sun. Brendan was understanding and walked his bike up too, even though he was perfectly capable of making it to the top without being a lazy retard like Sam and me. Carrigan was the only one to make it up the whole hill by the power of calf and pedal; such an athlete. Once at the summit, he began insulting us like Gollum until Brendan shut him up with a handful of sharp Nolan Ryan gravel, which resembled gray quartz, to which Carrigan hollered, "YOU CAN'T DO

THAT! I'M GONNA TELL MOM! YOU CAN'T DO THAT TO ME! MOM SAID!"

Kids.

When we finally crested the hill and looked over the steep drop I felt my stomach turn into the Everglades National Park. I looked over my Schwinn. It sucked. I was doomed to die on this descent, but couldn't turn back for fear of the eternal mockery of Carrigan, who was sans pubic hair.

I grinned at everyone like I was thinking, *Hell the hell yeah, boys! This is gonna be more fun than you can shake a divining stick at! Hell, yeah! Hell the hell yeah, guys! Hell! What the hell, right? Shit yeah.*

Sam looked scared. He had good reason. It was frickin' steep. All the brakes in the world looked like baby bunnies next to this gleaming grizzly bear of a hill. I probably looked scared too; no mullet with shaves in the sides could hide my velocity insecurities, no poker face could hide that I held a pair of Schwinn twos in this grand game of heroics. Bon Jovi's "Shot Down in a Blaze of Glory" started playing in my head. It gave me strength.

Without any warning or ceremony, Brendan suddenly shot off down the hill to my right, shouting defiantly at the gods, a lengthy, held out song of "WWWHHOOOOOOH!" Then Carrigan spit up a tornado of dusty rocks as he sped down after his brother; he didn't want to be outdone, that 4$^{th}$ of July firecracker.

Then. Pause. Nothing else happened. Sam and I just sat there with our bikes at our side, watching the Finnegan boys descend into eternal glory and flame. The hot summer breeze flitted through our hair and cooled the sweat on our temples.

After ten seconds, Sam and I finally looked beseechingly at each other with wimpy grins like we were both so super extremely excited to race down the hill and plunge to our infantile deaths. We were silently loathing G.I. Joe Hill each in our own way. We were responsible and cautious; we were little insurance adjusters in tiny-checkered vans. Steep hills did not compute for us. We sharpened our No. 2s at our mahogany desks. We stalled.

By this time the Finnegan clan was waaaayyyy down there, coasting with the nimble abilities of Mercury himself toward shimmering medals and olive-leaf accolades. (The Roman pines clapped their sappy branches and golden clovers fell from the heavens like honey from Elysium, an Irish gift from a multicultural Zeus for two foreign heroes who had spoken well by their physical prowess.)

After ten more seconds, Sam and I again glanced at each other. The time was now or never. I would *not* let Carrigan win the day.

"*You* go. You're bigger. I'll go behind you," Sam proffered. I shrugged my shoulders all cool and collected, like I had been just about to launch before my stupid little brother *interrupted* me with his baby babble. Sam = my own personal, faux-consanguineous Seamus. *My Antonia.* (No, I wouldn't read that for years to come.)

"No prob, doood," I uttered in reply.

And then I commenced balancing up and onto my Schwinn stallion, and off I went, gaining speed like a drunken blue jay through the sagging pine boughs, crackling in the heat and filling the air with sap song.

Sam watched from behind, and then finally started running alongside his bike, i.e., running his bike down the hill like a total coward. He called out to me, "Wait! Wait for me!" but I didn't hear him; all I heard was the crisp sound of Zeus' beard growing for me as I transformed into a veritable Hercules.

Despite my brave metamorphosis, I didn't make it that far down the hill, perhaps only fifty yards. You see, a big car suddenly came around the far bend out past the adrenaline-junkie Finnegans and raced up hill toward me in a massive cloud of white-hot dust. I descried it from afar and became utterly nervous because it was a mean-looking, rusty, old Ford truck with a roaring diesel engine; it obviously had never graduated from high school.

So I tried slowing down, but that didn't work: my inept Schwinn was incapable of safety on a gravel road. To be entirely honest, it was entirely my fault: I couldn't remember which brake (left/right hand?) was front/rear (?) and…so…I didn't want to run the risk of flying head first over my handlebars) I pulled over to the side of the road at full speed and awkwardly pumped both hand brakes at a measured rate.) The problem was that I pulled over too far to the right and couldn't correct my obligatory over correction. (Somewhere, far away, a DMV instructor was nodding his head superciliously.)

The truck passed by me at an alarming rate of speed in a massive, billowing dust cloud. (Clatter-clatter-clank-rattle. The strident pitch of hellhounds!)

I wobbled really, really fast up and down like Weebles on acid wobble, and the road, as if a bulldozer had quite recently made excessively fierce love to it, started dipping up and down and up again and down again in smooth-sinky divots, which were reminiscent of the smaller foxholes in the Huertgen Forest circa 1944. I wobbled more and more and then dipped up and down with the divot pattern before me at full speed, until I had absolutely *no* control whatsoever of my bike and only about one foot of road left to my right! My dust-covered ankle began whipping against milkweed and star thistle making a sound that even a banshee would flee from.

Then. Well. I crashed. Hard. Descending into the ditch, my foaming Stallion hit a good sized baby boulder, and I flew right the hell over my handlebars and hurled through the boiling summer air.

Even to this day I acutely remember what passed through my frenzied mind as I flew—like BATMAN himself. The smash hit movie had just destroyed the box office at the local Jackson Theater, the movie we'd seen just the night before; and there you have it. This is what flashed through my mind: THE JOKER'S PAINTED FACE IN ALL OF HIS SINISTER HECKLING! "Boooo Hooo! Yoooor gonna crash! Yooooor gonna crash! Boooo Hooooo Hooooo!" he guffawed. Yep, Jack Nicholson told me that this was gonna hurt. And it did.

My face seemed to land first and welcome all bits of gravel and dirt to lodge in its spacious pores. I suddenly became quite bloody: forehead, forearms, right lower jaw, bottoms of hands, finger tips, one elbow, both knees, one shin, right ear lobe at the very tip bottom, as if I'd had a bad ear piercing performed by Otis. Worst of all was my dislocated right shoulder. It felt like broken glass was under my skin.

I tried not to move much once I realized I had come to a complete stop (and lived to tell the tale). I lay there in the gray ditch for about forty seconds; my shoulder felt gummy, and my arm felt gummier: like a million red Gummi Bears were having an orgy under the blankets of my skin or, no, ...as if my muscles were melting like hot head cheese over limp rebar.

I continued lying there like the world owed me something fast until Sam finally made it to me, running up with his stupid wobbling bike, which he let fall over in a clatter as he ran the last few feet down to me, declaring, "HEY! What are *you* doing? *Stop resting!*" (I've never understood that to this day...resting? What? He saw me crash!) "We've got to go back home for dinner!" Then he perceived the full onslaught of just how bloody my face had become, and he commenced freaking out.

He bolted up away from me onto the road and began running around, bellowing animalistic yowls and screaming out, "Brendan! Carrigan!" He may have even screamed, "Oh, the humanity!" as my zeppelin bike burst into hellish flames a few yards up the ditch, but I don't recall it.

What made matters even crappier than they already were was that Sam, a headless chicken, began running around in long circles that soon enough spanned the entire width of the road and grew longer with each maniacal rotation until he ultimately was curtailed by the massive erosion ditch of desiccated red clay (a gaping devil's aperture) far over to the left side of the road, in which he fell. Hard. Frantically grasping at the air for ghosts. It was a long way for little Sam to fall. A six-foot drop to the rocky silt bottom, where he landed on his soft right arm and snapped it like a brittle twig. Snap.

Unbelievable. A dislocated shoulder and a broken arm in the same five minutes. The Jones boys in all their glory. I almost can't believe it, looking back, and yet I was there and experienced it all. Kids do the dumbest things ever, which makes life pretty funny as long as nobody dies.

Once Sam heard his arm snap he began screaming even louder than before. Once he noticed that it was flopping around like a limp trout whilst he was screaming he upped the screaming to an even louder volume. So, being the responsible older brother that I was, I dutifully, painfully got up and began my melodramatic injured-soldier journey toward my failing brother; "When Johnny Comes Marching Home" played somberly in the distance.

I would have to carry him on my dislocated shoulder to the hot LZ so the Huey could get us the hell out of Charlie's jungle, that is, if the napalm didn't melt us first. (Wait a minute...I just used two entirely different war allusions on the same page. Well, dammit, that's just how brutal this day was. It deserves copious and proper historical fanfare.)

Carrigan arrived first in his SR71 Blackbird, with Brendan not far along after—in his Huey helicopter. Their faces turned as pallid as Moby Dick seeing the ghost of Poseidon when they each got a good look at my ground-beef face. I might as well have had Saran Wrap around my head with a white Styrofoam yarmulke.

Brendan and Carrigan looked completely powerless, for once in their lives, like they didn't know if they should ride with Greg LeMond speed to summon the powers of the motherbreast Sinead or stay right with us and say a brief prayer as Sam and I died in the July heat, perhaps sticking us with the last vials of morphine left on the battlefield. Utter boyhood vexation.

A fat yellow grasshopper landed on my cheek and got stuck in the blood goo, kicking his striped barbed legs in consternation; I picked him off and impatiently tossed him onto the hot road, hoping he'd sizzle, pop, and die, uttering through my angry clenched ivories, "FFFFFFUUUUUUUUCCCKKKKK!" to the unmitigated horror of all around me. I had really dropped the F-bomb, loudly, with intent. So what? I was seriously injured, and *nobody* was helping me!

And then divine fortuity saved us all: a car cruised slowly up to us, appearing from a mirage out of nowhere. We were rescued...by an elderly couple in a behemoth Cadillac, which glistened in the hot sun with all its chrome and ugly mauve finish. It had a Dynasty/Dallas Landau top, mauve as well. (I don't know why Cadillac was still doing the Landau tops in the late eighties; I suppose they knew the blue-hair masses would continue purchasing them by the boatload. Denture target market.)

The lady in shotgun saw my face and exclaimed, "OH! Dick! They need our help!"

He nodded and grunted like a kind boar. I could hear the AC cranking behind the faux-wood dashboard. The automatic windows worked efficiently. As I climbed in I looked at what I was sitting on: mauve velveteen seats. Then I stressed out about getting blood on them and held my working hand under my chin so I wouldn't offend or stain with my kinetic blood. She saw me and admonished, "No! No, deary, don't worry about those old seats!"

Dick grunted again, not so kindly this time. I'll bet her name was Petunia; she positively reeked of rich elegance and old, million-proof magnolia perfume.

Sam entered and sat next to me—sobbing and scared. His arm was broken, poor bastard. Poor, poor bastard; he was the youngest soldier, marching at point, the soldier who's feet seem to sniff out an AP landmine. His powdery bones were irrevocably shattered.

The blue hair drove us heavily to the Finnegan fort.

That was the 4th of July, 1989.

We dedicated our bloody injuries to the formerly injured soldiers of the Revolutionary War. "Huzzah!" Then we drank barrels of whiskey. No, not really.

When we pulled up to the vertical, sawed timber gates of the fort, Sinead stepped out and gaped at my bloody body, dropping the red plastic bucket of laundry that was in her hands. She rushed us to her hospital in her country-blue minivan (an '88 Plymouth Voyager with faux-wood-paneled sides, V-6), where everyone knew her by name and gave us top-notch service. I remember the doctor that helped me was black, the first black man I'd ever seen in Amador County. His name was Moses. Needless to say, he was a sage

*PUSH MY LIFE INTO A DUFFLE BAG*

apothecary and led me out of painful Egypt. Perhaps he had an older brother that worked down at The Bass Hole liquor store by the Delta with a gold catfish watch. Perhaps.

After the hospital settings and scrapings and alcoholic swabbings we all went up to Pine Grove for 88 Burgers. It was a classic little burger hut that served HUGE cheeseburgers (dripping with the savory juices of heaven) and banana milkshakes. This made our Vietnam/WWII/Civil/Revolutionary War experience seem far away and but a dream, until the tangy burger sauce dribbled into an open face sore on my chin and stung like a minuscule ghost scorpion was stabbing my facial nerves. The image of a bathtub flashed across my mind.

Mmm. 88 Burgers. I'll always remember that the price that day came out to $17.76. Even back then I loved historical fodder.

The days after the biking fiasco were spent frequenting Sinead's hospital and having minor, local face surgery things to fix my ground-visage chuck. Sam got a fluorescent green cast. He was proud of it until it started itching and kept him completely from enjoying the loveliness of the Finnegans' expensive (light blue with white swirls; $$$) spa. He could only put his feet in. Carrigan made fun of him.

My shoulder mended fine although I hated the part were they popped it back into place. I didn't like thinking about or coming face to face with the grim fact that I had a skeleton deep inside me. Regardless, said youthful skeleton (bone scaffolding in German) was fixed, and I was able to throw the old hardball in no time, thus salvaging what was left of summer for fun boyhood high jinx.

This is the end of the 1989 bicycle anecdote. Fin.

Now let us zoom forward to when I actually left Stockton for almost good: the summer of 1991. The Finnegans asked me to come up once more and enjoy the country for some fresh air cornpone. So I did and enjoyed it very much, staying away from all bicycles. Eventually toward the end of August the holy mother Sinead approached me and evinced quite kindly that she thought I should stay even longer. "Would you like to attend school at Amador high with Brendan this year? Perhaps the whole year, for a different cultural perspective on life?" she inquired.

"Yes, I would like it very much," said I. (The whole school year away from Stockton? Was I hallucinating in the August heat?) "Yes, I would like it very much," I repeated, staring intently at her fine facial features with restrained elation, felicity, ebullience, rapture, jubilation, and exultation in my pounding heart.

"Cool. Why don't you give your mom a call and see if she's cool with it? We can work out the details later," she said. I loved it when she said things like "cool with it." She was certainly the hippest doctor in the United States of America.

Thus I began my teen career at Amador High School, catching a running mountain lion's golden back to school every morning on Ridge Road. It was my junior year.

Mom paid $250 a month in a luscious mailed check to the mighty Finnegans. I think that might have only covered my eating habits in all actuality, but the Finnegans were gracious hosts, and I was generously provided for under the auspices of their spacious white wings. I somewhat took advantage of this generosity, hot tubbing with affected extravagance almost every day and eating only the choicest diamond ice cream from a golden chalice. I lived it up. My king hat was huge. Ah…freedom from my crappy valley life. I didn't look back!

But then—something weird began happening to me. I slowly began to notice that my brain wasn't as normal as other people's. I noticed that I had growing, negative mental issues and insecurities. And then it got worse because I seriously began noticing that *I had indeed noticed* that I had these issues. Like a person looking into a box that's contained in another box, and then the person finds out that they're inside the first box deep inside the other box. A trapped feeling. Thus, I really freaked out.

It seemed to me at the time that I could *never* turn my frenzied, insecure brain off: I was continually afraid of things that perhaps didn't exist or would never ever really happen to me. I was always on the verge of being the personification of acute anxiety due to many a compulsion to have things *just so* in my ordered hours and living spaces. My fears and compulsions seemed to be vibrating with giant invisible muscles. I couldn't make the vibrating stop. I heard it all the time, especially at night when I tried to sleep.

It seems to me now that age sixteen is probably a normal age in which one starts to examine one's own head and personality objectively through the lens of cloudy adolescent subjectivity. I didn't like what I saw when I looked deep inside myself; parts of my mind were off-kilter and abnormal. My brain alternator seemed to run in irregular patterns of voltage that made my life engine belts howl with deviant disquiet.

First deviation: To come right out and say it, I started obsessing over Carrigan. Like he was my own son or something. No longer was I annoyed by him; rather, I was profoundly interested in him. He was twelve, supremely athletic (an amazing pitcher), bold, tough, good looking. I guess a kind of golden youth. He would have wrestled and beaten Alexander as a boy in Macedonia if he'd been born over 2,000 years back. He was in shape, healthy, wily, and a whole mélange of other character traits that I had *never* in my plump life possessed. But I didn't want to *be* him, not necessarily; I just wanted to be is best buddy (his father figure, since his real father was dead, and Luke Cromwell was too stoic)—his confidant—somebody whom Carrigan could trust—his best friend in the entire world. *Nope, not good enough!* My crazy compulsions would articulately scream. His best friend *in the entire universe!*

Yes. That works.

I had a crazy desire to always make him happy: make him laugh at my jokes, let him know that I was looking out for him, being the older leader and protector—big and strong like the bear I was. I liked that I could control him with my manipulative wit, as if he was my own little living action figure. I remember distinctly that it grew into absurd controlling extremes rather quickly as summer moved into fall.(Local shrinks surely would have jumped at the chance to examine me back then with yellow Mead notepads and expensive pens.)

For example, many a night I'd casually end up sleeping in his room and hanging out with him and his myriad Nolan Ryan plaques, Jerry Rice signed footballs, and other sportive regalia: expensive stuff owned by an important growing boy. Important stuff. I wanted to be important. I wanted to be expensive and necessary. Carrigan was my ticket, the punk kid with a solid fastball.

On those nights I'd ignore the older brother bore of Brendan. He was getting a bit preppy in my eyes—no more Giants caps or stadium windbreakers…just boat shoes and a frickin' leather briefcase thing that he took to school. Where had his Regent baseball bag gone? and opt for my golden boy; I tried implicitly to scare and excite him with my witty stories.

One ignominious night in particular, we got into a discussion about robbers, about how they were even tougher up in the woods because they had to be able to see in the darkness with no streetlights and be wary of raccoons, black bears, and the Yeti.

I told Carrigan, in a hushed yet excited whisper, that up in Pioneer, one robber had robbed six cabin-houses in one night and tied up all the residents—all without a sound, a getaway car, or an accomplice. I told him that he cut a jagged star into each captive's left forearm with a dull blade slathered in pine sap so it would sting for hours. I told him he had the stolen booty hidden out at a convenient drop off in the deep woods, and that the cops couldn't locate it. I told him that word around the county was that he was an old ninja from the Vietnam War and that he had been a P.O.W. and escaped with all kinds of learnéd moves…and also that he wore an actual camouflaged ninja suit when he robbed! Then I told Carrigan that another ominous word was buzzing around town that said ninja was moving *west*, down the foothills toward the richer two-story houses in Pine Grove, Jackson and Sutter Creek! *The Finnegan house was right along the robbing line!*

Carrigan was very quiet in his bed above me (I'd brought my sleeping bag in and was on the floor, feeling tough on the soft carpet).

"But we've got a new alarm system!" he blurted out, frightened like a beady-bulgy-eyed field mouse with a ninja owl spanning the night field from a black skeleton branch above.

I sounded the death knell. "It doesn't matter; his caliber of new-type robber has all kinds of scientific gear stolen from the military bases in Nevada! He can get in like a ghost, right after he disables the alarm system with, I think they call it a laser scanner or something. It has a gold diamond inside it as a power source; Special Forces ops. You know, the domestic home," I continued, *getting very convincing* and official sounding, using phrases such as this "stands no chance these days unless you sleep with a rottweiler and a shotgun, Carrigan. I've read all about this in the current *Ledger Dispatch*, and they get their info mainlined straight from the CIA in DC. It's federal-government mandated info, for the protection of U.S. citizens. You'll learn about the mandates later in high school."

I might as well have been smoking a cigarette in the dark. A Lucky Strike. No! A fat Cohiba cigar.

"And they also have secret inventions that can cut glass. Your alarm system doesn't tell you if glass is being cut, *now does it?*"

Hell, no, it didn't. Everybody in Amador County knew that.

Carrigan rolled quietly out of his baseball franchise logo comforter and flopped down next to me on the floor. Then he dragged the same great expensive comforter down upon his frightened frame and bundled up in a ball next to me, the informed warrior, the intelligent protector. I would kill the ninja before he peppered Carrigan with sappy ninja stars. I was a mighty bear, a veritable Kodiak.

And now I had accomplished my compulsive goal: to scare him into needing my protection. To be his dad at a weird sleep over party. I was pretty absurd back then. I don't really understand the psychology behind my actions, and thus I'm quite unforgiving toward my teenage self, wishing I could go back in time and slap myself upside the head, exclaiming, "What the fuck, dude?"

I wish Sinead had taken me to a therapist. I have a sinking feeling she knew I was troubled. And I know that she began keeping a watchful eye on me over the months. Her motherly kindness grew hesitant toward me little by little. Who could blame her? I haven't asked her about that weird year to this day. Even after sixteen years. No way. Too weird. Growing-up years are too weird; oft times they're best left at the bottom of a lake.

Second Deviation: we played baseball all the time back then at Mike Clark field in Pine Grove. Now, before playing, there was the obligatory calling of names so that teams could be chosen. I continually tried to work the odds right so that I'd be on Carrigan's team, but sometimes my quick wit calculations and sycophantic, pick-me-now-and-YOU-WILL-WIN stare didn't always work. And then my all-star son would be far from my intelligent grasp and irrevocably on the opposing team! Curses! Fie! Fie! Zounds!

I hated batting when Carrigan was pitching. It felt like trying to eat a slice of delicious pepperoni pizza squished inside a subway sandwich of mayonnaise, turkey, lettuce, and Swiss. It just felt wrong and tasted worse. I had a sensitive tummy. I would certainly gag.)

I'd shrug my eyebrows, lungs, and shoulders and then sulkily play really badly and lazily on purpose—all saturnine and stupid, fat looking. Jose Canseco would certainly have flipped me off had he been present. I would suck *that* badly, consciously hurting my team so that I could be the pinstriped martyr, and Carrigan could be "saved" by winning and looking good. I liked to have him look good.

In fact, I liked to have all the Finnegans look good, even Seamus. If I could have made his slobber liquid silver by scarring my forearms with snakebites and wasp stings I would've. I was that crazy about their perfection. They were my action figures. I figured I owed such well-wishing to them for all the hours logged in the hot tub. I also figured that if the Finnegans were winning at life then I was winning at life; and I don't mean the board game. As I lived among them every day I subconsciously thought, *This is what I missed out on growing up—a real family.* And I chewed, chewed, and chewy chew chewed on that mythical family turd for hours.

Carrigan was my favorite action figure demigod, and as the year wore on, Sinead became less of a demigod (smacking of 80% mortal) as Carrigan sprouted golden wings. If somebody had given me a sticker that said: PRESS, and a black camera with a giant flash bulb, I would've been the Carrigan Finnegan official paparazzi.

Meanwhile, Brendan and I grew further apart. We only hung out in the car to and from school or in front of the TV at night, watching inane sitcoms like *The Fresh Prince of Bel Air* and eating inane Crystal ice cream. He was 120% mortal.

That winter, the birth of 1992, I began to daily examine my burgeoning mental problems with shrewd scrutiny and alarming alacrity, a scientist of dark narcissism. I realized that I had taken on a singular form of depression, compounding my other issues. Not a slit-wrist depression exactly, just a selfish, gray-rain-cloud one: I wanted to be a proclaimed *victim* of someone or something at sometime or another all the time. And I wanted everybody to notice.

One night, a good-sized spider crawled into my can of Pepsi and drowned as I sat in the spa, oblivious. As I took a swig I just about puked, spewing out the candied-brown, drowned, and limp exoskeleton across the frosty weeds. Like an electric shock in the brain, I felt I'd been targeted by directly Mother Nature herself. *This spider knew he couldn't bite me 'cuz I'd see him, so he tried to bite my throat by hiding in this can! EVIL! WHY ME? THERE ARE, LIKE, SIX OTHER OPENED SODA CANS OUT HERE! IT'S NOT FAIR!* I angrily fomented, my brain fizzling like carbonated soda pop. I was the number-one victim of everything and everybody and every insect everywhere all the time for every reason ever. Behind every tree was a rapist redneck with a hickory, big-league slugger. I am now thinking of George Costanza's irrational insecurities, but I am not laughing. I was a paranoid person. I was a ridiculous person. I was still frightened of sharks and McDonald's bushes.

I didn't tell anybody about my problems, because to me they were not *real* problems (like the ones people in treatment centers on television's late night dramas: white robes, chattering mouths, bandaged arms). To me, they began to turn from negative problems into something else, something more palatable, more rational, more responsible—a more at-home feeling—something I could be proud of and nurture: my problems were simply me being *smart*.

I was smarter than most people and saw things they were too dense to perceive. I was acutely aware of a great many hidden things. I was cognizant of the true world: a world where four year olds get beaten bloody in bathtubs. A mean world. A Stockton world. Even if one lived in Amador County, there were still ex-Nam ninjas waiting to strangle you with really strong tiny wires that would slice into your throat and sever all your neck arteries in the blink of an eye. Nobody's trachea was safe. We all would be murdered; I was sure of it.

*Where's Carrigan? He needs my help!* my eagle mind screamed. The spider was in the water. The shark was in the air. Irrational rationalities.

The growing guilt of feeling like I was abandoning my mom, no—*betraying* her, made me feel even more irrational—more paranoid, like I was a bad person. Certainly Carrigan would realize I was betraying her and commence loathing my big presence in his home—which would lead to him telling his whole family what a jerk I was—then they'd hate me like rattlers and ultimately throw my big ass out into the frozen woods, and, of course, it would follow that the ninja guy would find me and know through innate P.O.W. powers that I was a fat horrible person—and—*then*, simply cut me into two jiggly pieces of flesh and betrayal; but that wouldn't be the end of the rational fiasco, because right there and then a gang of malevolent possums and a putrid posse of stinkbugs would find my dual corpse and begin feasting away! AH! I WOULD DIE AND END AND BE NAKED AND THERE WOULD BE DIRT AND GRAVEL AND BUGS AND VO5 SHAMPOO IN MY BLOOD AND SKELETON!

My mind was rapid. A train wreck of a brain. Irrational rationalities.

One day I accidentally stepped on my Biology teacher's new white Reebok sneaker (he was sporty, the varsity football coach, incidentally) and he leaped back, exclaiming (genially) "Whoa, you're on my shoe there, buddy!" I had big heavy feet. The squiggly lines of my old Nike traction sullied his snow-white sneaker like sin on a newborn. Across his toe area you could easily read the word "NIKE" in linoleum dust. I apologized and went to dust off his shoe, quickly/awkwardly—knocking my biology book off the sterile science experiment counter. He jumped back even further from me, exclaiming, *even more* genially, "HEY! Don't worry about it; they were too white anyway. They looked too new!" He leaned over and dusted off his fragile Reebok with a smile on his face. I smiled back nervously and felt just like a stinky mountain of hairy elephant dung. I picked up the heavy book with hatred in my heavy heart for just how loudly it had hit the floor, drawing every popular girl's attention to my elephant crappiness. I was the victim. Not the Reeboks.

All year I felt deep down that Mr. Lukens loathed my big presence for ruining his brand new, expensive, soft leather, consummately designed sneakers, white as snow. I knew it as surely as I knew that someday I would die. I also knew that behind his fragile amiability he was really planning ways of docking points on my tests for "squishing perfect amoebas under the microscope by rough handle-ization!"

Surprisingly, amid all my surreptitious irrationalities, I still had a lot of friends. My wit and funny personality saved me. Paradox. Even my being overweight and having plain looks were overlooked and indeed, kind of advantageous as I quickly became the BIG MAN on campus, following in the retarded footsteps of my real father. I was a Jones, big man of the Amador High School Buffaloes, weighing in at around 230 and standing a towering 6 feet 3 inches. I was huge, friendly, witty, and wouldn't harm a fly. Big bear. And people indeed liked me: the awe-inspiring Yellowstone spectacle.

Brendan had a lot of friends at school, who naturally became my friends; most of them were sporty and preppy, which rallied me to get going on my political crusade to be accepted and indeed craved by the upper echelons of high school.

Amador was a small school: about 600 kids in 1991, about a fifth the size of Stag high back in Stockton. Thus, big fish, little pond. (Thumbs up! From the cockpit of an f14 tomcat! With an American flag billowing in the breeze behind it and red, white, and blue electric guitars wailing in a slow, heroic ballad!)

My rise to big-fish fame was boosted not only by Brendan's contacts but also by my new love of staying busy within the scholarly schoolyard, so to speak. I was ACTIVE! I was a man creating my own destiny. In charge.

For the first time in my life: I exercised quite a bit (running, lifting, um, throwing baseballs at Carrigan) both at school and at the Finnegans; they really helped me get healthy! Lots of granola and Gatorade.

For the first time in my life I socialized an enormous amount. I moved from one group to another at lunch to make sure everybody still loved me and was

## PUSH MY LIFE INTO A DUFFLE BAG

cognizant of my big-man status. Even the freshman got some love. I joined the Student Leadership Class (S.L.C.) and used my outrageous acumen and magical whispers of elitism to become prominent there. At least, in my head I was prominent there. Oh, yes, also (and this is big) I began *announcing* at varsity basketball games, using my firecracker wit and booming radio voice to propel me into a veritable, golden empyrean of teen popularity. Announcing truly made me a big-bear-fish man. Everybody at Amador knew that I was *Theee* Voice of the Buffaloes on the court and off! I mattered and was indispensable. Finally. Bono Vox.

Oh, I forgot to mention that I whacked it a lot in high school (i.e. masturbated). Daily. High school boys of every generation will never admit to the fact that most all of them did or do the same. Daily. Sometimes I did this special kind of exercise twice a day, when I was feeling really healthy. I considered masturbation as part of my overall exercise regime. I'd read that it was "healthy and normal for adolescent boys to do it often" in my beloved UC Davis *Human Sexuality* book that I picked up for free in the junk bin at the school library. (I distinctly remember how I discreetly accomplished the task of picking it up: I spotted it from afar and maneuvered my way over to it like a spy so that nobody would think that I was a Pre-Med pervert. After all, I was only interested in the book out of a singular quest for resplendent medical knowledge. I slipped it into my backpack like it was a crown jewel, a red ruby, and quickly, as if a Dr. Pervert alarm might be sounded at any second, made my way to the nearest egress. I made it out of the library without being spotted, a giant smile in my face and in my pants. I was smarter than the decrepit library marm with her insipid horned beetle broach and dried up sexual brio.)

My UC Davis Human Sexuality book contained artful ash drawings of different sexual positions. I appreciated these drawings.

There were women of different ethnicities and different breast sizes portrayed. The black couple had subtle afros. The white male had big sideburns and a cowboy moustache. I didn't use this book merely for knowledge. The book instructed me that at age eighteen I would reach my sexual peak. So, I had better exercise a lot in order to be physically ready for the eighteenth-year sex party that would hit me like a ton of bricks in two years. Sexy bricks. Indeed. Be prepared. Sexual peak, prime, whatever. Exercise.

A ton of tits. Hitting me in the face. Exercise. Twice a day sometimes. (High school boys need freezing showers.)

As I exercised, I got a little thinner and looked a little better and started taking interest in actual, walking, breathing, talking girls—not just ones drawn in eruditely naked ash. I tried dating a couple real live girls, but had no success.

My date and I, continually and without fail, would end up with a *safe* group of people or, if I was lucky enough to get a girl alone in a dark theater, the movie would, no matter what, be a safe, laugh-out-loud, spill-your-Coke-on-my-lap, point, and-then-laugh-out-loud-some-more comedy. Coke out the nostrils like Old Faithful. (Damn comedies. They're nothing like an actual comedy, such as *Much Ado About Nothing.* Everybody draw a U shape on the white board—then label the different parts of the chronological comedy. Good. Learning is fun.)

I don't believe any girl truthfully found me attractive. Big men on campus aren't lusted over; they're hugged and cheered on. Hooray. I'd go home the loveless victim, the belle-less beast with cold, damp Coke pants, and exercise away my fears, hoping that any Finnegan ears weren't detecting odd noises in the tile and marble bathroom of twenty-five minute pretext dumps.

*But wait just one second!* It wasn't all just sad fancy. There was one poignantly perfect girl that cheered my lonely heart! I truly adored her, and she kind of liked me even though we never went out on a comedy-Coke date.

Her name was Monica; Monica of typing class. Man, was she ever cute. She had this lime-green Esprit tee shirt that would snuggle her curves and make me completely unable ot ytpe cuzz I waws sssekretliy steealieng glances at her glorious body and face. Soft like apricots. Visually candid like stars.

She was a brunette. She had eyes: oh man, oh man, did she have eyes! And she had a mouth with lips that curved up slightly at the edges whenever my wit prevailed, and the whole world blossomed in radiant ecstasy.

"Hey, your typewriter's really loud. I can't type. It's too loud. Can you please turn your typewriter off, Monica, until I'm finished? Some of us have to work around here," I declare, with perfect deadpan comic delivery.

"What? My typewriterrr.... What? You silly person!" Lips curving up slightly at the edges, chair swiveling in my direction. "Some of *us* have better concentration abilities than others; life is cruel," she rejoinds, grinning and begins typing really fast just to spite me: *click-click-click-cli-cli-click-click!*

"Life *iiisss* cruel, Monica; so I guess you'll have to go sit in the hall 'til class is over, since your typewriter is so loud it's causing students to fail this class," I reply, in control, flirting away with delicate ease like the man on the flying trapeze.

## PUSH MY LIFE INTO A DUFFLE BAG

She stops *clicking*, swiveling again in my direction, "Reeeeeeaaallly? Well, I honestly don't care about anybody else but myself. As long as I become the president then everybody else can fail." She begins banging on the typewriter keys, staring right at me maniacally, barely holding back her presidential, smoky laughter.

Looking back, Monica matched me wit for wit daily; she was like Elizabeth Bennett in *Pride and Prejudice*: always in control and willing to flirt, knowing she could navigate any situation to suit her objectives. If she didn't want to flirt with you she wouldn't, period. End of game. She always flirted with me. And I loved her for it.

She was in drama and musical theatre, smart and cool. Monica. *Sweet ESPRIT Monica!* She liked that I played baseball.

And here we have our next subject. I played baseball. Not only did I play baseball in the Finnegan front yard, but also on the Amador High professional varsity baseball team. I made the cut! Big man bats in another steak-and-gravy run for his bubbly high school career. And yet, still, nobody dated me, but it mattered not! I had my professional baseball validation. Everyday I could lay out my Amador High Buffaloes uniform in royal blue and white on my bed and stand back, arms folded, gazing at its majesty. I was part of a team, a team recognized by the entire community. I was just like Jose Canseco. So there. I didn't need a girlfriend. I was fine, irrational, and proud of it!

Well, not really. I wanted a girlfriend desperately. And I knew, deep down in my gut, that I was irrational and paranoid. I knew that it wasn't just me being "smart" all the time; my private Self-Reflection Sessions (walks) helped me to slowly realize and understand this.

Picture this: I'm going out for a long walk in the fields east of the Finnegan ranch at sundown. I'm smelling the fragrant grasses, I'm hearing the bird sounds, and I'm feeling the country air, quiet and footfall affirming. I'm feeling peaceful, and I'm forcing myself to ponder myself, my thoughts, my proclivities, my fears, everything, with judiciousness and objectivity. I'm getting better at being me. I'm becoming a better person. These solitary evening walks helped. Usually solitude renders the mad madder (examine Shelley's "Alastor"), but in my humble case, it forced me to see just how mad I was—and work to cope. Talking to myself out in those fields all alone was helpful, too. Once I even prayed. Many a field toad reared his bumpy head in vexation over my grassy twilight meanderings, for sure.

At this age of sixteen (1991-92) I was truly awakened to the fact that there was no more hiding from myself anymore. Smeagol had to face Gollum. I couldn't turn a blind eye to my oddities anymore. Social fears? Squeameries? Obsessive revelries via insecurities? I am now thinking that when I say, "No more hiding," I really mean, "No more hiding from the brain scars left by the past." Yes, that works. I had to climb into the bathtub once more, so to speak, and face the ancient monsters.

During those beautiful eventide walks I'd see Caleb hitting me, I'd see my mom flopping down another credit card at the shit store, I'd see Sam wishing I would go away, I'd see a Italian man without a head walking through the orange seventies with an unwieldy ghost erection throwing him off balance. (I'd never seen an actual photograph of my real father.)

With the onset of trying for the first time to get good grades, exercise, and succeed within the life-microcosm of Amador High, I had casually swept out all of the garbage in my life, but now there was this weird mental void that collapsed in on itself. I had no religion. I hadn't any fire in my heart. Thus, my childhood slowly rushed upon me like a dusty-boned, skeleton banshee. I stood in the field and heard it overhead. Then I could see it, way up there in the October sky, hovering over me and all the rest of the bruised children throughout time, bones all creaky rattley sounding and toothy jaws wailing mute bloody murder. Harrowing.

I saw it, and then I did something that surprised me. I bravely pointed up at it. Right at it. I wasn't afraid of it. It was just plain ugly, not scary. "You are not me," I said. "You are not welcome here," I declared, with a jolt of real trepidation. Then I raised my other arm, and instead of pointing I gave the banshee the finger.

When I got back to the house I grabbed a baseball and my mitt and headed immediately back out of the house. Biology homework could wait. I jogged a ways out away into the fields and began throwing the ball way up high into the air, feeling soothed by the sound it made as it came back and hit with a slap the inside of my competent mitt.

Up, up, up the ball would go by virtue of my powerful right arm, and then: SLAP! It hit the pre-molded pocket of my American-rawhide mitt. Soothing. Rawlings therapy. Manly and hinting of a cliché, but helping me nonetheless. At the time, I didn't know about culture or the art world. I didn't know the correct way of looking at paintings in order to be touched, assuaged, and refreshed by them. The only painting I even knew of was the Mona Lisa, because televised pop culture likes to eternally strip it down and make an ignorant, insipid mockery of it.

No paintings. No sculptures. No *Brothers Karamazov*. No *Paradise Lost*. No *Wasteland* or *Four Quartets*. No travel (which would force me to step outside of my minuscule world). Nothing. My only catharsis was baseball. And it worked.

I was a denimed Kevin Costner out in a cornfield—all mystic eyed and white-sneakered. I thought baseball was unflinching truth in a world of swirling vortex. It was my only fire escape. As I touched upon before, I did indeed play varsity baseball that year for the Amador Buffalos. This was a dream come true: I was out on the big green field, where hot chix could watch me and admire my sportive prowess; only problem here is that I didn't have much. I wasn't very good.

If a ball player could be judged on a skill level of 1-100 (100 being like Mark McGuire, Barry Bonds, or rookie of the year Carrigan Finnegan), then I, in my junior year glory would be about a 31. And that's generous. I sucked. My mind wanted me not to suck, but my instincts, body, and whatever else turns a human into a sport version of James Bond were all slow and stupid. Sometimes I flinched when at bat, frightened that the ball might hit me. This made me sad. I knew I sucked. I knew I was a bench warmer. I knew this and that and the other guys were seeing me know it and knowing it themselves. Even the mayflies knew it, gossiping of it in low tones to one another under their curved diaphanous wings.

Every time I threw the ball I worried I'd throw it too far or too short or off target. Every time somebody threw me the ball I worried I'd drop it. I was a tangled baseball of nerves out there on the green.

The only reason I even *made* the cut was the fact that my Student Leadership Class (S.L.C.), um, leader (that redundancy is funny), Mr. Larson, liked me and took pity on me. He was also the varsity baseball coach, by the by. He was a good man. He knew through his grizzled baseball instincts that I was tightly wound and that my adolescent stress could be greatly mitigated by him giving me a golden ticket within one of my many bitter chocolate bars. So he did. God bless you, Coach Larson, wherever you are. I hope you're still alive. You were really old.

And now for an American baseball anecdote; and, no, I do not mean the double I hit in that clutch game against the Linden Lions. I mean a real anecdote, not about achievement, but about the humorous trivialities that everybody loves, a laid back story. My buddy Troy Smith and I were in charge of maintaining the ballfield's nice, clean appearance. Everybody on the team had something extra-baseball-curricular to do so that Larson could instill a work ethic in us pinstriped rapscallions. Troy and I would meet on the ball field on non-practice days after school at 3:15. We'd walk around the school with a tiny white trash bag (the lame kind for under kitchen sinks; capacity: about two basketballs, no...a basketball and a small bunt cake worth of field junk). We'd pick up sticky Gatorade bottles, powdery orange Cheetos bags, ant-filled Snickers wrappers, human teeth, etc. This part of the clean up was mundane and dumb.

But the next part was awesome: we had to calibrate the pitching machine and make sure it was oiled and superlisclous for the next practice. Let the fun begin. We'd oil it and calibrate it like good-work-ethic boys, but then we did indeed have to try it out and make sure it worked right.

We'd put it on home base and aim it up and out toward the outfield; then we'd fire hot baseballs at 100 mph straight up and out into the banshee ether and watch 'em fly! They would just about pierce heaven, it seemed to us high school Hobbits.

When they landed they'd make 5-inch divots in the sod out in center field. (It was crazy powerful!) "Hardy har har," we'd snicker; later on, as Mr. Larson coached whoever was in the outfield: he'd trip, stop, look down, bend over, feel the divot, shake his head, look up at the sky, and wonder about baseball vendetta aliens. Then, even later on, he'd grunt and inquire, "Who's making all those marks out in the field? Do any of you guys have thick metal cleats? The school board pays out a lot of dough for this field." And everybody would lift up one of their feet and ceremoniously examine each cleat like good little, diligent baseballers, picking out sod and, on rare occasion, a used condom. The baseball field was government-protected mating-ground habitat for horny teens at night; this was commonly understood, but seldom spoken of in front of Mr. Larson.

Troy and I would examine our cleats too, with frumpled brows and tragically-concerned faces—then we'd look at each other and just about die of delicious joc(k)ularity. Those were good times, despite all the laps I had to run and jumping jacks I had to do.

(Now, is it just me, or was the jumping jack invented back in the Civil War days as part of a healthy soldier's workout or whatever? They seem so antiquated in movement and almost quaint, especially the name. Jumping Jack. Salt pork, hard tack, and Sharp's new model 1863 carbine.)

Troy Smith and I grew to be great friends. And then there was a third friend: Gabe Newton. They were both equally good at baseball and, well, girls (in a healthy way, not pervy or slutty, just good at actual dating—real gentlemen—opening a billion heavy mead hall doors for swooning, fragile lasses). They also got good grades. I was fortunate that they liked me. Thank you personality.

As our friendships grew we spent more and more time outside of the schoolyard together. I stayed the night like a bajillion times out at Troy's house, and the three of us stayed up late listening to Nirvana, Pearl Jam, Soundgarden, and other grunge greats. This was a good time to be into music; I'm really glad I wasn't in high school about five years earlier, when there was nothing but hair and mascara male crap on the radio. Indeed, I opt for the sable insight of Kurt Cobain over the glammy turds of Vince Neal. Flannel is so much more true to life than spandex.

The Red Hot Chili Peppers were also exploding at this time. I liked them because the hippest guy on campus (the Amador Johnny Depp, if you will) really dug them—even had a tour shirt! His mighty name was Logan Porto. Very intimidating. All the girls wanted to be on him, but he was too into poetry, elm trees, and metaphorical thoughts of death to notice. His ancient-looking leather-bound diary was his sex. Logan had long, grunge hair, too; thinking back acutely, he kind of looked like both Johnny Depp and Chris Cornell, but with chocolate brown eyes instead of lightning blue. Seeing how independent he was made me want to break my own rusty cage, like a Badmotorfinger. Sonorous allusion.

Music was as big as baseball to us cool Amador cats; it was our cultural dabbling point—along with Saturday Night Live, which we watched religiously—together—with Mountain Dew 2 liters in hand. And don't you ever forget the copious amounts of Taco Bell (some nights we'd drive 24 miles round trip to Jackson to secure our fast food fats). We weren't healthy snackers, but who is at the stupid age of 16? I even counted the endless amounts of white, iceberg lettuce in my tacos as my salad for the day. A weird combo: run lots of laps and then eat crap. I must have drunk at least ten truckloads of refined sugar that year in the form of satanic high-fructose corn syrup. Ah, you gotta give it to those soda-pop advertisers; they sure no how to kill us. America.

We three compatriots were an odd mix of one part jock, one part popular (synonymous), and one part nerd. And I say nerd because we started a Philosophy Club in April of that year, and it continued on into the next year.

We held it at lunch in the Drama room with Mr. Giles Turner at the helm. He was the illustrious drama teacher. Had been for twenty + years; he agreed to be involved with the club despite his busy thespian schedule. Well, actually, he agreed to lend us his giant '70s-smelling room at lunch whilst he munched his healthy, organic salad. (He was the only person in the world who actually, honestly knew the word "organic" in the year 1992, before it became the most popular word in the universe and beyond, circa 2001) discreetly and watched us believe ourselves to be supreme, enlightened thinkers.

None of us had ever read Plato, Aristotle, Kierkegaard, Rousseau, etc., but we weren't apologizing to Socrates for it, and we for sure thought we were the cerebral shit, I tell you what.

We'd lean forward and gesticulate gently as we dabbled in pointless gabble and sophistry. It's funny to me now; I wish I could go back in time and sit in at one of our airy, metaphysical meetings. None of us had beards. None of us had even heard of the simple allegory of the cave or could possibly define the word "sage." But we had good hearts. Yes, we were good men and true! And we were trying to grow (to issue forth greeny tendrils into the ether). Good for us! I like us back then: them-thar formative years of Mountain Dew philosophical midwifery.

My junior year in Amador County flew by faster than a hawk diving for a mouse. And I began to really enjoy life in the country—bright and shiny as a spotless credit record, which I falsely believed the Finnegans to possess.

# Chapter 10
# Blanket of Coldest Snow

But all good things must end: as the golden summer of 1992 hit mid-June. My time living with the Finnegans was over. Sinead had grown tired of me. She'd noticed that I secretly worshipped her son Carrigan and that my friendship with Brendan had cooled considerably. She didn't like this. My ostensible jolly persona didn't fool her. She knew I was dealing with some real issues.

Thus, she made the decision to no longer be the one to cope with me, because that would mean exposing her offspring to further Jones toxicity. Alert was the mother lioness; her protective claws were tapping my final seconds out on the stones. I had worn out my welcome. One year was enough. I'm sure Luke Cromwell had something to do with it. Bastard English invader. But who can blame him? It was high time I left.

So I packed my duffle bag and headed home to shitty Stockton: like an out-of-tune piano on fire with 200 pounds of dead catfish under the gleaming lid. Hot, shitty, stinky Stockton. I was not a happy camper. That was the end of my junior year, the end of Pine Grove in my life, or so I thought. As holy fate would have it, I would not stay in Stockton long.

My mother unwittingly and sadistically tortured me within the first two weeks of my being home: she told me to *travel back* up to Amador County heaven and grab my high school transcripts from the ancient secretary, who smelled like moldy, squishy avocados, in the A building at Amador High so that I would be all prepared for my lame senior year at Stag High. Crappy, crappy, crappy Stag High. "Sure, mother, I'll float on back up to Paradiso, gather up some sweet bunches of peachy cloud, and then tie heavy weights to my ankles so that I may descend back down into the Inferno; sounds great!" said I. And I got in my Volkswagen bug one fine morning and drove up into the foothills (like a white-tailed deer to procure my papyrus transcripts), my face sad with loss and exasperation. But then things got interesting, quite interesting, forsooth!

It was early summer. I had only been home a couple weeks and yet, here I was, fortunately—no…serendipitously back in the county of my juice-filled heart—all a-burgeonin' with the hopes and smells of piney goodness and coyote honesty. I loved the smell, even the dead skunks.

So, I hurried along and got my transcripts from the avocado lady without any problems. I'm forever amiable with secretaries. Then I hopped back in my mauve Volkswagen. (I forgot to mention that I acquired my first car: this bug, my junior year from an old lady in Sutter Creek; cost: only $300.00; mileage: only 102,000! A perfect first car, although somewhat banged up and louder than feral cats in heat.)

At last, with a resigned, deep breath, I readied myself for the long trip home. I started up the sputtering German engine. I sighed and put it in gear, moving forward slowly, taking it all in. The sun warmed the dusty windshield like a mother painting warm butter on her clear baby. A hot June breeze tickled my sweaty neck through the eternally rolled-down windows. It was approximately 95 degrees. The grass was all yellow, and the oaks were all sleepy. Bugs were singing and zipping around in the thick air. I sighed again, relishing the hot, sweet drama.

Was this it? Really it? The end of beautiful Amador County? *Please say no!* Was I to just drive back to Mordor now and prepare for darkness? It couldn't be. *How mundane and lifeless! How stifling to a young man's heart! How shitty! No!*

Wait. It was here, right here, that my thinking was pushed out of the way by my powerful stomach. My stomach's always been more mighty and domineering than my spineless brain. I was hungry. I was hungry. I was hungry. Okay, enough already! It was 4 p.m. Was it not? Supper time! Hungry Hobbit! Actually, more like Gollum; that's how hungry I was. Hamburgers. Fries. Banana shake. Hot and then ice cold and then hot again. Repeat. Wipe mouth. Ecstasy.

The immaculate and sexy red-and-white "Highway 88 Burgers" sign flashed across my Gollumesque mind. *Pre-ci-ous. Pre-ci-ous bur-gers. So squishy sweeeeet!* Yummy. An eight-mile drive up Ridge Road and then over and onto Highway 88, then add just one mile. 1,000 foot elevation up to a 2,300 foot elevation, speaking in foothill-elevation terms. Well, worth it. My foot hit the pedal, and my saliva elevated.

I would most certainly not start my Mordor year quite yet. Rather, I would rapaciously eat copious amounts of hamburger. I pulled out of the cracked asphalt parking lot and drove like a man en route to Christmas, through Sutter Creek, up Ridge Road, past all the wineries and that castle-looking house with the massive dry pond out front, past the Finnegan spread, past Surrey Junction, past the vet clinic where my future friend's pooch, Shortcake, breathed her last breath in '95, past the winding steeps, past Mike Clark field, and onward to Pine Grove and hwy 88—then, GLORIOUS 88 BURGERS...right before the Gold Post bar and alpine oblivion.

I ordered 3. Three burgers, fries, and an ice-cold banana shake, just like I prophesied a page back. Then I walked out to my dilapidated bug proudly, ready to devour my delicious carrion in private, like a portly northern Kodiak with a rare banana-flavored deer carcass shipped from a cousin sugar bear living around the equator. That's a woody-worldly analogy of predatorial connotations. (Incidentally, I remember always wrongly writing the word "commentation" whenever I meant the word "connotation" back in my inept high school days.)

Before I got into the bug I glanced around the parking lot and noticed a familiar face a few yards away next to a Geo convertible. And this familiar face seemed to notice me. I made the decision to say hello (insecurities over not quite knowing his name be damned; I was a friendly fellow!)

So I hollered over to him, "Hey! Would you remember a second-string center fielder if he was in the same parking lot as you?" I asked with the most radiant smile ever, jauntily traipsing over to him. The question was posed in a jocular way—disarming the entire universe and forcing bomb squads everywhere relax and crack open a cold one. And, wouldn't you know it, he smiled back and acknowledged me with sincerity. I wiped the sweat from my brow.

"Hey, BIG BEAR!" he hollered; he was a jovial fellow too.

My nickname to some of my sportier acquaintances at Amador was "Big Bear," which sounds like "Bear Hunter," my old step-grandfather; interesting. It worked.

I won't go into the details of our conversation, simply because I can't remember them. However, here is the point of our conversation: Larry, the Geo guy, did not like the fact that I had to leave the country and head back to Stockton. He was like, "That sucks. But, man, no, why don't you stay with us, instead, and stay at our house for your entire senior year?"

That's the gist. Angels got their wings somewhere up in the glistening heavenly city at the exact moment in time that Larry said those magic words. And I consented to look into it ASAP. Although overjoyed about the possibilities of the generous offer, I was still as cautious as ever. Who were these people exactly? Why did Larry feel it was fine and dandy to ask somebody his parents didn't even know to stay at their house for an entire year? Something was odd and out of place for sure. I needed proof of Slothicans sanity. So we decided to drive up to his dad's "textile" store right after I wolfed down my delicious burgers.

Larry's dad, Dick Slothicans, was a bit rotund, a bit greasy, but he extended his hand and was nice enough to me. Actually, perhaps too nice for a first meeting, agreeing with Larry that I should stay with them and saying things like, "No way in hell you're movin' down there; that's bullshit! You're staying with us!" I was assured by both father and son that it would be fine and dandy if I started living in their spare room thingy as soon as possible; which meant in about a month. I found out later that Dick actually knew me and already really liked me because I announced the Amador High basketball games with "real zazz and gusto!" Larry played on the team. All was good. I had already earned their trust.

But all wasn't so good. I soon found out that Dick was a bombastic, short-sighted man, with a quick temper and a smelly house. Regardless, I was happy as a clam to live out my senior year life in the golden foothills. I didn't have to pay any rent, either. When we finished negotiations in Dick's weird tee-shirt printing office on that hot August day, he grabbed the "company" phone and called my mother to kindly *inform* her of my new home. "As long as he'll eat what we put on the table then he can live for FREE," bombasted Dick, a corpulent, pallid wink to me where I stood, in the corner of the stuffy office, patiently smiling, feeling really weird and a tad nervous about Slothicans implications. After five minutes of discussion, Tallene consented to my staying on in Pine Grove for the upcoming year. I would be fed at no cost to her, I would be in the fresh air, and I would be taken care of. The deal was done in seven minutes total—entirely over the phone.

Thus it began. I was seventeen and in my first apartment. I was now a Pine Grove-ian on my own—autonomous of the patron Finnegans. I was ecstatic, but again, nervous. No rent? A year? Hmmm. Should I decline this offer? No! Why not?

Stockton sucks: My mother, Mr. Lincoln, and all of the tough gangsta parkas at Stag high. *No more questions, YOU!*

Thus began my glorious stay with the Slothicans. (Oh, God, the aftermath!) There was one prerequisite to my free apartment room. A prerequisite that shivered my timbers. Larry told me that I "had to play football" with him that very fall for the Amador Buffaloes. "We'll tear it up, Big Bear!"

Yuck. I hated football, but he was all buddy buddy about it, and I loved baseball, so maybe if I could go out onto the field with my football helmet on and a symbolic Louisville Slugger in my hand for placebo foolery I would be okay. Wouldn't *that* look funny. It's a rhetorical question, so no question mark, even though Microsoft is berating me presently.

"For sure you'll be a lineman, dude," declared Larry, looking me up and down. "You'll be good at pushing people around. A Chicago Bear. Oh, yeeeaah!" We chuckled like men.

Later that night as I lay in bed I was filled with a severe sense of trepidation: how was I to push other big guys around? I had no nerve! No gumption to kill and win! I was an announcer! Not a gladiator! What if I got really hurt? What if I allowed the QB to be sacked again and again? Would the other guys hate me? Would they beat me up in the showers? Would it really, honestly be me vs. the other team and my own team as well? Me vs. all manly men the world over? And, most importantly: would my prodigious girth show through my blue and white jerzee to all the hot cheerleaders? Would they subsequently vomit all at the same time when they saw the sweat lines of my Grand Canyon butt crack permeating the spandex material of my homosexual football pantaloons?

My mind raced and spun out of control. Fear gripped my brain like it was a deflated pigskin. All seemed lost. Football? Me? My eyebrows contorted as I looked to the ceiling. I remembered just how excited Larry was over the whole thing earlier that day, patting me on the back and crowing, *"We're gonna crush some skulls, buddy!"*

I loved crushing skulls, almost as much as I loved protecting skulls. Before permanently planting in Pine Grove, I had to endure one shitty month of Stockton summer before "hell week" (i.e., football training camp) started at Amador. I'd heard horror stories about hell week. There would be sweat for sure. I wasn't fond of sweat. Running. Getting naked in showers with other guys who had bigger genitalia and more well-positioned hair than I. My heart sank every time I thought about it. Baseball didn't require much showering.

I seriously hated football. But (And here I applaud my youthful charisma and courage!) I stood determined. I would slam into it like a freight train 'cuz it was keeping me in the foothills, dammit! It was a good deal through and through! I would kick football's burly American ass! *Tough me! Toot the tin horns!* So, I trained hard, like a Spartan who loved Pearl Jam, mashed potatoes, and slapping his insecurity in its soft face.

I started out said training by walking around a square Stockton block. Hard training, I tell you what: walking around a suburban block. Hell, yeah. I can see the sweaty Gatorade add now: Fat high school kid walks like hell. The end of the add would be me wiping my sweat-bead brow and chugging some antifreeze-colored electrolyte replacement fluid as if it were liquid life itself in a well-marketed form.

Then I began training harder: walking around the block twice. But wait! Then I stepped it up one frickin' notch: I JOGGED around the block—then around *two* blocks—then *three!* I began to actually feel better and get into a shape. Yes, indeed, hell week would be murdered by me, myself, and I. However, in actuality, I was almost murdered; my heart nearly exploded in the heat and sporty insecurities. Baseball practice was a cake walk in comparison.

Here's the funny part, the dirty secret I've kept forever from anyone and everyone I knew during that time: I faked a serious injury before the season even started. (Full-on wailing histrionics, I tell you—scrimmage game, half-ass ref running out and bending over me with a concerned frown on his face)! I let myself be pushed pretty hard by one of our own elephant lineman into a fleshy pile of adolescent spandex and cleats. Then they all huffingly arose from their grassy indentations, all except me because I had gotten "seriously injured."

What a shame. A gridiron tragedy, really. And what do you know, right *before* our very *first* real game vs. Linden! I was (not) crushed. My football dreams were (not) dashed to pieces. I let the team carry me off the field, my muddy arm extended down to my butt—showing that I had definitely injured my tail bone (whilst under the pile of lineman glory I had decided that it would be my tailbone I would pretextually injure. I mean, who could argue that I hadn't? Nobody would want to put their fingers into my sweaty butt crack to check—it was a flawless decision of sport lawyery).

Of course, I had to visit a chiropractor in Jackson [by myself—I drove myself—all ninja—I knew I wasn't hurt and didn't want anybody to find out];

a few teammates had seen me land pretty hard on my big butt right before the pile of husky boys buried me in a San Francisco dream. To them, I was hurt; they'd seen it. Case closed. Now I just had to see a chiropractor surreptitiously so all good football people everywhere would know I'd seen one. Case further closed. Football over, and good riddance!

Should I palm a fifty and leave it in said chiropractor's hand when we met and shook hands? Perhaps. Was that illegal?

The chiropractor told me in smart Latin doctor terms that my tailbone was incontrovertibly fine after the x-rays came back calciumifically benign. I glared at the x-rays incredulously, rubbed my upper butt with pain in my face, shrugged, shook the doctor's strong hand, sans fifty, thanked him, and asked if I should still look after my tailbone and treat it with some wholesome ice and TLC—to which he replied, "Yes, be cognizant of it and treat it with respect."

"Okay," I muttered, feeling not cool because I wasn't sure what "cognizant" meant. I left the chiropractor's office feeling like I'd let him down, not because my tailbone wasn't broken and I'd wasted his time, but rather, because he was an erudite man of anatomy and medicine and I did not know what the word "cognizant" meant, and he certainly could see it in my sweaty kid face. I think my hand was moist when I shook his ultra-cool doctor hand, too. Crap. I was such a dolt!

The next day at Amador I boldly lied to the whole damn school, telling my coaches and teammates that I had indeed destroyed my tailbone. I declined to show them the x-rays because they had accidentally been damaged by heat in my Volkswagen or something like that. I purchased a little secretary sitting pillow at K-mart for all of my classes so that nobody would dare question me. Instead, they'd show me respect and attention for being a wounded gridiron warrior. Especially the chix! Girls just love an injured butt, inflatable, red pillow from K-mart.

It was brilliant. It worked in all ways to my advantage: no more effing football, no more public penis showers, no more four-mile runs into Sutter Creek, no more impending wrestle battles with opposing team's mean meat-men linemen, and, also, bonus, now there would be endless attention from respected teachers once they saw my beautiful butt pillow (I considered teachers as equals, as colleagues in my teen-brain arrogance; thus, I liked them talking to me regularly considerably). There was also *exquisite* attention from all female faces: bubble gum chewing and Noxema fresh. All sorts of female

Amador caste-class levels would pay me due heed: freshman (bouncy), sophomore (smartening yet still bouncy), junior (sexually wise), and seniors (intercourse goddesses replete with smarts and faded paperback editions of *Catcher in the Rye* holstered in their faded Guess jeans back pockets which snuggled their respective booties snugly). (Oh, boy!)

I loved playing the injured victim. I loved using my little red pillow. I was an insurance agent's nightmare, and I didn't even know it. I had beaten almighty football at its own husky game.

Switch gears: The House of Slothicans. I was given a back-room house thingy that was oddly attached to the main house structure via an old, enclosed deck. I was happy, secretly, for the separate nature of it. The Slothican were somewhat indigent and somewhat emotionally off balance. I began to see this more and more as my yucky tenure endured itself into the winter and spring of 1993. (I was elated when I finally left, after graduating an accomplished senior from Amador. I never looked back.)

My separate room had no heat, but I was always hot, so it was okay; the Slothicans house was hotter than a blazing river of fire; *so* hot and humid that the blue sweat pants Dick eternally wore must have been glued to his big inner thighs. I suppose he found it, I don't know, cozy and comfortable? Lethargically halcyon? Sexy? Manly? Musky? I loathed the heat of that house.

I rather liked the coldness of my ghetto room-house. But its ghetto-ness had an acute downside. I remember one December night I left the window right above my bed (a faded mattress on the floor) open because the room was old and musty smelling. (There were energetic mice in the walls, too). I woke up around 4 a.m. shivering and noted with groggy severity that my blanket was completely covered in a thin, white blanket of snow about one inch in height. Magical and wintry. Like a fairy tale. I was so lucky. Should the walls perhaps have been composed of gingerbread sheet rock?

What made the room even worse was that it was a storage area for old, mysterious and somewhat nefarious Slothicans stuff: old framed pictures of penniless poordom displaying myriad toothless people, chunky metal objects with sharp edges, ancient faded magazines—some extensively pornographic in a neon-green 1984 nature, and, finally, a box of Larry's Star Wars toys from back in the day. This Star Wars box was actually pretty cool; and although I was a big teenager I still relished the opportunity to gently lift the old toys out of the box and scrutinize them as if they were priceless artifacts from another realm. The entire Ewok forest was in there: little huts and fake plastic trees in no way reminiscent of Radiohead. I'd continually say things to myself as I held the toys in my gentle hands, things like, "And just how much are you worth? You're a rare bird these days, a dying breed." It was as if I was the host of the *Antiques Road Show*, which, of course, didn't exist yet on PBS.

As the autumn progressed, Larry and I became closer friends, but I held him at a distance; though we didn't share a room, I treated him like a roommate, a pragmatic acquaintance who helped pay the bills, if you will. I didn't trust him yet with the details of my foggy young life. He seemed fine with the unspoken arrangement of our friendship. I was simply his buddy, somebody with whom he could relax; our nights spent together involved Pepsi, Orville Redenbacher microwave popcorn (butter out the wazoo), and HBO. Fine with me. I liked food and movies, especially free ones (although, I took care not to eat too much when Grendel Dick was waddling around the house.)

Larry had a giant female acquaintance named Bertha. She was frenetic, garrulous, and annoying. She was in love with Larry because he was smelly, like her: sport smelly, the death of hygiene smelly, rural smelly. By this time in my life I was fully armed with deodorant. Hence, I smelled like nothing but "ocean breeze" or "mountain rush" or "forest frolic with nymphs." No, that last one never existed, but if it had I would have purchased it religiously for its clever sexual connotation.

Being a responsible adult I made sure I wasn't smelly, but everyone around me was indubitably smelly. And they were by no means old-world Europeans, so they were in no way warranted to smell by mandate of an artsy, old-world culture.

I hated the Slothicans smells like I hated lots of things. I also hated that damn house. It was dowdy, dank, dark, and contained a thousand pictures of a thousand non-extant relatives (from who the hell knows where) lining the smoky, wood-panel walls. Cinder block stacks with old 2 x 4s were used as bookshelves, but not for books, rather, for cheap nick-knacks and yet more and more K-mart, "gold" framed pictures of untrustworthy family nutjobs. Oil cans and rubbers. Ten thousand cats drenched in fleas.

I simply must hereby mention the Slothicans dog: it looked like it was from the underworld—like a skeleton catfish with grave hair and a stinky-poop butt. Fufu was her name. Apt. Rhymes with PooPoo. Larry loved to squish the dog in his husky-man bosom and proclaim, "Fufu's sooooo cuuuuuuuute, isn't she, Big Bear?"

I'd change the subject and wish I were dead. The dog was fucked up; I simply must use harsh language here. I am, in fact, a dog lover, but I cannot stand for underworld dogs. Poor Fufu; it wasn't her fault she was a card-carrying Slothicans.

And now I must expound upon of the madness of King Dick—royal-blue sweat pants overseer of the stinky Slothicans estate, his regalia complete with eternal white/yellow cotton Hanes tee shirt: stained with years of an indolent, slothful, idle, slack, remiss, laggard, sluggish, heavy-footed, lagging, apathetic, loafing, dallying, languid, passive, asleep on the job, procrastinating, neglectful, unconcerned, indifferent, dilatory, tardy, dilly-dally, inattentive, careless, unready, unpersevering, lethargic, lifeless, flagging, weary, tired, and supine existence in the hick heart of Pine Grove. Forgive the exquisite hyperbole.

I suppose a little whiff of Stockton exists in every town, if one really looks for it; yes, even in the most pure country, foggy men and women maintain their ubiquitous benighted existence. Dick was foggy. He was truly bizarre: he led a failed life and yet exuded explosive pride, especially when it came to his choice son, Larry, replete in letterman jacket. He let Larry do whatever he wanted, whenever he wanted. Larry had a good heart, good grades, good attitude, so he kept out of trouble and moved onward toward his destiny at a casual pace. He was genuinely a good guy. A good friend.

Larry loved basketball more than he loved football or baseball combined. And he played on the varsity team, but was not by any means one of their starting five. Oft times I'd go out with Larry to a local court at Pine Grove Community Church and play a little basketball with Gabe Newton and Troy Smith. They were his friends too, which was greatly convenient. I played center during these games, not doing much at all for my team save rebounding, but it was good exercise and a wholesome bro time all around. Good for the heart, literally and figuratively. We'd bring along my little boom box and play Pearl Jam's "Ten" whilst doing hot b-ball moves on the carpeted court. It was all very high school. *Ah...I can hear the tape spinning now, "OHHUUUOOOHHHOHHH! EEEEVEN FLLOOOOOWWOOOWW—zaazeehhvaaahh like buhhtterrflies!" Eddie Vedder grungely howls as Larry goes up for a heavy jump shot. A lot of times there'd be little church kids watching us as if we were Greek gods on a celestial court of cloud and Orpheus McCready guitar lix.) My chuggles would bounce up and down the court and look really cool. Then I'd chug some orange Gatorade like a hero stained with my brothers' b-ball blood.*

This was around the time that I began going to church. I can thank the Slothican for that. And I humbly thank them in all sincerity, dismissing their Dickensian foibles right here and now. They had only begun attending church about six months prior, so naturally, I was brought along to the youth events by Larry, who was very enthusiastic about the whole God thing, "Youth group kicks ass, man! We play hoops, eat pizza, get into the Word, and chill. Its awesome!" he declared to me one day as we sat in his Geo Metro en route to meet Bertha for a movie in Jackson (the only movie theater in the county).

"Hmm, cool, yeah. Sounds fun," I muttered, insecure about meeting new people and God. But Larry pushed and pushed until I *finally* attended (dragged kicking and screaming, so to speak) and *frickin' loved it!* Food, happy people, games where I could innocently flirt with the nice, pretty girls and actually feel no pressure from athletic male monkeys. Youth group helped me. A lot. I believe profoundly in God and believe very strongly that He was moving the chess pieces in my little life quite cleverly.

Youth group led me naturally to Sunday morning service attendance at the Pine Grove, Evangelical Free Church: a wonderful place to feel accepted and genuinely loved during my shaky senior year. During this time, regular Thursday-night basketball games began between us pseudo-Christian high-school basketball players. The church youth pastor, Dean Amity, was actually only 40 years old and was, indeed, himself, a very good player; thus, he organized the grand games and played hard within them. Good times. God times. Michael Jordan and God playing one on one in our young hearts.

Usually I wasn't good enough or fast enough for these full-court, fast-paced battles, so I'd play for a little while and then step out so one of the younger kids could play. Everybody could see I was having trouble breathing, being six foot four and around 240 pounds, so why not just forget heroics and let them play the faster game they were all desiring to play (but weren't because they were all nice, Christian, and peacefully sensitive to my person). I'd gracefully bow out halfway through the first quarter and then cheer from courtside like a hearty big bear, growling loudly and purchasing wild forest berries from the snack lady.

One particular Thursday, Dick Slothicans was also courtside to cheer his son toward victory. Of course, Troy, Gabe, youth pastor Dean, and another guy, a junior: Ken, were better players than Larry, and as the game got intense Dick got hot headed and vociferously pissed off. Larry was being worked left and right.

Here's the play to remember: Larry went up for a crucial lay up and lost the ball when it was swatted hard out of his hands by Troy. Some friendly trash talking ensued like normal, and all was good and ended well. Larry and Troy high-fived, shaking their sweaty heads, like, "Man, what a game!" When all was said and done everybody went home happy and took much-needed showers (everyone except Larry; he didn't take many showers; it was awesome...especially when he hugged you like a brother).

Approximately three days later I was in the Slothicans living room on the phone with Troy, planning a SNL get together. I could almost taste the delicious Mountain Dew as I gabbed. Dick was sitting in his greasy easy chair, deliberately straining to overhear my conversation. Troy asked something about how long I had been at the game three days prior, if I'd seen how the game had gotten really intense. Yes, I had seen the game progress into an all-out battle. "Oh, yeah! I was still there long enough to see you swat Larry hard on that lay up!" We both chuckled. Good times. I hung up the phone.

Dick exploded. He was out of his chair in a millisecond, his hot breath bearing down on me. "I DON'T NEED THAT KIND OF BULLSHIT UNDER MY ROOOOF! HOW DARE YOU TALK THAT WAY ABOUT MMYY SON? THAT IS COMPLETE BULLLLLSHIIIT! HOW DARE YOU?" (meaty fingers pointing hard at me) this and that and this and that and life frustration and *"LARRY'S A BETTER BASKETBALL PLAYER THAN ALLLL THOOOOSSSEEE PRICKS! HE'S NBA MATERIAL! WHO THE HELL DO YOU THINK YOU ARE TO...."* and then I was rescued by Dick's wife, Daffy. God bless the woman! She raced over and tried her best to subdue his juvenile wrath, ultimately mollifying him by getting in between us and looking him straight in the eye with her solid, female Slothicans, no-bullshit powers.

I was shaken right down to my boots. He came out of nowhere. Images of Caleb's veiny forehead and Coors-colored eyes flashed like poison lightning across my tremulous brain. I went back to my room quickly. I cried. No lights on. Locked door. Head in my hands. It was scary. Was he sick of me eating their food and using their hot water? Was he just waiting for the right moment to put me in my place? Had I been being a little big brat? I would be careful never to be such a worthless brat again.

Later on, two days 'til Christmas, in fact, I was once more in the Slothicans living room by myself watching ESPN. Ma and Pa Slothicans were out saving the world, and the house was quiet save for Larry playing violent video games back in his room. I was enjoying myself, polishing off a pbj and listening to Chris Berman's sonorous voice on the television. But then I heard the Sega shut off and Larry's heavy footfalls come up behind me. I turned my head, somewhat annoyed. Larry approached and handed me a rolled up Steve Young (49ers quarterback) poster, saying, "Can you wrap this for me Big Bear? I gotta meet up with Rebecca (his new girlfriend) in five minutes, and I wanna get this thing taken care of so I can quit hiding it and put it under the tree. You're a good wrapper; can you do it while you're sittin' here?"

What else could I say, but, "Ah, sure." I didn't want him to think I was lazy. I had to earn my keep.

The tacky wrapping paper was on the kitchen table. I decided just to get it over with, so I put down my tasty pbj, got up, and trotted over to the kitchen. I would have to be fast lest Dick come home and think I was filching expensive Fritos or Pepsi. I finished in approximately four minutes. *A stitch in time saves nine;* an aphorism Larry had apparently never heard. Just then Dick and Daffy walked into the kitchen from wherever they'd been. (The front door of the house was in the kitchen). They were in good spirits. I was glad, but nervous about the Christmas contraband in my hot little hand. The poster was for Dick, of course, and I didn't want to spoil his juicy forthcoming Christmas.

(Footnote: the poster gift sums up the whole Slothicans lifestyle: Dick, a sixty-year-old man was receiving a five dollar K-Mart poster of 49er quarterback Steve Young from his seventeen-year-old son for Christmas; a kingly gift he would immediately hang on his dark bedroom wall.)

"What the hell is that?" inquired Dick, a gentleman and a scholar, his hot eyes fixed on the long cylinder wrapped with care in my hand.

I looked down at it. "This? A Christmas present," I nervously replied, my eyebrows raised, my heart flickering like a moth stuck to masking tape.

"It's a poster; who's it for? One of yer school friends? Do you wrap all yer presents here with our paper? I seriously hope not. Now, is it fer Larry?" he interrogated, elegantly, convivially, and with utmost diplomatic eloquence. The moth's other wing stuck to the tape, too much fluttering, moth dust was filling the air like pungent pollen. I shuddered deep down inside. There was no communicating with Dick.

Daffy immediately sensed my disquiet and rushed in for the rescue, saying, "Now, *Dick*, it's a *secret*. It's a present. Quit your prying, please." But this time he would have none of it. He glared at her as if to say, "You're just a woman; this is *man* business. Shut yer yap!" and then glared back at me. "Tell me what the hell poster it is, 'cuz I got Larry a poster for Christmas, and if it's the same one…" blah blah blah. His sweat pants blazed blue fire with detective zeal. The house got stinkier in the heat. The moth's abdomen exploded, spewing yellow guts all over my ribcage. FuFu was sniffing my shoes like a dung catfish with corpse hair, hunting for chicken liver betwixt my toes.

I tried to steady myself and answer like a man. "Um…no," and of course, I haven't a clue what I said. I somehow got out of it, though, and Dick got to open his poster on Christmas day with unfiltered, pure surprise and delight due to my taking a verbal beating. What a man.

I did *not* enjoy living within the spikey vine'd walls of the Slothicans kingdom. It tarnished my senior year. Even Stockton began to look very good to me as the fall months bumped into December, and my bedroom became a mousy ice cube of poverty. Larry, Daffy, Dick, and Titanic Bertha could all go into far away countries and get lost in humid jungles for all I cared. And let the silver back gorillas chase Dick around for a while. Yes.

My inner, dark disdain for the Slothican was tinged with guilt, because I certainly was living there for free and eating their animal-grade beef daily. So the whole shebang just made me feel sick. I tried my best to escape this sickness by practically *living* at school: joining a million clubs, doing extra-curricular crap for my senior classes, announcing as many games as my lungs would permit, and trying to flirt and date real girls No dice, no soap, no sweet kisses in the back of my tiny steel bug—just UC Davis ash drawings forever.

I also escaped by staying over myriad times at Troy's and Gabe's house. This was always fun. Their houses were actually clean as if normal middle class Americans lived there, which in fact they did. They weren't at all like the Slothicans bat-cave house. Side note: Larry and Dick were way into super heroes and wrestling). I pushed myself to be away from the house and Dick as much as I possibly could. And he, like all good passive aggressive old cusses, kept perfect mental notes of just how many times my presence was missing from under his sagging domain. He became really jealous, like a petulant child. There was no winning with him. Either he was sick of me or he missed me.

One night a happy coterie of us noble youths were in the Slothicans living room getting ready to head out to Taco Bell when we innocently started planning a fun get together BBQ at the park in the near future. Dick's radar ears picked up the signal and perked up. He stood from his greasy easy chair and interpolated, "Don't plan on him being there!" his meaty finger pointed harshly at me. Then he stomped out of the living room. Was he joking around? We all looked at each other in nervous confusion. I don't remember anyone chuckling to cover up the awkwardness. They all knew that Dick was…hmmm…what's the appropriate phrase? Um, oh yes: they knew that Dick was emotionally stinky. That works nicely. Emotionally stinky. Quite.

(I hereby have my novel revenge. Cerebral bullets of the brain, if you will—and you'd better believe I most certainly will! Just now my mind quickly whipped up the image of all the faded, crappy National Enquirers that sat next to the light-brown toilet in the Slothicans bathroom, so damn crappy I could scream with frustration!) For the first time in my young life, I began missing my mom's company. I began to see that she wasn't really such a bad person after all. The Unmoved Mover was working on my brain and heart for sure.

Dick died two years later. In 1995. It was some bacterial complication. I don't know what to say about that. It was and is still very sad. My heart hurts for Daffy and Larry. I'm sorry. Truly. Thank you for letting me live with you and for feeding me. Thank you for taking me to church.

But back to my senior-year winter. Christmas time at the Slothicans'. Big Bear on campus. This time would forever change the course of my life and leave me motherless, entirely alone in the world.

My mom's affair with Abe during the last few years had made her feel overly sexy, like she was sixteen again, bounteous, and sonsy. The problem with this was that she was indeed *overly* bounteous. She had become rather obese. And precious physical workings within her body were beginning to strain under the weight. Genetics, too, were a problem. Health was gone.

I don't know if she was fully aware of this growing problem. Rather, she seemed oblivious, opting for the red fog of bed romance with Abe; perhaps she felt her life slipping away as the house began shambling apart: weeds, leaking roof, mold, etc. Abe wasn't fixing things anymore. Let's be honest and frank right here and now, there was another big problem which pestered Tallene: her breasts were too big (and they seemed to be getting bigger by the day). These breasts made the Titanic look like the leg of a black ant scurrying over an ice cube. They were enormous, a strain upon the white landscape of her body. I'm sure her back was thinking, "What the hell is going on over there?" during this time. It was bearing all the weight.

The pain got really bad and finally alerted her to action that went beyond popping a million Advils. She resolutely decided to have a breast-reduction surgery no matter what the cost. The good, handsome, dark doctor told her that her mammaries were pulling at her back and causing irreparable bad stuff to happen. Those are unfortunately the only medical terms that my memory serves up.

So, the surgery was scheduled; Stockton surgery. Then it was rescheduled. Things were busy at the hospital and money was tight. Then it was rescheduled again, and Tallene sighed and sighed, clawing at the white Advil bottle. Then she suddenly got sick, and the whole hospital system seemed to wake from its stupor and brought her in for surgery, but at a different hospital. She went under the knife in early October (1992) at Sutter Memorial Hospital up north in Sacramento. Paperwork and morphine.

The surgery went swimmingly, like an old trout in an icy river. And she was rolled into the mission-accomplished recovery section of the hospital. Things seemed to be normalizing, even good. I was in Pine Grove at the Slothicans' at this time: discovering King Dick's madness and sitting comfortably upon my little inflatable red pillow.

I kept tabs on Mom over the phone. Like a good son. Like a great son: responsible and heartfelt. Mom was in recovery. Things seemed to be normalizing, on the mend. She'd feel better after her medical boob diminishing. And I would truly begin missing her, deep, deep down in my gut. Indeed. Things would be better from here on out. I would call her more and more, and we would chat like adults in a real world of bright pain and bright white light. After all, we would have grown closer through all the hospital shit…like real adults…with real things to do…things that seemed to be normalizing, on the mend.

But then she began complaining about some real pain down in the shadows of her body. Her intestines ached nonstop, like there was a little campfire smoldering inside. She was at home now, recovering normally. But the shadows and the campfire wouldn't go away. So she called up that fine dark doctor.

I followed along over the phone whenever Dick wasn't home and ruling the living room. I got nervous about life and death. My mother's voice had a tremor in it that I'd never heard before. The campfire was crackling as pine cones fell into it and the wind fanned it.

## PUSH MY LIFE INTO A DUFFLE BAG

So I decided to get in the damn Volkswagen and visit her on a Saturday. I couldn't go on Friday because I had an American History quiz. But on Saturday I went home. I left at 9 a.m. and packed a bologna sandwich wrapped in tin foil. Wonder Bread. French's mustard.

After a fifty-minute drive I entered the boundaries of Stockton and made a quick stop at Manny's burgers in order to purchase a Jones' family favorite, two Manny's deluxes with loads of relish. This would cheer up my old mom like fireworks on the 4$^{th}$ of July, for sure. I drove onward in my chuggy mauve bug to the old Oxford circle. When I got there, I was surprised to see the house looking so dowdy and forlorn.

It was Halloween time. Halloween night in fact. Orange and black outside. Candles and pumpkin pulp. Faces with teeth warding away evil spirits. I arrived home with my greasy white bag of steaming American hamburgers. I strolled up the walk, enjoying the orange, autumnal sky, the glorious chill in the twilight air, the redolent smell of dark green in the lawn. I didn't knock. I quietly let myself in and crept to her bedside. I wanted to surprise her. I had to be extra quiet, because the TV was muted.

"Hey, there, mother of mine!" I exuberantly proclaimed.

"Oh, son, come here, my baby," she said, not too surprised. We embraced. She smelled weird. The burgers smelled greasy. The house smelled close.

I stood back from her, smiling, I had made it, I loved her and was here to show her so. I looked her over. And my heart shuddered at what I beheld: she looked like somebody I'd never met in my entire life. She looked like a desperate, homeless stranger full of problems, somebody I would ignore on the street, holding my breath, averting my eyes, and hoping to God they wouldn't ask for a handout.

"How are you feeling? Are you okay? I brought some Manny's!" Big smile on my face! Thank God Almighty I had something to talk about. She wasn't hungry. I sat and ate both deluxe hamburgers with discretion, careful not to have any sauce on my face or fingers and using the burger wrapping papers as a spill protection plate on my lap.

We chatted.

I don't remember what we talked about that night; later on in our hospital meetings I remember *everything*, that is: once she was careening toward death. All I remember about Halloween is that she was spacey. Super spacey. Beyond Neil Armstrong. Beyond Roger Waters, David Gilmour, and the dark side of the moon. It was scary. The lunatic was on the grass. And the grass was full of weeds.

Her meds had changed her. Her body had changed her. Would I ever again really see *her?* Where had that quirky spark in the eyes gone off to? Where was her soul? Dammit! Who was this filthy stranger in her bed?

The stranger in her bed then began saying things that were out of left field. "Do you want some toast, or milk, son? But not burnt; it's not sour." I remember that particular one…others I would just be fabricating in order to make her sadder. I won't do that. It was surreal enough without any embellishment. I left shortly after that.

It felt too weird to stay, and I was getting impatient with her, being the selfish-asshole good son that I was. I had actually planned an escape route for the visit with my old mom; I had planned to visit for a loving amount of time and then abruptly leave in order to hook up with my old pal, Bret, in order to make a festive visit to the University of the Pacific haunted house. I was obliged to have a little fun, right? I mean, I'd driven *all* the way down there and spent depressing time with a sick person. Sure. I needed an uplift. I needed to be young. Teenagers deserve glowing chunks of gold just for being teenagers. The deserve the entire world to be handed to them.

I didn't like the smell of death. That was the weird smell I had smelled on her. It frightened me something fierce, like an invisible great white was swimming around in the house, awkwardly bumping into walls and working its pallid gills with a thrushing, invisible, salt-water sound. It was terrifying. And thus, I don't really blame me for being a spineless coward. Too many wasps. Too many monsters.

When I got back from the haunted house she was fast asleep; so I decided the best thing to do was to let her rest, undisturbed, and drive on back up to the Slothican'. She was druggy anyway; she wouldn't miss me. I drove the speed limit all the way home and listened to *Love Line,* a knowledgeable grin across my face. I loved sexual radio comedy. It was for adults, adults who were 11-16 years old.

A couple days later I heard the phone ring whilst I was checking my face in the bathroom mirror after dinner. Dick picked up the grungy phone, listened, and exclaimed, "Your momma's back in the hospital, man." Grandma Lulu was on the phone. Dick listened some more and continued, "Her gallbladders ruptured."

## PUSH MY LIFE INTO A DUFFLE BAG

A black cloud filled the room. And out of this black cloud came a lumbering wet black shark. I stood still against the wall so it wouldn't see me.

"It's okay, man," Dick assured me, hanging up the phone with a clink, waddling over and ultimately placing his meaty fingers upon my big back. I hated when he got all buddy buddy. He was a fake. And *no*, it wasn't okay.

I trudged out of the house and got into my Volkswagen, revving and revving the bubbly engine so it would warm up faster. Damn stupid bug. I drove the fifty minute drive in thirty minutes. I almost hit a deer, a skunk, and three possums. One of my headlights went out. A fat nurse at Sutter Memorial led me to her room. And there she was, looking completely wretched and sadder than Pearl Harbor.

She looked up and spoke. "Hi, son, my little boy; ooooh, you're here. That's good. The neatest thing happened just about an hour ago. Burt Reynolds stopped by to see how I was doing. Just to see *me*! Can you believe it? And he's a busy celebrity! He's a busy celebrity. So nice of him to take time out of his magazines; do you want some water?" she asked.

Then, later on in our sterile meeting, she asked me in a heartfelt tone, her chubby pink fingers on my forearm, "Can you record *L.A. Law* for me tonight?" I obliged, solemnly. I would record it superbly with my technical skills. 'Twas the least I could do. She absolutely adored *L.A. Law*. No problem. Nothing like TV shows to make you feel normal again. But. Then. She. Added, "Great! But hon, darling boy of mine," she patted my arm again and again, teaching me to listen and take her seriously, "make sure you turn the TV OFF, *completely* off," she implored. She looked me dead in the eye.

"Right!" I agreed.

"NO! You aren't listening!" Her voice got louder; it scared me. "You *must* turn it totally *off*, and be sure it's totally off, with black letters in the plastic." She shook her tired head, adding finally, "This little black boy keeps sneaking around and turning it on and off."

Grandma Lulu looked at me sharply as if to say, "Relax. Agree with her. Be cool; she's drugged. She's dying, and yes, little black boys *are* in fact terrorizing her house; it happens all the time. *Reader's Digest* is full of true stories like this."

I looked back at my mother, who was smiling at me. She was very fat, very pallid. The tubes were flowing with clear liquid. The machines were beeping and buzzing like excited jazz musicians.

"Got it," I said. "I won't let him, um, mess with the TV."

She nodded enthusiastically like a child. "He hides in the different cupboards when he's not turning the TV on and off. He's very tricky, but a real cutie. Children are so cute around here. But I dooo hate him; he's driving me nuts!" She chuckled, shaking her head and inhaling a big breath of Lysol air. "The little shit."

Wow. She said, "shit." Just out of the blue—to define a tricky little black ghost boy who didn't exist. Now this was actually quite funny, in an end-of-the-line, despairing way.

(Images of the deep south circa 1860 flashed across my mind. Shoeless. Muddy-bloody feet. Tattered clothing. Little affro full of lice. Kunta Kente getting to Harriet Tubman's hushed railway just in time.)

My mom was now certifiably crazy; and it wasn't just the meds. I was scared. I had already lost her. This stranger, bed person wasn't her...didn't even look or sound like her.

"Hey, hon, can you...nnneed to, you neeeed to deposit my welfare checks into the bank!" she blurted out.

Of course. This was normal. A normal request. (Checks? Plural?) I slowly nodded. "Sure thing." I could do that. Of course, I would need the account number and other such technically valid stuff. I grabbed a paper mate, a little napkin and asked her kindly for the number

"Oh, shuuurrrre: it's 555 5555 55555 555555," she matter of factly stated. I glanced at Lulu. She was staring at her daughter, Tallene, with her face full of bleak concern. I turned my head back to Mom and pretended to acquiesce. Then I stared hard at the napkin in my hands. I realized this number wouldn't do. I gathered up a little courage and asked, "What? It can't all be fives. You gave me, like, fifteen fives in a row. That isn't the account number, is it?" My eyebrows shot up kindly like *I* was the one at fault, *I* was the space cadet; *I* was stupid and full of death and IVs.

She suddenly looked confused for the first time. A sign of hope. A couple wires in her brain sparked and sizzled, but then poofed into silent coldness with a little gray smoke. "No, hon, I said two, two and the others..." she said, being kind to me. She was very patient with me, very proud to be my mother. She was gone.

She was speaking out through the fog, through the poisonous toxins in her brain, in her blood stream. The room filled with the warm sand of profound and inexorable sadness. All was lost. (The earth looked down at its soft belly, considering something violent, something symbolically sad; considering a deep, quick slice through the old skin: a hot gushing, big spilling, loud rushing of oceanic blood over all us sinners.)

Tallene looked into my eyes. I sensed the wires crackling once more, a hospital miracle! She was figuring something in her brain. She was clinging to a solid branch. She was really, really trying to break through. "No, wait. No, I said two; there aren't any fives," she said, continuing to figure and figure.

I felt God standing right next to me, to my right, next to all the flowers in pink plastic wrapping. He was staring at her, pulling for her. He folded his arms. His eyes were wet. He breathed deeply. I could hear it. I was all nerves and compassion, my eyes fixed on Mom's profound confusion over life and numbers. I looked deeply into her big, placid cow eyes. She looked beautiful at that moment, frozen in time.

I moved the conversation along. "What? Two? A couple twos and no fives?" I asked. I would wait forever if need be for her calculated answer; I would wait until I was a dry skeleton in the ruin of an ancient establishment of healing and medicine.

"No! That's not what I said." She patted my arm hard. She was frustrated.

"The social account number is 555 5555 5555, and then there's the 2," she declared, ending with a smile, confident and proud; she wasn't crazy after all. I nodded and scribbled the number five on the napkin. It almost looked like an eight I wrote it down so sloppily.

Then my nose itched, and I itched it, grateful for it earthly distraction.

Lulu leaned over and assured her daughter that I would deposit it in the morning and that the various bills would be paid on time. Some spittle shot out of her old mouth and landed in my mom's red hair when she said "paid." It was gross. I pretended not to notice, looking away toward the TV up by the ceiling on its swiveling-arm stand thing.

I would have to figure out an honest way of depositing the welfare checks; the people would just have to understand that my mom was nuts, especially once they knew she was dying in a cloud of white sheets and beeping droid machines. It wouldn't be a problem. Maybe 555 55555 555555 then 2 really was the actual account number. Maybe JFK really jumped out of the convertible and dodged the brain bullet. Maybe Lincoln grabbed the arm of John Wilkes Booth and punched his lights out. Maybe Eve threw that fucking apple straight back at that snake, smacking him right between the eyes. Maybe. Maybe Auschwitz, Dachau, and all the ovens never happened either.

Maybe people never die; they just take a holy silver train to the next station, reading the paper and enjoying a hot cup of coffee as they sit, beautiful forest scenery flying past out the streak free windows with a radiant blue sky that goes on forever and ever amen. I left the room and walked out of Sutter Memorial Hospital.

Burt Reynolds. A little black boy. Five. Then the 2.

I drove home. I had school in the morning, earlier than usual because the Philosophy Club was having its first annual breakfast. A whole three days went by like glaciers in winter.

"Your momma's in a coma!" Dick hollered out to me from the living room. I abruptly stood up, dropping my American History, current-events homework all over the dirty carpet and hurried to the one phone in the house, taking it awkwardly from Dick's meaty hand.

"How's my boy?" asked Lulu, with utmost sensitivity and care. "I'm fine," I muttered, leaning against the wood paneled wall. This was November 4, 1992. She was in a coma until later December.

I kept phone tabs with Grandma Lulu and J.R. during this foggy stretch. I didn't drive down to see her; what was the use? She was comatose. But then, to our great shock and surprise, on that gloriously cold and sunny day of December 20th, she miraculously came out of her coma. I remember all the frost on the fields in the early morning when I got the call just prior to leaving on my twenty-minute drive to school, which turned into a fifty-minute drive to Sacramento.

When I arrived at the hospital I quickly bypassed the fat nurse and made my way to her room. I was excited and scared, a combo of mixed emotions. And, when I beheld her there lying in bed with blinking eyes and extreme pallor, I became less excited and more scared. She looked awful. Inhuman, almost. She didn't remember much. She knew her name and her age, but not really who any of us were, though she felt strongly that we were important and perhaps really were family and not insidious imposters looking for loot. She had lots of slow, childish questions for us.

And the nurse kept coming in, indecisive on whether or not to kick us all out of her room. Pragmatism vs. idealism. It was a strange visit that lasted only fifteen minutes. Pragmatism won the day.

On Christmas Eve I rallied up some more nerve and drove down once more to see her. Lulu instructed me that now was a good time to visit; Mom had been "lucid" for a couple days now and even had walked around her room once with the aid of two nurses. This was extremely good news. But I had a problem: my Volkswagen had broken down literally the day before. And I had no money. No tools. No know-how. It was dead for now and sitting dumbly half way up the Slothicans driveway, caked in snow and mud. It had been snowing off and on for two days now, but at the moment of Lulu's beseeching phone call I could plainly see out the window that it had really picked up: white-out conditions even. PG&E and Caltrans were preparing for the worst. I scratched my head and hung up the phone. I stepped outside and looked at the sky, snow sticking to my eyelashes. God was silent.

Then the phone rang in the living room. It was Bertha. She asked if I needed anything and told me she was praying for my mom. In my desperate state I felt my ribcage quiver with sorrow and salvation as I asked her for a ride to Sacramento. "I'll be right over!" she exclaimed. I felt wretched for ever thinking ill of her. I was such a critical asshole all the time.

We drove down together. The little gray Honda was hot and stuffy, like always. And her oil light kept coming on, which worried me to no end. I thought the engine was going to explode at any second. She drove like a bat out of hell. It was her style. Damn the snow and ice. I felt an ulcer forming in my stomach as we sloshed down Ridge Road toward the quiet California central valley. There were old, empty fast-food containers covering the floorboards at my feet. It was disgusting. She was a slob. And I was an overly perceptive and abundantly critical asshole.

Once more I blazed through the lobby of the hospital en route to Mom. Her room had the same eerie, sterile light, the same beeping and buzzing, and the same oceanic smell. The stranger in the bed looked more alien than I'd ever seen her or even imagined she could ever be. The way she looked made the entire world seem like a pointless place, a mean, cold place, where the ultimate goal of all things holy is black hell in the corporeal form of ugly, noxious human body putridity and distention. Looking at her made life seem a real shit storm. A worthless exercise. Her hair was so red it looked like a clown's wig.

I walked up to her bedside and placed my hand on her arm. It sunk into the malleable flesh. She acknowledged me by winking slowly in my general direction. This tiny human movement cheered my heart and removed the black shit storm image from my beleaguered brain. My mom was in there somewhere. She couldn't speak because she was hooked up to a respirator and, at this point in the game, hadn't any vocal power left. I showed her my brand-new letterman jacket: blue torso, white leather sleeves, football patch I'd earned for doing absolutely nothing. It really should have been an advanced drama patch for top performance in solo acting.

She held a little white pad of paper that the nurse had given her in her left hand, and with an absurdly slow right hand she wrote the word, "sharp," and turned it to show me.

"Thanks, Mom," I replied. I did look sharp. I was her sharp son. I hoped she was proud and that that consanguineous pride would warm her foundering heart. She had done well by me. I hoped and prayed that my presence in my letterman jacket at her bedside would impress her more than Burt Reynolds ever would.

Then I went back home. I honestly thought she would last a good long while in that safe white room. Doctors were mythological gods in my book. Powerful creatures wielding powerful powers. I knew in my head that they would see to fixing her up just right. And I knew everything at the empirical age of 17. I had read books on doctors. College books.

I borrowed money from my buddy Troy's beautiful mother and fixed my Volkswagen; it was just the alternator. Rather inexpensive. No prob. Everything was under control. Even the ice on the roads was just nature's way of getting into the spirit of Christmas and not at all a personal ploy of God's to kick me while I was down. Things were steadily afloat on the black ocean. The black sharks were migrating slowly away.

I went back to Sutter Memorial on the 26th of December. The bug drove just fine. The new alternator seemed to give me better gas mileage. The drive was crisp and beautiful, my spirits high. And yet, once in that damn white room, I found it extremely difficult to keep them high. I could barely communicate with Mom. She seemed to have willingly placed one foot in another realm by this time. She was sipping her coffee and reading the translated headlines on that silver train. The scenery out her window was breathtaking. Holy wheels were spinning on perfect, smooth silver tracks. The darkness of God was hovering over the mountains in misty clouds of snowlight. One foot placed.

She scribbled slowly on the little white pad that she wanted me to clip her toenails. This request shocked me. She was still thinking of toenails?

"I don't have any clippers, Mom," I apologized, not really wanting to touch her feet.

She grew druggily impatient. I was treating her like a child, a child to be easily placated with ice chips in a tiny clear plastic cup. No. She wouldn't have it. I liked seeing the fresh, tiny fires in her eyes. "Ask the nurse," she drunkenly punched into the paper with black chunk ink.

I stood up and walked to the nearest nurse out the open door; she was no help, too busy saving lives. I walked back into the stuffy room. "They don't have any," I told her, sick of this toenail waste of time. Mom and I should be talking about old times or love or God or something like that! Not toenails! This wasn't at all like the movies. But she didn't give up; she breathed harder into the creamy wires and wrote, "GO TO GIFT SHOP CLIP MY NAILS!" It was all spelled perfectly, impressive. Synapses were firing brightly. I was instantly very mad at her and very impressed. I consented and was on my way; I even used my own money.

When I came back, I ceremoniously clipped her gross nails, thinking all the while of how I was just like Mother Theresa. I slowly, humbly, washed her feet, and felt better about our relationship. She was dying. So I clipped her nails. She smiled weakly at me. The smell of her potato feet clung to my fingers. I decided to try a little comic relief, "You used to wipe my butt; the least I can do is clip your nails."

Everybody chuckled, even the little black boy hidden in the medical supply cabinet amongst the cotton balls. Mom wiggled her toes awkwardly; she couldn't control them right. We shared a moment. That's the last thing I ever remember saying to my mother.

# Chapter 11
# Sod

She was back in a coma the next morning, by 6 a.m.

This new coma really pissed me off. "God" was playing games. Horrible games. In my gut I felt He really had nothing to do with it, but I was still angry Him. All He had to do was flip a sun switch, and Mom would be as healthy as a spring chicken. And yet He did nothing.

For Christmas I stayed in Pine Grove and had a lovely time with the Slothican. Super lovely. Simply delightful. Deck the halls. Oranges and chocolates. Fat people everywhere.

Then January and the new year came on strong. On the 5th, a Tuesday, Dick yelled toward the back of the house, "Your aunt's on the phone! HEY! YOUR AUNT'S ON THE PHONE!"

I ran toward the loudness. It had been a long time with no news, and I had been too cowardly to call. I didn't like my "relations" down in the valley, and I knew they'd be the ones answering the phone if I called, since my mom was nothing but a big coma. So I painfully eschewed every single natural impulse to call, and there were a lot of them, leaping upon me frantically like hospital ghosts in the wintry wooded night. I grabbed the phone from Alpha Slothican's hot hand.

Aunt: "Are you gonna come down and see yer *mother*? I tell ya, you'd better soon, hon; things're gettin' real bad down here…real bad."

Me: "Uh huh…really? Um. Okay, uh…how is she? What's happening? What are the doctors saying?" (thepowerfuldoctors).

Aunt: "Well, they tell me her organs are all failin' her one at a time; her entire body is just giving up the fight as of yesterday afternoon.… I…uh…" crinkling of the phone cord, "I'm gonna stop her dopamine. Her heart will then slow to a stop…I think. She gave us permission a while back and signed a doctor slip thing. She's going downhill fast and…in a lot of pain, honey. The doctors think it best." (themightiestdoctors)

An invisible little black boy hiding out in the Slothican house shot me right there and then with an imaginary elephant tranquilizer dart. It hit me in the spine and I leaned slowly into the phone.

Pause.

Aunt: "Do you want us to wait 'til you're here, honey? If you do, then you'll have to hurry; she's goin' pretty fast. What do you want us to do?"

Me, "No. I don't want to be there when it happens. Go ahead."

I thought of the long drive down to Sacramento, I thought of everybody waiting for me, awkward, looking at their watches, foreheads sweaty, wondering if I was breaking the speed limit on the icy roads; I thought of Mom in mute, excruciating pain. No way. Hell was on the phone and in the tires. I hated the entire universe with a soldier's quiet reserve. I did not want to watch her die. Let them do it. The hicks. They were good at icky life stuff like this. Poverty does that to you. I hung up. She said something else, but I hung up, cutting her off.

Click.

Dick looked low at me from across the room in his beige easy chair. He put down his paper. He was sad. Genuinely sad for me. He got up slowly and lumbered over to me. He hugged me, tight, then took a good long look at my face, but didn't say anything. I stared emptily right past him at the wall. The imaginary tranquilizer dart was working. The dopamine was stopping.

"Can you drive me down there? To Sacramento? To see Sam? I want to see my brother," I mumbled.

"Yes, let's go right away," Dick declared, rubbing my shoulder affectionately. He was all comfort and angels for me at that moment. Thanks, Mr. Slothican.

We crunched out onto the cold, frosty ground and slumped into his Geo. On our way down to the California valley he turned on the radio and let it play at a slow volume. Whitney Houston's "I Will Always Love You" from that *Bodyguard* movie came on. I thought of Mom dying, her heart slowly pumping to an irreparable stop. That song will be my mom dying whenever I hear it, for the rest of my life.

We got to where Sam was at Caleb's mother, Flora's house in Linden. She'd made a large bowl of salsa-rich, meaty taco salad for us all; comfort food. I hugged Sam tight like a big brother bear should. We didn't say much. We didn't need to.

I asked Flora if I could use the phone. I had Mom's hospital room phone number memorized. My aunt picked up the phone after one ring. "We're all still here; everything's still the same; we haven't done it yet," she said. I was shocked. I thought it was all over, but it wasn't. Whitney Houston was a fucking liar.

"Oh. Are you still going to?" I asked, feeling like a vile murderer with bloody forearms asking this cold, calculated, objective question. I hoped they were still going to. She was in pain. The mess needed to be over.

"Yes. We all decided to stop it in twenty minutes. Her organs are finished," she said, slowly, and with tact. I could hear other relations nodding in the white background.

"Oh."

"Are you *sure* you don't want…"

"No, I don't…want to be there when…" I trailed off, and she got the point. Frankness in the hard times. I was a soldier assessing a life-and-death situation and making a hard decision.

Aunt: "Tell yer brother about our decision; if he wants to come he's got twenty minutes to get here. Have him call us back if so."

Me: "Okay." I hung up the phone. I remember thinking that in an hour my mom would no longer exist. She was fast becoming a cold corpse—to be put in the ground and covered with cruel, lifeless dirt. Then my thoughts filled with a frightening avalanche of shiny bugs, fungus, rocks, rusty water, and freezing mud frost. Old skeletons ensconced in black loam. The smell of cold, moldering bones. Mom was dirt.

I looked at the kitchen clock, memorized its black-hand pattern, and then turned toward Sam in order to fill him in on all the dirt. But then I didn't. I couldn't. He stared blankly at me, scratching at his little knobby knees. The room was stupidly quiet. Everybody was waiting for my report. But nothing came out. The thought of Sam breaking down and crying made me sick to my stomach; I didn't want to see it. So I told him a partial truth: the family hicks were still there with Mom, making sure she was stabilized. They would call us back if the machines started beeping really bad news.

Everybody in the room looked suddenly confused, including Sam, and it donned on me that they all knew about the prospect of the dopamine being curtailed sometime soon and that I hadn't given them the next update on the imperative situation at hand. But regardless, nobody prodded me for answers, being that I was the disconsolate firstborn of fresh, new dirt. Twenty-two minutes passed, each one of them dreadfully slow.

Somewhere out in the golden beyond, Tallene's glorious spirit departed this earth. And her empty body began to stiffen. Some more time passed. About twenty more minutes. Then I allowed some more time to pass. About eleven minutes. Then I became extremely frustrated and stormed over to the phone, dialing the number with angry celerity. A nurse picked up, not a family member, a damn robot nurse. I immediately asked about Tallene Jones' condition.

"Mrs. Jones has expired...approximately thirty minutes ago," said the tranquil voice on the other side of the line. I was very polite in replying, and we finished up our serene, mandatory phone chat.

Then my inner voice screamed out so loud that my ribcage buckled, "SHE'S NOT A FUCKING GALLON OF MILK!" But my real voice remained placid. Calm. Adult. However, I did hang up the phone with a gentle slam. This alerted Sam, Flora, and Dick. They stared apprehensively at me from their corners with their whips and stools in hand. The Taco salad sat soggy and uneaten in its big wooden bowl.

I grinned at them: a huge silly grin. Sam didn't know Mom was indeed dead. None of them did. My grin got bigger. The joker. Dick shot a worried glance at Flora. My grin was scaring her.

"Mom's dead, Sam." Then I laughed. Out loud. Why? Why on earth did I laugh out loud in the face of so much sorrow? I don't know; maybe the tranquilizer took a turn for the madness in me. Maybe the dart hit a funny nerve. Shock. Real shock. We were all quite suddenly in shock. And each of us reacted differently. Dick went out for a stroll and a smoke in his big blue sweats.

Flora reached out for Sam, but he ran out the door and kept running, off into the cold, gray distance, looking perhaps for a large oak tree to lean against whilst tearing his clothes. Ashes on his head. Nothing in his wooden heart.

Caleb had been pacing around the outside of the house the whole time. I didn't know this. He'd been mourning quietly in his own way out by the back porch, smoking a Camel light or six. After I announced Tallene's expiration he opened the front screen door and walked slowly, purposefully past all of us toward the back bedroom. He knew. He must have been listening.

For some reason, I felt compelled to be with him. I certainly didn't want to be alone with Flora; she would try to comfort and mollify me like all older women do. So I walked back to him and held him as he bawled his eyes out on my sleeve. I was a lot bigger than he by that time. It was amazing, he cried and cried. (I'd *never* seen him cry a day in his life); I, on the other hand, couldn't physically cry. I could only examine his intense sobbing as if I was watching a movie, noting the depth and visceral punch of it all.

I was eerily Stoic, despite my world spinning like blazes of red, mute fury. I was completely soundless, like being thirty feet under water, lying down on the mossy mud floor, looking up toward the crystal surface, a cloudy sky above with wind and snow flurries filling the freezing white air. Somehow, the water's warmer than the air. Somehow, drowning seems lovely. Necessary. Like sleeping. Deeply. I thought to myself, *Mom's on vacation.*

The phone in the kitchen didn't make a peep.

# Chapter 12
# Hope Is an Alpine Lake

So now that Mom was dead, I was completely on my own. It was a perfect time for this to happen: I was just about to graduate high school and be a legal adult. Perfect time. I had lucked out.

January turned quickly into February, then there were some dead presidents' birthdays, a leprechaun, some painted eggs, and ultimately warmer weather. May opened the heavens and let in the Sierra Nevada sunshine; I was glad to see the windy, wet weather dissipate and ultimately vanish. Good old California, indeed.

Along with all this natural brightness came the end of my high school career. (Should that be an oxymoron?) I graduated with honors and a big smile on my face. I hung my graduation tassel (blue and white) on the rearview mirror of my bug and proudly watched it sway to and fro as I drove throughout the piney highways, crunching hot pine cones and blasting my crappy stereo like every other American eighteen-year-old.

I had made it. I was free to be an adult and tackle the world. Mom would have been so proud. She would have taken a lot of pictures. She would have beamed from the decorated bleachers.

In early June of 1993 I shook hands with the Slothicans and said farewell with hugs and kisses all around (all the while Fufu sniffing catfish-like at my sneakers); it was time to move away, away from everything that symbolized my new country life; time to forget and get to work down in the valley where I had a few family connections and a younger brother I was truly beginning to miss.

Three days prior to graduation I had arranged for myself a spacious place to live at a house owned by the parents of my old friend Buck Falstaff. Unfortunately, most the Falstaff kids save Buck were still youngsters, so the whole pile of the Falstaff clan pretty much lived there. There wasn't a lot of room for me. And yet, they were very nice people and agreed to let me stay with them for a time. This was the point in my life where I began to realize that I, myself, despite all my pride and self reliance, was in fact a foster, like Otis, Steve, Dolores, and all the others I despised. Life has a funny way of doing that kind of thing to you.

What was even more unfortunate than the ridiculous crowdedness of the Falstaff house was the incontrovertible fact that there was only room for me on the enclosed front porch. Seriously. I'm not kidding. Thus, I made my little room and bed out on said front porch with a springy old mattress from the Middle Ages and all of my life possessions piled into a far corner in big chunky boxes (getting perpetually damp with nightly dew). Here's the good news: no rent. Just like the Slothicans. I was a lucky lad! I would now be able to get a footing in the money world. Once I got a job, of course.

Looking back, it was very kind of the Falstaffs to take me in. They didn't have a lot of $$$. Nobody I really knew had any $$$. The Finnegans had a bit, but I didn't call them or see them much anymore. They did, however, send a card for me with a sad yellow lab puppy on it when Mom died. It had a check for three hundred dollars in it for food and life necessities. Very thoughtful. Sinead was always thoughtful. That money put gas in my car, food in my belly, and shampoo in my hair, Suave bright green, sour apple shampoo. It was only a buck at One Stop Market in Pine Grove. It was my favorite shampoo. It smelled like delicious candy. Luckily for me, the Lucky's supermarket a couple blocks away from the Falstaff homestead stocked plenty of Suave apple shampoo. They even stocked Suave strawberry shampoo. Little things in life have always made me happy.

The summer of '93 began with clean hair and a bright, go-get-'em-boy! attitude. I was of a ripe mind to pull myself up by my very own bootstraps and find my fortune and happiness. And Mom cheered me on up in heaven. Sometimes I could even hear her.

First things first: I grabbed some remnant carpeting from a discount carpet store and fully padded my exorbitant new pad: the (screen) enclosed front porch. I got permission to do this, of course, from ma and pa Falstaff. The carpet was teal with bright pink specks on it, office carpet: very thin and rough, yet still strangely padded so workers stilettos didn't make their feet ache at the end of a hard day of paper pushing. Carpet = Padding = Warmth = A Good Beginning. I was making virtue of necessity.

But despite all my efforts with the new warm carpet fort, I oft got too chilly out there in the wee hours of the night, even though it was late June. (Wind was the culprit). At these grouchy times I'd opt for the warmth of my air-enclosed Volkswagen, waddling out to it wrapped in teal carpet with bright pink specks. I'd plop the two front seats down and try to make room, but there was never enough. I slept somehow like an S in that car. Very uncomfortable. Very stressful. I suffered from lack of sleep that summer; a bad thing for any human with a functioning body. My eyes were dry and my voice was hoarse.

In late June I found out that our Regent Street house (the last tangible family vestige) was going into serious foreclosure. Big Brother was, of course, swiping it up because nobody was paying for it anymore. He swept in and locked it all up for safekeeping with a yellow tag on the front door that had a very large hand on it with the middle finger sticking up.

This yellow tag middle finger was nothing more than the natural progression of life, the healthy objectivity and logic of time marching stoically onward and paying heed to no one, but regardless of all rational rationality, all the marching pissed my shit right off. I had to fight, somehow; I had to find a way to keep the house a Jones' house. But this was a complete impossibility! And I knew it. The Joneses were penniless crap, a scattered people, fresh new dirt, even. There was no way to keep the house. Thus I became even angrier, deep down, sizzling in my ribcage. Frustration, enmity, and exasperation became my new Biblical names. I had to do something! The family famine was killing me!

On a hot Wednesday afternoon I picked up my Volkswagen keys and took action. I drove without hesitation over to the house just off the Oxford circle and, like a big Vietnam ninja, broke in at around 4 p.m. through the bathroom window with the faulty aluminum lock (hidden behind a giant oleander bush). (Later in life, I would chuckle to myself when listening to The Beatles' "She Came in Through the Bathroom Window" on *Abbey Road*.)

I almost broke the top of the toilet trying to gingerly get in without a sound. My weight shifted at the worst moment and I had to make awkward, quick physical adjustments to properly make it in. I knew there wasn't anybody in the house, but I still wanted to be quiet about the whole thing. I've always feared law enforcement. Maybe a little too much. But in the act of breaking in I had completed a very real act of defiance. I had crossed the line. I was fighting back, and it felt damn good! I didn't care about the consequences of "trespassing." This was *my house!*

And so, as I paced quietly around that old house, feeling all the walls and searching my tired memory for any honest home memories, I realized with a numb chill that the house itself no longer felt like home. It felt alien and cold and empty. It seemed to be laughing at me, only I couldn't hear its cackling laughter because the sound waves were in another dimension only heard by shrouded ghosts. And thus, I became bitter, physically taking it all out on the house, wanting to hurt it good.

First things first: I took my big heavy feet and kicked holes in all the walls. Big holes. Then I grabbed a knife that I found in the kitchen, on top of the empty, dirty, buzzing fridge, and began slicing up the carpet in deep lines that would take some time for any nosy government asshole to find. The carpet was dark, you see. The knife was big, sharp, and worked well. Every room received a floor scar and the carpet wailed in material grief as the blade separated its binding threads. Ancient carpet dust was swirling in the air. For a second, I smelled Dolores' cheap perfume.

Then, in a bit of a sweat, I spied a big syrup jug (Hershey's) left in an upper cabinet. I knew the bottle well; it had a big white pump for easy chocolate rivers and we used it back in the day to thoroughly coat our steaks, our potatoes, and our hungry faces. Dolores used to use it to thoroughly coat her entire naked body—then she'd dance for me as I smoked a fat cigar in a dark corner. Mom was sure that the little black boy had drunk it all, but she apparently was wrong because it was still very heavy.

I went right to work: vehemently throwing the massive jug down the cellar stairs. It broke at the bottom and exploded perfectly—much to my great and evil satisfaction. For once in my retarded life, there was a proper explosion. Kaboom! Chocolate all over the place for the cellar rats. Eat up, bitches. I love you all…and I finally agree with you about everything in this caustic world. It sucks. All of it. *Fuck the world!* The chocolate would dry and be a miserable mess that somebody would have to clean up with a sticky-as-shit mop for minimum wage. Good. Hopefully crunchy ants would cake up the mop as well and bite the poor hands that held it.

My next mission was to put a greasy imprint of my face on every window of the house; I did this slowly, starting from one side of my face at the ear and rolling over to the other side at the ear, squishing my nose on the way and leaving a horrifying, Medieval death mask imprint on the glass. I imagined a family moving into this house and their innocent little children seeing the window faces at night, shining in the orange street lamplight, from their beds and becoming petrified with absolute horror. Too petrified to call out for Mommy or Daddy. Sharks under their beds and hidden, black smoky evil between the walls. The death masks would scare 'em good. I was pleased.

At around 4:40 p.m. I cut a big, rectangular piece of carpet out from my bedroom (I don't know why; I was methodical rage flying on autopilot by then) and began lugging it out the front door to plop it down upon the front lawn for the whole Oxford Circle world to see. I've always been symbolic.

That's when I beheld the sobering sight of Mr. Johnny Law walking up the walk, resplendent with authority in the summer sun. He looked angry as hell. The nosy neighbors had ratted me out! Sonsabitches! *Fucking rich pricks!* I thought, my body filling with fear and loathing as the officer introduced himself.

Then he cut the mandatory police bullshit and grilled me good. "You mind taking me on a tour of this house, son? I just love to inspect these old homes for possible damage; you know what I mean? Houses are valuable things, valuable property protected by the law; and guess what: I'm the law. You mind telling me what you're doing here? You see this yellow tag property lock here?" He pointed at it.

I felt my guts turn to cold oatmeal. I was finished. And so I completely surrendered, admitting to everything, and giving him just what he'd asked for: a guided tour through the house like an incompetent real estate agent in purgatory. I was so nervous I almost puked. I'm not very tough once the police show up. I melt and apologize times a million.

I told him that I had lived there for years and years. I told him that my mommy had just died and was covered in dirt. I told him all about Burt Reynolds and even Abe Lincoln. I told him that Caleb used to beat me within those walls. I told him that I would have a poor, insignificant life because of this here house. I ended my supplication with an honest observance and admittance of my own gargantuan shittiness for breaking in through the bathroom window. And, wouldn't you know it, my lachrymose histrionics paid off! Pathos saved me! I had represented myself quite well in the face of the all powerful officer.

He stood quietly for a minute after I finished. He scratched at the back of his powerful neck with his powerful hand, looking down at the rectangular carpet piece in the living room by the front door.

He thought hard for us all. "You're lucky you lived here," he declared, pointing at my sternum with a powerful forefinger. "You were this close to being arrested, young man." He held his fingers an inch apart.

I gulped and nodded, sweat beading on my forehead. The house was hot in the late June afternoon. Blazing hot sun was blazing through the living room picture window, lighting up the stuffy emptiness of the house. I wondered how hot his dark blue police uniform was. It looked really hot. Slacks and a button-up shirt. It must be very hot. I hoped it didn't annoy him enough to think twice and book me for life. I shook like a leaf in my hi-tops.

My mind coughed up an image of Eddie Vedder flipping off the cop and running away into the California sunset, flannel flowing like sweet rebellion. Somewhere distant, a guitar would squeal through full-stack Marshal distortion! I was irrefutably *not* that rock and roll.

So I just stood there, nodding, focusing on the officer's polished black boots. They must be hot too.... Regret, regret, regret. But I rallied once more, "I don't know what came over me, officer," I lamented.

He was still angry, but listened and let it all soak in. Then he suddenly turned to me and put his hand on my shoulder, looking directly into my eyes, "You want to know something? My dad used to hit me." He paused for a moment, then continued, "Now get out of here. And don't ever come around this house again or you *will* be arrested on the spot."

And that was it. I ran to my Volkswagen bug and took off. The cop stood in the doorway, deep in thought, watching me leave,. I drove under ten miles under the speed limit all the way back to the Falstaffs'.

A little while after this emotional mishap I got a job at one of Stockton's many Godfather's Pizza emporiums. My somewhat "uncle" (whom I'd never really even talked to in my entire life; was he *really* my mom's brother?) was owner/manager there, so I had a free pass to a savory employment opportunity with cheesy wages.

Despite my luck I was not a happy camper: I hated it. I was thoroughly convinced that I was being controlled by people who were beneath me, people who were slathered in ignoble, juicy pepperoni day in and day out. Part of the reason for such supercilious thoughts was the erudite fact that I had recently begun attending Delta Community College. Fall was now in full swing. And despite all the chilly nights on my bedroom porch, I was beginning to make heady strides to rise above my toothless heritage. I was determined to be a smart donkey all the way.

Every morning, without fail, I listened to the NPR world news on my little boom-box radio as I got up and prepared for a day of community college scholarship and poverty pizza. I nodded, oh so pensively, as I heard phrases like, "The Dow Jones is down two percent today," as if I'd known it was on its way down and was an educated man of the pecuniary world. And speaking of educated man, I decided resolutely that within a short time I would be *through* with Godfather's and have a better job somehow involved with the sagacious professors at Delta, you know: doing research, filing, copying, being president of the college, kissing orphan babies for public photos, and lowering state taxes.

I loved school. I would get straight A's. I would just *have* to; there was no other option. I would *have* to give 120% if I wanted to rise above Stockton like a fiery phoenix. Odds be damned! Orphan or no!

And, wouldn't you know it, little old me began succeeding. The tangible signs began pouring in. I excelled on all my midterms and then my finals. All of my papers had remarks like, "YOU WIN!" and "I HAVE A DAUGHTER ABOUT YOUR AGE." Seriously, I was kicking some major valley ass. And, as a bonus, I finally got to use that *Human Sexuality* book in the actual, Medical, and Physical Human Sexuality class. It was still up to date and accepted by the faculty. I saved forty bucks! The ash drawings aided by making it so real and pleasantly visceral. Afros. Moustaches. Happy, communicative smiles. Sideways. Legs everywhere. Dorsal.

The only area I was totally sucking at was my physical labor job at Godfather's. I did not by any means have anything that even resembled a work ethic when it came to tomato sauce and mopping up. My wrinkly uncle seemed to me to be the epitome of somebody who'd given up on life, and I had quiet disdain for him: his baldness, his minuscule vocabulary. He was a mental midget ruling a land of pock-marked adolescent drones. I loathed the whole situation, the whole building, even the ugly hedges out front—the same hedges that smarted my forearms as I stooped through them picking up old cigarette butts with my latex hands. Man, I hated that job! Slavery! Serfdom! Ignorance! Clogged toilets!

In short, I was lazy and impatient when there was work to be done that I wasn't into. I felt like the world owed me something for all of the crap I'd lived through. But it didn't owe me jack, in all reality. I told my uncle again and again that I "really couldn't" work weekends because of this and that and that and this...too much important, cerebrally taxing homework or something like that. A belabored student. A congressman in the rough. He always acquiesced.

And then he always got all pissy—snatching up some other Oxy vs. saucefleem automaton to cover the shit shifts. I was too good to work weekends, being a community-college student, erudite and plump. I was too intelligent. I loved that word, "intelligent." It was my crimson flag of pride. Stockton would not hold me for long. I was a stubborn donkey kicking at the goads.

And then, to my great surprise, Stockton held me for a lot less long than even I expected. It held me for a little under a year! YIPPEE!

Let me hereby explain: I still had friends up in Amador County, namely: Larry Slothicans, Troy Smith, Bertha Hedgecock, and many sundry others. Ah, but there was somebody I haven't mentioned yet: a sharp girl with acute insecurity problems like me: Hattie. She and I had a happy friendship toward the end of my illustrious senior year. She was involved in many student-leadership-type groups at Amador, so we kept bumping into one another. She was also friends with Larry, family friends. Also (and this is important): she was a Community EV Free Church youth group leader. Boom: there you have it: Hattie was an inextricable component to my life in Amador County. I realized this fully only after I'd left. She also was intelligent.

So I started calling Hattie more and more and Larry more and more. (Now that I didn't live within the hot glare of Dick I totally didn't mind kickin' it vocally with Larry; he was always a cheerful fellow). I also began taking pleasant weekend drives up to Pine Grove for flippant fun: movies, nature walks, barbeque burgers, you name it. I recorded my college notes on cassette (i.e., me reading them) and listened to them in the bug in order to maintain Donald Trumpish success.

It was fun to get away, refreshing to the soul. Plus I was finally able to quaintly brag about my present community college scholarship. Vote for me: future governor of California. And they really listened. Since they all went regularly to Community EV Free Church in Pine Grove, I naturally started attending. More and more and more. This was spring and earliest summer.

God moved in for the kill like a lion.

I won't waste time explaining this abstract, beautiful notion simply because I can't do it justice. It's ineffable. He simply had me right where He wanted me and was patient, yet ready to make His vast love known to me. He was perhaps saddened by my life and was ready to fill me with glorious hope and quiet light so that I could heal. Thanks, Lord. Lord of myriad hosts. God of the angel armies.

First off, God steered the pastor of community in my direction. Turns out Larry's girlfriend Rebecca was Pastor Josephus' wily daughter. I didn't care for her much, but I loved and admired the successful Josephus…seriously. Here was the father figure I'd never had. Here was an accomplished man with degrees and compassion. Here was an attractive, compassionate, sensitive, bold, and sharp-as-a-tack man of God; Pastor Josephus and his church were like fresh springs of living waters in my life. I was quite surprised to find a pastor who was not pretentious and condescending. I thought the stereotype of the Bible-belt preacher was the norm for men of the protestant cloth: learned, yet fiery men who looked upon laypeople as inferior, soft, annoying, casual dolts, if you will. Apparently I was wrong; Josephus was in fact the opposite: easy-going, down to earth, even jolly! It was like I'd discovered living gold in California's mother-load country! EUREKA! A light shines in the darkness! Minuscule side note: I wanted to be Josephus.

"I must work hard to get to his level—no ifs, ands, or buts!" was my holy mantra, my daily meditation. I coveted his life. I truly adored him as somebody would a heroic protagonist in an Academy Award-winning movie. I took silent notes on how one should live their life by scrutinizing him every Sunday as he shook everybody's hand as they exited the church after cookies, coffee, and fellowship. He was so damn patient and amiable that it stupefied me. He was in control, a perfect saint, yet a practical business man. What really blew my mind is that he set up a meeting with me on a fine early May Saturday, complete with two mugs (one a 49ers '89 championship mug: red and gold, one a Hardin Simmon's University mug: purple and gold) of steaming Yuban coffee) and evinced immediately that he wanted to help me out; he wanted to make my life better, despite his busy-busy-busy-bee schedule.

"Where are you living now? I heard from Larry and Hattie that you're living on a *front porch* in Stockton? Is that correct?"

"Oh…yeeeeaah; that's correct, it's not as bad as it sounds." I sipped at my delicious coffee replete with six sugar cubes. I was implicitly overjoyed to be in Pastor Josephus' office (myriad tomes containing Greek and Latin filling the bookshelves), especially since I was soaking up all of his valuable attention. It was like Christmas. He was Father Christmas, and I was a child again.)

"POPPYCOCK!" he exclaimed, concern all over his face. "We gotta get you up here with us. Stockton is no place for a growing young man making his way in life," he declared, sitting back in his comfy, functional office chair. He was speaking my language. We were important business men attending to important matters. No longer was I merely a faceless soldier. I was out of the army. I mattered. We chatted.

The secretary interrupted us a few times with some files and declined phone calls, much to my great annoyance. Those people could wait. It was my time with Josephus. He really liked me. He respected my precocious intelligence. And he acted in that respect: he offered me this: I could easily commute to Delta College and yet *live* up in Pine Grove, thus continuing to completely attend Community EV Free Church and thus also continuing to completely fumble my way blindly toward the loving arms of the living God. Josephus wanted me in church: every Sunday, without fail, genuinely. He knew God was the best thing in the world and beyond, so he wanted me to have God in my life. Period. He was quite frank on this matter. I conceded, especially since he would start looking for a place for me to live that very day, using the Church Family connections.

Precisely one day later, after church no less, he found me outside by the birch trees during the post-sermon fellowship hour, as different families were slowly alighting to their hot cars; the parking lot was ablaze with soft golden sunlight:

"Who exactly are you living with, down there in Stockton…again?" he inquired.

"Oh, I'm living with the Falstaffs; they're nice people; they're are letting me stay with them rent free, but I mildly hate it," I said. I could be honest with Josephus, using gritty words such as "hate;" if I ever wasn't, he would call me on it.

"Oh, I see. Yeah, front porches don't work too well as bedrooms," he said, jokingly, hand to chin, thinking, looking off into the ponderosa parking-lot distance. The sun felt incredibly warm on that day. The air was clean and crisp. Daffodils were radiantly blooming along the church walkway. Bees were buzzing. Birds were chirping. God was singing an aria.

I held the church bulletin in my right hand, folded nicely, and looked off at my banged-up old bug, asleep in the glorious spring distance. I loved the foothills. I loved Community EV Free Church. I loved Pastor Josephus. I was pretty sure I loved God at the moment.

"You know something," he began, "there's a little apartment up the road at our retirement center that's now vacant. It's not very big, but the rent's free, and it's very clean. I actually lived in it eight years back when I was considering the pastor position here, before my family moved up from the bay area." A huge smile appeared on his face, and then he leaned in with a comedic spy impression, very subtle of course. His hand landed on my shoulder, and he humorously added, "A little church mouse has informed me that that apartment has your name on it!" He gently handed me the keys on a little leather keychain.

I almost began to cry. Seriously. I got a huge lump in my throat. My heart almost burst forth from my ribcage with the biggest KABOOM of explosive joy ever recorded in all of Amador County's history, the mining explosions of the 19$^{th}$ century notwithstanding!

I accepted immediately, shyly, thankfully, and respectfully. Pastor Josephus said, "You bet it's for you! We want you up here with us; we're your new family," and he gave me a big hug. He knew all about my mom's death and my hard life. He knew all about it and wanted to help any way he really could.

Just then the youth pastor, Dean Amity (the forty-year-old who was a great b-ball player), walked up with a big spring smile on his face. "What's up, guys?" he asked, patting my shoulder with good cheer.

Josephus informed him that I would be living in Pine Grove from now on and that he would love it if I could begin getting involved with the youth group in whatever capacity was open: perhaps events planning—including the big, annual, week-long visit to Bass Lake, the church's favorite summer camp down near Yosemite National Park. *Bass Lake was only a few weeks away!*

The image of sunscreen flashed across my mind. Sunscreen and Jesus Christ. Jesus Christ leaving his entire flock to come looking for me: lost and hanging off a cliff…in a lightning storm…bleating and bleating for help…slathered in pizza, snow, and mud…His staff extended downward…the little hook at the end of it grasping me and pulling me up into His arms.

Dean was very excited. "That'll be awesome!" (Definite youth pastor lingo; snowboards, super soakers, and hot-red electric guitars; juicy.)

Pastor Josephus added, "Maybe you could get him to do the announcing this year at camp. After all, he was *thee Voice* of the Amador Buffalos basketball team. I think the kids would love it."

Yes, they would love it. I would be vital and necessary at Bass Lake. Everyone would love me. They might as well begin the petition to change its name to Big Bear Lake in my honor.

My fate took a turn toward the mountainous heavens that sunny afternoon, May 1994. Rivendell and the house of healing. A mountain blue jay looked down at us and seemed to understand the greatness of the moment: my homecoming, my ascension into the mighty fold of beloved believers.

At around 2 p.m. that day, with an 88 burger and a banana milkshake in my belly, I raced on down to Stockton and informed the Falstaffs that I was, forsooth, leaving. I thanked them excessively. I hugged them. Shook all the hands. Buck looked upset, but I didn't care. I quit Godfather's, thanking my ostensible uncle for the job. He looked pissy. I didn't care. I'd find a Pine Grove job, perhaps collecting gold out of the wild mountain streams. I gathered up my paltry box of belongings and packed my bug full to its white vinyl ceiling. I popped in, turned on, and turned up Soundgarden's brand new album (tape), *Superunknown,* "Black Hole Sun" the song of choice, and then proceeded to backfire copiously. No bother; I smiled a huge smile and patted the dash, saying, "It's okay, girl; let's go!" And we motored on up, back up into the foothills! 3,000 feet up! I pretty much memorized the new album during the drive: one of the best things to do in life.

Then, well, I moved in. Arranging all of my life possessions took around twenty minutes. Easy. I took a deep, fresh air breath and looked around at my new kingdom. I was ecstatic. A fresh start. A new life.

School was almost done for the summer, summer of 1994...*mountain ranges better* than '93! All I had to do now was find a real job in Amador County and begin my own personal journey down the narrow road of sanctification. It was a pleasant road, a clean road. I was ready. I was one big pine-cone heart of joy.

Later that week Josephus asked where I was planning on getting my education *after* Delta. His daughter Rebecca would be attending Liberty University in Virginia first thing in the fall. He loved the school, Jerry Falwell, and the moral majority. He was on a big kick about it since he visited there not long before that. It was a Division 1 Christian University that was aflame with growth and real "integrity."

Enough said, I guess. "Liberty, huh?" I asked.

"Let me tell you. There are national leaders coming out of that great school. They are a Division 1 University; they've got all kinds of big sports and big academics going on there. You could announce at the basketball games in the big arena complex!" he bubbled. When Josephus was truly excited about something it was quite evident. He loved my announcing at the Amador games; it's first off how he got to know me. Rebecca was a basketball cheerleader, you see. Sports galore. America's gleaming vision of mental, spiritual, and physical health.

Naturally, I became "starry eyed" about L.U., wanting to please Josephus profoundly. I took some correspondence classes that very fall alongside my cake Delta classes. Life became peaceful like a river and began moving along at a surprising pace. However, I never actually set foot on the LU campus. Virginia was too far away. Rebecca, on the other hand, actually attended, but only one year, dropping out with ADD and a hunky new fiancé from Ohio who in no way resembled Larry Slothicans. For one thing he showered regularly. I hear they're still married. Two boys, one girl, respectively. It's Biblical.

I got super involved with the C.E.F.C. youth group that year. Part of this super duper involvement was due to my blossoming friendship with Pastor Josephus' son: John Roger. He and I hit it off immediately! We both loved Stone Temple Pilots, Nirvana, Soundgarden, Pearl Jam (oh, the camaraderie auspices of the Grunge movement), and the juicy, yet incredibly splendid Star Wars movies. All summer we cruised around in my bug looking for adventure and oft times finding it. Good times. I was eighteen and he only fifteen at the time, but surprisingly mature in spirit and mind. Our humor (in terms of our odd personalities) was distinctly extravagant, and we both "got" each other's comedic proclivities, subsequently honing one another. Our humor was Seinfeldian in nature, if that helps. All that we had in common: music, movies, comedy, and wit, most assuredly built a solid, granite foundation for what would turn out to be a lifelong friendship. We were equally enamored of fishing, too. He had a tackle box that could easily rival a bass pro-tour champion. The myriad lures glistened and rattled in the hot summer sun: Rapala balsa wood minnow floaters, crank baits, Mepp's lightning spinners, spoons, rubbery jigs, feathery poppers, chartreuse and rainbow Power Bait, and, yes, the obligatory crusty salmon egg canister were all represented copiously in said tackle box. A Plano forest-green-and-cream tackle box if memory serves. It had a curious smell.

Bass Lake was beautiful. Teal waters. Warm and soothing to the body. Plenty of bass to wrangle and catch from the rented red canoes.

Late June. Yosemite National Park. A hike to El Capitan. The pontoon boat was especially fun. My personal favorite.

I made many a LEVIATHANICAL splash from its rooftop diving board. And many an underling (13 year olds) giggled and pointed at my shirtless enormity. A veritable NFL lineman. The last Grizzly spotted in the California mountains. But I cared not! *Let them chuckle, and let me eat cake!* I wasn't ashamed of who I was, because apparently Jesus wasn't ashamed of me. Besides, the underlings weren't all that bad; they were kind underlings and brought me ice cold Dr. Peppers whenever I asked, since I was a good counselor and all.

John Roger and I fished for ages in the red canoes. He caught a smallmouth bass in the emerald shallows on his very first cast! I cheered, but honestly could've written "a smidgen jealous" on my freshly sun-screened arms with my finger. I was incapable of catching fish. I could plainly see the green bubbles pop up around the boat and therefore knew the bass were laughing at me deep down in the swaying weed beds.

Later on in the summer, August, there was the Bear River Retreat: a weekend affair complete with tents, raccoons, potato salad, trolling for trout on Roland Martin's big sparkly boat (outfitted with a live well and a beeping fish finder), and plenty of campfire hymns accompanied by acoustic guitars galore. (I don't know what contemporary worship leaders would do if the acoustic guitar had never been invented. They'd most likely perish forthwith.)

That August I began doing something I'd never honestly done in my life. I began praying a lot. Cleansing my soul of sadness. Cleansing, cleansing, and cleansing some more. It was hard to keep up, a real discipline. Ofttimes it felt like I was talking to myself in redundancies, blubbering like an imbecile, but I kept at it. Josephus told me prayer was hard, but in the end rewarding: God was a friend with whom dialogue was important. It was a relationship, active and breathing, thus it required input and work, like any rewarding relationship. God wanted to listen. God wanted for me to listen. And this was exciting because God was cool.

By fall I began making all kinds of new friends, friends of all ages that truly cared about my welfare: friends that would buy me lunch all over town, take me to movies and buy me expensive junior mints, invite me over for a dinner of caesar salad and chicken casserole, or perhaps Monday Night Football. Oh, the joy: I was *invited*, all the time—to everything. And nary a person tried to cram Christianity down my throat, no, they just invited me to everything and fed me quite well.

Real "Christians." Christ-like. Giving, not taking. Not jerks. They even wanted to hear about my mom's death. Wow. Nobody *ever* wanted that even *hinted* of in Stockton. "What was she like?" they'd ask, openness and compassion all over their faces. And then I would expound happily, feeling as though I were massaging my mom's sore shoulders in heaven.

One afternoon I sat with Dean out at Lake Tabeau in southern Pine Grove and spilled my guts about my past. I told him everything. How bad the beatings were, how much metal and *Playboy* there was, etc. "You watched *Faces of Death* how many times? And your mom pretty much killed herself and slept around? Caleb beat you with the metal side of a belt? Who's Dolores? What video camera? Otis who? Carrigan, your imagined *son?* Hmmm...okay, I see. I completely understand; and you know what? None of that matters; none of that is who you really are, but to be honest, those things will haunt you for a time. We'll have to do some real work to get you along the way to the new you, healing takes time, and sometimes life really sucks. I'm not gonna lie to you, because you already know," Dean explained. We sat a while longer on the big boulders, drinking in the fragrant eventide and watching the ducks bob for bugs in the grassy shallows.

Grace. Lakes will always mean grace to me. As will the peaceful Jordan Delta.

Larry, John Roger, and I kicked it all summer and fall, driving in my chuggy bug up to the myriad alpine lakes along highway 88 (Caples Lake, Silver Lake, Frog Lake, etc.), dining on Taco Bell extreme nachos (the chips were bright red, which we deemed radical) and perpetually listening to Soundgarden, Stone Temple Pilots (the *Purple* album, "Interstate Love Song"), and Nirvana at volume eleven in respect to Spinal Tap. Rock and Roll was freedom. Rock and Roll was life.

I remember one particularly poignant day high up in the alpine country, approximately 7,500 feet up. We parked off the highway by all these huge white granite boulders (with black golden specks glinting in the sun) alongside Caples Lake. Then we went for a stroll along the shore. All was quiet save for the holy mountain breeze. The air was extremely thin. John Roger picked up a flat stone and chucked it sidearm at the crystal surface of the water. It skipped seven times then sunk into the cold azure. Not bad. My turn. Thus, we commenced scouring the rocky ground for perfect stones which were easy to find at this altitude. And, further, we somehow stumbled upon a day of perfect tranquility…skipping rocks for millions of years it seemed…discussing God, the approximate ages of giant pine trees, high school (John Roger was going to be a junior in the fall so we were giving him pointers for upperclassman "success" at Amador), and various other scintillating topics.

And life thundered on blissfully toward truth and reconciliation. My life was good now. Still hard (I got a lame job at the Pine Grove Ace Hardware—a place packed with cynical, ribald fellows who hated God and illicitly me), but good. Community Evangelical Free Church and Delta/Liberty studies became me. New friends became me. The Good Shepherd became me. I was happy. A little hope crept into my heart like a slinky cat through a cracked front door. And like whistling in the dark, I beheld the glorious lightning, filling the cold sky with awesome beauty, banishing the winter of my life forever.

The summer of 1994.

Two years of said lightning hope passed by like a rifle shot in the Sierra Nevadas, and in 1996 I left for Fresno Pacific University. I took out school loans along with California student grants. I was poor and thus these worked out and were easily attainable. I was efficient when seeking higher education. Like a German auto designer. I graduated in two and a half years with resplendent grades. I received my BA in Social Science/Education. Plus, I ran track, *believe it or not*, for a couple of those years. I threw that shot-put like a mother! I still have my blue-and-white Fresno Pacific track windbreaker. I cherish it. University was fun. I'm proud of my years there. And God was always there, sitting next to me in class. I borrowing His books like a million times.

John Roger and I kept in close contact. He, of course, finished high school in 1997 and left for Simpson University up north. He was there, in Redding, Calfornia, for four years. His degree was in English Lit. Ha! Our majors glowered at each other and sized each other up like two wily cowboys in a one horse, scholarship town! At least this time I had caught the bass first!

To my supreme shock, his parents quite suddenly up and divorced in May of 1997 (the end of my first year at F.P.U.), right as he was gearing up for college. His dad had an affair with the church secretary. Cliché, yes, but it still hurts. Everybody in the county found out, and a walloping gossip tornado began churning up all the conifers. Needless humanity all over the place. Post-pastor Josephus left with the secretary that year and moved to Nevada, just outside of Carson City, where the cost of living was a lot cheaper than any inch of California, especially for the unemployed.

The entire church at that time was a heaping mess of, "What the hell do we do now?" Every time I visited for an oil change of my Christian walk I looked around at everybody's vexation and felt myself grow weary with the same vexation; I didn't have an answer, nor did they. And God certainly wasn't talking. Free will, as it turned out, was really real. I tried to assuage my weariness with rationalization. Things would turn out okay in the end; a new pastor would simply roll into town in like a Jeep Cherokee and begin fixing things. But wait, that didn't solve the personal problem of "What the hell do I do now? What about me? My life? My walk? My alpine lake?" Community EV Free Church had been my house upon the rock. And now it no longer would be. Was I destined to sink in the sand? No. I clung to God in my prayers like never before; and as it turned out, He was the real rock, the real refuge all along, not church or people. Imagine that. This is an important lesson to learn. Unfortunately, every constant believer learns it during his or her lifetime.

Mr. Josephus and what on earth he was up to in Nevada continually played upon my beleaguered brain. I felt personally, drastically let down by him. He had been such a hero, such a great man, and yet, I had to admit objectively to myself again and again that he was in fact a real, live human being, with flaws, battles, and problems, just like me, despite his seeming herculean heart.

I really hurt for John Roger, helping him cope over the phone during that year. I was just kinda "there" for him, which is a good thing to be. He trusted me since he knew I was one of the few people in his world who really understood how shitty it all was. What made things more shitty for him was the tumor that was discovered in his left shoulder joint that same May. It was removed at UC Davis hospital in San Francisco and quickly biopsied: benign. Profound relief. Providence like Ruth.

I visited him with our friend Cedric McPurdy whilst he recovered at the hospital; we brought him The Beatles' *Abbey Road* to complete his Beatles album collection. He was quite druggy, but happy to see us. It reminded me of my mom, weirding me out with her surreal, druggy behavior at Sutter Memorial. Hospitals can do that to you. White like bath tubs and sterile like comas. Endless wires and buzzing droids.

Over the years, he healed up nicely, just like me. I was proud to help.

After graduating from Fresno Pacific, my glowing B.A. adorning the wall in a rich mahogany frame, I continued my studies (M.A. fodder) and became a certified, California teacher. I now teach high school: American history. I love American history like a crazy person loves voices. And "madness is divinest sense." Thank you, Emily Dickinson. Your wit knows no bounds!

I also love kids. They need all the help they can get in today's bitter world. And I want to really help them along. I want to be the brand-new studded tires on their icy roads. I want to arm them with the gleaming weaponry of deep knowledge. I want to show them that there is hope at the end of everything. I want to be Gandalf the White, I suppose—yes, because he is just profoundly cool. Call me a "wizard-teacher." Wait, that sounds stupid. Well, whatever you do, don't call me Ishmael; Melville was funny but a bit long-winded! Just call me a "teacher." I think we've all had a teacher or two who changed us. Teachers that altered the course of our lives. Simply by caring about our lives and really doing their job. Yes. People need people...simple as that.

Looking back through the thunder storm of my young life, I realize that God has blessed me immeasurably. He's carried me most of the way: through the monstrous black clouds and the whirling, biting winds. I've ignored Him for great chunks of this storm, but He doesn't mind; He simply and silently continues to chase after me with open arms and a glimpse of peaceful paradise. I'm only just beginning to see that now; I see it shining through, boldly through all of the past monsters, the paper tigers, the crappy characters. God was and is bigger than them all: Dolores, Otis, Steve, mad King Dick, Abe Lincoln, precocious Carrigan, Stewart Vega and his unflagging momma, pock-marked Ogressa, Cadillac Ray, the old tobacco-stained man at the liquor store counter counting pennies, and yes: the great white shark himself: Caleb Stokes. *The whole smokey mess of them.* God pushed them all away, out of my life and into the frosty wilds of Siberia. I am no longer knee high to any of them. They're mere blips on the radar. I'm free.

And now I shall end my story with one more story. It is the tale of Caleb's death. Caleb didn't live a healthy life. He actually had hepatitis in the past and also a bad liver. Who can blame the liver—so much alcohol flowing hotly through it every day for many, many years. Crunchy aluminum cans. Yellow. But what finally took him was something else altogether, something more wicked, more acute: Caleb had a brain aneurysm.

He thought it was a bad headache at first and took a couple Tylenol. They didn't help. He was hangin' out with his hick brother Jethro, a.k.a. "Gunner," out at Jethro's shanty Linden ranch when a blood vessel in his brain suddenly burst open—applying lots of pressure in a vital brain area that can't endure such pressure. Grey matter under pressure. Not good.

As the story goes, the two were headed into town for something and were actually just getting into Gunner's truck when Caleb rubbed his forehead angrily with his wiry forefingers. "Damn headache!" he said.

His brother was like, "Oh, I hate 'em." This was precisely when he got more Tylenol from the house and they drove off toward town.

But his head kept hurting. Worse and worse. Even though it was an expensive, brand-name painkiller. By the time they got back, actually right when they stopped in the driveway, Caleb all of a sudden passed out in the passenger seat. Gunner called 911 and an ambulance arrived shortly after—a hot trail of dusty cloud in its wake.

"We need to take him immediately to St. Joseph's in Stockton!" said the people in blue and white, and they began loading him up on the Gurney. "Now hold on, he's got no insurance! He can't pay for that! You'll have to take him to the county hospital! Come on now!" fought Gunner.

The lady wheeled around on him. "If I don't get him to St. Joseph's within thirty minutes *he'll be dead.*" She wheeled back around and loaded blacked-out Caleb into the ambulance. He was beginning to look pasty and pallid. Gunner acquiesced, frustrated and scared in the hot sun. He really didn't like the thought of Caleb suddenly up and dyin' on him.

Note: this is the same St. Joseph's hospital that bought us out of our house on Wyndotte and sent us to the Oxford circle; it was the hospital right next to that damn liquor store that incited my bath tub beating.

They got Caleb to the hospital with the celerity of medical hummingbirds and quickly hooked him up to expensive, hissing machines. ICU. This literal dramatic movie scene occurred in January 1999. By this time, I was out of college and working on student teaching and certification stuff. I lived on Jackson highway just east of Sacramento in an old, yet spacious house: renting from a hospitable, adjacent Orthodox Church.

I got the call in the living room right before I was about to head out for a grand grocery shopping session, my list was full; it was going to be methodical fun. (I had a tad bit more money by then).

Caleb's sister's (deceased in 1988) daughter Rose (still alive, seldom-seen step cousin[?]) gave me the call. "Uncle Caleb's dyin'...you should come on over to St. Joseph's," she evinced to me through her hot tears. I think she's about my age. Maybe a little older. She continued, "Sam needs you to be here. Come on over, pleeeaaase, and please hurry!"

All right, for Sam. Groceries would wait.

My aforementioned friend Cedric McPurdy happened to be hanging with me that day. He's a patient, reverent kind of guy so when we got to the hospital he simply sat and looked at magazines in the waiting room for about a billion years, never complaining or uttering a word of protest. He's quite the gentleman, honestly, quietly understanding of a great many things. I left Cedric there and grimaced like, "Sorry. Look at magazines. Get some coffee. Sorry!" and then shuffled on down toward Caleb's room, a softball-sized lump in my throat.

And there he was, lying there on his little white hospital bed, utterly lifeless. He looked the same as always, just add a hundred IVs. Well, that's not exactly true, he looked more burned-out and ancient then I remembered. Like a dried up oak leaf, so brittle that a slight fall breeze would shatter him to bits.

I glanced at the nurse. She was cute as a button. Long, healthy, chestnut-colored hair. "Do we have a prognosis, yet?" I asked her directly, somewhat ignoring Flora, Sam, and Caleb's dead sister's daughter Rose. The room fell silent; I cared not: I wanted facts; this was a matter of life and death after all—screw sentimentality, tact, and Kleenex.

The nurse bravely replied, "Grim; the prognosis is grim." I pictured the grim reaper with lightning all jagged behind him. "There's a lot of swelling in his brain; it was a *full* aneurysm and a lot of time passed before we were called."

I nodded and nodded like I was important, like I was on this week's episode of *ER,* filling in for George Clooney, at home in bed with insidious flu.

She sternly, yet compassionately looked around at everybody in the room and declared (and I believe the others already had been told this or there's no way in all hell she would've just spilled it like this), "I don't think he'll last the night."

Quick as a whip (or belt), I stopped guest-starring on *ER.* Caleb was as good as dead. I looked him over. He was breathing, but still unconscious. He looked so old, but like normal Caleb, old like always, yet a new kind of old. He didn't look death-worthy—so it all seemed spinning and melting. Like it wasn't really about to happen. Death. The end of Caleb Stokes on the planet earth. Dirt and bugs again like Mom. I nervously scratched at my forearms. Hospitals; I've had my fair share.

About a half hour after this, Sam and I went out to get some lunch at the Hometown Buffet across the street. We were starving; we decided without speaking that we would have some quiet, powerful brother time. We hurried across the street in order to perform the family death ritual. It looked as if we were batting 2 for 2.

Once inside the restaurant we acquired our plastic, beige trays and began piling on the savory food, my treat. Then we sat and munched. Quiet as church mice. All I remember of our conversation was that I said something entirely stupid and cruel by trying to make a witty, upbeat joke in order to lighten a situation that was beyond any ray of weak winter sunshine. Sometimes the clouds are just too thick for my stupid jokes.

Sam's car, an old Mazda RX7 (white) was currently kaput. The transmission had exploded on him the week before and he had no money to fix it. I knew, being a logical, factual male, that Caleb had recently purchased a newer car: an '89 Ford Taurus, sparkly red, like the $$$ Ranger bass boats out on Lake Hogan.

Here's what I said. "Well, look on the bright side, you'll get a new car!" It was a really cruel thing to say. I'm so sorry I ever said that, Sam. Forgive me my stupid brain. Your big brother always laughs when he should cry. He'll never learn.

I remember his face: barely smiling after the comment, flushed white, hypnotically mixing his mashed potatoes, stewed carrots, and green beans into an edible pile. (The pile annoyed me. I hated it when people mixed different color food together on their plates.) We finished our Hometown Buffet meals and concluded our consanguineous therapy session. Sadly, nothing was achieved; no amount of buttery mashed potatoes or aluminum-cupped peach cobbler (with a fly vomiting on each sixth cup in collocation) was going to be our salvation. The foggy sadness had set in nice and thick. Visibility was nil. The vessel had burst.

*Already and unbeknownst to me or Sam, a silent figure crouched, a ghost, a little black boy, hiding in the shadows of St. Joseph's, behind the massive decorative plants, awaiting our return from lunch; the ghost boy cradled a heavy, elephant tranquilizer gun fully loaded. This figure was aiming for Sam this time. He'd already shot me seven years back.*

At around five in the morning, Caleb expired. Like a gallon of milk. Nobody got to say goodbye; his brain had already checked out. Sam mourned. Me too.

## Chapter 13
## When Minnows Reflect the Lightning

Right before that deadly January, I, incidentally, had spent Thanksgiving Day at Flora's house in Linden. The fields where frosty and gray. The cattle huddled their collective butts together, a brown-and-white rawhide wall in the face of the chilly wind.

Seemingly everybody who bore the name Stokes happened to be there at this time for food and filial fun: Lemon Shark Caleb, Flora, Sam, Stephanie, and Todd. Well, not everybody, Gunner was out hunting or rolling around somewhere, buck naked in muddy hogwash. Oh, yes, and Caleb's dead sister's daughter wasn't present.

Stephanie was Flora's granddaughter from some spooky specter Stokes child whose name eludes me entirely; I will here assume that they died in a car accident or modern stagecoach crash in the gold country. Rural roads are windy, dark, and very drunk. So orphans like Stephanie just make sense out in the country. Add stupid deer exploding all over the highway, and it gets even more dangerous! Shattered antlers, tongues, and knobby brown knee joints under quick black tires. Shit happens.

Todd was her eleven-year-old son. They shared one of the two little bedrooms in the Flora's quaint country house, cheesy quilts in baby blue and duckling yellow running amok. Sam occupied the other room: the dank master bedroom; this was November 1998, hence Sam was 18. Flora was very kind and oft times very generous (excluding the Oliver Twist time I needed a place to live—five years prior): case in point: Sam got her master bedroom and she slept on the couch every night, which was fitted with an old faded lavender sheet that I was presently sitting on that very Thanksgiving Day. A dowdy day. An odd, gray day, stuffy and full of aromatic American food. Despite said good food and Flora's good heart, the house was run down and disheveled. Forlorn is the apt word. It was mildly disgusting, too: fat, surreptitious mice, chunky carpet, yellowing floral wall paper, and a couple alligator lizards for good measure, their tails ever ready to pop off if the plump country mice got too close.

I was hesitant to sit on the couch, thinking that dirty, hillbilly sex had perhaps been performed on it, but then I remembered that Flora was in her early seventies and most likely was not having dirty sex regularly. The only heavy breathing she experienced these days was when she randomly exercised on her hot '70s exercise bike. It was a totally hygienic faded lavender sheet, so I plopped down and made myself comfortable. I would be a Stokes for the day. In my highfalutin mind, *I* was the certified generous person of the day simply because I was present for a crappy oakie get together. By all means I was far too intelligent to be hanging out with these people anymore.

Though I wouldn't admit it, I was (secretly) glad to be around some sort of family on Thanksgiving, my only other family was out of town or dead: LJ had just recently, died so Lulu was in mourning at her sister's in Los Angeles, Granny Mildred was dead, and, finally: Mom was most certainly *not* going to be eating turkey today.

We gathered around the overflowing table. Hot food. Steaming. All kinds of different colors, shapes, and sizes. Delicious. We ate. Flora's Turkey stuffing was superb! I had triple helpings of it. Honest.

After the holiday meal there was family fellowship time and easy conviviality, no alcohol present (Caleb had quit the bottle a few years back and freakishly stuck to it—doctor's warning! I was silently amazed). Sam and Caleb were utilizing the surprisingly new Nintendo 64 in the living room, so I decided to jump in on the fun. Game, Madden Football. Teams: Caleb: Jets (they sucked, but were his incontrovertible favorite team of all freaking time; I'll wager that the inimitable, eternally hirsute, sideburned Joe Namath had something to do with it), Sam/me: Niners, of course—what good Californian boy wouldn't? (Montana to Rice! The 30! The 20! The 10! TOUCHDOWN, 49ers!)

It was immense fun. We were comfortable and warm on a frosty day, all of us smiling, laughing, and slapping each other on the back like old war buddies...which in fact we were...well, old war enemies really. New miraculous chums.

Caleb was surprisingly good at the game. I looked him over as he moved his head awkwardly with each move of the controller, focused intensely on the screen; I surmised that perhaps the boyish fun of video games took his mind off bad beer during the off days. Did he have a Nintendo 64 at his house? His old/new life was a mystery to me by then.

Despite his perpetual, hot 64-bit football moves, Caleb starting getting his ass kicked by Sam, and yet he remained jolly the whole time, laughing and giggling at his own folly. (Fumble on the 7 yard line? Are you kidding me?), slapping his knee with delight—no sign of the old shark pride within him. No sign of competition. It was beautiful to behold. Like a dream. The lack of alcohol in his blood and perhaps his numerous gray hairs were changing him into a better, milder man.

I had a permanent smile drawn across my Thanksgiving face, so much so that the muscles in my face began to ache. Sam and Caleb, fightin' it out on the old gridiron: fumbling, intercepting, onside kicking, holding, face-masking, and ultimately Hail Marying for a winning score. Sam began laughing uncontrollably at one point in the 3rd quarter when he intercepted the ball and unwittingly ran the wrong way, wondering all the while why Caleb *wasn't* scrambling to tackle him. Caleb didn't utter a word, letting Sam trudge for a 52-yard gain before it dawned on him that he'd made an enormous mistake: sheer idiocy! Hilarious! All three of us burst out laughing as he turned around and tried to gain back some embarrassing lost yardage, being tackled immediately by Caleb's nearest wide receiver. All the food giggling in our stomachs made things even funnier. Our sides hurt profusely. The tiny video game men kicked and kicked their tiny running legs and shiny black cleats like minuscule spandex muscle spasms. They looked so awkward and goofy, juicy to the last yard!

This was one of the happiest moments of my life, sitting next to God on that lavender sheet couch, eating Hershey's kisses from a cherry red glass bowl, and watching a father and son coexist peacefully after so many years of bullshit.

I could hear Flora banging pots and pans around in the kitchen, cleaning up after the menfolk like all good oakie women are eternally enslaved to do. We didn't help out, being men and all, with our manly amusements (video games in the living room rather than smoking jackets in the drawing room; the times, they were a-changin').

After about two hours of such revelry, Sam stood up, put his controller down on the carpet, and said that he had a 6 o'clock appointment with the back bedroom television: a pay-per-view order: wrestle mania (no—I will *not* capitalize it), a special Thanksgiving pay-per-view *only* thing where the husky greased men hit each other over the head with giant, crispy-basted turkeys rather than aluminum chairs. Cranberry sauce would come out the loser's nose rather than blood. Gravy instead of sweat. A holiday special!

I grimaced. Wrestling was ignorant feces to me.

"Wrestling's fake, Sam," I offered, a grin on my face.

"Oh, shut up! It isn't fake. Come watch! You'll see!" he rejoined.

I declined the offer, reaching for another silver foil Hershey's Kiss.

I shot a glance at Caleb, he shrugged his shoulders; it was apparently fine for Sam to go off and sequester himself away from all other Stokeses for an hour; he was way into pro wrestling. Everybody knew it; it wasn't like it was a drug problem. I yelled out to him as he walked down the hallway, "Wrestling's compleeetely FAKE, Sam, and you know it!"

He rebutted, "HAW HAW!" an adroit argument that could stand up like a granite bulwark of acumen defense in any supreme court. Word up.

Quite suddenly, Caleb and I found ourselves alone together and indeed very tired of video games and pigskins. What to do. I considered helping Flora scrape chunky spatulas, but she was finished cleaning. I considered procuring for myself a little canned cranberry sauce with a dollop of copious whipping cream on top. I considered the fresh awkwardness of the situation. Caleb and I hadn't spoken in years before today. It got *really* quiet. And then he made a conclusive decision for both of us, which relieved my growing living room angst. He slowly leaned over to me from the old, country wing-backed chair and asked, "Can we talk?"

A blunt question, like lightning from a clear-blue sky. I was bewildered, but tried not to show it. "Sure," I replied, not knowing where he was going with this proposition. We were very alone in the quiet living room. Flora was now organizing the kitchen; Stephanie and Todd were out walking the sodden fields in full-belly, tryptophan hazes.

"Has your brother ever told you just how proud I am of you?" he said.

*WHAT?* My brain was alert like a startled deer. "No, he hasn't," I casually replied, kicking at the controller on the carpet. I avoided eye contact.

"I mean, just look at you," he gestured widely, "a college graduate! I never thought you'd have the ability to maneuver yer way up into college and actually finish. We all know this family has no money whatsoever, and perhaps isn't the brightest bunch of light bulbs, and still, you did it! All by yerself."

I nodded, as slowly as fog on a mountain, thoughtfully, looking blankly at the gray controller with rainbow buttons. Then he actually began holding back tears. Like a man. Actual tears. I could feel them vibrating in the air. A tiny lump began growing like a tiny seed sprout in my throat.

"Well, I just want you to know that there isn't a week goes by that I don't brag aboutcha to all my buddies at work. They all know yer really making a life for yerself. They know you've got yer head on straight, and that's worth a lot of salt in this world: a tough man's world."

"Wow. That's…cool. Thanks," was all I could reply, still avoiding his persistent gaze upon the right side of my face, which felt flushed.

"I want you to know that I call you my *son* whenever I talk about you to them, and I'm real sorry that Sam and I missed your graduation from college. Did you have the ceremony yet?"

I forced myself to look up into his wet, veiny eyes. "No, not yet; I'll walk in a formal ceremony this May, so you guys can come out to that if you wish." I offered, more uncomfortable than I'd ever felt in my entire life, but solid, really solid, thickly in the moment, like room temperature butter in April.

I nervously examined what I'd just said. *Did I really just use the word "wish"? If so, can he tell that I'm working excruciatingly hard to form real sentences?*

"Yes! You got it. We'll be there fer shure! This May; I'll have to bring out my new sunglasses; man, were they ever expensive; if you want we can go out to a fancy-schmancy lunch after, too, my treat, 'cuz I'm very proud of you. Very proud." His voice got a bit shaky at the end.

The whole house was vibrating invisibly, inaudibly. My heart was thick. My brain was tryptophanized. My mouth felt dumbly numb. Flora dropped a plate in the kitchen, exclaiming, "Dammit all!" which brought me back to earth and helped me collect my milky thoughts.

Was Caleb for real? Was he really praising me and my successes as a man? Was he really excited to see me walk in my scholarly robes? (He'd never actually make it to my graduation in May. He died in January.) Then things got even more poignant. "I've got *something else* that's been a mighty weight on my mind. I uh…I'm very, very sorry about how I treated you growin' up. I treated you really bad. *Really awful.* It was the alcohol, you know, it wasn't really me." He straightened up in his country chair and gesticulated in the air in front of him, fingers outstretched to augment the sad truth and power of his point, it reminded me of his lamplight storytelling out at the Delta seventeen years back. "That wasn't the real me. I was half monster back then; you get what I'm sayin'? I know I was half monster. I'll own up to it like a man."

I was motionless, soaking it all in. Mom was somewhere out beyond listening with rapt attention.

"Ye'r yer own man now; you can make yer own decisions about yer life, and whatever you want to think of me is your choice. You can totally hate me. I don't blame you if yer still mad at me for how I was back then; just know that I'm sorry…really, I am *so sorry*; I wish I could take it all back. I wish I could live my life all over again."

I nodded like a stupid cow. How does one go about replying intelligently to this kind of stuff?

I felt weak and big. Precious seconds passed. And then I finally mustered a mustard seed of courage. It was harder than anything ever, but I raised my head and looked up into his eyes. "I don't hate you. Life's too short to hate." That's all I mustered, but I was proud of it. The little aphorism sounded smart when it shot out of my mouth. I was sure Caleb was dumbstruck at the breadth of my mental capacities. I was a philosopher. Incapable of hatred. Which was total bullshit.

However, and despite my emotional prevarications, the truth of the matter was this: God and His magical Bible had been working on me over the years, whispering this and that, telling me to let go of this and that: things like wanting Caleb to get badly injured in a smash-'em-up car crash or get bit by a baby rattlesnake in some brown field far from any hospital. God wanted me to forgive him. And mean it. There's no shitting God.

"I forgive you," I muttered, almost inaudibly. It was like lifting a semi truck over my head.

Caleb froze, breathed it all in like a glorious orange summer wind, and leaned back in his chair. He took a deep breath and exhaled slowly, looking back at the paused game on the screen. The 49ers had just about sealed their victory over the Jets. All they had to do now was run the ball a few more times to run out the clock. Fans had already started to leave Candlestick Park in order to avoid the post-game traffic crunch. Life was too short to get stuck in traffic.

I decided not to tell Caleb anything about my cherished Christian faith; it was too holy a can of worms to open in front of him. Evinced forgiveness was enough for now. I had just taken huge steps. I was exhausted. Had I really forgiven the great white lemon shark, the paper tiger, the midnight murderer? Yes. I had. The world was a better place. This is what the people of Berlin must have felt like with their crowbars and sledge hammers in 1989.

And there we sat. Just the two of us. And he got really, really quiet—leathery hands gingerly up to his ancient face. He was crying. I couldn't believe it. I was not. I couldn't cry. I was a stoic, a statue, the hard, gray plastic camera that records the sad movie, not the actor in it. And I wasn't going to begin crying anytime soon; this was Caleb's deal, Caleb's problem. I had moved on, but nonetheless was very glad to hear him come to terms with his sadist past. It was high time the shark floated to the surface.

So I decided to comfort him, boldly reaching over and placing my stepson hand on his knee. We sat there quiet for a time. Just inhaling and exhaling. The California delta silently wound its way through the living room like living water, like the Holy Spirit. I could hear it. I could smell it.

Caleb was a wreck; he looked pathetic and washed up in his old, white tee shirt all faded and gross. He was a shadow—no, a withered skeleton of the youthful pitcher he once was long ago. His hair was wiry and coarse, falling out in tattered pieces; his scalp was shiny and ruddy, sadly showing in high detail the old skull just beneath the surface. He looked like death. He had really let himself go. A long time ago. And now he was in mourning. He knew he was the old stray dog out in the rainstorm.

I, however, was not going to expend the old emotional energy to fully take part in this dramatic scene; I wasn't one for such catharsis, such denouement. Maybe I hadn't truly forgiven him after all. *You cry this time, not me,* my mind declared, relishing the justice in Caleb's hot, dusty tears. I had done enough crying. I was sick of it. I was ready to move on. At long last the minnow was safe in the warm blue shallows, free to peacefully navigate the oceans of a wide wondrous world. The shark was sobbing. The shark was quitting. The lightning of God was illuminating the dark waters to the ends of their depths.

Although I held myself back, and although I didn't fully forgive him right there in that moment, I have to tell you that I felt a profound sense of joy in my heart. And I gave thanks to God, an arrow prayer straight up. I felt hope creep into the living room like a warm fog. I was finally in control of both myself and Caleb for the first time ever. I held all of the cards. I was confident, taking it all in at once like a young pilot cruising over New York City on a sunny Sunday morning in 1925. All bright white scarves and early skyscrapers. *I was newborn.*

Later that week I knelt by my bedside and allowed Caleb's old sins to drift out of my soul and off into nothingness like fire up into the night sky. I forgave him. Entirely. And God reached down to me and lifted the dead, reeking shark from off my back. And I truly loved Caleb, there and then.

Thanksgiving. Reconciliation. Old Testament style. The old stray dog out in the rainstorm was allowed into the Promised Land. Transparent angels stood in the corners of the room. I didn't know at that exact point in time, as I knelt there in the peaceful darkness, that Caleb was literally standing with both boots on death's doorstep. Just a little over a month later the mighty ocean took the shark with a great swell of a wave. So great was the swell, that the shark beheld the entire world and all its vast beauty from its top before he came crashing down in a glorious burst of foam, white as snow.

There have been moments in my life where the holy draws near, where loved ones embrace and glow like fire on the surface of the sun, inexplicable moments where John Field's "Nocturne #2" seems to mysteriously emanate from the very boughs of spruce and aspen alike along the shores of alpine lakes. And I cannot bear it. It is too much. My spirit is dumbstruck and my heart breaks.

These are the moments that make the eternal magic of life truly visible if only for a fleeting moment. These moments are not unlike a herd of majestic elk in a moonlit meadow you spot from a lonely forest highway, turning off your lights and pulling to the shoulder, letting your eyes adjust. You are not what is most important at that moment.

I have continually experienced acute moments such as these concerning the burning memory of my sweet mother. But oft times the boring side of life steps in and these special mother moments turn out to be a bit twisted and less than glorious.

Fore example, I'll be walking along, humdeedum, performing perfunctory tasks in the warm California valley and happen to pass a woman in a department store or on the sidewalk that just so happens to be the age my mom would be if she were still alive within the lovely tangible realm of this world. I will look and gaze and stare quietly at the woman and for a stinging moment actually panic a bit, thinking that she, in fact, is my dear, dead mother, without a doubt—in disguise—a completely thorough disguise. She was always very thorough.

I'll then irrationally rationalize that she faked her own death in order to meticulously escape her terrible life and begin anew: on her own: a fetter-free life to be lived to the fullest! A new woman!

At the precise moment in which I directly pass said woman in the department store or on the sidewalk, my brain will fire off a volley of hot bullets, *Look! She can't even look at me or acknowledge me as her son because she'll blow her cover. Amazing! Look at me, Mom...LOOK AT ME! PLEASE LOOK!* And I try and try to get her attention discreetly for about one second. But she never looks. She's too good at the game. A game that doesn't even exist.

My mom's gone. That's a concrete truth. I was at her funeral. Yet still I persist in this game. She's only on vacation, after all.

Speaking of her funeral, it was a real doozy. 1993. Bitterly cold. Lots of wet grass. Lots of misty clouds. Lots of people. Lots of flowers. Lots of words. For her funeral viewing, before the service, I made a special mix tape for her, including all of her favorite songs, "Lying Eyes" by the Eagles, an Elvis song whose name eludes me at the moment (it was from the early seventies and had a brass section in it; the chorus ended with, "because I love you too much, baby," with cheesy violins). The biggest song on the clear plastic Memorex tape was my mom's favorite song, "These Eyes" by The Guess Who. Wow. Just thinking about it gives me the chills. I had the tape playing at low volume in the background whilst people viewed my mother's body (caked makeup and folded hands across her stomach). As it was my turn to step up in line and view her for the last time, it seemed to me that all eyes began burning into my back, watching the son view the dead mother. It bothered me to no end, but I tried to shove it aside and fully scrutinize the big moment at hand: the last time I'd see her. I needed to memorize every inch of her face, and quick. And it happened that when I stood at the coffin and beheld her, yes, the very moment my eyes fell upon her the horn section hit for the chorus of "These Eyes" and the lead singer loudly sang out, "These eyes...ooh...are cryin'...these eyes have seen a lot of loves—but they're never gonna see another one like I had with you!"

I remember her closed eyes looked small and lifeless. No spark. Whenever I happen to hear that song I also hear the thunderous hooves of a thousand elk through a forest valley. And the moon is full to its radiant top with silver light. It doesn't matter if I'm in a grocery store or in an auto repair shop waiting room. The song still plays. And my soul awakens to the ineffable human experience surrounding me, like winter lightning that strikes you deeply, past the heart and into the eternal. There is movement among the silver shadows. There is purpose and beauty.

Life is a hard slog on bumpy trail, full up to the brim with leather belts and blueberry muffins. And we all must take our turn. Hopefully we will be the ones, the heartfelt thousands that bake the muffins rather than brandish the belts.

My young life was and is a dark forest in a windy thunderstorm: endless trees in the wet blue mists bend to the powerful tempest and sway like mad with frightened life in the wild night! Heavy black branches snap off and shatter upon the granite ground! Thunder explodes in massive white flashes—bone-jarring the earth off its deep foundations! And all is seemingly lost! All is chaos and terrible flashing flood fire!

...And yet, it is here that the world displays the very essence of hope.
*(Smack dab in the middle of the storm!)*
For here God is present.
Here God is moving.
And within the mighty tempest we finally see ourselves for what we truly are.
We are fragile as minnows.
We are hard as nails.
We are the lionhearted recyclers of human history.
And we love a good fight.